Chantelle Shaw lives on the Kent coast and thinks up her stories while walking on the beach. She has been married for over thirty years and has six children. Her love affair with reading and writing Mills & Boon stories began as a teenager, and her first book was published in 2006. She likes strong-willed, slightly unusual characters. Chantelle also loves gardening, walking and wine!

Growing up near the beach, **Annie West** spent lots of time observing tall, burnished lifeguards—early research! Now she spends her days fantasising about gorgeous men and their love-lives. Annie has been a reader all her life. She also loves travel, long walks, good company and great food. You can contact her at annie@annie-west.com or via PO Box 1041, Warners Bay, NSW 2282, Australia.

NINE MONTHS
TO TAME
THE TYCOON

CHANTELLE SHAW

A CONSEQUENCE
MADE IN GREECE

ANNIE WEST

MILLS & BOON

First Published in Great Britain 2021
by Mills & Boon, an imprint of HarperCollins*Publishers* Ltd,
1 London Bridge Street, London, SE1 9GF

www.harpercollins.co.uk

HarperCollins*Publishers*
1st Floor, Watermarque Building,
Ringsend Road, Dublin 4, Ireland

Nine Months to Tame the Tycoon © 2021 Chantelle Shaw

A Consequence Made in Greece © 2021 Annie West

ISBN: 978-0-263-28258-0

08/21

MIX
Paper from
responsible sources
FSC® C007454

This book is produced from independently certified FSC™ paper
to ensure responsible forest management.
For more information visit www.harpercollins.co.uk/green.

Printed and bound in Spain
by CPI, Barcelona

NINE MONTHS TO TAME THE TYCOON

CHANTELLE SHAW

MILLS & BOON

For Adrian.
We met on your sixteenth birthday,
still going strong on your sixtieth.
That's a lot of love!

CHAPTER ONE

'I DID NOT expect to find you out here alone in the dark.'

Lissa Buchanan tensed when a gravelly voice with a sexy Greek accent came from the shadows. She knew without turning her head that the voice belonged to Takis Samaras and her skin prickled.

'I thought you would still be holding court in the marquee,' he drawled. 'The most beautiful woman on the dance floor attracting the attention of every man in the room.'

'I wasn't trying to attract attention.' She was aware that she sounded defensive. She hated the party girl label the tabloids had given her. Her reputation in the media was not the real Lissa Buchanan, but she was not about to explain that to a stranger, even though he was the most intriguing man she had ever met. Her pulse rate had accelerated at Takis's casual compliment. 'Besides, my sister is the most beautiful woman at her wedding.'

'Eleanor is a delightful bride, which I assume is the reason Jace chose her for his wife,' Takis said drily.

'You seem surprised about Jace's marriage to my sister.' Lissa finally dared to look at Takis and nothing could have prepared her for her reaction to his potent masculinity. Never before had she felt such an intense sexual attraction. Beneath her bridesmaid's dress her nipples were hard, and the silk scraped across the sensitive peaks, creating a delicious friction.

The wedding ceremony had taken place at the town hall in Thessaloniki earlier in the day. Lissa's heart had missed a beat when she'd set eyes on Jace Zagorakis's best man. She had been conscious of his brooding presence and barely able to concentrate while Eleanor and Jace had made their vows.

Throughout the reception that was being held in a large marquee in the garden of Jace's beachfront house, Lissa had found her gaze constantly drawn to Takis. He was not conventionally handsome. Tall and powerfully muscular, but his chiselled face bore a grimly forbidding expression. On the rare occasions when he smiled, his teeth were a flash of brilliant white against his olive-toned skin. His jet-black hair was cropped short and beneath heavy brows his eyes were the colour of cold steel.

There was something uncompromising and at the same time fascinating about his mouth, which was both sensual and cruel. He was sleek and in the prime of physical fitness and he reminded Lissa of a wolf.

He shrugged. 'I confess I did not expect that Jace would marry. I have known him for a long time, and he has always been against marriage.'

'Ah, but who can understand the mystery of love?' she murmured.

'You think *love* is the reason why Jace's marriage to your sister took place at short notice?'

'What other reason could there be?' Lissa looked towards the main part of the garden, which was illuminated by hundreds of fairy lights, and saw Eleanor and her new husband emerge from the marquee. It was obvious that they only had eyes for each other. She sensed that Takis was about to say something, but he hesitated as his gaze followed hers over to the newlyweds.

'Perhaps you are right. I am not an expert on love,' he said in a cynical voice.

Lissa looked away from him, wondering why he disturbed her so strongly. She had sought a reprieve from socialising and taken refuge in a secluded corner of the garden where she could hear the soothing sound of the waves lapping against the shore on the other side of the wall.

She sensed that Takis had moved nearer to her, and he rested his elbow on the wall, trapping her against the old stones. She wasn't really trapped, but her feet seemed to be welded to the ground. His close proximity increased her awareness of the heat emanating from his body. Her eyes were drawn to him of their own volition, and she noticed the shadow of dark chest hairs beneath his white silk shirt. The spicy scent of his aftershave evoked a tug of response in the pit of her stomach.

'You have not told me why you left the party.'

She certainly wasn't going to admit that she'd felt envious when she'd watched him dance with a voluptuous brunette who looked as though she had been poured into her scarlet dress. 'I came outside because I want to be alone.'

'Liar,' he said softly. 'Do you think I hadn't noticed you staring at me at the reception?'

Had she been that obvious? Lissa's insides squirmed with embarrassment. He was the sexiest man she had ever encountered. The men she knew were mostly good-looking models or wannabe actors, but compared to

Takis they were boys. He would be an incredible lover. She did not know how she could be so certain, given her complete lack of sexual experience, but the ache low in her pelvis was a response to his smouldering sensuality.

She prayed that the darkness hid the blush she felt spread across her face. 'Are you suggesting I came out here hoping you would follow me?'

'Did you?'

'Of course not. I didn't realise you had noticed me. You were being eaten alive by the woman in the too-tight dress.'

Takis laughed and the husky sound was unexpected and utterly captivating. 'I apologise for disturbing your solitude. I'll go away if you wish.' He spoke with the confidence of a man who was fully aware of his effect on the opposite sex, of his effect on *her*.

'You can do what you want. I'm sure you will anyway.' It would be a dangerous mistake to believe that a wolf could be tamed, Lissa decided. 'Feel free to stay here and watch the moonlight on the sea. I'm going up to the house to wait for my taxi.'

'I believe you are staying at the Pangalos Beach Resort tonight. I am also staying at the hotel and it makes sense for me to drive you.'

The journey to Sithonia, a peninsula in northern Greece, took over an hour from Thessaloniki. The prospect of being alone with Takis shredded Lissa's composure, but she could not think of an excuse to refuse to go with him. 'Um…that's kind of you.' She did not recognise the husky voice as her own.

He shrugged. 'Jace gave me the responsibility of ensuring that you reach your hotel safely.'

So he had only offered to drive her because it was

his duty as best man and not because he was interested in her. Not that she wanted him to be, Lissa assured herself. But she hated the idea that she was a liability, which was exactly how her grandfather had made her feel when she'd been growing up.

'I am not kind,' Takis told her. 'Do not confuse me with your boyfriends with rich daddies who you have fooled around with on a beach in the Maldives or on a yacht in St Tropez. Your love life is an endless source of entertainment for anyone who reads the tabloids.' His jaw hardened. 'I am a survivor. I dragged myself out of a gutter and fought every step of the way to build my successful hotel chain.'

Lissa was infuriated by his sarcastic comments. How dared he judge her, especially as he did not know the first thing about her. She was about to tell him that it was no business of his how she lived her life. But she did not owe him an explanation.

She'd had years of practice at hiding her true feelings and gave a languid shrug as she forced herself to meet Takis's gaze. 'Presumably, *you* read the gutter press as you seem to know so much about me.'

In fairness she could not blame him for thinking the worst of her. She had never denied the rumours and gossip about her private life, and in fact she had deliberately sought the attention of the media, knowing that reports of her alleged bad behaviour were bound to infuriate her grandfather. One way or another she had been determined to gain Pappoús's attention.

Kostas Pangalos had become Lissa's guardian after her parents had died when she was a child, but he had been too wrapped up in running his hotel business to have time for his orphaned and traumatised youngest granddaughter. He had died sixteen months ago and had left Eleanor, his favourite grandchild, in charge of Gilpin Leisure.

That final snub from her grandfather had been a bitter blow for Lissa, and her brother, Mark, had been furious at being overlooked. Eleanor had appointed him as manager of the Pangalos Beach Resort, but Mark was struggling with his own demons and he'd left the hotel's finances in a perilous state before Jace had come along with a rescue package.

Lissa tore her gaze from Takis's mesmerising face and stepped past him. 'My brother-in-law is not responsible for me, and you are certainly not. I'll make my own way to the Pangalos.'

'Stop acting like a spoiled brat. Cancel your taxi and be ready to leave in five minutes.'

'You are unbelievably arrogant,' she snapped.

He did not deny it. His eyes were fixed on her face, and Lissa held her breath when he ran his finger lightly down her cheek. 'You are unbelievably beautiful. But you must know that.' His voice had deepened and rasped like rough velvet across her skin. 'I recognised you from TV adverts and photos in magazines when you were a model for that famous beauty company.'

His face was so close to hers that she could feel his warm breath on her cheek. Her heart missed a beat as he stared at her with smouldering intensity in his eyes. Lissa understood that look. Desire.

Ever since she'd reached puberty and her slender, gymnast's body had developed curves, men had wanted her. At first she had felt uncomfortable, but she'd discovered that the way she looked attracted male admiration, and it had been a heady feeling of power after she had been ignored by her grandfather. But although she had flirted with her admirers, she had never allowed or wanted things to go further.

The attention Takis was showing her filled her with trepidation as well as excitement. He was out of her league. Her brain urged her to step away from him as she would have done if he had been any other man. But there was something about Takis that made her want to respond to the sexual chemistry between them that was almost tangible.

He fascinated her in a way that no other man had ever done and made her wish she could throw off her inhibitions and insecurities. She wondered what it would be like to be kissed by him and was shocked to realise that she longed to find out.

His eyes glittered, and Lissa's heart gave a jolt at the idea that he had read her thoughts. He slowly lowered his face towards her, and she held her breath, mesmerised by his sensual mouth. Unconsciously, she ran her tongue over her bottom lip. Takis stiffened and jerked his head away from her, leaving her torn between relief and disappointment.

'Go and collect your things,' he said in a voice that suggested he was unaffected by the electricity that had crackled between them. It probably happened to him every time he met a woman, Lissa thought ruefully.

But her heart was still thumping after he had nearly kissed her. Why had he changed his mind? Even more puzzling was why she had hoped he would kiss her. She did not know him, and she definitely did not like him. His commanding personality and rampant sex appeal were too much of a threat to her equilibrium.

She was about to insist that she did not want a lift

to Sithonia, but the inflexibility in his hard expression warned her that this was a man who always got his own way. It occurred to her that her sister might have asked Jace to arrange for Takis to drive her back to the hotel at the Pangalos Resort. Eleanor had always been protective.

Lissa realised that she had no option but to accept Takis's offer of a lift. She muttered something unlady-like as she marched across the lawn towards the house and ground her teeth when his laughter followed her.

CHAPTER TWO

TAKIS HAD MET Lissa's type before. Self-obsessed and with a sense of entitlement that he found irritating. He had assumed he was immune to the feminine wiles of a pretty blonde, especially as his preference was for elegant career women who accepted the limitations of an affair with a man for whom commitment was a no-go area of discussion.

But Lissa was not merely pretty. He sent a sideways glance at her sitting next to him in the car. She was beautiful. Stunningly, breathtakingly beautiful. It was easy to see why the camera loved her exquisite bone structure, the high cheekbones, perfectly symmetrical features and wide eyes that were intensely blue and reminded Takis of the blue-domed churches on Santorini.

Before the wedding, Jace had been impatient for his bride to arrive, but Takis's gaze had swerved from Eleanor in her wedding finery to her bridesmaid wearing a cornflower-blue silk dress that moulded her slender figure and small, high breasts. He had been unprepared for the impact of Lissa's smile, which held an unexpected sweetness and a vulnerability he told himself he must have imagined. Not so long ago, Lissa had dominated social media sites, and the tabloids had been obsessed with her racy lifestyle, although recently she had not been in the public eye.

During the reception Takis had been lured by the sweet melody of her voice while she'd chatted to him about her life, which seemed to be one long round of parties, he thought cynically. Inexplicably, the sound of her laughter had evoked an ache in his chest. He could not remember a time when he had laughed and not immediately felt guilty.

And he'd had to remind himself of the stories he'd read about Lissa's numerous liaisons with male celebrities who were as famous and as pointless as she was. There had also been rumours of recreational drug-taking, which she'd denied, but it had been reported by various sources that she'd been dropped by the beauty company she had represented. Lissa was trouble with a capital *T*, and he had only agreed to Jace's request to drive her to the Pangalos hotel because it would have been churlish to refuse.

Who was he kidding? Takis mocked himself. He had been unbearably tempted to kiss her when he'd found her in the garden. Thankfully at the last second his brain had overruled his libido, but it had taken every bit of his willpower to resist Lissa's lush mouth. Sexual attraction had sizzled between them and the truth was that he had seized the chance to spend some time with her on the journey to Sithonia.

He glanced at her again and saw that she was holding up a small mirror in one hand and a tube of lipstick in the other. Takis felt a tightening in his groin as he watched her slide the lipstick over her lips, outlining their sensual shape. His mind flashed back to when he was sixteen and living in his father's house in the remote mountain village in northern Greece where he had been born.

Takis knew when he stepped into the kitchen that Spiros was out, probably drunk and brawling in a bar. The tensions at home evaporated when his father was not there.

His stepmother was peering into the cracked mirror over the sink as she painted her mouth with lipstick. He leaned against the door frame and watched Marina. His gaze was riveted on her glossy lips and he felt embarrassed that he could not control the hardness beneath his jeans. His eyes met hers in the mirror and he felt an illicit thrill of desire.

Marina was only a few years older than him. And not technically his stepmother as his father had never married her, even though she had given Spiros another son. It was whispered in the village that Giannis was a bástardos, *but people were careful not to say so in front of Takis, who loved his little half-brother fiercely.*

Marina spun round from the mirror. 'Do you like my lipstick?'

He stared at her scarlet lips, and powerful, urgent feelings throbbed inside him. 'Yes.'

'You want to kiss me, don't you?' Her hips swayed as she walked across the room. She stood so close to him that her breasts pressed against his chest, and he almost forgot to breathe. 'I know you are planning to go away from here. Take me and Giannis with you, and every night you can do more than kiss me. You can have me, Takis.' She brushed her tantalising red lips over his. 'Help me escape from this godforsaken village and your father, and I'll make a man of you.'

* * *

Takis had been powerless to resist his stepmother's advances. Helplessly caught up in his teenage crush on her. He could not have predicted that his actions would have diabolical consequences for her and Giannis...

He swallowed hard and forced his mind away from the past and the little boy who would be a man now, had he lived. The memories were too painful and his guilt too great a burden. Something inside him had died with Giannis, and Takis had vowed on the day his brother had been buried that he would never again lose control of his emotions. For nearly twenty years he had found it easy to keep his pledge, and in truth he'd never met a woman who had tempted him to break it.

'You have missed the road where we are meant to turn off.' Lissa's voice jolted Takis from his thoughts and he cursed beneath his breath as he braked and turned the car around.

'You're very quiet,' he drawled once they were heading in the right direction. Lissa's chatter about people he'd never met and had no interest in would be better than wallowing in the black pit of his past. 'Have you run out of things to say?'

'I talked about myself quite enough at the reception,' she said with a rueful smile that had a peculiar effect on his heart rate. 'It's your turn to tell me about yourself.'

'What do you want to know?'

'Are you married?'

He laughed despite himself. 'Subtlety is not your strong point. I'm not married, and I have no plans to marry, ever.'

'Surely you will get married when you have children?'

'I do not want children. The responsibility of fatherhood holds no appeal for me.' Takis kept his eyes on the road but he sensed that Lissa gave him a curious look.

'I thought all Greek men hope for an heir to continue their family name.'

'Not me. I am the only living descendant of my father.' His fingers involuntarily clenched around the steering wheel as he pictured the heartbreakingly small coffin that had contained his brother's body. 'It is my intention that there will be none after me to carry the name Samaras.'

'Is your father dead?'

'Yes.'

'What about your mum?'

'She died a few years ago.' He had paid for his mother's funeral when he'd been informed of her death by the man she'd been living with. But Takis had not attended to pay his respects because he'd felt nothing for the woman who had abandoned him before he'd been old enough to go to school. *Like he had abandoned Giannis.* Guilt tasted like bitter bile in his throat.

'My parents are both dead too. They died when I was a child, and me and my brother and sister went to live with my grandparents. Nana Francine died not long after. She was heartbroken at losing Mum. I think my grandfather resented the responsibility of bringing up three children.'

'I have heard that Kostas Pangalos was a formidable character.'

'Pappoús was a bully,' Lissa said flatly. 'He made a fuss of Eleanor because she reminded him of our mother, but he didn't care about Mark or me.'

There was a faint tremor in her voice and Takis sensed that she had been hurt by her grandfather's rejection. He could not help feeling sympathy for the little girl who had suffered the devastating loss of both her parents and had felt unloved by her grandfather. He knew what it was like to grow up without love.

He frowned, acknowledging that Lissa was not what he had expected. According to the various online platforms that had been obsessed with her latest hairstyle and the clothes she wore, she was as hard as nails, a beautiful heartbreaker and rampant social climber. Out of the corner of his eye he saw her run her fingers through the jaw-length blonde hair that framed her striking features. *Theos!* She was insanely beautiful.

He forced his attention back on the road. At the wedding reception, men had watched her. Takis had noticed the leering looks they'd given her, as if she were somehow public property, and he'd felt furious and inexplicably possessive.

His turned his head towards her once more and his gaze collided with her deep blue eyes. She hastily looked away and he was intrigued by the blush that stained her cheeks. Her air of innocence had to be an act, but for what purpose? he mused. It was wasted on him. He knew all the manipulations and the games that women liked to play.

'You said that you have known my brother-in-law for some time.' Lissa broke the tense silence that filled the car.

'We met while we were working as labourers on a building site. I had no family, and Jace took care of his mother after his father died. We were both desperate to earn money, but we were teenagers and lied about our age so that the site foreman would employ us.'

The weeks and months after he had left his village

had been tough. He had been homeless, penniless and half-mad with grief at the loss of his brother. Jace's friendship had saved him from sinking further into a dark place, Takis acknowledged silently.

'Jace and I supported each other as we developed our careers,' he told Lissa. 'Fate lent a hand when we were lucky enough to share a substantial prize on a lottery ticket. The money allowed Jace to set up his property development company, and I established Perseus, my hospitality and leisure business.'

'Perseus is a character in Greek mythology, isn't he?'

'Yes, he was the slayer of monsters.'

'It seems an odd name for your hotel business. You could have had Zeus, the King of Olympus. Or Hephaestus, the Master of Construction, as you once worked on construction projects.'

Takis silently owned to feeling surprised. 'Have you studied Greek mythology?'

'Not formally, but I'm fascinated by ancient Greek history and I've read a lot of books about it. The Acropolis Museum and the Parthenon are on my wish list of places to visit. Have you been there?'

'No,' Takis admitted. His apartment in Athens overlooked Greece's most famous heritage sites, but he rarely took time off work for leisure pursuits.

He had no intention of explaining that he'd chosen Perseus, the monster slayer, as a constant reminder of the monster who had lurked inside his father, and perhaps resided within him too.

Spiros had become violent when he'd lost his temper and Takis had endured many beatings from him. He did not know if his father's behaviour was the result of a genetic mutation or if it could be passed down from one generation to the next. But Takis was not prepared to take the risk of having a child of his own. The world would be a better place when his bloodline died with him.

Without a family, or any emotional ties, he had single-mindedly set about making his fortune. He'd been hungry for success, determined never to return to the village close to Greece's border with Albania. The region was blighted by poverty and unemployment and his father had scraped a living by rearing goats—the only livestock suited to the rugged landscape. But life as a goat herder had held no appeal for Takis.

Giannis's death had left a void in his heart, but he'd discovered that his lack of emotions allowed him to be hugely successful in his business dealings. Taking risks did not scare him when he'd already lost the only person he had loved. He'd earned a reputation for ruthlessness as he'd built his empire. From the outside he appeared to have it all. Money, several homes around the world and a constant stream of beautiful women in his bed. But it all felt meaningless. His success meant nothing to him when he carried a secret so dark and shameful that he had never spoken of it to anyone.

Takis mentally shoved his memories back into a box labelled *Do not open*. 'The first hotel I bought in Mykonos was in a bad state of repair. I developed it into an award-winning, five-star hotel, and I own four other luxury leisure complexes located in the Cyclades islands, as well as two high-end hotels in Athens.'

He frowned when he heard a tiny snore and glanced at Lissa. Evidently she had been unimpressed by his achievements for she was fast asleep. He grimaced.

Evidently, the only subject that Lissa Buchanan was interested in was herself.

The Pangalos Beach Resort was up ahead now. He turned on to the driveway lined with tall cypress trees and parked the car next to the flight of steps leading up to the main entrance. Light from an overhead lamp streamed through the car window and highlighted Lissa's exquisite features.

Her sideswept fringe had fallen across her face, and Takis had to restrain himself from reaching out to brush her hair off her cheek. Her long, spidery, black eyelashes flew open and her gaze locked on his. The shadows disguised the blue of her eyes, but he saw her pupils dilate and heard her breathing quicken—or was it his own breaths that were unsteady?

Takis swore silently. He did not want to feel so aroused that his erection strained beneath his trousers. He could not remember being so profoundly affected by a woman—except for one woman a long time ago when he had been young and fired up with testosterone. His stepmother had taken advantage of his feelings for her. He had longed for tenderness and affection, but Marina had seen him as a means of escaping her life with his father.

Lissa blinked and Takis sat back in his seat as she came fully awake. 'Sorry.' She yawned. 'I remember you were talking and then I must have nodded off. Did I miss anything?'

'I apologise for boring you with my life story,' he said drily.

'Oh, I always fall asleep on car journeys.' She sat upright and shook her head so that her baby-fine hair swirled around her jaw, drawing his attention to her slender neck. The atmosphere inside the car was combustible, sexual tension lacing the air, and Takis was sure she must be aware of the intense attraction between them.

He was relieved when Lissa opened the door and climbed out of the car. He did the same, but when he followed her across the gravel driveway she stumbled and would have fallen if he had not shot his arm out and caught her.

'Ow! My ankle.'

He helped her over to a low wall so that she could sit down and hunkered in front of her as she rubbed her ankle. 'Why do women wear ridiculous shoes?' he asked impatiently, inspecting her high-heeled sandals.

'I love my heels. I'm too short without them.'

'You had better take your shoes off in case your ankle swells.'

He watched her unfasten the delicate straps and slide the impractical sandals off. She gave a deep sigh as she wriggled her toes.

'Can you manage to walk?' He straightened up and tore his eyes from her cute toes with the nails painted in sparkly pink varnish.

'I'm sure I can.' She stood up carefully, but when she tried to bear weight on her injured ankle she gave a yelp and sat back down. 'I'll stay here for a bit. The pain will probably go in a few minutes.' She tilted her head and looked up at him. 'Thanks for the lift.'

Takis exhaled slowly. 'I can't leave you out here. I'll carry you into the hotel.'

'There's really no need.'

He ignored her protest and leaned down to scoop her into his arms. She weighed next to nothing, and he was struck by how fragile her slender figure felt beneath her silk dress as he held her against his chest.

'Put your arms around my neck,' he ordered, puzzled by the tension he could feel in her body. She was behaving as if she had not been this close to a man before. An idea he immediately dismissed when he reminded himself of the tabloid stories about her energetic love life with interchangeable boyfriends.

'There is an entrance to the private apartment at the back of the hotel,' Lissa told him as he was about to walk up the front steps of the hotel.

Following her directions, Takis came to a door in a secluded courtyard and waited while she retrieved a key from her purse and gave it to him. He inserted the key in the lock, shouldered the door open and stepped into a hallway where a lift took them to the top floor and directly into the apartment.

He carried Lissa into an airy sitting room and glanced around curiously, aware that Jace had lived in the apartment when he was a boy and his parents had part-owned the hotel, until Kostas Pangalos had conned Dimitri Zagorakis out of his rightful share of the business.

Takis deposited Lissa on the sofa and had every intention of bidding her goodnight and leaving. Except that his body refused to obey his brain. He stared down at her as she leaned back against the cushions. Her hair framed her face like a pale golden bell, and her eyes were astonishingly blue, while her glossy, red mouth promised carnal delights that sent a throb of desire through him. She threatened his self-control more than any other woman had done.

'Would you like a drink? My brother left a bottle of

whisky behind when he left.' Lissa stood hesitantly then walked across the room without any sign of discomfort. 'Or there is some brandy,' she said as she opened a cabinet and inspected the contents, 'but it has probably been here some time. My grandfather used to drink brandy. What do you prefer?'

'I don't want a drink. I see that your sprained ankle has miraculously recovered,' he said sardonically.

She shrugged. 'The pain has worn off. When I was younger I used to compete in gymnastics competitions. I fractured my ankle during a routine, and it still twinges occasionally.'

'Are you sure you did not pretend to injure your ankle to lure me into your apartment?'

'Of course not. Why would I?' Lissa sounded genuinely surprised. But she was as changeable as a chameleon, Takis thought grimly. He was bored with playing games. Did she really not feel this desire between them? He stepped closer to her and saw her eyes widen, the pupils dilating.

'Because of this,' he said thickly. His heart was banging against his ribs. He had to kiss her. He wanted to taste those lush, red lips that pouted prettily at him. But he was in control, he assured himself as he slid his arm around her waist.

She gave a soft gasp but did not pull away from him. Her tongue darted over her lips in an unconscious—or was it a deliberate?—invitation.

Lissa had captivated him from the moment he'd seen her at his best friend's wedding, and with a low groan Takis hauled her against him.

CHAPTER THREE

THIS TIME HE was actually going to kiss her. Lissa saw the intent in Takis's eyes as he tightened his arm around her, bringing her body into even closer contact with his. She was conscious of his hard thigh muscles and the solid wall of his chest. She heard the unsteadiness of his breaths and found that she could hardly breathe at all.

She had wondered what it would be like to be kissed by him. To experience his wickedly sexy mouth sliding over hers. And now the fantasy was about to become reality. Her heart clattered against her ribcage. She could not allow a stranger to kiss her. It was crazy and so out of character for her. But he did not feel like a stranger. Takis had fascinated her the instant she'd seen him at her sister's wedding, and even though her brain advised caution it was outvoted by the torrent of desire that swept through her. She sagged against him and tilted her face up to his.

Takis made a low noise in his throat and brushed his mouth over hers. Once, and then again, taking little sips as he teased her lips apart with the tip of his tongue. Lissa's senses were assailed by his evocative scent, sandalwood cologne and something earthier and male that was uniquely him. She could hear her blood thundering in her ears and felt the hard thud of his heart beneath her hand when she laid it on his chest.

With a soft sigh she parted her lips and capitulated to his sensual demands. His kiss was beyond anything she had imagined in her virginal daydreams. It was not the first time she had been kissed. But she had not had anywhere near the number of boyfriends as had been reported in the gossip columns. She had cultivated a party girl reputation to rebel against her grandfather, who had cared so little about her, but the truth was that at twenty-three she was embarrassed by her inexperience.

Takis pulled her even closer, making her aware of his powerfully muscular physique. His hands felt cool through her silk dress and yet left a trail of fire across her skin as he feathered his fingers down her spine and then clamped hold of her hip to pull her against his hard thighs. His other hand shaped her jaw, angling her mouth so that he could deepen the kiss. His lips were firm and masterful, and she melted in his fire. He had awoken her desire, which had been dormant since she was seventeen, when her first boyfriend had cruelly destroyed her trust along with her reputation.

Lissa did not want to think about him. She kissed Takis unguardedly, parting her lips beneath the pressure of his, and then tentatively dipped her tongue into his mouth. He made a feral noise like the growl of a wolf, and she felt empowered by the realisation that this impossibly gorgeous man desired her. At last he lifted his mouth from hers, but only so that he could trail kisses over her jaw and cheek. His beard felt abrasive against her skin and when he gently nipped her earlobe with his teeth, a shiver ran through her and she pressed herself closer to his hard body.

'*Thélo na se do,*' Takis muttered. Lissa wondered if he was aware that she spoke Greek. Pappoús had insisted that his grandchildren learn the language of his birth. She knew Takis had said, *I want to see you.*

The implication of his words shattered the sensual spell he had cast over her. She tensed when he moved his hand to her nape and tugged the ribbon of her halter-neck dress. In the past, photographs of her wearing a skimpy bikini had appeared in the tabloids, but she had never taken her top off in front of anyone, except for that one shameful incident when she'd been seventeen. The memory made her go cold, and common sense replaced the fire in her blood.

'No.' She pulled free from Takis's arms and quickly retied the straps at the back of her dress. 'I… I can't,' she said huskily. 'We need to stop.'

His eyes narrowed, but he dropped his hands to his sides and made no move towards her. 'Why?' he demanded, frustration evident in his curt voice.

'We only met for the first time today.' A part of her wanted to give in to the wild feelings Takis had aroused in her, to throw caution to the wind and return to his arms. But he was moving too fast. 'I just think we should slow things down a bit instead of rushing into a relationship.'

Takis's dark brows shot up. 'What kind of relationship were you thinking of? If you were hoping for a grand romance I must disappoint you. But I was under the impression that we both want the same thing.'

'And what is that?' She was chilled by his cool tone.

'To spend the night together.' He frowned when she made a choked sound of denial. 'You flirted with me at the wedding and reception, *koúkla mou.*'

'I am not your *doll*. Maybe I did flirt a little. You are very attractive.' She knew she was blushing and wished she were more experienced. 'It was harmless fun. I didn't expect you to kiss me…and for things to get out of hand.'

His grey eyes were as hard as tensile steel. 'You were throwing out signals that you wanted to sleep with me.'

'I certainly was not.' She glared at him, as furious as Takis clearly was. Her conscience pricked that she had responded eagerly to him. His kiss had been a revelation, but while she had been discovering her hitherto unknown sensuality, Takis believed that she had been leading him on.

'I think you should leave,' she said shakily.

'I agree.' He strode across the room and paused with his hand on the door handle, turning his head to give her a glowering look. 'Do you get a kick out of teasing and tantalising a man?' he said contemptuously.

She drew a sharp breath. 'I have the right to say no.'

'Of course.' He roamed his eyes over her flushed face and lower to the betraying hard points of her nipples jutting beneath her dress. 'Perhaps you do not know what you want, *koúkla mou*.'

'Perhaps not,' she said in a low voice. 'I've never done anything like this before.'

'What do you mean?'

Lissa let out her breath slowly. 'The truth is that I'm a virgin.'

Takis stared at her in silence for a few seconds and then he laughed. It was not a pleasant laugh, and it grated on Lissa's fraught emotions. 'How do you explain the stories in the media, detailing your affairs with idiotic young men who crave fame and adulation as much as you do?' he demanded.

She flushed and said defensively, 'Everyone knows that the tabloids depend on scandalous stories to sell more copies. Most of the stuff they print is made up or exaggerated.'

'It is you who is a fantasist if you think you can convince me that you are as pure as snow.'

'Isn't that a case of double standards?' she demanded. 'It's okay for a man to have a playboy reputation, but a woman is a slut.'

'I certainly do not believe that. Women are entitled to a sex life as much as men. But the point I was making is that you are claiming to be a sexual innocent when the evidence is to the contrary.' He swept his icy gaze over her. 'You might play games with other men, but don't try to play them with me.'

'Get out,' she snapped, goaded beyond endurance.

'Don't worry, I'm going.'

He went without another word, but the loud slam of the door behind him spoke volumes. Good riddance, Lissa told herself. He was arrogant beyond belief and she hoped she never saw him again. But her traitorous body did not share the sentiment and she ached with sexual frustration that she'd never experienced before, as well as an inexplicable sense of hurt.

She walked listlessly into the bathroom to remove her make-up before moving into the bedroom where she stripped off her dress and donned a distinctly unsexy nightshirt with a picture of kittens printed on the front.

Damn Takis Samaras, she thought angrily as she climbed into bed and pummelled the pillows into submission. Why on earth had she blurted out to him that was a virgin? She had never confessed the truth to anyone else, not even her sister. She felt humiliated by Takis's refusal to believe her and angry with herself for confiding in him.

As she was about to switch off the lamp, Lissa remembered to take her medication. Eighteen months ago she had been diagnosed with an overactive thyroid and been prescribed tablets to adjust her thyroid levels. Thankfully, the worst symptoms of hyperthyroidism—weight loss, exhaustion and feeling nervous and agitated—were now under control.

At the time that she had become ill, the tabloids had alleged she was addicted to class A drugs. The story had gained credence when she had been photographed looking painfully thin and drawn, stumbling out of a nightclub. Had Takis seen *those* photos and assumed that she was the party girl portrayed in certain sections of the media?

It might explain his behaviour, although it did not excuse it, she thought grimly. The best thing to do was to try to get some sleep and forget about Takis. But when she closed her eyes, she pictured his brutally handsome face. The taste of him was still on her lips and there was a heavy sense of regret in her heart.

Regret for kissing him. Regret for asking him to stop.

Takis glanced moodily around the packed ballroom where women in brightly coloured dresses flitted like butterflies and men wearing dinner suits resembled penguins. The charity fundraising ball for the Zagora-kis Foundation was hosted every year by Jace in Thessaloniki, but this year the venue had been changed to the Pangalos hotel. Takis had cited work commitments as an excuse to stay away. Yet here he was, nursing a stiff Scotch in one hand while he scanned the crowd for Lissa's distinctive platinum-blonde bob.

He could not rationalise to himself why he had changed his mind and decided to attend the party. The hotel evoked unwelcome memories of his previous visit when he'd carried Lissa up to the private apartment where she had stayed after Jace and Eleanor's wedding. For the past month, Takis had tried unsuccessfully to forget the one woman who his instincts warned him to avoid. But his mind kept replaying those moments when he had taken Lissa in his arms and covered her lush, red lips with his mouth.

Her passionate response had fuelled his desire like a flame to tinder. But then she had pulled back and he'd glimpsed uncertainty in her eyes, a wariness that had puzzled him until he'd reminded himself that she was no doubt playing a manipulative game. He had rejected the idea that her air of innocence could be real when everything else told him it was a lie. Her accusation of double standards was not true. He did not care how many lovers she'd had, but he put a high value on honesty.

He'd stormed out of Lissa's apartment in a furious mood made worse by the nagging ache in his groin. But his anger had been as much with himself as with her. He did not understand why he had come on to her so strongly, or why he'd reacted so badly when she'd rejected him. He'd never had a problem if a woman had said no to him in the past, although it did not happen very often, he acknowledged wryly. He was ashamed that when Lissa had called a halt to their passion he'd reacted like a hormonal adolescent. She made him feel out of control and he knew how dangerous that could be.

Takis's thoughts turned to himself as that teenage boy on the cusp of manhood, his body a riot of hormones and his heart craving love that his parents had never given him…

Marina wound her arms around his neck and tugged his mouth down closer to hers. 'I bet you've never kissed a woman before. Shall I show you how it's done?'

Takis swallowed hard. His youthful body was so aroused it hurt, but although he hated his father, he felt some loyalty to Spiros. 'You are my father's woman,' he muttered.

She laughed softly. 'One kiss won't hurt.'

He looked into her dark eyes and felt a rush of emotions as he clumsily pressed his mouth to her lips. His body shook when she parted her lips beneath his. He kissed Marina with all the love in his lonely heart. But there came the sound of heavy footsteps in the hallway, warning him that his father had returned to the house.

Takis hastily stepped away from his stepmother, but she grabbed hold of his arm. 'Promise that you will take me and Giannis away with you or I will tell Spiros that you kissed me,' she hissed.

'If you do, he will kill me.' Takis had suffered his father's violent temper many times.

Marina shrugged. 'You had better start making plans for us to leave.'

The truth had soon become clear to Takis. Marina had manipulated him for her own purpose. In that moment she had shattered his youthful, trusting heart and he'd learned the painful lesson that love was for fools. He had crept out of the house the same night, determined to escape his stepmother's machinations. Days later, he'd learned that his father, Marina and Giannis had all died when a fire had raged through the house.

Takis had not mourned Spiros. He had felt some guilt that he'd refused to help Marina get away from his father. But far more devastating had been the realisation that he had abandoned his little brother to a terrible fate. If only he had stayed he would have saved Giannis from the inferno or died trying.

Takis took a swig of whisky and forced his mind away from the memories that would haunt him forever. In the ballroom, the ongoing battle between the disco music and the white noise of countless conversations was a welcome distraction. He caught sight of Jace and Eleanor dancing close together. The tender expression on his best friend's face as he looked at his wife startled Takis. He had assumed that Jace's marriage was a business arrangement that would allow him to claim back his family's share of the Pangalos hotel. But from what Takis could see, Jace appeared to be captivated by his fair and gentle Eleanor.

As for that sister of hers… His brows snapped together when he thought of Lissa. It irritated him to have to admit that he was disappointed she was not at the ball. He had been certain she would be at the highly prestigious social event. Partying was what Lissa did best, everyone knew that.

Pride had prevented him from asking Eleanor if her sister had remained in England. Jace had mentioned that Lissa worked at Francine's, the hotel in Oxford owned by Gilpin Leisure. Eleanor had inherited the business on her grandfather Kostas Pangalos's death. Jace had also mentioned that Lissa had been prevented by a clause in her grandfather's will from accessing her trust fund until she was twenty-five. Perhaps it was for that reason that Eleanor had employed her sister, Takis mused. He could not imagine flighty Lissa holding down a mundane job as a hotel receptionist.

A commotion over by the doors that led to the terrace caught his attention. An argument had broken out between two young men and they squared up to each other until a figure stepped between them.

Lissa.

His heart slammed into his ribs. Why was he surprised that she was at the centre of trouble and more than likely the cause of it? His fingers clenched around his glass as he lifted it to his lips and took another gulp of whisky. Every muscle and sinew in his body was taut and he could hear the hard thud of his pulse in his ears.

Takis told himself that his reaction to Lissa was no different from that of every other red-blooded male in the room. Her beauty made her the focus of attention and tonight she looked stunning in a sparkly silver sheath dress that moulded her slender figure. The low-cut gown was strapless and had the effect of pushing her small breasts high. A side-split in the long skirt revealed a shapely leg and a tantalising glimpse of a lacy stocking top when she walked.

He moved his eyes back up to her exquisite face, framed by her blonde hair that flicked against her jawline. She was his hottest sexual fantasy. He must have imagined a vulnerability about her when he'd kissed her. There was no mystery to Lissa Buchanan. She could bring a man to his knees with a smile on those lush lips of hers that promised sensual nirvana.

He had to have her, Takis realised. Bedding her was

the solution that would free him from his inconvenient obsession with her. He beckoned to a waiter and put his empty glass down on the tray but declined another drink. His heart was racing, and he did not need alcohol when anticipation surged through his veins like a powerful drug as he strode across the ballroom.

CHAPTER FOUR

LISSA FROZE WHEN she spotted Takis threading a path through the crowd on the dance floor towards her. She had only decided to attend the charity ball after her sister had mentioned that Jace's best friend could not make it. No way did she want to run into the most arrogant man on the planet ever again.

She was having a perfectly nice time at the party, or so she tried to convince herself. Plenty of men had asked her to dance, and she'd drunk champagne, although she had learned from bitter experience to stick to one alcoholic drink, and she could make a glass of fizz last all night. She had laughed and flirted and pretended to be the glamorous socialite everyone believed her to be. Only she knew that the truth was very different.

The evening had felt flat, flatter than usual. Until she saw Takis was here and fireworks exploded inside her.

He halted in front of her. His grey eyes gleamed like polished steel and his chiselled features were utterly mesmerising. Lissa could not look away from him or greet him as coolly as she would if he was any casual acquaintance. Her breath was trapped in her lungs and her mouth had dried.

Takis looked dangerously sexy dressed all in black—

an elegant tuxedo, a silk shirt open at the throat and his bow tie hanging loose around his neck as if he had impatiently tugged the two ends apart.

'I didn't think you would be at the ball,' she blurted out, cringing that she appeared so gauche.

'I wrapped up a business meeting quicker than I'd expected and I arrived a few minutes ago. What was all that about?' he drawled. At her puzzled look, he said, 'I suppose the two young colts were fighting over you?'

She blushed because he was so close to the truth. Jean-Claud Delfour's family owned a vast wine estate in the Loire Valley and Tommy Matheson was the son of an American billionaire. They were at the ball as representatives of their families, who had made large donations to the charity that Jace headed. Lissa had met the two young men on the London party circuit.

'They've drunk too much,' she said with a shrug. 'I'm not a piece of meat to be fought over. *I* choose who I want to dance with.'

Takis's gaze dropped to her bare shoulders and his mouth crooked in an enigmatic smile. 'Choose to dance with me.'

It sounded like an order that she had no intention of obeying. But somehow she was standing so close to him that her cheek was against the lapel of his jacket and he slid his arm around her waist. He captured her hand in his and pulled her even closer to his whipcord body.

It had to be then that the DJ swapped the frenetic disco music for a slow jazz number, Lissa thought despairingly. While she danced with Takis she felt as though they were the only two people in the ballroom, in the universe, moving in perfect synchrony to the slow beat of the music. She was fiercely aware of his hard thighs pressed against her, and his hand at the small of her back exerted pressure to bring her pelvis flush with his.

His warm breath fanned her cheek as he murmured, 'You didn't call.'

Lissa remembered the text message she had received from him days after her sister's wedding. She'd left the Pangalos hotel early the next morning to avoid any chance of running into Takis again and had spent several hours at the airport, waiting for her flight to London.

Back in Oxford, she had thrown herself into her job at Francine's hotel, where she had been the general manager since Eleanor had married and moved to Greece. Lissa was grateful to her sister for giving her the chance to work in the family business. It was something she had wanted to do—more to prove that she could rather than a burning desire to be a hotel manager. Her grandfather had accused her of lacking a strong work ethic after he'd seen newspaper pictures of her sunbathing on beaches in exotic locations around the world. Out of stubborn pride she had not told him that she fitted her modelling work around studying for a diploma in hospitality management.

Pappoús had made her feel worthless, but Lissa had hidden her true feelings behind a mask of bravado. Accepting the modelling contract had given her financial freedom. She had pretended to be an irresponsible party girl, partly to annoy her grandfather, but her public image was also a defence to stop anyone discovering that the real Lissa Buchanan felt *lost*.

The text from Takis had flashed on to her phone's screen one evening, and her heart had pounded as she'd reread it countless times. She did not know how he had got hold of her number and wondered if he had asked her sister for it. He had included his own contact details and the message simply read:

It would be good to hear from you.

She tilted her head up to his face and her heart missed a beat when her eyes meshed with his glinting gaze. 'Did you expect me to want to speak to you after you were so vile? You're cute, but not that cute,' she said drily.

His husky laughter rolled through her, and she felt inordinately pleased that she had amused him. She was transfixed by his smile and the flash of white teeth in his darkly tanned face. But it would be unwise to lower her guard against a wolf, however docile he might seem.

'I am definitely not cute like a little puppy dog.' His smile disappeared and the sudden grimness in his voice sent a shiver through Lissa. 'You should keep away from me.'

'Difficult, considering our current position,' she murmured. Her feet momentarily lost the rhythm of the music and Takis tightened his hold on her waist as she stumbled. She did not understand why the bleakness in his voice made her heart ache.

'As a matter of fact, I came to your apartment the morning after we argued to apologise for my behaviour, but the maid said you had already left for the airport.'

'I had an early flight,' she fibbed, smiling at him. Her heart lifted with the knowledge that Takis regretted the unpleasant way the evening of the wedding had ended as much as she had. She was willing to put it behind them and move on. But move on to what exactly? She did not know what Takis wanted from her, although the hungry gleam in his eyes gave her a fair idea. She could not ignore their white-hot sexual chemistry, but was she brave enough to throw herself into the flames?

Perhaps he had the ability to read her mind. He drew her even closer to him, and desire tugged in the pit of her stomach when she felt the hard proof of his arousal beneath his trousers. 'Shall we start over?' he suggested.

Her breath caught in her throat. He fascinated her more than any man had ever done. 'I'd like that,' she said shyly.

A frown briefly appeared on Takis's hard-boned face, but then he smiled, although the expression in his eyes remained speculative. And all the while they danced hip to hip. Lissa's breasts were crushed against his chest and the fire inside her burned hotter, wilder, out of control. Takis muttered something beneath his breath as he swept her across the ballroom and out of the door on to the terrace. A few guests were standing around chatting and he steered Lissa over to an empty corner.

'Are you staying in the private apartment here at the hotel?'

'Jace's mother and her nurse are using the apartment, and I have a room in the staff quarters.' Lissa sighed. 'My room is the size of a broom cupboard and has a view of the car park. But I made a last-minute decision to attend the ball and the hotel was fully booked.'

'I am in the penthouse suite, which has a private roof terrace and a pool where guests can swim naked beneath the stars if they so desire,' he drawled.

Lissa's mind ran riot as she imagined him naked. She

had been acutely aware of his muscular body beneath his suit while they had been dancing. She wondered if Takis had chosen his words deliberately to seduce her. To let her know what would happen if she gave in to the desire coursing though her.

The answer blazed in his eyes, and her heart skittered. After their last disastrous meeting she had tried to convince herself that she disliked him, that she should forget him, but she had failed on both counts, she acknowledged with a sigh.

Her tongue darted across her lips. 'Do you desire?' she whispered. 'To swim beneath the stars, I mean.'

'I do.' The dark intensity of his voice set every nerve ending on Lissa's skin alight. 'Would you like to swim with me?'

Her pulse was racing so fast that she felt dizzy, unmoored and uncharacteristically reckless. She had the sense that she was standing at the top of a precipice and about to leap into the unknown. 'Yes,' she whispered.

Takis caught hold of her hand and lifted it up to his mouth. He grazed his lips over her knuckles and Lissa felt a sensation like an electrical current shoot up her arm. She watched his dark head descend and anticipation ran through her as he angled his mouth over hers. She wanted him to kiss her, there was no point denying it to herself.

She parted her lips and glimpsed a fierce gleam in his eyes as he claimed her mouth with arrogant possession. His kiss was even better than she remembered, hotter and more intense, and she melted against him, helpless to resist his passionate demands.

All her adult life Lissa had refused to be the kind of woman she had allowed her grandfather to think she was. She had hugged the secret of her virtue to herself when Pappoús had criticised her after reading reports of her wild lifestyle. But Kostas was dead, and Lissa could barely remember why she'd engaged in a stupid battle of wills with him. She no longer had to be in awe of an old man who had disapproved of her. She could do whatever she wanted.

Takis's warm breath filled her mouth and his raw, male scent intensified her longing. He broke off the kiss at last and stared intently at her, his expression half-hidden in the shadows. And then he tilted his head back and looked up at the dark sky, studded with diamonds.

'It is a perfect night for swimming beneath the stars, *koúkla mou*.' He held out his hand, and after an imperceptible hesitation Lissa linked her fingers through his.

Takis ushered Lissa into his penthouse suite, and as she heard the door close with a soft snick she was beset with doubts. When they had left the ballroom and entered a lift, there had been other guests besides them. But now she was alone with the most enigmatic and sinfully attractive man she'd ever met. And somewhere on the way up to his hotel suite the reality of what she was doing had sunk in and her confidence had deserted her.

'Would you like a drink?'

It was tempting to settle her nerves with alcohol, but the one and only time she had been drunk had ended with her very public humiliation.

'No, thank you,' she said stiffly. She was aware that she sounded like a teenager on a first date, and the truth was that she had never really moved on from the deeply upsetting incident when she'd been seventeen.

Takis's eyes narrowed when she stepped away from him, but he made no attempt to touch her. Lissa reminded herself that she had been alone with him in her apartment the previous time they had both stayed at the Pangalos hotel. But tonight was different. She had responded to his passionate kiss and encouraged him to have expectations that, though she'd desperately wanted to, she hadn't been sure she could deliver.

'I don't usually do this,' she told him in a low voice. 'Go to a hotel room with a man I barely know, I mean.'

'No?' His tone was sardonic.

Lissa bit her lip, feeling at a loss to know how to explain that she was not the person he believed her to be. That she had courted scandal and lived up to her party girl reputation to provoke her grandfather, but that she was now ashamed of her childish attempts to gain Pappoús's attention.

Takis shrugged. 'You came here of your own free will and there is nothing to prevent you from leaving. No chains across the door.' He strode across the room towards the glass doors that slid open smoothly when he flicked a switch on the wall. 'I'm going for a swim. Join me, if you wish,' he drawled as he stepped outside.

The only chains were in her mind, Lissa realised.

She looked over at the front door of the penthouse and felt a hollow sensation inside at the thought of walking away from Takis without exploring the powerful chemistry they shared. Did she have the courage to overcome her inhibitions and behave like any other single, twenty-three-year-old woman? There was only one way to find out.

The sound of a faint splash from outside drew her over to the glass doors. Light from the penthouse spilled on to the terrace, but the pool was dark and Takis was a shadowy figure cutting through the water. He swam several lengths before he stopped and hauled himself half out of the pool, resting his elbows on the tiles.

'So you've decided to stay.' Nothing in his tone gave an indication of his thoughts.

'Yes.' Trying to ignore the frantic thud of her heart, Lissa walked across the terrace, her stiletto heels clipping against the tiles. 'But I don't have a swimsuit.'

Takis grinned. 'Neither do I.' He heaved himself out of the pool with a lithe movement and stood a little way off from her. Water streamed down his body, running in rivulets over his broad chest and washboard-flat abdomen.

Lissa's gaze followed the tracks of water down to his black boxers that sat low on his hips, and she felt relieved and just the tiniest bit disappointed that he wasn't completely naked. A partially clothed Takis was enough for her to cope with. At the ball he'd looked magnificent in a tuxedo, but the sight of his bare chest with a smattering of dark hair that arrowed down to the waistband of his boxers set her pulse hammering. He was so *male*, so virile and potent, and she felt intensely aware of her softer, feminine body.

'Presumably you are wearing underwear, which is not so different from a bikini,' he said. 'Do you need me to unzip your dress?'

'I can manage.' She could do this, Lissa told herself. Undoing her dress wasn't a problem as it had a side zip, but undressing in front of Takis tested her resolve to throw off the shackles of her past.

Silver sequins sparkled like tiny stars as the dress slipped to the floor, leaving her in her stockings, stiletto shoes, lacy knickers and strapless bra. She had worn less on the beach, she reminded herself.

Takis uttered a low growl of admiration that caused her nipples to harden. Before her nerve could fail, she kicked off her shoes and peeled her stockings down her legs. 'Which end is the shallow end?' she asked him when she walked towards the pool.

'It's all one depth. I am a couple of inches over six feet and I can stand on the bottom, but I doubt you will be able to as you are much shorter than me. I left the underwater lights off so that we can swim by starlight.'

Lissa stared down at the dark depths of the pool and her stomach muscles clenched with fear. Why on earth had she thought that this was a good idea? 'I'm not a confident swimmer,' she admitted. 'I don't like being out of my depth in water.' She was way out of her depth with Takis before she'd even dipped a toe in the pool, she thought. Panic made her breathing erratic.

Takis jumped into the pool and disappeared beneath the surface. He reappeared and slicked his wet hair back from his brow. 'I'll stay close to you so that you can grab hold of me if you feel nervous.'

Terrified was a more accurate description. Her phobia of deep water had started when she'd been a child. She stood on the top of the pool steps and was aware of a dryness in her mouth and her rapid heartbeat. She felt an urge to run back into the penthouse. But she could not spend the rest of her life running away from scary situations, Lissa thought, feeling impatient with herself. She wanted to change who she was, and change began with simple steps.

Steeling her nerves, she put her foot on the second rung of the steps and then the third, slowly lowering herself into the pool until her shoulders were beneath the water. She stretched her leg down but could not feel the bottom with her toes. Taking a deep breath, she swam a few strokes, but panic overwhelmed her and she felt herself sinking. She splashed frantically and swallowed a mouthful of water.

'Be calm. I am here.' A pair of strong arms wrapped around her waist.

Lissa clutched Takis's shoulders. 'It's no good. I can't do it. Will you take me back to the side, please?'

'Try to relax,' he murmured. 'Why do you dislike being in a swimming pool so much?'

She thought about giving a flippant excuse that her hairstyle would be ruined if she got it wet. But something in Takis's steady gaze made her want to confide in him.

'My parents drowned when I was ten. They were in Sri Lanka to celebrate their wedding anniversary.' Her voice shook. 'They went away and never came back.'

'That was a terrible tragedy,' he said softly. 'Have you ever sought help to overcome your understandable fear?'

She shook her head. 'I've never told anyone. It sounds silly, but when I'm in the water I imagine how scared Mum must have been when she was caught in a strong sea current and couldn't make it back to the beach. My dad tried to save her, but he was swept away too.'

Takis brushed a strand of hair off her cheek. His eyes were silver-bright in the darkness. 'I promise you won't drown. Will you trust me to keep you safe, *koúkla mou*?'

There was no reason why she should trust him, yet oddly she did. 'Yes,' she whispered.

'You need to build your confidence in the water by learning to float. Try to relax and I will support you while you lie back.'

Lissa attempted to follow his instructions, but when the water filled her ears she panicked and grabbed his arm. 'It's no good. I'm hopeless.' Her grandfather had often told her so, and she'd never had a reason not to believe him.

'Nonsense,' Takis said calmly. 'Can you feel my arm beneath your back? I won't let you sink. Try again,' he encouraged.

Her second attempt was more successful. The sensation of water in her ears made her feel terrified that it would cover her face and she'd be unable to breathe. But she trusted that Takis would not allow her to sink and gradually her muscles unlocked as she discovered that there was no need to thrash her arms and legs frantically in an effort to stay afloat.

After a few minutes Takis dropped his arm away from her so that she was floating on her own. 'Well done,' he said. 'It takes courage to face up to fear. You have taken the first step and I have no doubt that you will become a more confident swimmer.'

Lissa was not used to being praised. More often she had been criticised by her grandfather. She felt a spurt of pride in herself for starting to tackle her fear.

'Thank you for being so patient.' She gave Takis a shy smile and he looked puzzled for a moment before his answering smile set her pulse racing.

He placed his hands on her waist, drawing her towards him and turning her around so that her back rested on his chest and the water lapped around her breasts. 'Look up at the sky,' he bade her.

Lissa tilted her head and caught her breath as she stared at the glittering canopy above them. There was no moon, and the black sky was filled with more stars than she had ever seen. 'It's incredible,' she said in awe. 'I've always lived in a city and never noticed how bright the stars are because of the light pollution.'

'When I was a boy I used to climb the mountain near my home, and when night fell, the stars seemed close enough to touch.'

'That sounds lovely. Is it a pretty place where you grew up?'

He gave a short laugh. 'I have not been back there for twenty years. The scenery attracted a few tourists in the summer, but there was no work or prospects for the people who lived there. I climbed the mountain hoping to see a better place on the other side of it. I couldn't wait to leave.'

Lissa wanted to know more about his past, but his terse tone warned her to curb her curiosity. She stared up at the stunning light show in the sky. Nature at its most glorious. Her senses became attuned to the rhythmic rise and fall of Takis's chest that felt like a wall of steel behind her. His strength made her feel safe and the heat of his body pressed up close to hers was intoxicating.

She let her head drop back a little more so that it rested on his shoulder. The night air was so still that she heard his breathing quicken, and his hands tightened on her waist. Her heart gave a jolt when she felt his body stir beneath his boxers, and the hard proof of his arousal nudged her bottom.

'I'm curious,' he drawled, turning her in his arms so that she was facing him. 'Why did you accept my invitation of a night-time swim when you have a fear of deep water?'

'I didn't think we were actually going to swim,' Lissa admitted. Her heart missed a beat at the glint in his eyes.

'Ah, so was stargazing the attraction?'

She could pretend to agree, but she had been putting on a pretence for much of her life. It was time to be honest with herself and with Takis.

'You are the attraction,' she whispered.

CHAPTER FIVE

'YOU TAKE MY breath away,' Takis said huskily. He pulled Lissa closer to him so that her breasts brushed against his chest. 'Wrap your legs around me,' he instructed as he waded through the water, carrying her over to the edge of the pool.

He lifted her on to the tiled floor and heaved himself out of the water. Catching hold of her hand, he led her over to a circular daybed and drew her into his arms once more. His eyes gleamed in the darkness and the predatory expression on his face once again reminded Lissa of a wolf. A mixture of excitement and faint apprehension sent a shiver through her.

'Are you cold?' He picked up a towel and blotted the moisture from her shoulders, and then ran his finger lightly over her décolletage, down to the edge of her bra. 'Your wet underwear needs to come off,' he murmured.

Lissa looked down and saw that her bra had turned see-through, and her nipples were two dark outlines jutting through the material. Her common sense told her that she should wrap the towel around her and return to the penthouse to change into her dress. But her feet refused to obey her brain and she did not move when Takis reached behind her back and unfastened her bra.

As the flimsy underwear fell away from her breasts, she stiffened, remembering the humiliating events that had followed when she'd allowed her first boyfriend to see her naked breasts. She had been unaware that photographs of her had been taken until they had been made public.

But she reminded herself that she had put her trust in Takis in the pool when he had helped her to overcome her fear of drowning. She released her breath slowly, but at the same time her heart rate accelerated when she saw the expression in his eyes.

'Eísai tóso ómorfos,' he said. 'You are so beautiful,' he repeated in English.

A dull flush spread over his angular face. He lifted his hand and touched the pulse thudding at the base of her throat, and then he lowered his head and pressed his mouth to the same place before feathering kisses along her collarbone.

He lifted his face to hers, and Lissa's lips parted involuntarily as he claimed her mouth in a deeply sensual kiss that lit a fire inside her. The last remnants of her tension eased, and she gave a soft sigh when he slid his hands down from her shoulders and stroked the sides of her breasts.

His fingers drifted over her dainty curves, as if he were learning her shape by touch as well as by sight. She caught her breath when he finally brushed his thumbs across her nipples.

'Do you like that?' he murmured as her nipples hardened beneath his caresses.

'Yes.' His touch was addictive, and she wanted more. Need and longing were emotions she had never felt for any other man, certainly not to this degree. Her teenage crush on Jason had not prepared her for the sweet flood of desire that pooled between her thighs as Takis gently rolled her nipples between his fingers. 'Oh,' she gasped. 'Yes.'

He made a rough sound in his throat that sent a tremor through her. 'Do you have any idea what you do to me?' he rasped. 'I tried to forget you, but I failed.' Frustration was evident in his voice.

'I couldn't forget you either.' Lissa whispered the words against his lips as he kissed her again. He tumbled her down on to the daybed and stretched out beside her, trailing kisses down her neck and over the slopes of her breasts.

She felt his warm breath on her nipple and her heart gave a jolt. She'd never permitted a man to put his mouth on her breasts, but now she silently willed Takis to do just that. He flicked his tongue across one tender peak and then the other, and Lissa could not hold back a sob of delight.

She clutched his shoulders and felt the ripple of powerful muscles beneath her fingertips. The pleasure he wrought with his mouth on her breasts was so intense that she moved her hips restlessly, desperate to assuage the insistent throb *there* at her feminine core.

Takis moved his mouth back up to hers and kissed her with mind-blowing sensuality. He demanded her complete capitulation, and she gave it willingly, sliding one hand into his jet-dark hair, while the other explored the hard line of his jaw, covered with stubble that felt abrasive against her palm.

He took everything she offered and demanded more. His tongue plundered the moist interior of her mouth, eliciting a response that she could not deny him. He draped one heavy thigh across her legs and captured her wrists in his hand, pinning them above her head. And then he put his mouth on her breast and sucked her nipple in a highly erotic caress.

He transferred his attention to her other breast and Lissa was vaguely aware that the thin cries she could hear came from her. But she could not control her reaction, as the pleasure Takis evoked with his hands and mouth on her body drove her mad with longing.

Her breath left her on a shuddering sigh when he tugged her knickers off and pushed her legs apart. She had never been naked with a man before and a tiny voice inside her asked if she was ready to take this next step. The answer had to be, *Yes!* She was a twenty-three-year-old virgin and she wanted to take charge of her life and finally explore her sensuality with this fascinating man.

Takis traced his fingers along her inner thigh, moving inexorably higher. A quiver of anticipation ran through Lissa when he cupped his hand over her feminine mound.

'Relax,' he murmured as he stroked her moist opening. But it was impossible to relax when everything he did was shockingly new. She gasped when he pressed his thumb over the hidden nub of her clitoris. The sensation was indescribable, and she instinctively arched her hips towards his hand.

Takis gave a husky laugh and slipped a finger into her slick wetness. 'Tell me how I can give you pleasure, *koúkla mou.*'

His voice intruded on the sensual spell he had woven around her. The realisation of what she was doing made her heart clatter against her ribs. Takis was kissing her mouth again while he moved his hand in a rhythmic motion. He stretched her a little wider so that he could slip another finger into her molten heat.

It felt so amazingly good when he swirled his fingers inside her. Each movement of his hand drove Lissa higher and her breathing quickened as she felt herself nearing an orgasm. When Takis lifted his head and stared down at her, she could not bring herself to meet his gaze. Not when his fingers were still deep inside her, swirling in an insistent dance that made her quake. She skimmed her hands over his chest, tracing the arrowing of hairs down to his boxer shorts. Through the still-damp material she felt the hard ridge of his arousal push against her hand.

'I want to make love to you, Lissa. Thinking about you has driven me crazy for weeks.' He withdrew his fingers from her trembling body and propped himself up on an elbow, slipping his hand beneath her chin and forcing her to look at him.

'Before we take this any further I need to make something clear.' The sudden coolness in his voice sent a prickle of warning across her skin. 'I'm not looking for a relationship. I want you, but for one night only. That's all I'm offering. One perfect night together.'

She was glad that Takis had been honest, while trying to ignore the sinking feeling in her stomach. She shouldn't feel hurt because he had set parameters and insisted that sex was all he wanted. *Why would he be interested in you as a person or want to get to know you better?* taunted a voice inside her that reminded her of her inadequacy.

'What have you got against relationships?' she asked him.

He shrugged. 'My life is my own. I work hard and

play hard and I choose not to have personal commitments. I enjoy sex and I'm good at it.' The heat in his gaze sent a lick of flames down to Lissa's feminine core. 'But sexual ecstasy is simply that,' Takis drawled. 'It has no higher meaning, and it is not a connection between souls. I know this because I do not have a soul.'

She stared at his hard-boned face and sensual mouth that she found utterly fascinating. There was no rational explanation, no right or wrong. She simply wanted to make love with him.

'One perfect night,' she murmured.

His wicked smile stole her breath. 'Do not doubt it,' he said softly as he cradled her cheek in his hand and dipped his head towards her, slanting his mouth over hers.

His kiss blazed through her and she parted her lips, eager to respond to his sensual demands. He lay down beside her and roved his hands over her body, exploring every dip and curve. The scrape of his jaw on her breasts was a sensory delight that made her shiver as he skilfully heightened her anticipation.

Takis pulled off his boxers, freeing his erection, and Lissa drew a swift breath when she felt the hard length of his arousal nudge between her thighs. She wanted to explore his male body, but when she ran her fingers along his shaft, he groaned.

'There's no time for that. I have to have you now,' he rasped. His urgency fuelled her own longing for him to assuage the sweet throb of desire between her thighs, but she was confused when he rolled away from her and reached for his jacket, which he'd left on a chair. Understanding dawned when he took a packet of condoms from the pocket and quickly prepared himself.

He knelt over her and slipped a finger inside her, his eyes glinting like molten silver when he discovered how wet she was. 'You are ready for me, *koúkla mou*.'

Lissa felt a flutter of anticipation as he positioned himself between her legs and slid his hands beneath her bottom. It was actually happening. Takis was about to make love to her. She *was* ready. So hot and needy. His wide shoulders blocked out the light of the stars and she could not see the expression on his face.

'Bend your knees,' he murmured, and when she obeyed, he eased forward and Lissa felt his swollen tip push between her silken folds. She tried to prepare mentally and physically for him to possess her. But then he made a harsh sound in his throat and thrust into her, and it *hurt*, and she snatched a sharp breath.

It was not possible, Takis told himself. He must have imagined that Lissa's body had initially resisted when he'd entered her. He pulled back a little way and stared down at her. An alarm bell rang in his mind when she evaded his gaze, but his eyes were drawn to her lush mouth, reddened from his kisses, and all he could think of was how desperately he wanted to kiss her again.

She was so tight and hot. His brain was sending him a startling message, but he could not comprehend the possibility that she had not done this before. He tried to move and withdraw from her, but it felt like his shaft was being gripped in a velvet glove and he could not fight the tsunami of need that swept through him.

'Am I hurting you?' he bit out. He felt dangerously out of control.

'No…' she whispered slowly. She moved her hips as if trying to find a more comfortable position. The ripples of her internal muscles squeezing his shaft very nearly made Takis come there and then. 'It feels better now,' she said in a small voice that was like a kick in his guts.

He should stop. He would stop. But somehow, instead of pulling out, he sank deeper into her and groaned as every nerve ending on his body thrummed with expectation. He was greedy for more, and when he fought his desire and again pulled back, Lissa clutched his shoulders and arched her hips in mute supplication, and Takis was lost.

He supported his weight on one elbow and slipped his hand between their joined bodies, seeking the tight little bud of her femininity. He caressed her with his fingers and simultaneously set a rhythm, slow at first as he pressed deeper. He withdrew and pressed again, quicker now, each thrust harder than the last as the storm inside him built.

It was elemental and fierce and uncontrollable. With a sense of shock, he realised that he was about to be overwhelmed. He clenched his jaw, but he was no longer the master of his body and he gave a savage groan at the moment of release as pleasure ripped through him.

Takis's chest heaved with the effort of dragging oxygen into his lungs. Deep shudders racked his body and in a distant corner of his mind he acknowledged that he'd just had the most incredible sex of his life. However, he was aware that the same could not necessarily be said for Lissa.

Had it really been her first time? His brain could not process what had happened. He'd never lost control so spectacularly. The questions in his mind demanded answers. If Lissa had been a virgin, as he suspected, what was her agenda? Women always wanted a piece of him. He'd learned that lesson when he was sixteen. Unwanted memories surfaced. Marina's triumphant smile, and the sickening realisation that she had taken advantage of his tender feelings for her.

He lifted himself off Lissa and rolled on to his back. He had to know the truth. 'It was your first time, wasn't it?'

'Yes.' Her voice was a thread of sound.

A host of unwelcome emotions churned inside Takis. Guilt, confusion and anger, mainly with himself but also with Lissa. 'Why didn't you tell me? If I had realised, I would have been gentler.'

'I did tell you,' she said, still in that small voice that made him think he had ruined something that could have been, *should* have been, beautiful.

He swore silently when he remembered how he had dismissed her claim of sexual innocence. He'd been convinced that she was playing a manipulative game, and perhaps she was, he thought grimly.

'So, what were you hoping for?' His eyes had become used to the semi-darkness and he saw her puzzled expression. 'Did you expect something in return for your virginity?'

'I had no expectations,' she said quietly. 'To be perfectly honest, I found the whole experience underwhelming.'

Underwhelming! Takis's male pride smarted, but he conceded that Lissa had good reason to feel underwhelmed by his performance.

She got up from the daybed and hurried over to where her dress was a glittering heap next to the pool.

Cursing beneath his breath, he pulled his trousers on and strode after her.

'What are you doing?'

She had stepped into her dress and was struggling with the zip. 'Leaving, of course. I can't go back to my room naked. Oh, this wretched zip.'

'Careful, or you will rip the material.'

'Like you care!' She slapped his hand away when he tried to help. The zip was stuck halfway up her dress. She clutched the bodice against her breasts with one hand and picked up her shoes with the other. 'Goodnight.' She swung round and promptly tripped over the hem of her skirt, which was too long without her high heels.

Takis caught her before she fell and turned her to face him. The glimmer of tears in her eyes tugged sharply on his conscience.

She had been speaking the truth when she had told him she was a virgin.

And she had been speaking the truth when she'd said she wasn't expecting anything from him. His instinctive accusation had been wrong.

Which meant that he had behaved appallingly. He released his breath on a ragged sigh as a single tear slipped down her cheek. 'Don't go,' he said gruffly. 'Stay and talk to me.'

She shook her head, but she did not move away from him, and he felt a faint tremor run through her slender body when he put his hand on her waist. 'What is there to talk about?' she whispered. 'I'm done, Takis.'

But he wasn't done with her. Nowhere near, in fact. 'You could start by explaining why the tabloids printed all those stories about your private life, which were patently not true.'

She avoided his gaze. 'It's complicated.'

'That doesn't surprise me, *koúkla mou*,' he said drily. He had thought he knew everything there was to know about Lissa Buchanan, but she confounded him and intrigued him more than any woman ever had.

He threaded his fingers through hers and led her over to a glass door that opened directly into the master bedroom of the penthouse suite. When he switched on the bedside lamp he was struck by how fragile Lissa looked. Her blue eyes were huge and shimmered with tears. She tucked her hair behind her ear, and something moved inside Takis as his gaze lingered on her delicate features with those exquisite cheekbones.

'I'm sorry your first time was a disappointment.' Takis felt a need to put his arms around her and simply hold her, but he sensed that her composure was close to breaking. He ran his finger lightly down her cheek. Her skin was as soft as a peach and he liked the soft flush that bloomed on her face. He liked it way too much.

His voice deepened. 'I regret my crass behaviour. If I had realised...' He shook his head. 'I listened to gossip and rumour and did not take your inexperience into account.'

CHAPTER SIX

LISSA'S LEGS GAVE way, and she sank down on to the edge of the bed. The stinging sensation between her thighs had eased, but the restless ache there was worse. She felt unfulfilled, overemotional and a little bit sick.

She did not know what she was doing here, why she had stayed with Takis instead of insisting on returning to her room. She did not understand why she had given herself to him and become the kind of woman her grandfather had believed she was. She had always been a disappointment to Pappoús, and now she was disappointed with herself. All the reasons why she had agreed to have casual sex with a man she hardly knew now seemed flimsy, and she felt cheap.

She tried again to pull up her zip, but it wouldn't budge, and she held the bodice of her dress tightly against her breasts. Takis drew up a chair close to the bed and sat down, stretching his long legs out in front of him. When she darted a glance at him, his expression was unreadable, but she sensed that he was angry, although whether with her or himself she couldn't tell.

He folded his arms across his bare chest, drawing her attention to the ripple of muscles beneath his satiny skin. 'You owe me an explanation.'

Lissa flinched at his steely tone. 'I don't owe you anything.'

He said nothing and she let out her breath slowly when it occurred to her that Takis was the only person who had asked her for the truth. Her grandfather had believed every dirty lie printed about her, and even her brother and sister had avoided mentioning her private life whenever juicy details were aired in public.

'It started when I was seventeen,' she said flatly. 'I was invited to a party by a guy called Jason. He was a singer, and I had been to some of his gigs in bars around Oxford. All the girls at school fancied him and I was amazed when he showed an interest in me.'

Anger made tears prick her eyes as she remembered how gullible she had been and how flattered she'd felt when Jason had asked her to be his date at his party.

'He was trying to break into the music business and had his own record label funded by his millionaire father,' she told Takis. 'I was unaware that a photographer from a music magazine and a journalist who worked for a local newspaper had been invited to the party. Jason plied me with alcohol. I thought I would look sophisticated if I drank cocktails, but I got horribly drunk. I don't remember who persuaded me to take my dress off and dance on the table in my underwear.'

She bit her lip. 'Jason suggested we go outside for some fresh air. I let him kiss me, but I'm sure I didn't agree to him taking my bra off. There was a lot of fuss and people and flashing lights, but I was too out of it to know what was happening. Luckily, one of my friends insisted on driving me home.'

Lissa dropped her gaze from Takis's impenetrable stare. 'The next day, the headline on the local newspaper was something along the lines of *Singer's Sex Romp with Star-Struck Groupie* and there was a photo of me, half-naked and in a compromising position with Jason on the bonnet of his father's Rolls-Royce.'

She had felt mortified and *used* when she'd realised that Jason had set her up. 'It was bad enough that I had been humiliated in my home town, but worse was to come. A tabloid newspaper got hold of the photo and they published an interview with Jason in which he said that I was an obsessed fan who had stalked him and begged him for sex because he was famous.'

Takis frowned. 'I assume the guy lied because if he had admitted that nothing happened between you there would not have been a scandalous story and he wouldn't have got exposure in the national press.'

'That's exactly it.' Something loosened in Lissa's chest, like a knot that had been tightly tied unravelling. 'It was a fantastic publicity stunt for Jason. Radio stations started playing his music and he was even offered a place on a reality TV show.'

'Why didn't you deny the story and demand that the newspapers retract it?'

'I didn't know who to make a complaint to. And, anyway, no one would have believed me. My own grandfather didn't.' She grimaced. 'When Pappoús saw the picture of me in the papers he was furious and accused me of bringing shame on the family. He said my behaviour could damage his reputation, the reputation of the company. Not once did he question if what had been written about me was true. I was still at school, for heaven's sake. But he was so ready to believe the worst of me, so I let him.'

'You should have been able to count on him to defend you,' Takis said in a clipped voice. Lissa wondered if he was talking from experience.

Pappoús's failure to protect her when she had needed his support had been the most hurtful part of the whole unedifying episode. In her mind Lissa heard her grandfather's coldly condemning voice.

'You always want to be the centre of attention, just like your father. I never liked him, and I was disappointed when your mother married him. He won a few prizes for showjumping, but he didn't have the work ethic to succeed in business, and you take after him.'

Lissa realised that Takis was waiting for her to continue. 'A result of my unwanted fame was that my photograph was spotted by a scout for a model agency. Their client was a well-known cosmetics company. Sirène were looking for a fresh face to launch their new brand, and they chose me. The brief was a sassy, city girl with an attitude, so I acted the part to convince everyone I was that girl.'

She shrugged. 'I went to parties and met loads of handsome men, but I wasn't interested in any of them. Everyone was playing a game, trying to get noticed and desperate to boost their profile. I was a model for a famous brand and that made guys want to be photographed with me. In the world of celebrity there is no such thing as bad publicity.

'Whenever a scandalous story about me appeared in the tabloids, my grandfather called to say how ashamed he was of me. The *only* times he phoned were to give me a lecture and tell me that I would never amount to anything. I realised that I could get Pappoús's attention by behaving badly. But he had no right to judge me,' she said bitterly. 'He never knew the real me.'

Takis leaned forward in the chair and his grey eyes glittered beneath his thick lashes. 'So who is the real Lissa Buchanan? Why weren't you interested in any of those other men you met at parties?'

'There was no spark,' Lissa admitted. 'I never felt attraction, awareness, whatever you want to call it…until I saw you at my sister's wedding.' She looked away from him. 'But I was wrong.'

He frowned. 'In what way?'

'I thought you felt the spark too. But just now when we…' She felt her face burn. 'It was fairly obvious that I didn't know what to do. The earth didn't move for you… so I must have been mistaken to think you desired me.'

Takis swore. 'The issue was that I desired—*desire*— you too much.' At her puzzled look, he said roughly, 'I have never lost control like that before. The world didn't just move, it spun off its axis. I was impatient, desperate, and they are not words that I have ever used, let alone felt.'

He stood up and raked his hand through his hair. 'Why did you choose *me* as your first lover? Did you get swept up in the romance of the wedding and mistake the sexual attraction between us for love?'

Lissa shook her head. 'I don't believe in love at first sight. How can you fall in love with someone when you know nothing about them? When you know nothing about yourself? I am not the party girl the tabloids made me out to be, but I spent a long time pretending to be that person, and the truth is I don't know who I am,' she admitted.

She met Takis's gaze and said candidly, 'When my grandfather died, I made the decision to take charge of my life and make choices that feel right for me. I chose to have sex with you because I wanted to.' She smiled ruefully. 'And because you are incredibly attractive and sexy, and you promised me one perfect night.'

Takis looked faintly stunned for a few seconds, but then he walked over to the bed and took her hands in his, drawing her to her feet. 'A promise that I have every intention of fulfilling,' he said softly. 'Will you allow me to make love to you with the consideration and care that I should have shown you the first time, Lissa *mou*?'

Her foolish heart skipped a beat to hear him call her *his* Lissa. She wasn't his and never would be. But everything she had told Takis was true. She was on a journey of self-discovery and curious to explore her sensuality. Instead of replying to his question, she lifted herself up on to her toes so that her face was almost level with his and pressed her lips to his mouth.

He immediately took control of the kiss and made a muffled sound in his throat as he slid his tongue between her lips and explored the moist interior of her mouth with mind-blowing eroticism.

Lissa had not entirely believed Takis when he'd told her that he had lost control because he'd wanted her too much. But now the spark blazed into an inferno and his passion scorched her. His mouth and hands were everywhere on her body; his lips moved over her jaw and cheek before sliding up to explore the sweet spot behind her ear, while his fingers gripped the top of her dress and tugged it down to her waist.

He cupped her bare breasts in his big hands and rubbed his thumb pads over her nipples, making them instantly hard. Lissa was desperate for him to replace his fingers with his mouth. She flushed with embarrassment when she realised that she had spoken out loud.

Takis gave a throaty laugh. 'Patience, *koúkla mou*. Good things happen to those who wait.'

'I don't want to wait,' she muttered. 'I want you.'

He muttered something incomprehensible as he stripped off his trousers and tumbled her down on to the bed, removing her dress completely. His body was a symphony of sleek, bronzed skin and impressive musculature, and he was unashamedly aroused. Anticipation sent a quiver through Lissa when he skimmed his hand over her stomach and pushed her thighs apart. He claimed her mouth again in an intensely sensual kiss that drove every thought from her mind, and she gave herself up to the exquisite sensation of Takis gently parting her womanhood and sliding a finger into her slick heat.

His caresses soon had her body clamouring for more, and the ache low in her pelvis became an insistent throb that she instinctively knew only his complete possession would assuage. But when she tried to pull him down on top of her, he laughed softly and shifted his position so that he was kneeling over her. She snatched a breath when he bent his head and kissed his way along her inner thigh, higher and higher until he flicked his tongue over her ultra-sensitive clitoris.

Lissa made a choked sound and gave up trying to tug his head away from between her legs. She ran her fingers through his luxuriant black hair and arched her hips towards his mouth as he pleasured her in the most intimate way imaginable. Takis reawakened her desire with his wicked tongue, and she curled her fingers into the satin sheet as pleasure built inside her and became an unstoppable, irresistible force. It was too much, not enough, she wanted more, wanted… Bliss.

She came hard against his mouth and gave a sharp cry as her orgasm made her shake from head to toe. But her body sensed there was something more than this sweet delight, something even better.

As if he'd read her mind, Takis lifted his head and murmured, 'That was just a taster, *koúkla mou*. And you taste like nectar.' He donned a condom with a swift efficiency that reminded Lissa he had done this countless times with countless women. She wished that she were more experienced and knew how to pleasure him.

But her insecurity dissolved when she saw the hunger glittering in his eyes. 'Tell me if it hurts and I'll stop,' he murmured as he positioned himself between her thighs, and she felt the swollen tip of him press against her opening. This time there was no sharp sting, just a wonderful feeling of fullness as he eased slowly forward. It felt so unbelievably good. She realised that she had been holding her breath, and when she relaxed and her eyes met his, it was like the final link of the connection between them. Body and soul, except that Takis had insisted he did not have a soul.

'It doesn't hurt,' she assured him. 'Don't stop.'

He withdrew from her almost completely and then thrust again, a little harder this time, making her gasp as she realised how powerful he was. He filled her, completed her, took her over with each measured stroke as he set a devastating rhythm.

Reality faded, and Lissa decided that if none of this was real, if Takis's big body driving into her was simply an erotic dream, then it did not matter if she arched her hips to take him even deeper inside her and wrapped her legs around his back so that they moved together in perfect synchrony. Each thrust took her closer to a place that hovered frustratingly out of reach. Her breaths came in sharp pants, and she dug her fingers into his shoulders.

Sensations were building to a crescendo deep within her and tiny ripples of pleasure began to ripple out from her central core. Takis slipped his hand between their joined, sweat-slicked bodies and found her hidden pleasure zone. One flick of his thumb and simultaneously another powerful thrust of his body drove her to the edge. He kept her there for seconds that seemed to last for eternity before he gave a final twist of his hand, and she shattered.

The intensity of pleasure was beyond anything Lissa had imagined she could feel. As the shudders of sexual rapture slowly subsided, she realised that Takis had not finished. He started to move again, supporting his weight on his elbows as he set a pace that was wilder than before. Faster. Harder.

Her body welcomed each thrust of his steel length and impossibly she felt her desire stir again. She gloried in his possession and held nothing back. She was his. The words were a litany inside her head, and she whispered them into his mouth when he claimed her lips once more and kissed her deeply. He reared above her, his jaw clenched and his eyes gleaming hotly, and then he gave a savage groan as his big body juddered, and Lissa trembled beneath him as she followed him into the fire.

For a long time afterwards he remained on top of her and their bodies were still joined. His mouth was pressed against her neck and she felt the thunderous beat of his heart gradually slow. Eventually, he moved across the mattress to deal with the condom. His silence stretched Lissa's nerves and she wondered if there was a protocol she should follow. Her inexperience of the situation made her tense and turned Takis into an ominously silent stranger.

'You were right.' Her voice sounded over-bright.

He turned towards her and propped himself up on one elbow. 'About what?'

'You are good at sex.'

'I would take that as a compliment, except I know you have nothing to compare my performance with,' he said with amusement.

She quickly lowered her lashes to hide the emotional storm raging inside her. 'Well, I wasn't disappointed.' She strove for the same cool tone that he had used, as if she could convince herself that she was unaffected by the passion they had shared.

Takis lifted his hand and brushed her long fringe off her face. 'Neither was I disappointed. But I knew I wouldn't be. At Jace and Eleanor's wedding I don't know how I kept my hands off you, and later when I drove you back to the hotel…'

A dark flush ran under his skin. 'I don't usually come on to a woman so strongly. The truth is that I had desired you before we ever met. For a while, your face was on billboards everywhere, department stores, airport lounges, and whenever I turned on a TV it seemed that there was an advert showing the face of Sirène. You. Beautiful, sexy…every woman wanted to be like you and every man wanted you.'

'They wanted who they thought I was. My image was created by a PR agency and accepted without question by the media. Until you, no one ever asked or cared who I really was.'

Takis frowned. 'But then, quite suddenly it seemed, your photograph was replaced with that of another model on adverts for the cosmetics brand, and there were rumours you had been dropped as their representative.'

Lissa shifted up the bed and leaned against the headboard. She knew it was ridiculous to feel shy after what she and Takis had done but she pulled the sheet over her breasts.

'My contract with Sirène was for three years, but I became ill a few months before it was due to finish. I lost a lot of weight, and there were other unpleasant symptoms. I felt anxious a lot of the time and my body would tremble uncontrollably. The tabloids jumped to the conclusion that I was a drug addict.'

'Are you fully recovered from your illness?'

'I have an overactive thyroid. It's a lifelong condition, but it is controlled with medication and I have regular check-ups with my GP.'

'Did you hope to return to modelling?' Takis asked.

'I was offered another contract, but my grandfather had died, leaving Eleanor as head of Gilpin Leisure. I jumped at her offer of the position of assistant manager at Francine's hotel.'

Lissa gave him a wry smile. 'You look surprised. I didn't get the job through nepotism. While I was modelling, I also studied hospitality management. Eleanor gave me a trial period, and I have shown that I can run the hotel successfully. My grandfather refused to give me a chance,' she said bitterly. 'But I proved him wrong. When Eleanor married Jace she appointed me as general manager of the hotel.'

She fell silent, feeling embarrassed that she'd probably bored Takis with her life story. He'd admitted that he had desired her when he'd seen photos of her as a beauty model. She had been his fantasy woman…he must have been disappointed when he'd discovered that she was a virgin.

He swung his legs off the bed and did not say anything as he stood up and walked into the en suite bathroom. Lissa stared at the door, which he'd shut behind him, and wondered if he was giving her a subtle message that it was time for her to leave.

She stood up gingerly and picked up her dress from the floor, to discover that the silk lining was caught in the zip and no amount of tugging would free it. Takis walked back into the bedroom and lifted his brows in silent query when he saw her clutching her dress.

'I don't know what happens next.' She bit her lip. 'I was going to go back to my room.'

'What happens next is that you are going to soak in the bath I have run for you.' His smile made Lissa's heart perform a somersault. The wolf looked almost gentle. 'I thought you might be feeling sore.' He held out his hand to her, and after a brief hesitation she placed her fingers in his and allowed him to lead her into the bathroom.

The bath was a huge, sunken affair, filled to the brim with foaming, fragrant bubbles. 'First we went in the pool, and now I am to have a bath. I'll look like a prune,' Lissa joked to disguise her uncertainty as she stepped into the tub. The mirror revealed that her usually sleek bob was dishevelled, and her mascara was smudged. It was a far cry from when she had been the glamorous face of Sirène.

She looked different and she felt different. It wasn't

just the slight tenderness between her legs; she felt as though she had been set free from the rules she'd imposed on herself because she'd needed to prove that she was better than her grandfather's opinion of her. There was a whole great mess awaiting her in the morning, she thought ruefully. But the way Takis was looking at her made her forget everything and focus on him when he joined her in the bath.

'You have never looked more beautiful than you do right now.' He gently touched the red patches on her breasts where his beard had scraped her. 'Your skin is so pale, and I have left my mark on you.'

Not only on her skin, but she did not tell him that she would never forget him. Perhaps every woman remembered their first lover, she thought. But then Takis kissed her and she stopped thinking. He drew her down into the foaming water and picked up a sponge, which he slid over every inch of her skin, paying particular attention to certain areas of her body until she was trembling with longing.

She gasped when he slipped his hand between her thighs and his fingers unerringly found her molten heat. Her own hands were not idle, and she enjoyed making him groan when she touched him, tentatively at first, but she became bolder and circled his thick shaft with her fingers.

'Enough,' he growled. He lifted her on to his lap so that she was straddling his thighs and her pelvis was flush with his. His lips paid homage to her breasts as he entered her with a hard thrust. Water sloshed over the sides of the bath, and the bathroom floor was flooded by the time he scooped her into his arms and carried her through to the bedroom.

* * *

Lissa wished the night would last forever. But when the first glimmer of light in the sky heralded the dawn, she studied Takis's autocratic features, which were softer in sleep, and stole one last kiss from his lips before she slid out of bed. He had insisted that he only wanted one night with her, and she could not bear to stay there, only for him to remind her of that. She held her breath when he stirred, but he did not wake up, and she quickly pulled on one of the hotel's bathrobes, gathered up her dress, underwear and shoes and let herself out of the penthouse.

CHAPTER SEVEN

Sunlight dancing across his face woke Takis from a dreamless sleep. Too often his nights were disturbed by nightmares of Giannis trapped by the flames in the burning house. But this morning he felt a deep sense of contentment. The pleasurable ache in his muscles was not surprising after he'd spent hours making love to Lissa. Sex with her had been incredible. But now there were protocols that he hoped she understood.

From experience, Takis knew that waking in the morning with a new lover could be tricky. Women who had seemingly been happy to accept his no-strings rule the night before sometimes turned into clinging vines when it was time to say goodbye. The situation with Lissa was more complicated because she had given her virginity to him.

The possessive feeling that swept through him was inexplicable. The gift of her innocence had been un-asked for, and he was appalled that on a deeply fundamental level he liked the fact that he was the first man she'd slept with.

Remembering her passionate response when he'd made love to her made him instantly hard. Lissa may have been a virgin, but she had proved a willing and eager pupil and she'd quickly learned how to please him. He had known from her husky moans and the way she'd trembled in the throes of every orgasm he'd given her that she had enjoyed the night as much as he had.

He rolled on to his side, expecting to find her lying next to him, but there was just a faint indentation on the pillow where her head had been. She was not in the bathroom or outside by the pool and her sequinned dress and shoes were missing, which could only mean one thing.

Takis swore. Once again Lissa had surprised him, and he did not like surprises. Had she left without waking him because she was upset? The idea made him feel uncomfortable, but it had been her decision to sleep with him, he reminded himself. She was not his responsibility, but that did not stop him selecting her number on his phone.

She answered on the fifth ring. Evidently she had not been expecting him to call. 'Takis? Good morning. How are you?'

He gritted his teeth. Anyone listening to her cool voice would think she was talking to a casual acquaintance instead of the man she'd spent the night having passionate sex with.

'I was surprised when I woke and found you had gone.'

'I thought that was the idea,' she said quietly. 'I'm in a taxi on the way to the airport for my flight back to England. You were fast asleep when I left, and I decided not to disturb you.' There was a pause, and then, 'I should probably go. Thank you for a perfect night.'

'It was my pleasure,' he said drily.

Forty minutes later, Takis leaned back in the plush leather seat of the helicopter that was taking him to

Athens. He could not understand why he was in such a foul mood. The night he'd spent with Lissa had lived up to all his expectations, and it should have been enough. It *was* enough, he told himself. He had never needed anyone. And no one needed him. He avoided close relationships because if he did not allow himself to care, he couldn't be hurt or feel responsible for someone else's happiness. He was better off alone, and he had never doubted it.

When he walked into his apartment on the top floor of a modern development he owned in the city centre, he acknowledged that the sleekly luxurious but impersonal decor reflected his ethos on life and relationships. He did not form attachments and he shunned all ties. It was true that he'd bought his villa on Santorini because he had been drawn to its picturesque charm. The agent dealing with the sale had remarked that the villa with extensive gardens and access to a private beach would be an ideal family home for when Takis married and had children.

But that wasn't going to happen. He had no need of a wife. Work was the only mistress he cared about. Success was satisfying, but nothing could fill the emptiness inside him. He didn't want it filled. He deserved it.

Lissa was the most complicated, confusing and confounding woman he'd ever met, Takis frequently reminded himself over the following weeks. He was determined to put her out of his mind and focused on his latest project, the acquisition of a hotel and leisure complex in Santorini that he'd had his eye on for a long time. The negotiations over the price he was willing to pay were lengthy and intense, and when the deal was finally signed, he celebrated on the neighbouring island of Mykonos, where some fifteen years ago he had bought his first hotel in the Perseus chain.

Sipping vintage champagne in the hotel's nightclub, Takis acknowledged that he was at the top of his game. He was a self-made multimillionaire, and any of the women in the club would be his with little effort on his part, but none of them captured his interest.

In an effort to forget Lissa, he had dated several beautiful women, and there had been occasions when he'd been snapped by the paparazzi leaving a club with a stunning brunette or a gorgeous redhead. But the tabloids were unaware that he had escorted his dates home at the end of the evening and politely declined all invitations and pleas to stay the night.

He finally admitted to himself that he missed Lissa, which was crazy because he usually never gave an ex-lover a second thought. He had tried keeping his distance from her, but he found himself thinking about her a lot.

Evidently she had taken him at his word when he'd stipulated that he only wanted one night with her, and she hadn't called or messaged him. But that hadn't stopped Takis's heart lurching whenever his phone pinged, and his disappointment when Lissa's name did not appear on the screen inevitably soured his mood.

The situation could not continue, he decided. He would have to see her again, and a new business deal he was on the verge of completing would give him the perfect opportunity to get in touch with her. Overfamiliarity bred boredom, he told himself. If he had an affair with Lissa, he was confident that her novelty would wear off and he would be freed from the unaccountable hold she had on him.

* * *

Lissa glanced out of her office window at the rain beating against the glass. The dismal weather reflected her mood, which turned even bleaker when she looked at her computer screen. The photo of Takis with a beautiful woman clinging to his arm was in a Greek newspaper that Lissa was reading online. She did not know why she tortured herself with needing to know what he was doing, and with whom. It was bad enough that every time she spoke to her sister, Eleanor recounted another story about Takis's love life that had appeared in the gossip columns.

Frustrated with her inability to get over him, Lissa deleted the screen image of Takis's starkly handsome face. Since she'd returned to Oxford after spending the night with him at the Pangalos hotel she had focused on work. In an effort to keep busy, she had also enrolled in an interior design course and discovered that she had a natural flair for design.

At school, art had been her passion, and she'd planned to study design at university. But she had got caught up in her modelling career and at the same time had decided to study hotel management because she'd hoped that when she showed her grandfather her qualifications he would be impressed and apologise for doubting her ability to work for the family hotel business. Pappoús had died without knowing how hard she had tried to win his approval, Lissa thought heavily. In many ways she was glad. She had spent too much of her life feeling unwanted by her grandfather, lacking self-worth.

Her phone pinged, and her heart flipped as she wondered if Takis had sent her a message. He hadn't, and she felt angry with herself for hoping that he had. She had wasted enough time moping over him and it had to stop. On impulse she decided that maybe she should accept an invitation to dinner from Andrew, a solicitor she had met at the sports club. She picked up her phone but hesitated before placing it back down on her desk without making the call. Andrew was a nice guy, and it wouldn't be fair to have dinner with him while she was fixated on a devilishly sexy Greek.

Organising the staff rotas was not Lissa's favourite task, but she was glad of the distraction as she opened the relevant computer file. The head chef and sous chef had had an argument and she tried to make sure they were on different shifts, but tonight the hotel was hosting a dinner for a hundred and fifty guests and Ben and Alex would have to work together. Sorting out issues among the staff was a part of hotel management that Lissa knew she did not excel at. It was probably her own insecurity that made her want to please everyone, she thought ruefully.

Her phone rang and she quickly quashed the hope that it was Takis. She smiled when her sister's name flashed on to the screen. 'I have two pieces of news,' Eleanor said after they had exchanged greetings. She sounded excited. 'I'm pregnant.'

'That's wonderful! How does Jace feel about becoming a father?'

'We are both over the moon. I'm expecting a little girl.'

'Oh, El, I'm so pleased for you. Are you suffering much with pregnancy symptoms?'

'Not really. In fact, I didn't realise I was pregnant for a while. But I can't stand the smell of coffee.'

Lissa glanced at the cup of cold coffee on her desk

that she had been unable to drink. The effects of an unpleasant stomach bug were still lingering, and she had gone off coffee. 'What is your other news?'

There was a slight hesitation before Eleanor spoke. 'I have decided to sell Francine's. Jace intends to concentrate on running his property development business, and I want to be a full-time mum when the baby comes. But I'll ensure you remain as manager of the hotel.'

'Surely that will be a decision for the new owner.'

'Takis assured me that all the staff will be offered new contracts with his company.'

Lissa's heart clattered against her ribs. 'Takis? Do you mean that *he* is buying Francine's?' She must have misunderstood, she told herself frantically.

'Yes, he is keen to add the Oxford hotel to his Perseus chain.'

'But he can't. You can't sell Francine's...' Lissa tasted blood in her mouth where she had bitten down hard on her lip.

'I'm sorry, I didn't realise you'd be so upset. I know that the hotel is part of Pappoús's legacy, but you and he did not see eye to eye.'

'Francine's is a link to our parents,' Lissa choked.

'We have to let them go,' Eleanor said gently. 'It's time to move on. I expect Takis will contact you soon to discuss the management position.'

Somehow Lissa forced a bright voice as she congratulated Eleanor again on her pregnancy, but at the end of the phone call she felt numb with shock. The prospect of having Takis as her boss was mind-blowing. It would be unbearable to work for him and perhaps see him regularly when he visited the hotel. She would have to resign and look for another job. But she did not only work at the hotel. Francine's was her home, and it would be a huge upheaval to leave.

There was a knock on the door, and her assistant, Pat, walked into the room. 'I saw you had left your coffee to go cold. I've brought you another one.'

'Thank you.' Lissa blenched as the strong aroma of coffee assailed her.

'Are you feeling all right? You haven't seemed yourself lately,' Pat asked with a motherly concern that tugged on Lissa's emotions. 'Maybe you should see a doctor.'

'I have an appointment with my GP this afternoon. I had a blood test to check my thyroid levels and I should find out the result today.'

'You young girls don't eat enough, if you ask me. I hope you'll have time for dinner before the function this evening.' Pat paused on her way out of the door. 'The florist has finished arranging the flowers in the dining room. The tables look lovely. It will be a late night for you, I expect.'

It certainly would, Lissa thought with a sigh. Francine's hotel hosted many functions throughout the year, but the Lord Mayor's dinner and dance was the most prestigious event in the calendar. The invitations stated carriages at midnight, but Lissa knew she would be helping to clear up after the party until the early hours.

The rain eased off in the afternoon and she decided to walk to her GP's surgery.

'Unfortunately, the results of your blood test went astray, and I have only just received them,' Dr Williams explained. 'Your thyroid levels are higher than they should be, and I will change the dose of your medication.' She hesitated before continuing. 'There's something else. The blood test also shows a positive result for pregnancy.'

Lissa stared at the doctor, feeling sure that she must have misheard. 'I can't be pregnant,' she croaked. 'I have missed a couple of periods, but I wasn't concerned because it has happened before.'

'Certainly, a thyroid condition can affect a woman's menstrual cycle, resulting in light or irregular periods. But you are definitely pregnant.' The doctor gave Lissa a sympathetic smile. 'I can see that this has come as a surprise. I'd like you to make an appointment with the midwife as soon as possible so that you can be booked for an antenatal scan.'

It couldn't be true, Lissa thought numbly. She couldn't be expecting a baby. Takis's baby. But little things fell into place. Her tiredness and odd reaction to certain smells, especially coffee. The feeling in the pit of her stomach when her sister had revealed her own pregnancy. Her breasts were more tender than usual, and when she had shopped for a new bra she'd found that she had gone up a size.

But she *couldn't* be pregnant. Takis had used a condom each time they'd had sex. She froze when she remembered how he had started to make love to her in the bath. Could it have been then? The how and where were not important, she thought heavily. The fact was that the man who had told her quite clearly he never wanted children was the father of her child.

Lissa walked back to Francine's hotel in a daze, barely able to comprehend that a new life was developing inside her. She had never really thought about having a child because she had been advised that her thyroid condition could make it difficult for her to conceive. This baby was a miracle, but Takis was unlikely to see things that way. He was going to be furious when she told him her news.

She remembered the excitement and pride in her sister's voice when Eleanor had announced her pregnancy and said that Jace was delighted. But Lissa did not have a relationship with her baby's father, and she hadn't spoken to Takis for months. In fact, it was four months since she'd slept with him, she realised when she did a mental calculation. It was astonishing that she had reached that stage in pregnancy without being aware she was carrying Takis's baby. To complicate the situation even more, Takis was the new owner of Francine's. Which made him her boss.

It would not be long before her pregnancy was noticeable. Even if she did not tell him that the baby was his, he might guess, and she had a fair idea of how he would react. She thought of leaving Oxford and looking for another job and somewhere for her and the baby to live. But Lissa's conscience insisted that Takis had a right to know he was going to be a father.

If he refused to support his child, she would manage. She had some savings from when she'd earned a high income as a model, although she'd lent her brother money so that he could clear his debts. Mark was receiving treatment for his gambling addiction and she could not ask him to repay her while he was trying to get his life back on track.

At least she had her inheritance. Her grandfather's will had prevented Lissa from accessing her trust fund until she was twenty-five, but her sister was the trustee and had made the money available to her. It would help when the baby was born. But Lissa knew she would have to go back to work and all her friends who were working mothers went on about how expensive child-care was.

Somehow she got through the rest of the day and tried not to dwell on her secret while there was so much to do, preparing for the Mayor's dinner-dance. But being pregnant was such a momentous, life-altering event and every time she thought about the future she felt terri-fied. She popped up to her apartment to change her dress for the evening, and when she studied her body in the mirror she noticed signs of her pregnancy that she'd previously missed. Her breasts were fuller, and her usually flat stomach had a small curve. Emotions that she had held back all day flooded through her. She was scared, but also excited at the thought of having a baby.

When she had been diagnosed with an overactive thyroid, and the endocrinologist had explained that the condition could affect her fertility, she had felt sad that she might never be a mother. It had been something she knew she would have to deal with in the future, if she fell in love with a man and wanted to marry and have a family. But against the odds she was pregnant, and she felt awed and thrilled and still not quite able to believe it.

Just before seven o'clock, guests began to arrive and gathered in the bar for cocktails. Lissa checked the din-ing room, which looked elegant with the tables dressed in white and gold. Once tonight's event was over she would have time to make plans, but for now she must focus on her job.

The door leading to the kitchen flew open and one of

the waitresses ran out. 'Miss Buchanan, Ben and Alex had a fight, and Ben has gone.'

Lissa stared at Kate. 'Gone where?'

'I don't know. He stormed out, saying he wouldn't be coming back. What are we going to do about the dinner?'

What indeed? Lissa tried not to panic. The guests were expecting to sit down to a five-course meal, and she was without a head chef. She hurried into the kitchen and found Alex nursing a fat lip. 'You will have to be head chef tonight,' she told him.

'But—' Alex began to protest.

Lissa turned to the junior chef. 'Jo, you will be sous chef. Everyone else will muck in and help, including me.'

She picked up an apron and was about to put it on when a voice that had haunted her dreams came from the doorway.

'You should not be in the kitchen. Do I need to remind you that your duty as manager of the hotel is to be front of house to greet the guests?'

Lissa spun round, and her heart leapt into her throat as she stared at Takis. It was too soon. He shouldn't be here. Not yet. Not before she'd had time to steel herself.

'I... I wasn't expecting you,' she stammered.

His brows rose but the expression on his hard-boned face was unreadable. 'Evidently not,' he drawled. 'I arrived a little while ago and waited for you in your office. But I find you refereeing a fight between the kitchen staff.'

'I—'

'Are you going to call the staff agencies and request a replacement chef?'

'The recruitment offices will be closed now.'

Takis frowned. 'So what *are* you going to do?'

'I'm sure we can manage,' Lissa assured him, trying to sound more confident than she felt with the torrent of emotions building inside her. 'I'll see if I can get hold of Ben and persuade him to come back to work.'

'Don't bother. I never give second chances.' Takis's hard gaze swept around the room and every one of the staff stood a little straighter. 'My name is Takis Samaras, and I am the new owner of Francine's. Tonight you are all on trial. Do well, and you will keep your jobs. But if you fail to meet my expectations, you're out.'

No one said a word, and everyone suddenly became very busy plating up the first course. Lissa hurried out of the kitchen after Takis. He was talking on his phone and she took the opportunity to study him.

He was wearing black trousers and a matching rollneck sweater, topped with a black leather jacket, and he was as gorgeous and sexy as she remembered. She fancied that his face was leaner, his sharp cheekbones more pronounced, and the predatory gleam in his eyes made him look even more wolflike.

Her body responded to his rampant masculinity. Her nipples tightened and she felt an ache between her thighs. With a flash of despair she wondered why he still affected her so powerfully. Her hand moved involuntarily to her stomach and she tensed when Takis's eyes roved over her. Would he guess her secret? She was conscious that her black velvet dress was a little tight over her breasts.

He slipped his phone into his jacket. 'I've just spoken to the manager of the hotel I own in London. They have a chef available who could take the head chef's place, but the journey time to Oxford is an hour and a half, and it would probably be nearer to two hours because of some local flooding where the river has burst its banks.'

Lissa suddenly remembered a gastropub beside the river that had had to close temporarily after the cellar had flooded. 'I have an idea,' she told Takis. She took out her phone and found the number for the White Hart. Five minutes later she had arranged with the pub's manager for the head chef to work at Francine's for the evening.

'Good,' Takis said when she explained that she had found a replacement chef. 'But the argument between the kitchen staff should have been dealt with before now. It was your responsibility to take charge of the situation.'

'Ben has had some personal problems…'

'He should not have brought them into the workplace. Your role as general manager is to ensure the smooth running of the hotel. It is not only the kitchen staff who need to impress me if they want to keep their jobs. I expect one hundred percent commitment from everyone, including you.'

'You're a fine one to talk about commitment,' Lissa burst out angrily.

His gaze narrowed on her flushed face. 'I suggest you set aside your personal feelings while you are at work.'

'That won't be hard. I do not have any personal feelings for you.'

He closed the space between them and stared down at her. Lissa had forgotten how tall he was and felt glad that she was wearing four-inch heels.

'We will continue this discussion later,' Takis said

in a low, intense voice that sent a quiver of awareness through her.

'Don't,' she whispered, as much to her foolish pounding heart as to him. Her conscience prodded her to tell him about the baby they had conceived that night in Greece. But she could not bring herself to blurt out her momentous news while they were standing in the busy hotel foyer.

'I must go…and do my job,' she said stiltedly as she stepped away from him and hurried off to the cocktail bar to greet the town's mayor and other local dignitaries.

Much to Lissa's relief, there were no further problems, and the dinner-dance was a great success. The guests began to depart at midnight, but it was another hour before the last car to leave turned out of the hotel's gates. Lissa went into the kitchen to check that the staff had transport home. She phoned for a taxi for one of the young waitresses who had stated her intention to walk through the city centre at night alone.

'It's only a ten-minute walk, Miss Buchanan. Taxi drivers charge the earth after midnight.'

'I'll pay for the taxi, Becky. I want to be sure you arrive home safely.' Lissa glanced across the kitchen and discovered that Takis was leaning against a counter. He was frowning and she guessed he had overheard her conversation and no doubt disapproved. She would let him know that she had paid the waitress's taxi fare personally, and not out of hotel expenses.

By the time she had locked the front door after everyone had gone, Lissa felt sick with tiredness, and her heart sank when she walked past her office and saw Takis sitting behind her desk. His desk now, she silently amended as she stepped into the room.

'These are very good,' he murmured, flicking through her folder of interior design ideas.

'You have no right to look through my private folder,' she said stiffly.

'I do if you were working on your designs when you should have been carrying out your job as the hotel's manager.'

'Those particular sketches are my ideas for refurbishing some of the hotel's bedrooms.' Lissa bit her lip. 'I heard you tell the staff at the end of the shift that their jobs are secure. But what about me? Will I continue to manage Francine's?'

He drummed his fingers against the desk. 'I plan to install an experienced manager from one of my other hotels. Francine's is dated in the way it operates, and frankly it fails to provide the high quality of service that I demand.'

Shocked and dismayed, Lissa closed her eyes, desperate to stop the tears that threatened to spill from them. She couldn't lose her job. Not now. When she opened her eyes again Takis had moved and was standing in front of her. 'I proved tonight when I found a replacement chef that I can think on my feet. I'm good at my job. You can't fire me,' she pleaded.

He lifted his hand and tucked her hair behind her ear. 'I have other plans for you, *koúkla mou*.'

The spicy scent of his aftershave assailed her senses, and a tremor ran through her when he slid his hand beneath her chin and tilted her face up to his. Lissa's body responded wildly to the sensual promise glittering in his grey eyes as he lowered his mouth towards hers.

With a low cry she pulled away from him. 'No. You

don't understand. I need my job at Francine's because I… I'm pregnant.'

Takis rocked back on his heels but he said nothing. His muted reaction was worse than if he'd exploded in rage. Lissa wished he would say *something*. Anything would be better than his ominous silence.

'Congratulations,' he drawled at last. 'Is the father of your child pleased?'

His voice dripped ice, and a shiver ran through Lissa. Did he really not understand what she was telling him?

Shakily she tried again. 'You are the father. I'm having your baby, Takis.' His furious expression shredded her nerves, but she continued. This time with conviction. 'I realise that you probably don't welcome the news. But I intend to support the child on my own. That's why I'm asking you to allow me to keep my job.'

CHAPTER EIGHT

THERE WAS A roaring noise in Takis's ears. He could not think or breathe. He felt the hard thud of his pulse, of his temper rushing like boiling lava through his veins. It could not be true. Lissa must be playing a cruel trick. Hadn't he learned years ago that all women were manipulative? And had once believed Lissa to be the same?

He realised that she was waiting for him to say something. But he could not bring himself to speak. Did not dare. His throat had closed up and his heart was trying to claw its way out of his chest. He stared at her, searching for some sign on her slim figure that she was expecting a child.

There was something different about her, he realised. Earlier tonight when he had seen her again for the first time, he had been stunned by her radiant beauty. The way she had seemed to glow from within.

Theé mou!

Even if she *was* pregnant, there was no way it was his baby, he reassured himself. He held on to that. His vocal cords relaxed, and he bit out one word. 'No.'

'For God's sake, Takis. There are employment laws in England. Pregnant women have rights, and you can't simply dismiss me.'

'No,' he repeated harshly, trying to convince himself as much as her. 'I am not the father of your baby.'

Lissa seemed to grow taller and she lifted her chin and met his gaze proudly. 'You know damn well that I was a virgin until I met you.'

He could not deny that indisputable fact. But he wasn't fooled by her look of wide-eyed innocence. He couldn't be. 'You must have taken another lover after you slept with me,' he said coldly. The sensation of an iron band crushing his chest was lessening as his brain kicked into gear.

'Do you really believe I hopped into another man's bed immediately after I'd had my first sexual experience with you?' Lissa demanded.

Takis wanted to believe it. The alternative was unthinkable.

'You are the only man I've ever had sex with, and whether you like it or not I am expecting your baby.' She took a step towards him. 'Please believe that I never meant for this to happen. I only found out today and I am as shocked as you.' She placed her hand on her stomach and said softly, 'An accidental pregnancy is not such a terrible thing. We are going to have a baby.'

Rejection roared through Takis. And fear. Gut-wrenching fear. He could not be responsible for a child. Not again.

'I do not want a child. I told you that fatherhood holds no appeal for me.'

He did not doubt that she was pregnant. And now that the initial shock was subsiding, he realised that he did not doubt quite so strongly that the baby was his. Even as he fought against the very idea. He was the most untrusting man on the planet, and yet he had no reason not to trust Lissa. He did trust her. She had never lied to him. But how could *he* be a father after he had behaved so irresponsibly in the past? Takis was certain that he did not deserve to have a child. A child did not deserve him.

'Fine.' Lissa spun round and marched across the office. She had almost reached the door before he realised that she actually intended to walk out.

'Where are you going?'

'To bed.' She put her hand on the door handle and sent him a withering glance over her shoulder. 'I started work at six a.m. yesterday and it is now a quarter to two in the morning, which means that I have been on duty for nearly twenty hours. Does that show enough commitment to my job?' Her sarcastic tone made Takis grit his teeth.

'We have things to discuss,' he bit out.

'What things?' She opened the door. 'I have informed you that I'm pregnant and you stated that you do not want to be a father. So don't be.'

Cursing beneath his breath, he strode after her and slammed the door shut before she could walk out. 'What do you mean? Am I *not* the father? Do not play games with me, Lissa,' he warned her darkly.

She turned to face him. 'This baby might be unplanned, but he will be loved, is already loved by me. I told you about my pregnancy because it was the right thing to do, but I don't want anything from you. I'll go away somewhere, and you will never hear from me again. When my child is older and asks about his father, I will say that you are dead. Better that than for him to find out that he was not wanted by his father.'

Did she mean it? Takis's jaw clenched. Just because

Lissa had not made demands yet, it did not mean that she wouldn't do so. He hadn't wanted a child, but a child had been conceived. *His* child. Could he really walk away from his own flesh and blood? The answer hit him like a punch in his solar plexus. Of course he couldn't.

Takis felt the same sense of being caught in a trap that he'd felt when his stepmother had played a cruel game with his teenage emotions. One he had tried to escape by leaving home, leaving the half-brother he'd adored behind. He could never forget or forgive himself for abandoning Giannis to such a terrible fate. Had never confessed what his actions had led to.

He raked his fingers through his hair, unsurprised that his hand was unsteady. 'Why did you refer to the baby as him?' he asked Lissa.

She shrugged. 'I just have a feeling that it's a boy. I'll be able to find out the baby's sex when I have a scan and I can text you the result if you would like to know.'

She was so cool, Takis thought savagely, aware that his own emotions were dangerously close to exploding. He placed his palms flat against the door on either side of her head and watched her eyes widen in response to the sexual chemistry that had always been a potent force between them, and still was, he acknowledged.

Lissa stared at him. 'If you give me twenty-four hours to pack up my things and write me a reference so that I will be able to get another job, I promise you will never see or hear from me again.'

He believed her. She'd left without waking him after she had given her virginity to him. Lissa was perfectly capable of disappearing, and he would spend the rest of his life wondering if his child was safe or needed his protection. It would be a new kind of hell, a different version of his nightmares.

She sagged against the door and closed her eyes. Takis was struck by how fragile she looked. The dark smudges beneath her eyes were a stark contrast to her pale skin. 'I'm exhausted,' she whispered. 'We both need to calm down. Perhaps we will be able to talk more rationally tomorrow.'

Concern replaced his anger. Lissa was pregnant and Takis acknowledged that his behaviour was unacceptable. Without saying another word, he scooped her off her feet and held her against his chest.

Her lashes flew open. 'What do you think you're doing?'

'You were about to collapse,' he said gently as he opened the door and carried her through the hotel foyer.

Her blue eyes flashed with anger. 'I don't need your help.'

'Yes, you do.' His jaw clenched, determined. Lissa and the baby were his responsibility. *God help them*, he thought grimly. 'You will have to direct me to your living quarters.'

She sighed as if she realised that it was pointless to argue with him. 'Go through the door marked *Private* and there is a lift up to the apartment on the top floor.'

Her head dropped on to his shoulder and she was asleep by the time Takis carried her into the apartment and located her bedroom. He looked down at the silky blonde hair that curled against her delicate jawline. She was so beautiful. He felt a fierce tug of desire in his groin and was furious at his unbidden response to her. This was not the time.

He resented the hold Lissa had over him. He'd come

to Oxford intent on rekindling their passion so that he could get her out of his system. But she had dropped the bombshell of her pregnancy and he had no idea how to proceed.

He laid her on the bed and unzipped her dress. She hardly stirred when he removed the dress and her shoes but left her bra and knickers in place. When he pulled the duvet over her, he thought how young she looked. He swore softly. What a goddamned mess.

Takis knew he should try to sleep, but his thoughts were too chaotic. He explored the apartment and in the kitchen found a bottle of brandy, which he carried into the sitting room. Getting blind drunk was tempting but would not solve anything. Lissa was pregnant with his baby. It was his worst nightmare come true.

He remembered the first time he had met his baby half-brother. He had loved Giannis from the moment he'd looked inside the pram and seen a tiny infant with huge, dark eyes. Giannis had grown into a sweet-natured little boy who had adored his big brother.

Takis took a long swig of brandy, unable to hold back the memories that surged into his mind. He had not discovered what had happened until a few days after he'd left his home and travelled to Thessaloniki, where he'd happened to meet someone from the village.

'Will you go back for the funerals?' the man had asked him. 'You haven't heard? There was a fire. Your father tried to escape from the burning house, but he was killed when a wall collapsed on top of him.'

Takis had not cared about the fate of his father. 'You said funerals.' Sick dread had curdled in the pit of his stomach. 'Did my stepmother...? And Giannis? Not him,

please, no, not him.' A howl of agony had been ripped
from his throat when the villager shook his head.

'Marina and her little son both died in the flames.
It's lucky you were not there, or you could have lost
your life too.'

Guilt was his punishment, Takis brooded now as
he refilled his glass. He should have stayed at home to
protect Giannis, but in a fit of pique and fury with his
stepmother he'd run away. Oh, he'd told himself that he
was leaving because he wanted a better life than that
of a goat herder, but the truth was that he'd wanted to
pay Marina back for breaking his heart.

When he had returned to the village he had been
overwhelmed with grief at the sight of the blackened
shell of the house, and at the mortuary three coffins.
He'd walked straight past the largest coffin, hesitated
next to the wooden box that held Marina's body and
crumpled to his knees beside the smallest coffin.

It had been so pathetically small. That's what had
struck him the hardest. Giannis had been just five
years old. Imagining his little brother's terror when
he'd woken in the night and found he was trapped by
the flames had fuelled Takis's nightmares ever since.

He prowled around the room and stopped in front of
the bureau where several framed photographs were dis-
played. The little girl with pale blonde hair was unmistakably Lissa, and he guessed that the attractive couple
on either side of her were her parents. They looked a
happy family, but family was something Takis had no
concept of. He had grown up with a violent father and
a stepmother who had tried to seduce him.

How did his upbringing equip him to be a successful
parent? The truth was that it did not, which was why he

had decided that he would not have children. But he remembered the words Lissa had thrown at him: he was going to be a father, whether he liked it or not.

Perhaps Lissa's pregnancy was a chance for him to atone for his past mistakes, Takis brooded. If he was honest, the responsibility of becoming a father terrified him. But he would not abandon his child like he had abandoned his brother. He must claim his baby.

Fragments of a dream flitted through Lissa's mind. Takis arriving unexpectedly at the hotel, his furious reaction when she'd told him about the baby. Her eyes flew open and she could feel her heart pounding. It hadn't been a dream. Light was filtering through the curtains into her bedroom. She checked the time and was horrified to see that it was ten o'clock before she remembered that the deputy manager would be on duty.

She had been dead on her feet at the end of the dinner-dance. Takis had brought her to the apartment, and he must have removed her dress and put her to bed. Her stomach rumbled, and she knew she should eat for the baby's sake. She wondered if Takis had spent the night in the hotel or whether he had driven back to London. He'd made it clear that he did not want the baby, and there really was nothing for them to talk about. She certainly did not want a maintenance payment from him. She and her baby would be fine on their own, Lissa told herself.

She pulled on her dressing gown and headed for the kitchen but stopped dead when she looked into the sitting room and saw Takis sprawled on the sofa, where he had obviously slept. His shirt was creased and the dark stubble on his jaw was thicker, but his rumpled appearance did not detract from his dangerous sex appeal. Lissa felt her nipples harden, and even though her dressing gown was made of thick towelling she folded her arms over her chest as Takis raked his gaze over her.

'Why didn't you use a room in the hotel?' she asked him. 'Two of the suites were empty.'

'I stayed in your apartment to be close to you in case you needed anything during the night. There was also the possibility that you might try to disappear,' he said drily.

Her legs felt wobbly and she sank down on to the sofa. 'I don't have anywhere to go.' The reality of her situation was sinking in. She would soon be without a job or a home. She supposed she could go and stay with her sister in Greece while she tried to organise her life, but the future was frighteningly uncertain.

Takis shifted along the sofa towards her. 'You are still very pale.' He picked up her wrist. 'Your pulse is going crazy. Is a fast heartbeat normal in pregnancy?'

'I'm not sure.' She did not tell him that his close proximity as he rubbed his thumb lightly over her wrist might be why her pulse was racing. 'My thyroid condition can cause problems during pregnancy and I'll have to have extra check-ups to make sure the baby is developing okay.'

He stood up and grimaced when he ran his hand over his rough jaw. 'I need a shower and a change of clothes, and then we will talk.'

Lissa noticed his holdall, which he must have brought from his car last night. She directed him to the guest bathroom and went to the kitchen to make tea and toast. She reminded herself that they were adults, and without the heightened emotions of the previous night it was surely not beyond them to have a cordial discussion. She would not prevent Takis from seeing his child if he wanted to.

As she carried the tray into the sitting room, it occurred to her that she did not even know if he drank tea. They had created a new life together, but her baby's father was a stranger.

Takis walked into the room, and Lissa's heart crashed against her ribs as she made a mental inventory of him. Faded jeans hugged his lean hips and he wore a grey cashmere sweater that clung lovingly to his muscular chest. His hair was damp from the shower. He had trimmed the stubble on his jaw, but he still looked like a pirate. He was devastatingly attractive, Lissa thought with a rueful sigh that he could still affect her so strongly.

'This is fine, thank you,' he said when she offered to make him coffee if he preferred it to tea. She'd noticed he winced when she explained that she only had instant coffee.

Lissa forced herself to eat half a piece of toast, but it tasted like cardboard and swallowing became an ordeal as her tension grew. 'You wanted to talk,' she reminded him.

He put down his cup, the tea untouched, she noticed.

'You and the baby are my responsibility.'

His coolness quashed her tiny hope that there could be a happy outcome to their conversation. She remembered when he'd made love to her and his eyes had blazed with heated passion. Now Takis was a remote stranger, and Lissa's heart sank when she realised that he viewed her pregnancy as a problem that he was determined to solve.

'I don't want to be your responsibility,' she said sharply. 'I've had enough of feeling like a burden. That's what I was to my grandfather. You don't have to be involved. I have money of my own and, as I told you, I plan to go back to work after the baby is born.'

'How do you propose to combine bringing up a child with a career?'

'I haven't worked out the details yet. But I will be fine,' Lissa insisted. 'I won't deny you visiting rights if that's what you want.'

He shook his head. 'I have a duty to ensure the welfare of the child we have created and your welfare. There is an obvious solution to the situation we find ourselves in.'

She gave a helpless shrug. 'It's not obvious to me.'

'We will marry as soon as it can be arranged,' Takis said smoothly.

'Marry?' Lissa stared at him incredulously. 'I'm not going to marry you. There's no need.'

His hard-boned face showed no emotion. 'You do not think it is important for the baby to be legitimate?'

'Nobody cares about that these days. Marrying simply to conform to outdated values is a terrible idea.' Without giving him a chance to speak, she said fiercely, 'I don't want to marry you. It's a crazy idea.'

'Nevertheless, it *will* happen.' He sounded implacable, and Lissa felt a ripple of unease. Takis could not make her marry him, she reminded herself. 'Marriage will give us equal parental rights,' he continued. 'If you refuse, I will seek custody of my child.'

She jumped up from the sofa, breathing hard. 'You wouldn't win. Courts rarely separate a baby from its mother unless there are exceptional circumstances.'

'Would you be prepared to risk a legal battle that could drag on for months or even years? The costs involved with solicitors' fees and so on are likely to be exorbitant.'

'I don't believe this,' Lissa said shakily. 'You told me that fatherhood does not appeal to you.'

His jaw clenched. 'It's true I would not have chosen to have a child. But neither of us have a choice. You are pregnant and we must both do what is best for the baby.'

Takis was like a tornado tearing through her life, Lissa thought frantically. She felt agitated and panicky and her heart was beating alarmingly fast. 'I can't breathe,' she gasped. The room was spinning. She flung out a hand to grab hold of the back of the chair.

'Lissa!'

Takis's voice came from a long way off. It was the last thing she heard before blackness engulfed her.

CHAPTER NINE

'ARE YOU SURE the baby is all right?' Lissa asked the nurse who was pushing her in a wheelchair along the hospital corridor.

'Baby is fine. Your pregnancy was constantly monitored while you were in intensive care, but you will feel more reassured when you have an ultrasound scan later today. We'll get you settled in your room first.'

Lissa glanced around the pretty room they had entered. It was decorated in shades of pink and reminded her of a luxury hotel room. 'This doesn't look like a hospital ward.'

'Mr Samaras arranged for you to have a private room,' the nurse explained as she helped Lissa on to the bed. 'Would you like me to put your photographs on the bedside cabinet? Mr Samaras brought them in,' she said as Lissa looked puzzled when she saw two framed photos of her family that had been on the bureau in her apartment at Francine's hotel.

She remembered that whenever she had opened her eyes Takis had been sitting next to her hospital bed. But her memory was vague. The doctor had explained that she'd been rushed to the hospital by ambulance and admitted to the intensive care unit after she had collapsed.

'You experienced a thyroid storm, which is a rare complication of hyperthyroidism. Your thyroid levels were dangerously high, which caused your blood pressure to soar. The condition can be fatal if it is not treated quickly.' The doctor was confident that Lissa's pregnancy should continue normally with her thyroid condition controlled with medication. Although there was a risk that that she could go into labour prematurely.

'How long have I been in hospital?' she asked the nurse.

'A week. You were very poorly for a few days. That handsome fiancé of yours has been very worried about you.'

Fiancé? Lissa's memory was becoming clearer. Takis had demanded that she marry him, but she had never agreed she would. Thankfully, her baby was unharmed by what had happened to her. She wondered if Takis had been worried about the baby, or if he'd hoped that her illness would put an end to her pregnancy. Tears filled her eyes as she lay back on the pillows.

She must have slept because when she awoke, Takis was sitting on a chair beside the bed. Her heart flipped as she studied him. He was as gorgeous as ever, but there were grooves on either side of his mouth that had not been there a week ago.

'How are you feeling?' he asked. Nothing in his voice or shuttered expression gave a clue to his thoughts.

'Better,' Lissa told him. 'You don't need to be here. I'm sure you must want to go back to Greece to run your business.' She bit her lip when his heavy brows drew together.

'I have stated that you and the child you are carrying are my responsibility.' He ran a hand through his hair. '*Theos!* It is my fault that you nearly died,' he said harshly. Lissa had never seen him so unrestrained.

'How do you work that out?'

'Your thyroid condition means that pregnancy is a higher risk for you. I should have been more careful when we had sex.' A dark flush ran along his sharp cheekbones. 'There was one time in the bath when I was reckless.'

'There were two of us,' Lissa said quietly. 'I was reckless too.' Takis could not spell it out any clearer that he regretted her pregnancy.

The tense silence was broken by a knock on the door, and a nurse entered the room. 'I've come to take you for your ultrasound scan, Miss Buchanan. Would you like your fiancé to accompany you?'

Lissa glanced at Takis. 'Well, do you want to see your baby?'

His eyes narrowed at her challenging tone. He seemed to be waging an internal battle with himself. 'I would like to be at the scan,' he said in a tense voice.

In the scanning room Lissa had the sense that everything was surreal. She hadn't had much time to assimilate the news that she was pregnant before she'd been taken ill, and the time she'd spent in intensive care was a blur. A nurse helped her on to a bed and the sonographer smeared gel on to her stomach. When she was lying down her bump was barely discernible.

'Every pregnant woman carries differently,' the sonographer assured her. 'But your baby is definitely in there. This is the heart.' She pointed to a tiny, flickering speck on the screen. 'And here we have the head and spine.'

Lissa held her breath. Her eyes were fixed on the

image on the screen. It was real. In a few months she was going to have a baby. A little person of her own who she would love, and who would love her. She felt overwhelmed with emotion and fiercely protective of the new life that she would soon bring into the world. A new life she would never let feel like a burden to her.

'The baby is a bit smaller than I would have expected for your dates, but there is no cause for concern at the moment,' the sonographer explained. 'I can tell you the sex if you would like to know.'

Lissa looked at Takis. He had not spoken during the scan and she had no idea what he was thinking. 'It is your decision,' he said. There was nothing in his voice to give a clue to how he felt at seeing his unborn child. Perhaps if they knew whether she was expecting a boy or girl, Takis would feel more of a connection to the baby.

'We would like to know,' Lissa said to the sonographer.

'You are expecting a boy. Congratulations.'

Lissa's heart leapt. A little boy! She wondered what he would be like and imagined a baby with dark hair like his father. She had felt him stiffen when they had been told the baby's gender. How did Takis feel about having a son? She glanced at him and was startled by an expression of stark pain on his face. She turned her head back towards the screen and the image of their tiny son. When she looked at Takis again, his hard features were once more unreadable. But Lissa could not forget his devastated expression or help but wonder what it had meant. Whether he truly feared fatherhood or if it was something more.

He pushed her wheelchair back to her room and ignored her protest that she did not need his help as he lifted her on to the bed. The brief moments when he held her in his arms evoked a sharp tug of longing in Lissa, and she swept her eyelashes down to hide her expression from his speculative gaze.

'Thank you for bringing these from home,' she said, picking up the photographs of her family.

'I thought you might like to have them. How old were you when the photos were taken?'

'Ten. The picture of me with my mum and dad was taken at a gymnastics competition. I'd won a medal and they were so proud of me. Mum had been a gymnastics champion and she encouraged me to take up the sport.'

She held up the other photo. 'This was taken on a family holiday to Ireland before my parents flew to Sri Lanka to celebrate their wedding anniversary. It was the last picture of them before they died.' Her heart gave a pang as she looked at her parents smiling faces.

'You had a close relationship with them?'

'I was the spoiled, youngest child, and my brother and sister probably resented all the attention my parents gave me,' she said ruefully. 'But we were a happy family.' She remembered family events, birthdays and Christmases that her parents had made so magical. They had made her feel safe and secure and loved, and that was what she wanted for her baby.

She looked at Takis. 'Why did you ask me to marry you?'

He frowned. 'You know why. You are pregnant with my baby.'

'Yes, but why insist on marriage—really? I've told you that you don't have to stick around.'

His jaw clenched. 'I will not abandon my child. He

is my heir. It would make no difference if you were expecting a girl,' he said before Lissa could speak. 'I am determined to protect my son and provide for him. My business interests have made me wealthy and I can give him a good lifestyle and the best education. Everything that I did not have,' he added.

Lissa nodded. 'I'm not so naive as to think that money and the privileges it brings are not important. But it is far more important that our son grows up knowing that he is loved unconditionally.'

Takis did not respond, but perhaps men did not feel the surge of devotion that expectant mothers felt to their unborn children—that she certainly felt—Lissa mused. It would be different when the baby was born and Takis held his son in his arms. She had to believe that. She wanted to believe they would create a family unit that she had craved after her parents had been cruelly snatched from her.

'I will marry you,' she told him, trying to ignore the lurch her heart gave, the feeling that she had taken a leap into the unknown. 'My brush with death, or at least serious illness, has made me see things more clearly. No one can predict what will happen in life. My parents went on holiday and did not return.'

She swallowed the lump in her throat. 'If we are married and something should happen to me, I'll have the reassurance of knowing that my son will still have his father, and there will be no question over who should bring him up.'

Takis frowned. 'Nothing is going to happen to you.'

'You can't be certain. I'm not being pessimistic, just realistic.' She sighed. 'After my parents died my father's cousin and his wife offered to have me and my brother and sister. But my grandfather was the next of kin and we were sent to live with him. Pappoús didn't want Mark and me, and he only took an interest in Eleanor because he groomed her to take over the family's hotel business.'

Lissa wished Takis would say something. His lack of enthusiasm was a reminder that he believed it was his duty to marry her. She was once again someone's responsibility. At least that's clearly the way he felt. It was a far cry from the romantic dreams she'd had when she'd been a little girl of meeting her Prince Charming. But she'd stopped believing in fairy tales as well as Father Christmas and the Tooth Fairy when her parents had died. More than anything she wanted security for her son. Which meant she must marry her baby's enigmatic father.

'I will make the arrangements for the wedding to take place in Greece,' Takis told Lissa. His voice was clipped, his emotions tightly controlled. He knew from the slight quiver of her bottom lip that she was hurt by his brusqueness.

Frustration surged through him. He had never wanted to marry or have a child, but fate, or more truthfully, his spectacular lack of control when he'd had sex with Lissa and his hunger for her had run wild, meant that he would soon be a husband and a father.

He was going to have a son. The shock of it ripped through him. If he had not attended Lissa's scan, he might have been able to distance his emotions from the situation. But she had looked at him with such fierce hope in her eyes that he'd found himself agreeing to go to the scanning room. And in truth he had been curious to see his child.

It had been worse and at the same time more incredible than he could have imagined. The images on the screen of his baby had been surprisingly clear, and the sight of a tiny beating heart had made his own heart clench. Right then, he had made a silent vow that he would give his life to protect his child, as he should have protected his brother years ago.

Memories slid from their lair in his mind. They were always there, waiting for him to drop his guard, and as soon as he did, they tormented him.

'Where are you going? It's night-time.'

Giannis's sleepy voice had come from the mattress on the floor that he'd shared with Takis.

'Can I come with you?'

'Not this time, agoraki mou.*' Takis had knelt and pulled his little brother into his arms. 'I have to go away for a while. Don't cry. I promise I will come back for you soon.'*

He'd felt Giannis's hot tears on his neck as sobs had shaken the boy's skinny body. 'I don't want you to go, Takis. Stay with me...'

That was the last time Takis had held his brother. He had returned to the village only once, to carry Giannis's coffin into the church. Even after all this time his grief was still raw. He had betrayed an innocent child's faith, his word had meant nothing and the memory of Giannis's tears would haunt him forever.

Lissa was looking at him and he did not understand why he felt such an urge to confide his secret shame to her. There could be no absolution for what he had done. He glanced at the photograph of her with her parents. There had been so much love in her voice when she'd spoken about them.

Something inside him cracked as he thought of the reason why she had agreed to marry him. Marriage would ensure that he was the baby's legal guardian. Lissa had suffered the devastating loss of her parents, and she was determined to spare her child from rejection, which was how her grandfather had treated her.

'I give you my word that I will protect our son, always,' he said gruffly. He would make sure he kept it this time.

Her blue eyes widened. Those beautiful blue eyes, the colour of the summer sky, that had cast a spell on him the instant he'd met her. But he would not allow her to bewitch him with her mix of innocence and sensuality again, Takis assured himself. He could not.

'And love.' She stared at him, and he wondered if she had noticed him flinch at the word. 'You will love our son, I hope. That's the deal.'

It was not his deal and never would be, but Takis did not tell her that his heart was buried on a mountainside with a little boy he had betrayed.

'You should rest,' he said briskly, avoiding Lissa's gaze. 'As soon as you are well enough to be discharged from hospital we will fly to Athens so that I can organise the necessary paperwork for us to marry. I would prefer a simple ceremony and a minimum of fuss.'

'I'd like my sister to be my bridesmaid.' A pink stain ran along her cheekbones, emphasising her delicate beauty. 'Our marriage is a practical solution to the situation we find ourselves in. But Eleanor won't understand. She married Jace for love. I don't want her to worry about me, especially while she is pregnant. It would be better if we pretend that our marriage is real.'

'There is no reason why anyone else should know

the truth of our relationship,' Takis agreed. But as he roamed his eyes over Lissa another truth hit him. A strap of her nightgown had slipped down to reveal a slim shoulder and the smooth slope of her breast, and he felt a white-hot flash of desire in his groin.

This was the reason he found himself in a situation that required him to marry, even though he had never wanted a wife, and still did not, Takis thought furiously. This uncontrollable desire that he'd never felt so intensely for any other woman. When he had met Lissa months ago he'd been unable to resist her sensual allure, but he'd limited himself to one night with her. However, their one perfect night had resulted in her conceiving his child and had changed the course of his life.

But he *would* control his body's response to her that made his heart rate quicken and his blood thunder through his veins. He was determined that their marriage would be on his terms, but Lissa's suggestion to allow other people to believe they were marrying for conventional reasons made sense, Takis decided.

'We will live in Greece,' he told her. 'I own a penthouse apartment in Athens, but it is not a suitable place to bring up a child. Do you have any preferences on the kind of house you would like?'

'So I am to have a choice?'

He narrowed his eyes to hide his irritation at her sarcastic tone. 'I would like to bring up my son in Greece. I assumed you understood that, but if you object strongly I suppose I can consider moving my business base to England.'

'I don't mind living in Greece. But I want us to discuss things. I am an adult, not a child who you can tell what to do,' Lissa said with some asperity. 'Marriage is about compromise.'

'I will try to remember,' he said evenly. Compromise was not a word in Takis's vocabulary, but he would put his ring on Lissa's finger and thereby claim his child before she discovered that fact.

CHAPTER TEN

THE WEDDING TOOK place at the civic hall in Athens a month after Lissa had been discharged from hospital and Takis had brought her to Greece. Jace and Eleanor flew in from their home in Thessaloniki, and Lissa shed emotional tears when she hugged her sister.

'It's so exciting that our babies will be born only a few months apart,' Eleanor said when they were in the waiting room before the ceremony. She gave Lissa a thoughtful look. 'I'll admit I was surprised when you told me you are pregnant. I didn't realise that you and Takis were together, although it was obvious at the charity ball that the two of you couldn't take your eyes off each other. Was it love at first sight?'

'It was,' Takis answered for Lissa. She tensed as she looked around and found he was standing behind her and must have overheard the conversation with her sister. He smiled urbanely at Eleanor. 'At your wedding to Jace when I was the best man and Lissa the chief bridesmaid, we both felt an instant connection, didn't we, *agapi mou*?'

He met Lissa's startled gaze and the indefinable expression in his eyes made her tighten her fingers on the bouquet of freesias that he had surprised her with before they'd driven to their wedding. She reminded herself that they were pretending to be in love so as not to arouse her sister's suspicions. Lissa knew that Eleanor would be concerned if she guessed the real reason for her decision to marry Takis.

They both wanted security for their son, but Lissa was starting to realise that she hoped for more than a sterile marriage of convenience. Her pulse accelerated when Takis slipped his arm around her waist. There had been no physical contact between them in the run-up to the wedding when they had lived at the house that Takis had leased in a leafy suburb of Athens.

The rental house was sleek and modern, but in Lissa's opinion the decor was unimaginative. Since she had left her job as manager of Francine's hotel she'd focused on the interior design course she was studying online. There was minimalist and there was boring, she'd told Takis when she ordered brightly coloured cushions to bring life to the living room. Takis had merely raised his eyebrows and disappeared into his study, where he spent most of his time when he was not at the Perseus hotel chain's head office.

Lissa had the sinking feeling that he wanted to avoid her, but she had reminded herself that the situation was odd for both of them. They were almost strangers, but once they were married she hoped they would begin to build a life together and create a family unit ready for when they welcomed their son into the world.

She looked down at the engagement ring on her finger. The previous day her hopes of building a relationship with Takis had been boosted when he'd unexpectedly joined her for dinner. Most evenings she dined alone because he did not return from work until late. But when she had walked into the dining room, she'd found him waiting for her and her heart had performed a somersault.

She had been reminded of the first time she'd met him at her sister's wedding when she had been desperately aware of his smouldering sensuality. Nothing had changed, she'd thought as her pulse had quickened when she'd smelled the distinctive spicy scent of his aftershave.

'I have something for you,' Takis had said after the butler had served the first course and left the room. He'd handed her a small box, and Lissa's heart had thumped when she'd opened it to reveal a ring with a deep blue sapphire surrounded by diamonds.

'It's beautiful,' she'd said huskily.

He'd given her a brisk smile and picked up his wine glass. 'Your sister would think it odd if you did not wear an engagement ring.'

I don't care what anyone else thinks, she had wanted to tell him. For goodness' sake, walk around the table and kiss me! But she hadn't dared say the words out loud. Instead she had slipped the ring on to her finger and sternly reminded herself that their marriage was a practical arrangement and Takis was not likely to have gone down on one knee when he'd presented her with the ring.

Lissa pulled her mind back to the present and realised that Eleanor was speaking to Takis.

'How did you persuade my sister to have a small ceremony? It was always Lissa's dream to have an over-the-top wedding with dozens of bridesmaids and hundreds of guests and an amazing dress. Although you look lovely,' Eleanor told Lissa quickly. 'A cream suit is so elegant, and you will be able to wear it again.'

'A big wedding would take a long time to organise.' Lissa quickly made the excuse, conscious that Takis was looking at her speculatively.

'Lissa is still recovering after being seriously ill,' he explained. 'It is better that she does not have too much excitement.'

There was no danger of her getting overexcited when her fiancé had barely paid her any attention, Lissa thought wryly. She slanted a glance at Takis as they walked into the wedding room, and the glittering look he gave her made her wonder if he had read her mind.

The wedding officiant greeted them, and the civil ceremony began. In a surprisingly short time the officiant pronounced them married. Lissa's heart missed a beat when Takis bent his head and brushed his lips over hers. It had been so long since he had kissed her, and she could not hide her response to him. Her body softened as she melted against him and parted her lips beneath his. She trembled with desire that only Takis, *her husband*, had ever made her feel.

He hesitated for a fraction of a second before his arms came around her, drawing her even closer to him so that her breasts were crushed against his chest and she felt his hard thighs through her skirt. She put her hand on his chest and felt his heart thudding as erratically as her own.

The heat of his body spread through Lissa, causing a molten warmth to pool between her legs. Instinctively, she pressed her pelvis up against his and felt the hard proof of his arousal.

He still wanted her. That at least was a start. She

smiled against his mouth and heard him give a low growl as his tongue tangled with hers. The doubts she'd felt that she was doing the right thing by marrying him faded. They had never discussed one crucial aspect of their marriage, but she could feel the evidence of Takis's desire for her. Tonight was their wedding night, and she was sure he wanted to make love to her as much as she wanted him to.

A discreet cough from the officiant broke the magic. Takis lifted his mouth from Lissa's and looked faintly stunned when he realised that they had made a very public display. She heard Jace give a throaty chuckle, but Takis was grim-faced when they walked the short distance to the restaurant where they were to have lunch.

It was late in the afternoon when Eleanor and Jace left for the airport to fly back to Thessaloniki. A car collected Takis and Lissa and took them to his office building, where a helicopter was waiting on the helipad to take them to Santorini. He had explained that he owned a villa on the island.

It was a perfect location for a honeymoon, Lissa thought as the helicopter flew over the sea, which was dappled with gold in the sunset. From the air the island's half-moon shape around the rim of the caldera was clearly visible. The coastline was dramatic, with towering volcanic cliffs and beaches with unusual black sand.

'The scenery is spectacular,' she said as the helicopter dipped lower and a village with square, whitewashed houses came into view. 'The buildings with blue domed roofs are churches, aren't they?'

'Yes, they're popular with tourists who want a photo opportunity,' Takis told her. 'Santorini, and the other, smaller islands nearby were formed after a massive volcanic eruption thousands of years ago. The crater that was left after the eruption is the only sunken caldera in the world and the lagoon is said to be four hundred metres deep.'

The villa stood alone on a headland and had incredible views of the sea. Lissa had expected Takis's island home to be modern and minimalist, but the coral-pink exterior was the first of many surprises. Inside, there was colour everywhere; green and terracotta tiles on the floor, walls painted a soft cream, and in the living room there were brightly patterned cushions scattered on the sofas. A vase of vibrant yellow chrysanthemums stood in the fireplace.

'This is lovely,' she commented. 'I didn't think you were a cushions kind of person.'

'My housekeeper Efthalia is responsible for those,' Takis said drily. 'Her husband, Stelios, also works for me as a caretaker and driver. The couple live in the staff cottage.' He gave Lissa a brief smile. 'I suggest you rest before dinner. You look tired.' He moved towards the door. 'I have a couple of calls to make.'

No woman wanted to be told that she looked tired, especially on her wedding day. Or be left alone by her new husband. Lissa stared at the door after Takis closed it behind him and wondered what phone calls were so important. She was being oversensitive, she told herself. The truth was that her pregnancy did make her feel more tired. She was showing now, although she suspected that her bump was partly due to the wonderful meals the cook at the Athens house had prepared.

She climbed the stairs to the second floor of the villa and found the master bedroom, but not her luggage. A connecting door led to another bedroom, and she spied her suitcase. Her clothes had been unpacked and hung in the wardrobe. Perhaps the housekeeper assumed she would use the second bedroom as a dressing room, Lissa thought as she slipped off her shoes and lay down on the bed. She would close her eyes for five minutes and then go and drag Takis out of his study if she had to.

When she woke, it was dark outside the window and someone had switched on the bedside lamp. The nap had revived her, and she was looking forward to an intimate dinner with Takis. The dress she had bought for her trousseau was a scarlet sheath made of jersey silk that clung to her new curves. She ran a brush through her hair that she'd recently had trimmed into her usual jaw-length bob, applied scarlet gloss to her lips and sprayed perfume on her pulse points before going downstairs.

As she walked through the villa, Lissa was surprised to hear from outside the whir of rotor blades. She stepped into the garden, and her stomach swooped when she saw Takis walking towards the helicopter.

'Wait!' Her muscles unfroze and she tore across the lawn. 'Where are you going?' She cursed as she stumbled in her high heels and pulled off her shoes. 'Takis?'

He turned around slowly. His hard-boned face was expressionless, and in the darkness that seemed to press around them he was a forbidding stranger. 'I came to your room to say goodbye, but you were asleep, and I did not want to disturb you. I must return to Athens.'

'Must?' Temper beat through Lissa. 'Why?' He made

no response and she said huskily, 'Explain to me how our marriage is going to work when you go out of your way to avoid me. We hardly spent any time together in Athens and I understood that you work long hours. But you brought me here to your villa, it is our wedding night and I thought...'

Her voice trailed off when he lifted his brows in that arrogant way of his that made her feel small and insignificant. She'd had a lot of practice at feeling insignificant when her grandfather had taken no interest in her, Lissa remembered bleakly.

'Why would we spend time together?' Takis sounded surprised. 'The only reason we married is so that our child will be born legitimate. We agreed that in public we will give the impression that our marriage is real, and your sister was convinced by our performance.'

'Was it a performance when you kissed me? Because it didn't feel like you were pretending.'

She had made the decision to marry him knowing that love was not involved. But she'd believed that they wanted the same things in the marriage, friendship, security for their child and yes, sex. She'd hoped that their physical compatibility would be a base on which to build their relationship, and she was sure she had not imagined the gleam of desire in Takis's eyes at their wedding.

'This conversation is pointless,' he said, stepping away from her. 'I have an early morning meeting in Athens before I'm due to fly to St Lucia to view a hotel that I am considering buying.'

'You're going to St Lucia without me?' Disappointment tore through Lissa. 'I thought we had come to Santorini for our honeymoon.' He could not have made it clearer that he was not prepared to make room for her in his life. In Athens she'd thought he was giving her time to recover from her illness, but now she realised that he regarded her as a nuisance. Would he think the same of their son when he was born? she wondered sickly.

'You have everything you need at the villa.' Frustration clipped Takis's voice. 'The staff will take care of you.' He started to walk towards the helicopter and Lissa followed him.

'When will you come back? What am I supposed to do while you are away?'

'You are on a paradise island and I'm sure you will find plenty to do. Stelios will drive you to wherever you want to go.'

Lissa noted how he avoided her first question. She watched him climb into the helicopter and wondered how she could have been so stupid as to think he might want to spend time with her or get to know her. She should have realised when he'd mostly ignored her in Athens that he wasn't interested in her. But this was not just about her.

'What about when our son is born?' she demanded. 'Will you use work as an excuse to hide in your office and ignore him too?'

Takis closed the door of the aircraft without answering her, and the *whomp-whomp* of the rotor blades grew louder. She would not cry, Lissa told herself sternly. He wasn't worth her tears, but her vision was blurred when she watched the helicopter take off. Moments later it was a beacon of light in the dark sky, taking her fragile hopes for her marriage with it.

Takis stared out of the helicopter at the night that was as black as his mood. Even as the glittering lights of

Athens grew nearer he fought the temptation to instruct his pilot to fly him back to Santorini and Lissa.

When she had run across the garden wearing a sexy dress that had surely been designed to blow any red-blooded male's mind, he'd come close to forgetting that he could not have her. Could not allow himself to have her. He was determined to resist his desire for her. The damage had already been done and she was pregnant with his child, but he was not going to compound his folly by becoming more involved with her than was necessary. By letting her believe they could have anything more.

When they had arrived in Athens a month ago Lissa had still been fragile after her illness. Takis could not shake the guilt he felt that he was the reason she had almost lost her life. Her thyroid condition had become acute because of a hormonal imbalance caused by her pregnancy. He had taken a stupid risk one time when he'd made love to her and he would have to live with the repercussions.

He felt another stab of guilt as he remembered her disappointment when he'd left her behind on Santorini. *Theos*, he had not done anything to give her the idea that he'd taken her to the island for a honeymoon, he assured himself. He had kept his distance from her. Except when he had kissed her at their wedding, he recalled grimly. He had only meant it to be a token, a nod to convention when the wedding officiant had pronounced them married.

But Lissa had kissed him back and he'd been lost the instant he'd felt her mouth open beneath his. She had tasted like nectar, and he'd been powerless to fight his desire for her, which had rolled through him like a giant wave, smashing down his barriers. His wife tempted him beyond reason, which was why he had left her at the villa and instructed his pilot to fly him back to Athens.

The nagging ache in his groin mocked him. He could not give Lissa the relationship she wanted. Not even a purely physical one. And maybe she wanted more than that. He'd caught her looking at him with a wistful expression on her pretty face that had set alarm bells ringing in his head. He had married her because she and the child she carried were his responsibility. His to protect. But he felt uncomfortable when he thought of her accusation that he would ignore his son when he was born.

Takis could not imagine what it would be like to have a son. He did not know how to be a father. His own father had been a violent bully, and the only lesson Takis had learned from his childhood was how to survive. But love and tenderness? He knew nothing of those things.

When the helicopter landed at the house in Athens, he went straight to the private gym and worked out for hours in a bid to forget that this was his wedding night, and his beautiful bride was miles away. Eventually, when he was physically exhausted, he took a punishing cold shower before he crawled into bed, only for his dreams to be tormented by fantasies of having Lissa beneath him and hearing her soft cries of pleasure when he drove himself into her body.

Work was a distraction that Takis was glad to immerse himself in. He spent four days in St Lucia, finalising a deal to buy a hotel complex that would be a valuable addition to the Perseus hotel chain. To his annoyance he found himself imagining what it would be like if he had brought Lissa to the Caribbean with him and they'd honeymooned in one of the luxury lodges.

If they'd made love on the private beach where the pure white sand ran down to an azure sea.

Back in Athens he spent long days at his office and when he returned to the house every evening he refused to admit that he missed Lissa being there, even though when she had shared the house with him he had avoided her as much as possible. Something that she had noticed, he thought with a stab of guilt, remembering her accusation when he'd left her at the villa that he used his work commitments as an excuse to stay away from her.

He must have imagined that Lissa's perfume lingered in the rooms at the Athens house, but he retreated to his study, which was the one room she had never entered, and tried to concentrate on financial reports for his expanding business empire to take his mind off his wife, who intruded on his thoughts with infuriating regularity.

A week passed, and another. Lissa phoned him several times, and the calls were invariably tense as she demanded to know if he intended to avoid her for the rest of her pregnancy, and beyond that, what was going to happen when their baby was born?

'I don't care if you want nothing to do with me,' she told him. 'But our son will care when he is old enough to understand that you have rejected him.'

But for the past couple of days Lissa's name had not flashed on to his phone's screen, and there had been no terse conversations, which had made Takis feel uncomfortable and guilty and unable to explain that he did not know how to be a father, or a husband for that matter. He had no role model to follow, apart from his own drunkard father.

The tenderness that he sensed Lissa hoped he would

show their child, and perhaps her, simply was not in him. Maybe it had been once, but Giannis's death had made him hard and cold. It was impossible to change who he was, Takis thought, justifying his behaviour, and tried to ignore his conscience, which taunted him that he was afraid to try to change.

He flew to Naxos to visit the hotel he owned on the island and deal with an issue that needed to be resolved. His suspicions that the hotel's manager had been fiddling the accounts and moving money into a personal account proved correct. Takis fired the manager, whom he had trusted, and he was in a foul mood by the end of a frustrating day.

'I thought you should see this,' his PA said when they boarded the helicopter. Rena handed him a tabloid newspaper. 'Page three.'

Takis turned to the page and managed to restrain himself from swearing loudly when he stared at the photograph of a group of young people fooling around in a beach bar in Mykonos. He knew their type. The beautiful people, rich, bored, minor celebrities. Lissa was at the centre of the group and her smile seemed to mock him. His temper simmered as he read the caption above the photo, which had been taken the previous day.

Tycoon's new wife parties with friends in Mykonos without her husband!

Lissa's male friends were heirs to huge fortunes. They spent their time drifting around Europe's flesh-pots and had probably never worked a day in their lives, Takis thought furiously. Fury shot through him. What was Lissa playing at?

He called the direct number of the manager of the Mykonos hotel, Perseus One, and learned that Lissa had checked in two days ago and was not due to leave until after the weekend.

'There has been a change of plan,' Takis told his pilot. 'You are to fly me to Mykonos before you take Rena back to Athens. I am planning to surprise my wife.'

CHAPTER ELEVEN

IT WAS DUSK when the helicopter flew low over Mykonos and landed in the grounds of the hotel. Perseus One was the first hotel Takis had bought when he'd established his hospitality business and he was proud that he had developed it to a level of breathtaking opulence demanded by its millionaire and billionaire clientele.

The marina was full of luxury motor yachts, and the hotel's casino was packed. On an island renowned for a party atmosphere, Perseus One was the place the rich and famous flocked to every Friday evening when a well-known DJ hosted an all-night party.

Takis strode into the nightclub and scanned the crowded dance floor. Lissa's pale blonde hair made her easy to spot. She was dancing with a guy who Takis recognised from the newspaper photo was Tommy Matheson—a lethargic young man whose only pursuit in life was spending his father's billions.

Lissa looked stunning. She wore the red dress she'd worn the last time Takis had seen her in Santorini. It clung to her newly voluptuous breasts and the swell of her belly where his child lay.

Anger surged through Takis when he saw how other men looked at Lissa as if they were imagining her naked. How dared they gawp at her? She was *his*. He was stunned that he felt possessive and jealous. They were not emotions he had ever experienced before or known that he was capable of feeling.

He strode across the dance floor and dropped his hand on to Lissa's shoulder, spinning her round to face him. The idiot she had been dancing with beat a hasty retreat after one look at Takis's grim face.

'What the hell are you playing at?' he demanded, raising his voice above the pounding disco music.

Lissa tilted her head and looked at him. She did not seem surprised to see him. 'I'm dancing and enjoying myself,' she said coolly. 'Is there a problem?'

He ground his teeth together. 'I have warned you before not to play games with me, *koúkla mou*.'

'Or you will do what, precisely? Take me to a pretty villa and leave me alone with no companionship and nothing to do except ask myself why I agreed to marry you?'

Her sarcasm further enraged him. 'You are carrying my child,' he snapped. 'Do I need to remind you of the reason why it was necessary for us to marry?' His eyes were drawn to the rounded swell of her stomach beneath the tight-fitting dress. Pregnancy made Lissa even more beautiful and sensual, and Takis longed to caress her gorgeous body. He clenched his fists to stop himself reaching for her. 'You are my wife and I do not appreciate you making an exhibition of yourself in public.'

Her eyes flashed, and he realised that she wasn't as calm as she made out. In fact, she was very, very angry. 'I don't understand why you should complain about me socialising with my friends. You have made it clear that you are not interested in spending time with me.'

She shrugged off his hand and carried on dancing, moving her hips sinuously to the pulse of the music and sending Takis's pulse skyrocketing. He clamped his arm around her waist. 'I want to spend time with you now. We're leaving.'

She glared at him. 'You can't *frogmarch* me out of the nightclub.'

'I think you will find that I can. Keep walking,' he advised her, 'unless you want me to carry you out of here.'

Lissa must have realised that he was serious, and she huffed out a breath as she walked beside him across the lobby. A lift whisked them up to the private suite that Takis kept for when he visited the hotel.

'Why do you object to me meeting my friends?' She rounded on him.

'I object to you courting the attention of the paparazzi.' Takis thrust the newspaper into her hand. 'A photo of my wife flirting with another man in a hotel that I own is not the sort of publicity I want for my business. You have made a fool of me.'

Lissa stared at him. 'I wasn't aware that the photo had been taken, or that it was published in the tabloids. What, do you think I wanted this to happen?' she demanded when he looked disbelieving.

'It's an occupational hazard. You attract attention.'

'You think I deliberately sought media interest?' She paled. 'Well, if that was my plan, it worked. You have been avoiding me for weeks, but when you saw my photo in the newspaper you couldn't get here fast enough so that you could criticise me, just like my grandfather used to do.'

'The situation is not the same,' Takis growled, guilt

knifing him in his gut when he saw the shimmer of tears in Lissa's eyes. He guessed they were tears of anger. She was trembling with fury, and the air between them crackled with temper, hers and his.

'It's exactly the same,' she snapped. 'The only way I can get your attention is by behaving badly in public.'

'We are not in public now, and you have my undivided attention.' He did not know if he had moved or if Lissa had, but he was standing in front of her, so close that he saw her eyes darken and he heard the sudden quickening of her breaths. Takis was aware of the exact moment the spark between them caught light. He could not resist her, he didn't even try.

He bent his head and claimed her mouth, kissing her with a desperation that on one level appalled him. He had no control when it came to this woman. An alarm rang in his mind, reminding him of the one other time he had abandoned all control when he had kissed his stepmother. This was different, he assured himself. He was not an impressionable teenager who had been convinced that his stepmother's occasional kindness to him was a sign of affection. Marina had broken his youthful heart and taught him that trust was a fool's game.

He lifted his head and stared at Lissa's lips, softly swollen from his hungry kisses. A hectic flush highlighted her cheekbones, and Takis knew she felt the tumultuous desire that was a ravenous beast inside him. He tightened his arm around her waist, bringing her body into even closer contact with his. But he tensed when he felt a rippling movement where her stomach was pressed against him.

'Was that…?' He could not disguise his shock.

Lissa smiled. 'Your son is saying hello to his daddy.'

Takis was shaken. Even at Lissa's scan, when he had seen the image of a baby on the screen, he'd felt a sense of unreality. But the movement he'd felt within her belly was not an inanimate image. It had been made by a tiny foot or fist. His son. A child he had never wanted, but nevertheless the baby deserved to have a kind and caring father. Takis did not know if he had those qualities in him. He rather doubted it. If he allowed himself to soften even a little, he might just fall apart.

He stepped back from Lissa and saw her stricken expression. Takis knew he needed to say something, but the longer the silence stretched between them the harder it became to think of anything that she might want to hear.

'Our son will be born in a few months and you had better get used to the idea,' she said in a low, intense voice that had more impact on him than if she had shouted. 'You promised to protect and love him, but I have seen no evidence that you will do so.'

'I promised to protect and provide for my child,' he corrected her. 'He will want for nothing.'

'He will want his parents to love him. Every child needs to be loved, and when they are not it causes terrible damage. I know, because my grandfather withheld his love from me, and I felt worthless. I won't allow you to make our son feel that he is unwanted by you or a burden,' she told Takis fiercely. 'I won't allow it.'

Lissa opened her eyes and looked around at an unfamiliar room before she remembered that she had spent the night in the second bedroom in Takis's private suite at the Perseus hotel. She had intended to return to her own room, but Takis had arranged for her things to be brought to his suite and she had deemed it safer not to argue with him.

They had both needed to calm down after their blazing row over the photo that had appeared in the tabloid newspaper. Lissa forced herself to be honest about her decision to meet Tommy in Mykonos after she'd seen on a social media site that he was visiting the island, which was a popular party venue. She'd felt lonely and abandoned at the villa in Santorini. Damn it, Takis had abandoned her.

It *had* occurred to her that the paparazzi would probably be in Mykonos, keen to snap pictures of Tommy and his celebrity friends. She hadn't consciously hoped to provoke a response from Takis, but in the cold light of day she was sickened by the realisation that she'd behaved like she used to do when she had desperately sought her grandfather's attention.

Lissa ran her hand over her stomach and felt the little fluttery movements of her baby kicking. It was an incredible sensation that she had wanted to share with Takis. But his expression when he'd felt their son move had been hard to describe. He'd looked shocked, but there had been something else in his eyes. There had been fear, Lissa realised as she recalled Takis's expression. It had only been a flash of emotion before his features had reassembled into those hard angles that she found so fascinating.

Her stomach rumbled and taking care of her baby instantly became her top priority. Trying to fathom the mindset of the stranger she had married was fruitless anyway. She slipped on the silky robe that matched her negligee and stepped on to the balcony. Her heart missed a beat when she found Takis sitting at a table spread with a variety of breakfast options.

'Come and eat,' he said, standing up and holding out a chair for her. As always, he looked gorgeous in black jeans and a cream shirt, beneath which Lissa could see the shadow of his dark chest hairs. His eyes were hidden behind sunglasses, and she wished she'd worn her shades to hide the evidence that she'd cried herself to sleep last night.

'What a view,' she murmured, wanting to distract his attention away from her. On one side of the hotel was the old port and beyond it the white cubed buildings of Mykonos town. An iconic windmill stood on the hill above the town. Lissa turned her head the other way and gave a soft sigh at the sight of the turquoise Aegean Sea sparkling in the sunshine.

'Perseus One offers the best views of the island. It's one reason why I bought the hotel.' Takis poured tea into a cup and placed it in front of Lissa. She buttered a freshly baked roll and filled a bowl with berry fruits and yogurt. Incredibly, the tensions of the previous night had eased.

'How did a boy from a poor village become one of Greece's most successful entrepreneurs?' she asked him.

He shrugged. 'It was hard at first. I was sixteen when I left my village and hitched a ride to Thessaloniki. I had no money and slept on the streets until I found work as a labourer on a construction site. I think I already told you it's where I met Jace.'

She nodded. 'The two of you became friends.'

'We shared the same drive and ambition. Jace supported his mother, but when he went to prison I looked after Iliana. It was the very least I could do after Jace had saved my life.'

He saw that Lissa was shocked. 'We were attacked by a gang. One of them attempted to stab me in the back and Jace punched him. Witnesses were paid to lie and say that Jace had started the fight. He was found guilty of grievous assault for which he was given a prison sentence.'

'That was terribly unfair. Poor Jace. Eleanor said that you and Jace are as close as brothers.'

'I guess we are.' Takis was silent for a moment and then released his breath slowly. 'I had a half-brother who died when he was a small child.'

'I'm sorry.' Lissa waited for him to add more to the tiny snippet of information about his past. But she sensed he had retreated into himself and had told her more than he'd intended.

'Soon after Jace was released from prison our fortunes changed when we won two million euros on a lottery ticket,' Takis continued. 'We shared the money equally and came to Mykonos because we'd heard that it had a great party scene. This hotel was for sale. It was derelict, but I saw its potential. I used my winnings to buy the place and turned it into the most exclusive resort on the island. At the same time I put myself through college, studying every evening, and gained a business degree.'

'You make it sound easy, but you must have worked incredibly hard,' Lissa murmured, feeling huge respect for him. The people she knew, people like Tommy Matheson, took their wealthy lifestyles for granted. They had been handed them. It's what people had believed of her too.

Takis looked at his watch. 'My helicopter pilot has just arrived from Athens and we will leave for Santorini in an hour.' His brows rose when Lissa nodded. 'I expected an argument.'

'We did enough of that last night,' she said ruefully. The state of their marriage was the elephant in the room that neither of them had addressed. There would have to be a discussion, but this morning there was a precarious connection between them that she did not want to break. 'Besides, it's too nice a day to argue.'

Takis grinned, and Lissa's breath snagged in her throat. He was impossibly sexy when he smiled. 'For once we both agree on something, *koúkla mou*,' he murmured. 'I propose we call a truce for today.'

'That's two things we agree on.' She smiled back at him and her heart lifted as she felt a little spurt of hope that they could work things out. 'Who knows, we might actually get the hang of this marriage thing.'

Lissa had assumed that the helicopter would take them directly to the villa in Santorini, and she was surprised when they landed in the grounds of a grand-looking building on the island.

'I thought you might like to see the hotel I purchased a few months ago. The building has been undergoing extensive renovations and I plan for it to open next summer,' Takis explained as he ushered her through the front door.

The hotel's main lobby was still a shell, but Lissa immediately saw its potential. Sunlight streamed through the huge windows, and the views of the caldera were breathtaking. 'I'm guessing that you can watch the sunset from this side of the hotel.'

Takis nodded. 'The rooms in the original part of the building were once caves that had been carved into the mountainside and were used to store wine. The hotel has been extended and there are fifty guest rooms and suites.'

He gave Lissa a tour of the ground floor and pointed out the various function rooms. 'As you can see, there is still a lot of work to be done inside. I asked a few interior designers to pitch a concept for the hotel and they all suggested it should be a party venue. Admittedly the designers came up with different themes, but essentially it would have the same club vibe as Perseus One in Mykonos.' He rubbed his hand over his stubbled jaw. 'I'm not sure it will work as well here.'

Lissa followed him through a set of doors and stepped on to a patio. From outside it was clear to see that the hotel had literally been carved out of the cliff in a series of terraces. A few rooms, she guessed they were the suites, had private pools. Far below, the sea was cobalt blue and made a stunning contrast to the white walls of the hotel and the vivid pink bougainvillea that tumbled over the balconies.

'Santorini has the reputation of being the most romantic of the Cyclades islands,' she said. 'I think you should make romance the theme of this hotel. Perseus One is where people go to party. But say a couple met at the nightclub in Mykonos, and a year or so later they wanted to return to Greece to get married. The Santorini hotel could offer wedding packages.'

She walked across the patio, which jutted out from the cliff so that it appeared to be floating above the sea. 'This would be a perfect setting for weddings. And you could also promote anniversary packages. People like to return to the place where they were married.'

Lissa warmed to her theme as ideas bounced around her head. 'I see Perseus One as the young, hip hotel for singles who want to have a good time and perhaps find romance. You could name this hotel Aphrodite after the goddess of love. The concept here is a little more grown-up, still fun but the decor is elegant and tranquil, and instead of a nightclub you have a restaurant that offers fine dining.'

She blushed when she realised that she had been talking non-stop. 'Sorry, I got carried away. I'm sure you have a vision for your new hotel.'

'I do now, thanks to you.' Takis took off his sunglasses and the gleam in his grey eyes made Lissa's heart flip. 'I really think you're on to something with the wedding venue suggestion. Which leads me to the reason I brought you here.'

A woman walked across the foyer towards them. 'This is Zoe,' Takis introduced her. 'Zoe, I would like you to meet my wife, Lissa.'

As they exchanged greetings Lissa immediately liked the Greek woman's friendly smile.

'Zoe is an architect,' Takis explained. 'My idea is for you to design the lobby and function rooms and Zoe will work alongside you to advise you from an architectural perspective.' He smiled at Lissa's stunned expression. 'That is, if you decide to accept the contract I am offering you.'

'Seriously?' she asked huskily. She wanted to work when the baby was older, but instead of returning to hotel management she had been thinking about starting an interior design business. 'Why have you asked me when you could hire a more qualified and experienced interior designer?'

'I was impressed with your designs at Francine's hotel when I looked through the portfolio that you had left on the desk. I also know that you recently completed an online design course and were awarded a diploma. While we were in Athens I overheard you phone your sister to tell her of your success,' Takis explained when Lissa looked puzzled. 'I wondered why you did not share your news with me.'

'I didn't think you would be interested,' she confessed. She remembered when she was a child, feeling proud that she'd won a prize at school for an art project, but when she'd rushed home to tell her grandfather, he'd told her that drawing pictures was a waste of time. She couldn't bear to have had Takis react in the same way.

'I like your idea of making the hotel a wedding venue,' Takis said. 'The name Aphrodite is a nice touch. You have the vision and artistic flare, and Zoe will help with the structural elements of your designs.'

'I would love to accept the contract.' Lissa could not hide her excitement. Ideas for the Aphrodite's lobby were already forming in her mind. 'This is an incredible opportunity for me. I won't let you down,' she promised Takis. She felt overwhelmed by his faith in her.

Maybe things were starting to fall into place, Lissa thought later when they had returned to the villa and she immediately set about turning the garden room into a design studio. She had been hurt that Takis had kept his distance after their wedding when he had left her in Santorini and returned to Athens. But earlier he had opened up a tiny chink when he'd talked about himself. She felt a connection with him because, like her, he had experienced tragedy in his life. The death of his younger brother. She only wished he'd revealed more. Why hadn't he?

Lissa frowned as she remembered his strange reaction when he'd felt the baby move inside her. He'd looked horrified, and the almost tortured expression on his face had been the same as at the ultrasound scan when Takis had stared at the baby's image on the screen. Was his reaction something to do with his brother's death?

He had not planned to have a child, Lissa reminded herself. Undoubtedly, he had been shocked when he'd learned of her pregnancy, and it was not surprising if he was taking some time to come to terms with the prospect of fatherhood. But he was the one who had insisted on marrying her and she was glad of his determination to claim his baby.

The rapport she'd felt with Takis today filled her with hope that they could make a success of their marriage. She certainly wanted to. She wanted him, Lissa admitted, feeling a sharp tug of longing in the pit of her stomach when she thought, as she so often did, of all the wonderful ways he had made love to her on the magical night they had spent together. It seemed like a lifetime ago when they had swum beneath the stars at the Pangalos hotel. She had been plagued with insecurities she'd had as a result of her grandfather's coldness towards her, but now she was going to be a mother and she had discovered that she was strong and fierce and utterly determined to protect her child from feeling rejected by his father.

She sighed as her mind returned to Takis. After their perfect night together she had crept from his bed while he was still sleeping, afraid that if she stayed she might not be able to hide how much he affected her. She had returned to Oxford and tried to get over him. But she never had. Night after lonely night she had ached for him, and the ache was worse now that he was back in her life, but not in the way she wanted.

Lissa's stomach grumbled, reminding her that it was time she fed her baby. She had asked the housekeeper to make moussaka for dinner because it was Takis's favourite. But when she went into the dining room she was surprised to see only one place had been set on the table.

Efthalia came in, carrying a casserole dish. 'Kyrios Samaras told me that he would not be staying for dinner,' she explained.

With a sinking heart and a sickening sense of déjà vu, Lissa looked out of the window and saw the pilot climb into the helicopter. Was Takis planning to abandon her once more? Disappointment brought tears to her eyes, but she blinked them away as anger swept through her in a hot tide of temper. She would not let Takis do this to her. To their baby.

She hurried across the hallway and burst into his study. 'You have asked me several times if I was playing games, even though I've always been honest and open with you. Now I'm asking you the same question.' She glared at him. 'You had better have a good explanation for why you are leaving me and our baby again.'

CHAPTER TWELVE

TAKIS CLOSED HIS laptop case with a decisive snap, but Lissa noted that he evaded eye contact with her. 'I am returning to Athens because it is where my business is based.'

'You could work remotely from the villa just as easily as if you were in your office.'

'Not everything can be managed online. I prefer to meet my executive team face to face.'

'You are making excuses.' She bit her lip. 'I thought you would stay in Santorini and we would both be involved with the plans for the refurbishment of the Aphrodite.'

'You don't need me here. I trust that you will do a good job, and you can discuss your design ideas with Zoe.' He started to walk towards the door, but Lissa planted herself firmly in front of him. 'You said you were bored and had nothing to do. Now you have the hotel project to occupy you.'

'Is that why you gave me the contract?' She felt sick with the realisation that he had been humouring her. That he did not really have any faith in her, he was merely trying to find a way to amuse her while he was gone. The pleasure she'd felt that he had chosen her to design the Aphrodite evaporated, leaving anger and hurt in its place. 'I am not a child who you need to keep entertained.'

'You are acting like one. I gave you the design contract because I like your ideas. I need to be in Athens, but you will remain here in Santorini to oversee the work on the Aphrodite.' Frustration edged into his voice. But there was something else too that Lissa didn't quite recognise. Desperation. And it bolstered her.

'The real reason you're leaving is because it suits you for us to live apart,' Lissa asserted as he stepped past her. 'What are you afraid of, Takis?'

He turned in the doorway and frowned at her. 'What do you mean? I'm not afraid of anything.'

'I think you are lying.' She should have quailed at the glowering look he sent her, but temper won over common sense, which urged her to remove herself from the conversation and the room with her dignity intact. 'I think you are afraid of me.'

He walked back to her. Not walked, *stalked* like a wolf hunting down its prey, Lissa thought when he smiled, showing his white teeth. But he did not smile with his eyes, and his hard gaze bored into her. 'Why would I be afraid of you, *koúkla mou*?' he asked, his voice deceptively soft, but she heard the bite behind it.

Lissa did not know what came over her then. Perhaps it was the memory of the way he had kissed her at their wedding with a hungry passion that had lit a flame inside her. Or how he'd kissed her the previous night in Mykonos and the taste of him lingered on her lips still.

Maybe it was simply because she wanted to, she decided as she stood on tiptoe and balanced herself by putting her hands on his shoulders. 'I think you are afraid of this,' she whispered against his mouth, and then she kissed him.

He stiffened and clamped his hands over hers as if he intended to pull her away from him. His mouth was an inflexible line, and Lissa was sure she had lost whatever silly battle she had started. He didn't want her, and his rejection was nothing new, she thought bleakly. She was an expert at being rejected. She dipped her tongue into his mouth, wanting one last taste of him, and to her amazement he gave a low growl from deep in his throat. The sound was shockingly erotic and raw with sexual need.

He dropped his hands and wrapped his arms around her, hauling her up against his whipcord body. His lips moved over hers as he took control of the kiss and the fire inside Lissa became an inferno. She felt Takis shake and knew that she was shaking too. When she finally tore her mouth from his and stepped away from him, his eyes glittered, and he looked stunned.

'Damn you,' he said thickly. 'What do you want from me, Lissa?'

'I want a proper marriage.' The words burst from her. 'When you insisted that we should marry for the sake of our baby, what did you envisage our relationship would be like? You must have thought about it,' she said when he frowned. 'Is your plan for us to always live apart? You in Athens and me here in the villa? And what will happen when our son is born? Will you ignore him as you do me? Because if that is your plan, to be an absent father like you are an absent husband, it's not good enough.'

'The baby is not here yet,' Takis said icily. There

was no sign in his cold eyes of the hot desire that had blazed there moments ago.

'We should use the time before he arrives to learn more about each other and discuss how we want to be parents. But how can we do that if you keep running away?'

'I am not *running away*,' he said furiously.

'Why don't you want to spend time with me?' Her voice rose with the hurt and anger she could not hide. 'I am the mother of your child. Don't you want to know what kind of mother I will be, or don't you care?'

'*Theos*, Lissa.' He raked his hand through his hair. 'What do you want from me?' he repeated harshly.

'I want to know what kind of father you will be. What kind of husband, and whether you actually want to be married to me—because that is not at all clear.'

She swallowed as a thought occurred to her. 'You left me to spend my wedding night alone after you dumped me here. Is that because you have other interests in Athens besides your business?'

Takis stared at her and she saw the exact moment he grasped her meaning. He looked outraged. 'Do you think I have a mistress in Athens?'

'I don't know what to think,' she said flatly. 'I might not have much experience of these things, of men, but I know you are a highly sensual man, and we are not...' She flushed. 'You are not satisfying your desire with me.'

'So it stands to reason that I have another woman? I did not *dump* you at the villa,' he gritted. 'I have provided—'

'So you keep reminding me,' she cut him off. 'But our baby will need more than material things. He will need a father who comforts him in the night and reads him stories. A hands-on father, not one who lives miles away and bangs on about how he provides and protects, when as far as I am concerned you do neither.'

He stepped closer to her, a dangerous look in his eyes that made her tremble, but with excitement, not fear. Takis seemed dumbfounded that she had questioned him, but it was vital for her to discover if he would be a caring father or if he would treat their son with the indifference her grandfather had treated her. Lissa had never really understood why Pappoús had disliked her, and she had certainly never dared to ask him. But for the first time in her life she was standing up for herself and fighting for what she wanted, for the marriage she wanted, and it felt good.

'Is this another attempt to get my attention?' Takis ground out. He was breathing hard and his eyes were like a terrible storm, dark and ominous. This was the man behind the mask, Lissa realised with a jolt. Takis was not the unemotional rock of granite that he wanted her to believe. His emotions were exposed, stark and savage on his face. She understood that he hoped if he looked menacing she would back down. She did not fully understand why he still needed to keep her at arm's length, but she had come this far, and retreat was not an option.

She met his tormented gaze boldly. 'If it is, what are you going to do about it?'

Takis hauled Lissa into his arms and slammed his mouth down on hers. He was willing to do anything to stop her asking questions that he did not know how to answer. He kissed her to prevent her from challenging him in a fierce voice and with an even fiercer expression on her face as she demanded to know what kind of father he planned on being.

He hadn't planned any of this. He hadn't wanted a child, or a wife, let alone a wife who forced him to ask himself the same questions she had flung at him. And he still did not know the answers. All he knew was that he wanted her beneath him, on top of him, any which way as long as he could bury himself in her molten heat.

He roamed his hands over her body, discovering her round curves, which distracted him constantly. Even when he'd removed himself to Athens after their wedding—so that he was on the pulse of his business, he assured himself, not because he had been *running away*—Lissa had been a distraction. He had spent his nights in a fury of sexual frustration, but he'd told himself it would pass. If he kept away from her, his desire for her would fade. And then he'd seen the photo of her in the newspaper and he'd seized the excuse to rush to Mykonos to claim his wife.

'What kind of marriage do *you* want?' he asked when he finally lifted his mouth from hers, but kept her body clamped against him. The rock-hard proof of his arousal straining beneath his trousers mocked his belief that he had any control where Lissa was concerned. And he no longer cared that she knew the effect she had on him when she smiled her beautiful smile that tugged on something deep inside him.

'I want you,' she said simply.

Her honesty was his undoing and demanded that he be honest with himself. He could not fight his need for her. Takis had prided himself on never needing anyone, but pride was a lonely bedfellow, and he was tired of always being alone.

'Do you want me to do this?' he asked thickly as he slanted his mouth over hers again and kissed her with fierce passion. He felt her tremble as he trailed his lips down her neck and pressed his mouth against the pulse that was beating erratically at the base of her throat.

His hands trembled with need as he unfastened the buttons on her blouse and traced his finger over her sheer, pale pink bra. 'Pretty,' he growled. Her blouse fell to the floor, followed by her bra, and Takis groaned as her breasts spilled into his hands. 'Prettier,' he said thickly as he rubbed his thumb pads over her dusky pink nipples and felt them swell and harden to his touch.

He looked into her eyes, which were deep blue pools, deep enough to drown in. She made him think of summer skies and laughter, and for the first time since he was a teenager he wondered if there was hope for him. He wanted to step out of the darkness into Lissa's golden light.

Her skirt was made of a stretchy material that moulded the firm swell of her pregnant stomach. Takis was fascinated by her new shape, her sensual roundness where once she had been angular, and he could not get enough of her voluptuous breasts. He tugged her skirt off and his eyes roamed over her lace panties.

'Are you sure?' he asked her. He did not know how he'd bear it if she had changed her mind, but he needed to give her the chance to reconsider, because if he made love to her there would be no going back. She would be his. He would no longer be able to stay away.

'I'm sure,' she murmured.

His heart thudded as he pulled her knickers off and

lifted her up, sitting her on the edge of his desk. He cupped her breasts in his hands and bent his head to take one rosy nipple into his mouth. She gasped as he suckled her, leaning back and supporting herself with her hands on the desk so that her body arched, and her breasts were presented to him like ripe, round peaches that he feasted on hungrily.

Her guttural moans ran right through him, all the way down to his shaft, and made him harden even more. His body was impatient, but it wasn't surprising for he had not done this for months, not since the night he'd spent with Lissa at the Pangalos hotel. But even though he felt like he might explode, he was determined to control his hunger until he'd satisfied hers.

Takis dropped to his knees and pushed her legs apart so that he could trace his lips along her inner thigh. She made another of those husky moans as he licked her moist opening and pushed his tongue inside her. He felt her fingers slide into his hair and shape his skull while he caressed her intimately until she was panting, and he knew she was close to climaxing.

'I want you,' she told him in that fierce way of hers that tugged on something inside him. Her eyes were huge and dark with desire and her blonde hair curled against her flushed cheeks. She was the most beautiful thing he had ever seen, and he did not deserve her beauty, her smile. Takis knew it, but he could not help himself. He unzipped his trousers and freed his erection. He was harder than he had ever been, and he needed her now. He positioned himself between her thighs and pressed forward, sliding into her with a smooth thrust that drew a gasp from her.

'Am I hurting you?' he muttered, his mouth against her neck.

'No, it's just been a while since we last did this.'

He registered her words and knew he should feel appalled by the possessiveness that thundered through him, but instead he felt strangely humbled that she was his and his alone. He pulled back almost completely and then thrust again, deep into her velvet heat, into the sweet embrace of her femininity, and it felt like he'd come home at last.

Lissa wrapped her legs around his hips as he began to move, carefully at first, but when he sensed that her urgency was as great as his, he increased his pace and the intensity of his thrusts, taking them both higher. It couldn't last, but he gritted his teeth and fought for control. His hands gripped the edge of the desk and he felt the moment she tensed.

'Takis...' She sobbed his name as he drove into her again and felt her shatter around him. And he came almost instantly, his orgasm sweeping through him so that he shuddered with the pleasure of it that had never been this intense with any other woman.

After a long time he withdrew from her and adjusted his clothes. 'Are you all right? The baby...'

'We are both fine,' Lissa assured him softly.

There was a whole great mess in his head that he would have to face sometime, Takis acknowledged. But not now. He did not want to think of all those questions of Lissa's that needed answers. Tonight he simply wanted to be with her, and so he swept her up into his arms and carried her up to his bed, where he made love to her again and again until they collapsed exhausted in each other's arms.

Lissa fell asleep with her head resting on his chest. Takis placed his hand on her stomach, and his heart stood still when he felt the baby kick. He swallowed hard, unable to assimilate the feelings that stirred inside him. Was this tenderness, this ache beneath his breast-bone when he imagined his son? He wished he could be a better man than he knew he was and a better father than the one he was afraid he would be.

'Who is Giannis?'

Takis turned his head on the pillow and met Lissa's cornflower-blue gaze. He had woken to a sense of con-tentment that he hadn't felt for months. Perhaps even years. But he tensed when she said, 'You were dream-ing and called out the name Giannis.'

She rolled on to her side and propped herself up on her elbow, drawing the sheet over her ripe breasts that Takis would admit he was addicted to touching.

'I apologise if I disturbed you. I occasionally have nightmares.' He tried to sound casual, hoping that Lissa would not pursue the matter. But he should have known it was an unrealistic hope. He was learning that his wife was tenacious as well as fierce.

'What are your nightmares about?'

Takis exhaled deeply. 'Giannis was my younger brother.' He answered her first question. 'Half-brother, technically. We had the same father but different moth-ers.'

'I remember you said that your brother died when he was a child. Was he ill?'

'No.' Takis swung his legs over the side of the bed and pulled on his trousers before walking over to stand by the window. Outside it was another beautiful day in

Santorini, with the sun shining in an azure sky on to the turquoise sea below. But in his mind he pictured the barren grey mountains around his village, the scrubby grass that had sustained his father's herd of goats. The blackened, charred remains of the place he had called home, although it had never been one. Not in the way the villa felt like home, but he suspected that might have something to do with the fact Lissa was here.

'There was a fire. Giannis was killed in a house fire along with my father and stepmother.'

'How terrible!' Lissa's voice was very soft. 'How did it start? A house doesn't simply burst into flames,' she said when he swung round from the window and stared at her.

'It was thought that my father dropped a smouldering cigarette on to the sofa before he fell asleep. No doubt he was drunk.' Takis shoved his hands into his pockets and clenched them into fists. 'His body was discovered by the front door so it's assumed he must have tried to escape. My stepmother and brother were asleep upstairs. The fire was ferocious and swept through the house. They didn't stand a chance.'

Lissa's eyes were fixed on him. 'You were the only one of your family to survive. Oh, Takis.'

He could not bear her sympathy. He did not deserve it. But suddenly he could not bear the secret shame that had weighed on him since he was sixteen. He knew if he told Lissa the truth, the gentle expression in her eyes would turn to disgust. Only perhaps then she would understand why she and their son were better off without him.

'I was not in the house. I had abandoned my brother when I left the village a few days before the fire.'

Her brow wrinkled in a tiny frown. 'You didn't abandon him if he was with his parents.'

Takis snorted. 'My father was a bully with a filthy temper and a habit of using his belt on me. As for my stepmother, Marina was much younger than my father. She was barely eighteen when she gave birth to my half-brother. I was eleven when Giannis was born. He was the cutest baby and toddler. When he grew older, he was my shadow. I was the person he wanted if he grazed his knee.' Takis swallowed. 'He adored me, and I him. But I betrayed his faith in me. I left him when he was five years old and I never saw him again.'

Lissa slid out of bed and wrapped the sheet around her to cover her stomach wherein lay another innocent little boy, who had no knowledge of his father's cowardice, Takis brooded, conscious of a terrible ache in his chest.

'Why did you leave?' she asked.

He wondered why he was still telling her any of it. Perhaps it was so that she would stop looking at him with a light in her eyes as if she saw something in him, some goodness that he knew did not exist.

'My stepmother tried to seduce me,' he said tautly. 'I was sixteen and thought I was in love with her. I convinced myself that she loved me, and so I kissed her. Marina had known that I was planning to leave the village and go to the city to look for work and make a better life. She wanted me to take her and Giannis along, and she threatened to tell my father that I had tried to force myself on her if I refused.'

He turned his head towards the window once again and the stunning view from his villa. Other men envied him his wealth and success, but he was empty inside, and until he'd met Lissa that emptiness hadn't bothered him overmuch.

'I felt a fool when I realised that Marina had been stringing me along,' he admitted rawly. 'My teenage pride was crushed, and I couldn't bear to see her again knowing she had been laughing at me. So that night I left.'

He sensed that Lissa had crossed the room to stand beside him, but he could not bring himself to look at her. 'I thought that Giannis would be safe. My father had some fondness for him and did not beat him. I had the crazy idea that I would find work, save some money and go back for Giannis when I could support him.'

Grief caught in his throat. 'I promised him that I would go back for him. He begged me not to leave him, but I went anyway, and he died in the fire.'

'You couldn't have known what would happen. No one can see the future,' Lissa said gently.

'You don't understand,' he ground out, his shame a savage torment that had never left him in all these years. 'I was in a temper because of what my stepmother had done. I left because I wanted to show her that I did not care about her, like she didn't care about me.'

Takis made himself turn around to face the condemnation that he was certain would be in Lissa's gaze. But there were tears in her eyes, not judgement.

'What else could you have done but leave?' she asked quietly. 'You were sixteen. A boy not yet fully a man, and your stepmother took advantage of you. If you had somehow managed to take her and Giannis away with you, what kind of life would they have had? You told me that you slept on the streets when you first arrived in the city. How could you have taken care of a child when you lived rough and begged for food?'

She stepped closer and put her hand on his chest. 'The fire was a terrible twist of fate, but it was not your fault that Marina and Giannis died. For twenty years you have believed you were to blame for an accident that you couldn't have prevented. Isn't it time you learned to forgive yourself, for our son's sake if nothing else?'

Takis stared at her and realised with a jolt of shock that her tears were for him. 'You asked me what kind of father I will be. My only experience of a father was the monstrous man who failed me every day of my childhood. I wasn't there for my brother when he needed me. I failed Giannis. You can see there is a pattern here,' he said harshly. 'There is no guarantee that I will not fail my own child.'

'I don't believe that,' Lissa said softly. 'I don't believe that you are in any way like your father.'

'How can you be sure? You do not know me.'

'Then let me know you.' She stood in front of him and held his gaze, that fierce light that he was beginning to recognise was a part of her shining in her eyes. 'Stay here with me so that we can learn about each other, for our son's sake.'

CHAPTER THIRTEEN

TAKIS STAYED BECAUSE he could not bring himself to leave her. This woman who confounded him and amazed him more with every day that he learned something new about her. His wife was wise, Takis discovered. She understood there was a darkness inside him, and bit by bit he started to open up to her.

They lived at the villa, but not separately like when they had lived in the house in Athens before they'd married. Takis shared his bed with Lissa, ate his meals with her and spent all his time with her. They talked and laughed and made love endlessly, but he still could not get enough of her. Most days he worked in his study for a few hours and Lissa went into her design studio and made plans for the Aphrodite hotel.

Occasionally Takis had reason to go to his office in Athens, but he always returned in the evening, and when he climbed out of the helicopter and watched Lissa hurry across the garden to meet him it was like the first time he had ever seen her. That kick in his gut and the feeling that his life would never be the same again. Which, of course, it wouldn't.

Soon Lissa was in the third trimester of her pregnancy and before long Takis would have a son. He did not know how he felt about that. He still avoided thinking about his imminent fatherhood or what kind of father he would be.

'Life is about choices,' Lissa told him. 'I don't believe we are born with our destiny mapped out in advance. We control our own destinies, as you did when you chose not to be a goat herder in a poor village and instead built a business empire. Just because your father was a brute, it doesn't mean that you will be like him.'

Takis wanted to believe her, but sometimes in the middle of the night, when he lay in bed with Lissa curled up asleep beside him and felt his baby kick, he saw Giannis's face and heard the little boy's sobs. *Don't leave me!* It occurred to Takis that if he maintained a distance from his son when he was born, the child would not love him as Giannis had loved him, and so would not be devastated if his father failed him.

Takis set his complicated thoughts aside as he walked into the villa. This evening he and Lissa were to host a party to celebrate the completion of the refurbished Aphrodite hotel. His wife was very talented and she had done an amazing job. As he'd known she would. And Takis had shamelessly used his contacts to make sure everyone else knew it too. The guest list read like a who's who of Europe's social elite.

His meeting in Athens had overrun so he'd changed into a tuxedo before the helicopter had brought him back to Santorini.

Lissa was in their bedroom. Takis halted in the doorway, transfixed when she turned towards him. 'You look...' Words failed him.

'Like a whale?' she said drily, but Takis heard uncertainty in her voice and something inside him cracked.

'Beautiful,' he growled. She looked like a goddess in a gold floor-length gown. The off-the-shoulder bodice framed her ripe, round breasts. Her dress was made of some sort of shimmery material that skimmed over the big mound of her stomach.

Takis had noticed that she often touched her baby bump, and now she placed her hands on her belly in a protective gesture that made him want to fall to his knees and worship her. His child's mother would never abandon her son like Takis's mother had abandoned him. Like he had abandoned his brother. His son would always be loved.

He was aware of a host of emotions that he did not want to define. Because he was afraid, whispered a voice inside his head.

'You look incredible,' he told her as he walked over to her and drew her into his arms. '*I ómorfi gynaíka mou.* My beautiful wife.'

Fireworks exploded inside Lissa when Takis slanted his mouth over hers and kissed her. There was passion in his kiss but also a beguiling tenderness that dismantled the defences she tried to maintain around her heart to protect it from her husband. To protect herself from falling in love with him. She suspected that she was not doing very well on that score.

He groaned and pulled her against his whipcord body, as close as her swollen belly would allow. But Lissa jolted back to reality and regretfully broke the kiss.

'We can't,' she gasped, snatching air into her lungs. Takis's eyes gleamed like molten steel as he stared down at her. 'We can't be late for the party,' she reminded him. 'It is an important night for you, the opening of the tenth hotel in the Perseus chain.'

His chest heaved as he released a ragged breath. 'Tonight is *your* night to shine when your designs are unveiled. As badly as I want to make love to you, and I do, desperately, I will make myself wait for a few hours. You deserve your time in the spotlight and the accolades for your work that I know you will receive.'

He reached inside his jacket and withdrew a narrow box, which he opened to reveal an exquisite necklace and drop earrings made of rose gold and set with white diamonds.

Lissa's eyes widened when he held the box out to her. 'I can't accept...'

'Please. I had them made for you.'

Swallowing hard, she turned towards the mirror and attached the earrings to her lobes while Takis stood behind her and fastened the necklace around her throat.

'They're dazzling,' she whispered, tracing her finger over the diamonds sparkling on her décolletage. The jewellery was beautiful, but it was the expression in Takis's eyes, a softness that had not been there before, that made Lissa's heart turn over.

'You will dazzle our guests,' he said thickly. 'While we are at the party I will be imagining you wearing the diamonds and nothing else, which is exactly what will happen later tonight.' He slid his arms around her waist and placed his hands on her stomach just as the baby gave a hard kick.

His expression shifted and for a moment there was a look of such intense pain on his face that Lissa caught her breath. Takis had appointed one of the top obstetricians in the country to oversee her pregnancy, and he paid for Dr Papoulis to fly to Santorini every week for the antenatal appointments. But she still did not really know how he felt about becoming a father, or how he felt about her, for that matter.

They had grown closer since he'd moved into the villa and their marriage was working out better than Lissa had dared hope. But something was missing. Love was missing. She tried to convince herself that what she had with Takis, friendship, mutual respect and their physical compatibility, was enough. But it did not feel enough.

Sometimes she wondered if she was destined to spend her life longing to be loved, and it hurt because she had so much love inside her to give. She wondered what would happen if she were brave enough to tell Takis of her feelings for him. But if she did, and he did not feel the same way about her, it would drive him away.

Takis stepped away from her and picked up her wrap from the bed. 'We should go,' he murmured as he handed it to her, 'or we will be late.'

He drove them along the winding coast road to the hotel. Butterflies leapt in Lissa's stomach when she stood with Takis in the Aphrodite's opulent lobby to greet the guests. She had hoped that her dramatic designs would make an impact when people entered the hotel, and the favourable comments that she overheard seemed to indicate that she'd pulled it off.

'I am proud of my hotel and incredibly proud of you,' Takis told her later in the evening when he found her in the wedding room. 'You did not need to feel nervous. Everyone is blown away by your creation of a unique venue that has an ambiance that is both welcoming and unashamedly luxurious.'

'How did you know I was nervous?' she asked.

'I know you, *koúkla mou*,' he said softly. 'There is an English expression, you wear your heart on your sleeve.'

Lissa hoped he could not really tell everything that she was thinking and feeling. For the first time ever, she was glad to be interrupted by a journalist, who came into the room and asked for an interview. It helped that the journalist was not a member of the paparazzi and worked for a prestigious interior design magazine.

'What was your inspiration for the wedding room and the stunning terrace where open-air weddings can take place?' the journalist asked.

'Since I was a little girl, I imagined getting married in a beautiful, romantic setting, and I wanted to create a fairy-tale venue where brides and grooms can have a truly magical wedding of their dreams.'

'You must have wished that the Aphrodite had been finished in time for your own wedding,' the journalist commented.

Lissa felt Takis's gaze on her and wondered if he was remembering the functional room in the civic hall where they had married purely because she had conceived his child. She needed to remember the reason why he had married her. 'A wedding is special wherever it takes place,' she said to the journalist, hoping she sounded convincing.

Those butterflies inside her started fluttering again when Takis drove the car away from the hotel at the end of the evening. Although he told her she was beautiful, she felt insecure about her pregnant body. When they walked into the villa he swept her into his arms and carried her up the stairs to the bedroom, ignoring her pleas to put her down because she weighed a ton.

'Do you not see how beautiful you are?' he murmured as he freed her from the bodice of her dress and made a feral sound in his throat as he cradled her bare breasts in his hands. He tugged her dress down over her stomach so that it slid to the floor, leaving her in her tiny, lace knickers and the diamond necklace sparkling at her throat.

She stared at their reflections in the mirror. His tanned hands cupped her pale breasts, and streaks of dull colour ran along his cheekbones. He rubbed his thumb pads over her nipples until they were pebble-hard and rosy pink.

'You are a goddess. *My* goddess,' Takis told her in an unsteady voice that clutched at her heart. He stripped off his clothes with an urgency that thrilled her, and then he sat her on the edge of the bed and sank to his knees in front of her. He pushed her thighs apart and worshipped her with his tongue and his clever fingers until she sobbed his name.

'Lissa *mou*.' He murmured her name like a prayer as he slowly eased his swollen length inside her. She gasped as he filled her, and he hesitated and withdrew a little way.

'Am I hurting you?' His gentle concern curled around her heart.

'Only when you stop,' she muttered as she wrapped her legs around his hips to bring her pelvis flush with his.

He laughed softly. 'I have no intention of stopping until you scream my name, *koúkla mou*.'

It was the sweetest threat Lissa had ever heard and

she gloried in his fierce possession as he thrust deep, over and over again. She could deny him nothing. She was conscious only of Takis driving into her, taking her higher, and then holding her there at the edge for time-less seconds. He slipped his hand between their bodies and gave a clever twist of his fingers, and his name left her lips on a sharp cry as she shattered.

He hadn't finished with her and built her up again with his skilful caresses so that she climaxed twice more. Only then, when she was flushed with ecstasy and utterly replete, did he take his own pleasure with a hard thrust that tore a groan from his throat.

Afterwards he lifted himself off her and cradled her against his chest. Lissa loved the warm afterglow as much as she loved the amazing sex, but as she hovered on the edge of sleep a thought niggled in her mind. Takis had seemed to enjoy their lovemaking, but he had been different tonight, more controlled. They had just shared the most intimate moments that two people could experience, but despite their physical closeness he was still unreachable.

The baby was due in eight weeks, and Takis was con-cerned about Lissa flying in the helicopter and insisted on them returning to Athens to be closer to the private maternity hospital where she was booked to give birth. He had bought the house that he'd previously leased, and Lissa spent happy hours designing and overseeing the decoration of the nursery. She had been worried that Takis might spend hours in his study, as he had done in the past, but the close relationship that had developed between them in Santorini continued to flourish.

He had encouraged Lissa to set up her own interior

design business. 'There is no need for you to work and I know you want to be a full-time mother for a while, but you are amazingly talented, and you could take on design contracts when the baby is a bit older, if you want to.'

Lissa had glowed with pride at Takis's praise. For a long time she had believed her grandfather when he had told her that she would never be good at anything, even after his death. But she had proved to herself that she was not worthless. She was no longer the person who had hidden her insecurity behind a party girl image that had never been the real her. She was a woman growing in self-confidence, a wife, and soon to be a mother.

The next step on her journey to what she hoped would be her very own happy-ever-after was to be honest with Takis about how she felt about him. Once, she would have been too afraid of rejection to contemplate such a daring step. But she had a good reason to overcome her fear, Lissa thought when her son kicked so hard against her ribcage that she caught her breath. Even if Takis did not love her, she had to know if he would love their baby. If he could love their baby.

All these thoughts came to her early one morning when the new dawn made the world seem full of possibilities. And because she had become brave, and before her nerve failed her, she rolled on to her side in the bed, which was no easy task when her big belly was cumbersome, and her eyes met Takis's sleepy gaze.

'Kaliméra, koúkla mou.' His sexy smile almost stole her the words she was about to speak.

'I need to tell you something. I'm falling in love with you.'

* * *

Takis froze and his gut twisted into a knot of fear. Love had ripped his heart out and left a void in his chest ever since he had thrown a handful of earth on to Giannis's coffin. He didn't have any love to give. How had he let this happen, let things get this far?

'Take my advice and don't,' he told Lissa curtly.

She dropped her hand from his chest, and he hated the look of hurt on her face, hated that he was the cause of it.

'Why complicate things?' He made his voice softer, realising that he needed to reassure her of his commitment. 'We have become good friends as well as good lovers. I respect you and I admire your talent. I'm hoping that when the baby is older, you will accept a position with my Perseus hotel chain as an interior design consultant.'

He lifted his hand to smooth her long fringe off her face and felt the knot inside him tighten when she turned her head away, but not before he'd glimpsed the disappointment in her eyes. Disappointment with him. She shifted across to her side of the bed. It was a very big bed, and the chasm that he sensed had opened up between him and Lissa was widening by the second. But what was he to do? Takis asked himself. He had not asked her to fall in love with him. The idea of it appalled him. Lissa deserved better. He was dead inside, and he couldn't change. Maybe he did not want to change, suggested a snide little voice inside him. Maybe he was too much of a coward to try.

'We will create a family for our son like the happy family you once had,' he sought to reassure her. Takis had no experience of a happy family, but he knew family was important to Lissa and he was prepared to promise anything to see that light in her eyes again. 'It is my responsibility to make a success of our marriage and I will not fail to do the best for our son and for you.'

Lissa nodded as she got up out of the bed, but she did not look at him. He wondered if that could be enough for her.

Over the next two weeks Takis did his best to prove that he was committed to their marriage, even if he could not give Lissa the romantic dream she hoped for. Thankfully, she had not said anything more about her feelings for him. That morning, when she'd dropped a boulder into the still pool of their relationship, he had handled it badly, he acknowledged. She had locked herself in the bathroom for a worryingly long time, eventually emerging with flushed cheeks—from having had a bath, she'd told him—and suspiciously bright eyes that neither of them mentioned.

They both tried to carry on as if nothing had happened, but he felt edgy and he sensed that Lissa had withdrawn from him. One Saturday, Takis suggested a trip to the Acropolis Museum. They spent a few hours wandering around the exhibition halls before climbing the steep path and steps up to the top of the Acropolis hill to wander around the breathtaking Parthenon, built as a temple dedicated to the goddess Athena.

'What an incredible view,' Lissa murmured as they stood and looked at the city spread out before them. She rubbed her lower back and Takis frowned when he saw her wince.

'Are you in pain?' He led her over to a bench. 'Sit for a while. We shouldn't have spent so long in the museum. Too much standing is not good for you.'

'A bit of backache is normal at this stage of my pregnancy.' She took a sharp breath. 'I've been having some of the practice contractions that the obstetrician said might happen.'

'*Theós!* Why did you not tell me before we climbed to the top of the hill?' Fear greater than he had ever felt before made Takis's heart clench.

'I'm fine.' Lissa focused on her breathing, like the midwife at the antenatal classes had told her. She'd woken with mild backache that morning but hadn't paid much attention to what had been no more than a niggle. When Takis had suggested visiting the museum her foolish heart had leapt at the chance to spend time with him away from the house, which had felt claustrophobic since she'd mentioned the L word.

His horrified expression would have almost been funny if it hadn't made her want to weep. Pride had got her into the bathroom before she'd let her tears fall, and pride had made her stick a plaster over her wounded heart and carry on as if she did not feel utterly broken by his rejection.

'We must go home,' Takis said now in a tense voice. She couldn't work out if he was annoyed or concerned. She let him help her to her feet and was glad of his hand beneath her elbow when a pain shot across her stomach. By the time they had walked back down the hill and climbed into the car, the tightening sensations were happening with alarming regularity. Her labour could not have started six weeks early, Lissa tried to reassure herself. But the next contraction was so intense that she gave a cry.

'Takis…' She hesitated. 'I think the baby is coming.'

He swore and pulled out his phone to call the maternity hospital. 'They know we are on our way,' he told her after he'd instructed the chauffeur to drive faster.

'It might be a false alarm.' Lissa gritted her teeth as another sharp pain tore through her.

'Mr Papoulis and his obstetrics team are preparing for you to give birth.'

Takis had never seemed so remote but for once Lissa wasn't thinking about him. 'I'm scared,' she said on a sob. 'It's too early for the baby to be born.'

Their son didn't think so. She needed an emergency Caesarean. Lissa's blood pressure was soaring, and the baby was in distress, so she was rushed into Theatre and given an epidural anaesthetic. Everything became a frightening blur of bright lights and urgent voices from medical staff dressed in green operating gowns.

But then Takis appeared beside the trolley where she was lying. His eyes locked with hers as he clasped her hand in his strong fingers, and she clung to him as if he were a lifeline. She could not see over the screen that had been put across her stomach, but Takis suddenly gripped her hand tighter. '*He's here.* The baby has been born.'

'Is he all right?' Lissa asked fearfully. The silence seemed to last for an eternity before she heard a shrill cry as the baby took his first breath. Tears streamed down her face when a nurse placed the tiny infant on her chest for a few moments, but then he was wrapped up in blanket ready to be whisked away to the neonatal unit.

'His name is Elias,' Lissa told her nurse, who was writing the labels to go around the baby's fragile wrist and ankle. She understood that her baby would need special care, but her arms ached to hold him, and her heart ached for love that she hoped her son would feel for her. Love that her husband could not or would not give her.

Takis stared at his baby son lying in the incubator with wires and tubes attached to his tiny body. It was impossible to believe that this scrap of humanity would survive. He blamed himself for Elias's premature birth. Lissa should have been resting, not traipsing around a museum. It was he who had not been able to give her the love she deserved. Who had suggested they leave the confines of their home to escape the emotions left unspoken, but which hung in the air. He was sure that was the reason she had gone into early labour.

His heart clenched. The baby had a mass of dark hair and reminded him of Giannis. *Theos!* Takis had not wanted a child, but his son was here, fragile and terrifyingly vulnerable. He had promised that he would protect his son and provide for him, and he would gladly do both. But more than that? He remembered how Lissa had looked at him and said fiercely, 'You have to love our child.'

Love, that most unstable of emotions that risked pain and heartbreak. He did not want to take the risk and feel the pain of loss. He dared not love his little son.

'What kind of father will you be?' Lissa had asked him. Now he had the answer. Elias's father was a coward, and if Lissa knew the truth, no doubt the light in her eyes that shone so brightly when she looked at him, that light that made him want to be a better man, would dim.

CHAPTER FOURTEEN

LISSA EXPERIENCED A rollercoaster of emotions in the first tense week after she'd given birth prematurely. She felt a mixture of joy and fear when she looked at her tiny baby in an incubator. But Elias was a fighter and day by day he continued to thrive.

She stayed in the hospital with the baby for a further three weeks and learned how to feed and bath Elias so that very soon it felt natural to be a mother. Takis visited every day. He brought her flowers and gave her a beautiful sapphire-and-diamond bracelet, but what she really wanted was for him to kiss her instead of prowling around her hospital room like a caged tiger. His edginess made her edgy, which in turn made the baby cry, and she was relieved when he left.

'Do you want to hold him?' she asked when they had brought Elias home, a month after his birth. Takis had carried the baby in his car seat up to the nursery. He shook his head when Lissa carefully lifted the baby out of the seat.

'Let him settle into his new environment. I expect you will need to feed and change him.' Takis was already at the door. 'I'll tell the nanny to come and help.'

Lissa frowned. Takis had only held Elias a couple

of times, and on both occasions he had seemed reluctant to do so and had handed him back to her after a
couple of minutes. But the baby was so tiny and fragile, and she supposed that Takis felt nervous. Initially
she had argued against having a nanny, but Maria was
an invaluable help, especially as Elias needed feeding
during the night.

Lissa was sleeping in the bedroom adjoining the
nursery, and at first she was so wrapped up in mother-
hood that she did not allow herself to wonder why Takis
showed little interest in his son. He had gone back to
his old habit of disappearing into his study when he
was at home, and he went to his office every day, often
working until late.

But as another month passed, his indifference became more apparent. Lissa blamed herself because the
good relationship they'd established before Elias was
born had cooled to the point where she and Takis rarely
saw each other. If only she had not confessed her feelings for him, they might have been able to resume their
marriage, which hadn't been perfect but had been better
than the divisions between them, which she had no idea
how to deal with. They were still sleeping separately,
even though Elias had settled to one nightly feed, which
the nanny gave him. Lissa did not have the confidence
to move back into the bedroom she had once shared
with Takis, and he did not suggest it.

Her insecurities flooded back. Why had she forgotten that he had married her because she had been expecting his baby? A baby he took as little interest in as
he did her, Lissa thought bleakly. She remembered how
Takis had insisted that she was his responsibility. He
had married her out of duty, and all the time in Santo-

rini, when she had been falling in love with him, she had meant nothing to him.

Worst of all, he had broken his promise to love his baby. Although, when she thought back, she realised that Takis had never actually made that promise. He had said he would give his son his name and the benefits of his wealth. That he would protect him. But that wasn't the same and it wasn't enough, Lissa thought, anger replacing her deep hurt.

She imagined a future where she was desperate for Takis to take notice of her. Desperate for his affection and love until bitterness crept into her heart and she despised him as surely as he would despise her. Something broke inside her then. It wasn't selfish to want to be loved. With hindsight she realised that when she'd been a teenager and still grieving for her parents, she had needed her grandfather to love her. She deserved so much more. And now she knew what she must do. She must save herself from her loveless marriage that broke her heart daily.

Takis let himself into the house and dropped the bunch of flowers that he'd bought on his way home from the office on the hall table. The flowers were a peace offering that he hoped would break the impasse between him and Lissa. She had looked so unhappy lately and he knew he was responsible.

She did not understand why he had distanced himself from her and Elias, and he could not explain that he was protecting them. And, if he was honest, he was protecting himself. She had once taunted him that he was afraid of her, and it was true. He recognised that he was in danger of becoming attached to her.

The only way he could control emotions that he did not want was to put up barriers. He'd thought she hadn't noticed. But lately he had caught her looking at him with a vulnerable expression in her eyes that made his heart clench. She wanted more than he could give her, and they were going to have to negotiate a way around that for both their sakes.

He checked the ground-floor rooms before going upstairs to the nursery, expecting Lissa to be there. Elias was asleep in his crib. Takis glanced at the baby who reminded him so painfully of Giannis and quickly left the room. He found Lissa in the bedroom where she'd slept since she'd brought Elias home from the hospital. She stiffened when she glanced over her shoulder and saw him.

'I wasn't expecting you home so early,' she said flatly.

Takis roved his gaze over her slender figure. She looked amazing in jeans and a T-shirt, and it was hard to believe that she had given birth only two months ago. He wondered what she would do if he tumbled her down on the bed and removed their clothes before making fierce love to her. Sometimes he'd caught her giving him a hungry look that made him think she wanted to resume their physical relationship as much as he did.

It was then that he noticed the suitcase on the bed and the pile of clothes next to it. Foreboding dropped into the pit of his stomach. 'What is happening?'

'My sister has invited me to stay with her and Jace in Thessaloniki. I've only seen baby Acacia a couple of times and it will be nice for Elias to meet his cousin. Jace is sending his plane.'

Takis couldn't explain the relief that rushed through

him. 'I should have thought to arrange the trip. You will enjoy spending time with Eleanor.'

Lissa closed the zip on the suitcase. 'Yes. And when I come back to Athens I want a divorce.'

He jerked his head back as if she'd slapped him. His heart was thudding painfully hard. 'I don't understand, *koúkla mou*,' he said carefully.

'*Don't* call me that,' she snapped, her eyes blazing. 'I'm not your doll. We both know that I am not anything to you.'

'That's not true.' He felt like he was standing in a field of landmines and an explosion could wipe him out at any moment. 'You are my wife, and the mother of my son.'

'You wanted neither.' Her mouth trembled and she looked away from him and stuffed a sweatshirt into the suitcase. 'I could cope with your indifference if it only affected me, but it will affect our son. I won't let Elias grow up wondering why his papa doesn't love him. It's too cruel.' She dashed a hand across her eyes. 'I'm going to take him back to England. I'll find a job in hotel management that hopefully offers accommodation, and you won't have to see us ever again.'

Takis felt the walls of his fortress start to crumble. 'That is not what we agreed.'

'I know our marriage was meant to be a practical solution when I became pregnant,' she said in a strained voice. 'But it's not working for me and I have to end it.'

Fear cracked through him. 'Tell me what I have to do to make it work,' he gritted, unable to control his desperation that made him feel physically sick when he realised that she was serious about leaving him.

Tears shimmered in Lissa's eyes, but there was determination on her face, determination to leave him and take their child with her. 'You have to love me. And we both know that's not going to happen.'

Takis stared at her. 'We can work this out…'

'How?' she choked. 'I love you, and it's tearing me apart to know that you don't love me. I understand why after Giannis died you shut off your emotions. But another little boy needs your love. Elias is your son, but you ignore him, and it breaks my heart to think he would suffer the pain of rejection that I felt when my grandfather had no time for me.' Lissa lifted her chin. 'And I deserve more than a sham of a marriage.'

Takis silently applauded the self-confident woman she had become. The one who stood up for herself, for her son.

'I deserve to be loved,' she said fiercely. 'I want my freedom so that one day I can fall in love with someone who will love me back unreservedly.'

She walked over to the door. 'I forgot to bring Elias's car seat from downstairs. He will wake from his nap soon, and I have booked a taxi to take us to the airport.'

Takis watched her leave the room. He was frozen inside, and his lungs burned as he dragged in a breath. He ran a shaky hand over his eyes. Lissa had told him that she loved him, and in the next breath announced that she was leaving him. So was her first statement a lie? Just like his stepmother had lied about loving him all those years ago?

But the schoolboy infatuation he'd felt for Marina was nothing like the powerful feelings he had for Lissa. The truth hit him like a thunderbolt. Love. He had denied it and assured himself that he was in control of his emotions. Love hurt. Why would he risk the searing pain he'd felt when his brother had died? Instead he had been a coward and withheld his love from his baby son.

He strode down the corridor, opened the door to the nursery and walked across the room to the crib. A pair of blue eyes surveyed him unblinkingly, and then Elias smiled and Takis felt his heart shatter into a thousand pieces.

'I stayed away from you because I was scared,' he told the baby rawly. His throat felt like he'd swallowed broken glass. 'Scared I might drop you or do something wrong.' He swallowed hard. 'Scared to be your papa because I don't know how to be a father. But I will learn. I promised your mama that I will love and protect you always.'

Life was about choices, Lissa had said. Takis chose not to be a monster like his father had been. Chose to learn from his mistakes. He would be the best father he could be, he promised Elias. Taking a deep breath, he reached into the crib and carefully scooped his son into his arms.

The baby was so small and breakable. Was he holding him tightly enough? Too tight? Takis slowly released his breath and held Elias against his shoulder. The baby's dark hair felt like silk and he smelled…of baby, Takis thought as tenderness swept through him, and a wave of love so strong that it hurt his heart.

Lissa had said that he must forgive himself for Giannis's death in the fire that Takis now accepted had been an accident that he could not have prevented. He had punished himself for twenty years and buried his heart in an icy tomb. But the ice had gradually thawed in the warmth of Lissa's smiles and the light that blazed in her eyes when she looked at him. Only him.

'Your mama is wise and beautiful, and you have her eyes,' he told his son. He looked towards the door and saw the nanny holding a bottle of formula.

'Would you like to feed the baby?' she asked, offering Takis the bottle.

Not this time, but he had a lifetime to bond with his son, and he would, Takis vowed. 'I'll leave Elias with you,' he told the nanny. 'I have something important to tell my wife.'

Lissa walked back into the bedroom with the baby carrier and stopped dead when she saw Takis unpacking her suitcase. Her emotions couldn't take much more. She felt raw and did not even bother to wipe away the tears that coursed down her cheeks. She put the carrier on the floor and sagged against the door frame.

'Don't,' she choked. 'Just don't. I need to go.' She forced herself to look at him and her stupid heart broke all over again. He was so gorgeous, but he didn't want her, he'd never wanted her, except for on one perfect night. She sniffed inelegantly and knew she must look a mess. Her mascara wasn't waterproof, and she had cried enough tears to fill an ocean. 'You have taken everything else. Can't you at least let me have my dignity?'

'I love you.'

Her heart skittered as Takis said the words she'd longed to hear. But she shook her head. He was only saying them because she was leaving.

'No,' she said with tremulous effort. 'Don't play games with me.' Takis had said those words to her more than once. He had been suspicious of her and so furious about her pregnancy. More tears filled her eyes when she thought of darling little Elias, who would never have his father's love.

She pressed her finger against her quivering lips, hating that she was falling apart in front of Takis. She was aware of him moving and tensed when he drew her hand away from her mouth. He was so close that she breathed in his heavenly male scent, and she ached with longing.

'I knew I was in trouble the minute I saw you,' he said heavily. 'I'm not a big fan of weddings, but I couldn't refuse when Jace asked me to be his best man. All eyes were on the bride, except for mine. You stole my breath.'

He let go of her fingers, which he had been squeezing hard like a drowning man clinging to a life raft, and lifted his hand to brush her long fringe off her face. 'You stole my heart. I fell in love with you, but I fought my feelings and insisted that our marriage was a solution to a problem.'

'My pregnancy was a problem for you,' she said dully.

The expression in Takis's eyes made her tremble. 'I told myself that I did not deserve to be happy, but even that was an excuse. The truth is that I was afraid to acknowledge how I felt about you because all I knew of love was that it had nearly broken me. When Giannis died I made a pact with myself never to allow love into my life. I didn't need it, and I certainly didn't want it. But I couldn't forget you.'

He ran his finger lightly down her cheek, tracing the path of a tear. 'I thought if I kept you at arm's length I would be able to control what is in here.' He pressed his hand against his chest. 'But my heart knew the truth, *agapi mou*, and it beats only for you.'

'Takis.' She could not speak when her heart was beating so hard it hurt.

'If I beg, will you give me a chance to try to win back your love?'

She swallowed. 'I can't.'

Takis paled beneath his tan and closed his eyes. 'I'm sorry for how I treated you. I know I don't deserve your love.' He pinched the bridge of his nose and Lissa's heart turned over when she saw that his eyelashes were wet.

'It wouldn't be fair to Elias. I can't bear the thought of him feeling worthless because his father doesn't love him.'

'I adore our son,' he said urgently. 'I swear I will spend the rest of my life making sure that he knows how special he is.'

Takis slipped his hand under her chin and gently tilted her face up to his. 'You humble me with your courage. You were heartbroken when your parents died, but you are willing to love again. I have seen your devotion to Elias, and I wish…' He swallowed hard.

He tried to smile and failed. 'Big boys do cry. Especially when they have lost the person they love most in all the world, the universe.'

Finally, Lissa believed him. 'You haven't lost me, my love,' she said softly. 'I am right here, and that's where I want to stay, forever.'

He kissed her then, with such tenderness, such *love* that Lissa felt as though her heart would burst.

'I love you,' she whispered against his mouth as he drew her down on to the bed.

'You are my world. You and Elias.' The reverence in

Takis's eyes filled Lissa with joy. 'You are everything and I am nothing without you,' he said deeply.

They undressed each other with hands that trembled, and Takis told her over and over again how much he loved her before he worshipped her body with his mouth until she could wait no longer and lifted her hips towards him. When he entered her and made them one, it was like the first time, beautiful and new and shining, and Lissa was dazzled by this love of theirs that was brighter than the brightest star and would blaze until the end of time.

A week later, the helicopter flew over Santorini, but instead of going to the villa it landed in the grounds of the Aphrodite hotel. The hotel had not opened for guests yet, so Lissa was surprised to see several cars parked on the driveway.

'Maria will take Elias for a walk in the pram,' Takis told her as he ushered her into the hotel.

'Is an event taking place here today?' Lissa asked.

'A wedding.' His eyes gleamed with an expression she could not decipher. It did not happen often for they no longer had secrets from each other.

She walked into the wedding room and saw that a long table was set with delicate crockery, champagne flutes and a stunning floral display down the centre of the damask tablecloth. The pure white roses intertwined with spikes of purple lavender and sprigs of fragrant rosemary were exactly what she would have chosen for her dream wedding, Lissa thought wistfully.

Outside on the terrace, chairs had been arranged in rows facing the arbour, which was swathed in white voile and decorated with roses. Beyond the romantic arch was that amazing view of the caldera, and the sky and the sea were as blue as the sapphire on Lissa's engagement ring.

It was astonishing how the bride, whoever she was, had incorporated every detail that Lissa had drawn on her designs when she'd planned the wedding venue.

'I hope I haven't forgotten anything,' Takis murmured. 'I used your designs to create the wedding setting.'

'I hope the bride approves,' she said lightly, trying not to show her disappointment that another woman would enjoy *her* perfect wedding.

Takis smiled. 'I hope she does too.' He captured her hands and linked his fingers through hers. She was stunned when he dropped down on to one knee. 'Will you marry me, Lissa *mou*? Here, today, in front of our family and friends, and will you let me show you how deeply I love you for the rest of our lives? All of this...' he glanced around at the beautiful wedding setting '... is for you, for us, so that you can have the wedding of your dreams.'

'B-but we are already married,' she stammered.

'The ceremony will be a blessing of our marriage and a renewal of the vows we made to one another.'

'Oh, Takis, I love you so much.'

'I love you, *kardia mou*.' He framed her face with his hands and lowered his mouth to hers to kiss her with tender devotion.

'Are we really going to have a wedding ceremony today?' Lissa asked several blissful minutes later when he trailed his lips over her cheek and nuzzled the tender spot behind her ear.

'We are.'

She gave a rueful glance down at her strap top and denim skirt. 'I'm not dressed to be a bride.'

'I left your sister to organise your wedding dress and she delivered it to the hotel just before you arrived. Your brother is here too.'

'Eleanor is here in Santorini? Did she know you were planning all this?'

'I needed her help so that I could make our wedding perfect.'

She smiled at him through her tears. 'I thought you were not a fan of weddings?'

'I will love ours, because I love you, *koúkla mou*, and I'll do anything to make you happy.'

'That's easy. You just have to keep loving me.'

Takis caught hold of her hand and led her up to the honeymoon suite. 'Your dress is hanging in the wardrobe. I am under strict orders from your sister not to take a look at it.'

'How long do we have before the ceremony?' Lissa murmured. She met his smouldering gaze and recognised his hunger, which was as urgent as hers.

'Just long enough,' he growled as he scooped her up into his arms and carried her over to the bed. And then he was kissing her like she had longed to be kissed, wildly and passionately, his tongue tangling with hers while his hands made short work of undressing her.

She felt the thunder of his heart beneath her fingertips when she skimmed her hands over his chest, tracing the arrowing of rough hairs down to where his arousal was thick and hard. When he eased into her, he told her how much he loved her. He kept nothing back as he whispered the secrets that were no longer hidden in his heart and were all for her.

* * *

Later that afternoon, Lissa stared at her reflection in
the mirror and decided that this must be a dream. Her
wedding dress was from the pages of a fairy tale, an
exquisite concoction of ivory tulle and lace with an off-
the-shoulder bodice and a full skirt adorned with tiny
pearls and diamanté. Her brother, Mark, escorted her
down to the terrace where her friends from England
had gathered with Takis's friends, who had welcomed
her into their social circle in Athens. Eleanor was there
with Jace and their baby daughter, and Elias was asleep
in his pram.

Her eyes flew to Takis, who looked impossibly handsome in a light grey suit, a navy blue shirt and silvery
grey tie. Her husband who loved her. It was in his eyes
when he gazed at her in a kind of awe, and in his husky
voice when he whispered that she was the most beautiful bride there had ever been.

When they renewed their vows he slid a stunning diamond eternity ring on to her finger, where it sparkled
as brightly as stars next to the blue sapphire engagement ring and her wedding band.

'The honeymoon suite has a pool where we can swim
beneath the stars,' Takis whispered against her lips.

'I didn't pack my swimsuit.'

He grinned. 'Neither did I.'

Dinner was a noisy, happy affair as the wedding party
laughed and chatted and toasted the health and happiness of the bride and groom. It was all a little too much
for the youngest guests, and as the sun sank into the sea
and the sky turned pink and gold, Takis carried his son
across the terrace to show him the breathtaking sunset.

Jace was there, cradling his little daughter in his arms. 'Do you remember how we used to say that we would never get married, and we definitely didn't want children? What happened?' he asked ruefully.

'Love happened.' Takis grinned. 'We have come a long way, my friend. Who would have guessed that we would end up with our own families?'

'I have no regrets,' Jace said. 'How about you?'

'I am the luckiest man in the world.' Takis looked down at his angelic son before he turned his head and gazed at his wife, who was the love of his life. She looked over at him and her smile was full of love and promise for tonight when they would be alone. 'No regrets,' he said softly.

* * * * *

A CONSEQUENCE
MADE IN GREECE

ANNIE WEST

MILLS & BOON

Once again, with feeling, thank you
to Abby Green, Anna Campbell and Efthalia Pegios,
for your help when I needed it.

PROLOGUE

'ARE YOU SURE you don't want to join me?'

Strato slitted his eyes against the sun, taking in the top-less woman in his superyacht's swimming pool. Her breasts bobbed in the water but her blonde hair was dry and perfectly styled.

'No. You carry on.'

If he wanted to swim he'd dive off the boat. The waters in this part of western Greece were like crystal. And when Strato swam it was a workout, not a loll in a pool he could traverse in six strokes.

And if he wanted a woman…

That was the problem. He didn't want this woman.

Four days had been ample to remind him he didn't like mindless chatter. That celebrity gossip was no match for an intellectually stimulating discussion or a sense of humour.

And that manufactured passion was no substitute for the real thing. She was enthusiastic, or able to feign enthusiasm, yet there was something lacking.

Strato frowned. There was always something lacking.

The problem, he realised with sudden insight, was with *him*, not her.

He'd avoided deep attachments and emotional relation-ships since he was old enough to understand their inher-ent danger. He'd spent his adult life with women content to abide by those restrictions. Ones who enjoyed a good time and a good party. Yet he grew increasingly restless and dissatisfied.

That accounted for his spur of the moment decision to invite Liv and her friend aboard. But instead of enjoying their company, he increasingly avoided them. At least previous lovers had been engaging and there'd been mutual respect and interest.

She pouted, tilting her head coquettishly. 'If you don't want to swim, I could give you a massage.'

Strato shivered. What he wanted was to be left alone. He didn't want bony fingers kneading his shoulders as a prelude to sex that would leave him feeling even emptier than before. If he needed a massage his sports masseur/personal trainer was aboard.

'Perhaps you'd prefer something else?' a throaty voice purred. Strato turned to see his other guest emerge from indoors. She moved sinuously, hips forward and shoulders back, showing off her lean model's body.

Her long hair swung around her shoulders as she watched him from the corner of her eye. Beneath the translucent jewelled caftan she was naked. Her lips curved in a smile that was half invitation, half hungry.

Strato knew her real hunger was reserved for his wealth.

He suppressed a sigh. He was being unfair. He'd got what he asked for. Restlessness had impaired his judgement. It had been his mistake inviting Liv and Lene on this trip, and not just because he'd overestimated their appeal.

He'd specified fun, sex, luxury and no strings, all temporary. But it was clear they thought the term *temporary* was negotiable, already blatantly hinting about longer-term relationships.

Strato couldn't allow them to harbour hopes about permanency. The very thought made his nape prickle.

'Maybe you'd like to join the pair of us?' Lene pulled off her dress with a flourish to reveal her elegant body, then dropped the fabric, stepping into the shallow end of the pool. She beckoned her friend. 'Maybe you'd like to watch me and Liv together and then join in?'

She reached out and stroked her friend's bare flesh from shoulder to thigh.

Two pairs of assessing eyes fixed on Strato. He felt the

weight of their calculation. They weren't motivated by desire. Except the desire to please him so he'd keep them in luxury and shower them with expensive trinkets. Or maybe, in a moment of weakness, decide to make one his long-term lover.

Strato smiled and took off his sunglasses. Instantly two smiles, gleaming and perfect, answered as the women moved closer together.

What they didn't know was that his expression hid a surge of disgust. Self-disgust at that.

Had he really thought a cruise with these two would be amusing?

Amusement was the last thing he felt. There was a metallic taste in his mouth and his flesh tightened as distaste stirred.

He'd known what they were. As they'd known what he was. Notorious for his wealth, low boredom threshold and refusal to be caught by any woman.

'Thanks for the invitation, ladies.' He rose and their gazes raked his body.

Okay, maybe he did them an injustice. Their interest in his body wasn't totally manufactured. But that didn't alter the essentials. This wasn't working.

'My apologies, but something has come up unexpectedly.'

He gestured towards the study he'd left minutes before. Let them think he'd received news that required his attention. That would afford them some dignity when he gave them their marching orders.

'Do carry on and enjoy yourselves. But I'm afraid I have to change my plans and regrettably you'll need to return to Athens today.' He paused for that to sink in. 'My helicopter will take you back at sunset, or earlier if you prefer. From there a chauffeur will take you wherever you like.' He nodded. 'Thank you both for your company. It's been memorable.'

He turned and walked across the deck, tuning out the sound of gasps.

His efficient secretary appeared from inside as Strato reached the side of the boat. As ever he was there just when he was needed. 'Fix it please, Manoli. And a suitable gift for each of them.'

Strato stood for a moment, looking across the water to the small island a couple of kilometres away. He breathed deep, drawing in the fresh, salt-tanged air as an antidote to the unpleasant taste on his tongue. Then he executed a perfect dive into the green depths and began swimming.

CHAPTER ONE

STRATO CROSSED THE soft white sand of a tiny beach, heading for a cluster of trees. The swim had made his blood pump and with it had come a possible solution to a business problem that had kept him awake into the night.

It suited him to concentrate on that, rather than the error he'd made inviting Lene and Liv aboard.

He dropped to the sand where an overhanging branch provided shade and stretched out, telling himself to focus on the difficulty his Asian headquarters had raised.

Sometime later a pulsing noise made him look up. There was his chopper, rising from the yacht's helipad. His guests must have decided to head back to the city straight away, to seek out some new sponsor as soon as possible.

Strato's mouth twisted. His lapse of judgement with that pair had left him feeling strangely…diminished. He frowned over the sensation.

Could it be that his deliberate choice of shallow, undemanding relationships was making him shallow too?

But he could see no way to avoid that. He didn't want people trying to get close. Yet most of the women who were happy with short, physical relationships didn't really engage his interest any more.

Plus, increasingly, they took his warning that he didn't do relationships as an invitation to try. They didn't understand that Strato Doukas had no hidden soft spot. No secret urge for a spouse or family.

His pool of shade turned suddenly icy.

There'd be no wife or family for him.

He tasted bile at the thought. The lessons of his childhood would never be forgotten. His father had seen to that.

Ruthlessly he thrust aside the tainted memories. Far better to focus on work, one of his antidotes to a past best forgotten.

But before he could concentrate on his Asian business issue, he caught sight of a small boat, white with a painted trim of aqua and red, puttering towards the island.

Strato sighed. He wanted solitude, not a bunch of day trippers. But as he squinted into the sunlight he saw just one figure, wearing a wide straw hat and bulky shirt.

The little vessel approached till it was off the rocky tip at the end of the beach. A picnicker? It had better not be a paparazzo.

The intruder whipped off the wide hat and Strato stared. A she. With dark hair almost to her waist. His eyebrows rose. Hair like that wasn't something you saw every day.

Nevertheless, he must focus on this logistics problem…

With one swift movement the big shirt came off to reveal a figure that actually snared his breath.

Just as you didn't see hair like that often, nor did you see bodies like that, at least in his social circles.

She twisted and bent to stow the hat and shirt and he registered her suppleness—always a plus—as well as her spectacular curves. The newcomer had an hourglass figure. The sort that, sadly, seemed to have gone out of fashion.

After his slim-to-the-bone guests this week, the ripe swells and tantalising dips of this woman's figure drew his gaze like a beacon. He watched as she wriggled her hips, pushing down a pair of baggy shorts to reveal more lush curves. Even the dowdy dark one-piece swimsuit didn't detract for it fitted like a second skin.

His lips curved. Perhaps he wouldn't mind meeting a picnicker after all.

Yet instead of coming ashore, she put on a mask and snorkel and lowered herself off the far side of the boat, heading into deeper water. For five minutes he watched, curious about the back-and-forth pattern of her swim.

Whoever she was, she was in little danger of drowning.

Those long legs kicked powerfully and she moved with grace and precision. But eventually she swam to the headland and past it, out of sight.

Probably just as well. He'd come here to be alone. The last thing he needed was another woman distracting him. He stretched and rolled over, turning away from the water.

Cora jammed the hat more firmly on her head as she picked her way across the rocks, eyes on the ground. Only when she reached the sugar-fine sand did she look towards the shady grove she'd taken to using for her lunch break.

And discovered she wasn't alone.

A figure lay in the deep shade.

No one else came to this tiny islet, except in the height of the summer season when occasional day trippers from the main island might stop. She turned to survey the water. The only boat in sight, apart from the little wooden one she'd borrowed from her father, was a huge, sleek cruiser in the distance. The sort that looked more at home in Piraeus or the Bahamas than in this forgotten corner of Greece.

Cora frowned, noticing the single set of footprints emerging from the sea.

People who cruised the world in those swanky big yachts didn't swim four kilometres for fun. Had his boat sunk? He couldn't have come ashore in last night's storm. The footprints were too fresh.

Frowning, she headed up the beach. She hoped he wasn't injured.

Her stride slowed then stopped as she got closer. A man lay on his side, his back to her.

He was naked. The same dark olive colour from his wide, straight shoulders, down the curve of his tapering back to tightly rounded buttocks and long, hairy legs.

Cora swallowed. Surprise dried her mouth and caught her lungs. She felt her eyes widen.

This man was big, she realised. Really big, with long limbs and a toned, fit body.

She was used to fit, athletic men, given her work. Yet she didn't think she'd ever seen one like this.

Would he look as spectacular from the front?

A tiny breeze riffled his dark hair but he didn't move. Her eyes strayed to a discoloured area spreading from the shoulder he lay on, up towards his shoulder blade.

Her frown deepened. An injury? Not blood, surely?

Dropping her canvas holdall, she rushed up to him, the tang of fear on her tongue. Was he breathing?

She bent and a hiss escaped her. Shock and relief. Not blood. That wasn't a recent injury. It was old scar tissue. A burn or—

Muscles rippled under dark gold skin and he rolled over, his shoulder sliding against her ankle, making her jump back.

Spectacular was the word. She had an impression of streamlined power, of formidable energy before she forced her attention up. Yet that momentary survey of his naked form had her heart thudding. Spectacular was definitely the word. Spectacular all over.

Cora swallowed hard and focused on his face. A broad brow. Severe, straight black eyebrows and beneath them slitted green eyes.

Poseidon. That was who he looked like.

Every Greek had seen likenesses of the mighty sea god, the personification of male strength and beauty. Surely if the old stories of gods appearing to mortals held any truth, Poseidon would have eyes like that. Stormy. Assessing. The colour of the sea she'd just swum in.

Cora's mouth dried. 'You're alive.'

'You were expecting a corpse?'

The fine hairs on Cora's arms rose and something unfamiliar breathed into being. As if that deep, amused voice woke something dormant within her.

She stiffened and took another half-step back.

'I wasn't sure what to think.' Maybe she'd had too much sun. When she met that probing green gaze her vision seemed to blur at the edges.

Cora broke eye contact and looked past him, frowning.

'You've got no towel, no clothes.' Amazing how tough it was not to let her gaze dip to his lower body. One quick look had already revealed he was built on the same monumental scale all over. Heat rose to her face.

Those straight eyebrows arched. 'Is there some rule that says I must have them with me at all times?'

'I wondered if you'd had an accident.'

'Is that why you were bending over me? To give me mouth to mouth?'

Her gaze dropped, past a long, straight nose to his smiling mouth. His mouth was beautifully formed, almost too beautiful for a man. Except that the rest of his features, from his solidly carved jaw to the high-cut planes of his cheeks, were so overtly masculine. A deep groove bisected one cheek where his wryly amused smile rose more on one side than the other.

There was no way you could call it a dimple.

A dimple implied something cute and appealing.

This face, this smile, was sardonic, not cute. As for appealing... Her thrumming pulse was proof of that.

But Cora was no fool. He might be incredibly charismatic, with that sexy, quintessentially masculine body. But there was a sharpness about him she didn't like.

As any Greek who knew their myths could tell you, the ancient gods weren't kind, caring creatures. They were dangerous.

This man was too. Every feminine instinct sensed danger. The danger not of violence but of primal awareness between male and female.

It showed in the sharp speculation belying that ostensibly lazy stare. In the way his gaze flickered to the damp patches where her breasts pressed against the worn denim shirt. And in the way that smile broadened into something like interest as he saw her noticing.

And above all in the fact he didn't make a move to cover his nakedness, just lay there, as if inviting her to appreciate his assets.

'Right. Well, if you're okay, I'll go.' This might be the only deeply shaded spot on the tiny island and she might be long overdue her lunch but—

'How do you know I'm okay? You haven't checked my pulse.'

Strato surveyed his Nereid with curiosity and a surprisingly sharp jab of pleasure. For she was definitely a Nereid, a sea nymph.

She'd been the one snorkelling. Her hair hung in long slick locks and there were crease marks on her face from her goggles. Besides, even the frumpy shirt and long baggy shorts couldn't hide her phenomenal body.

But then he'd had the advantage of seeing her luscious body in all its glory and he had an excellent memory.

Her eyebrows pinched and wide golden-brown eyes met his with a mix of impatience and suspicion that was as obvious as it was novel. Women didn't usually look at him that way.

Usually they looked eager.

He lifted a hand to his forehead and saw her attention drop to his biceps. Suspicion narrowed her eyes.

Okay, it was an obvious move, drawing attention to his muscles. But he'd seen the way those eyes had widened as she'd looked him over, dwelling for a second on his penis. He understood that look. Had seen it so often from so many women over the years. Annoyance had stirred at her dismissal. She'd actually been turning away when his words stopped her.

This woman was definitely different. After that first appreciative stare she'd kept her attention on his face.

Strato found that intriguing. Almost disappointing.

He shouldn't want female attention. He'd just sent away the two women who'd joined him for sun and sex.

Either he was so supremely shallow that he couldn't stand being ignored by a lovely woman. Or so world-weary a hint of novelty grabbed his attention—and other parts, making them stir with interest. Neither said much for his character.

Ruefully he decided he might be both. Though no one else would dare voice such an assessment. Not when Strato Doukas commanded billions.

He added cynical to the list.

'Are you all right? Did you hurt your head?'

Strato realised his palm covered his forehead and it might look as if he had a headache.

For a nanosecond he contemplated lying. But he preferred the truth, even when it was brutal. Better the truth than hiding from it. He knew first-hand how perilous it could be, not facing facts head-on.

His mouth tightened and in response a frown gathered on her brow.

To his amazement Strato felt warmth lick behind his ribs. Warmth that had nothing to do with sexual interest but with the fact this woman he didn't know was genuinely worried about him.

It was bizarre.

He paid a host of staff extremely well to cater to his every need. He didn't need a stranger's worry. Yet her words stirred something deep inside that he hadn't experienced in a long time.

Raking his fingers through his hair, he gave her a deliberately languid smile, refusing to dwell on his instinctive reaction to her simple kindness. That felt too much like weakness. 'No, I'm not injured. Do I look it?'

Satisfaction scudded through him as he watched her

swallow, as if fighting her instinctive response. Because she liked what she saw?

Shallow, Doukas. Definitely shallow.

But better than dwelling on his response to her concern.

'Good. I'm glad you're okay.' Her voice had a throaty edge that rippled across his libido.

She didn't look glad. She looked strung too tight. Strato liked that. He also liked the way her nipples stood erect against her shabby shirt, making him wonder if those plump breasts would feel as spectacular in his hands as they looked.

But shallow though he might be, he was also ruthlessly honest with himself. Which left him thinking about why her interest pleased him. Because it counteracted that momentary jab of unexpected connection he felt? Gave him something to concentrate on other than the emptiness growing inside?

He heard himself saying as she made to turn away, 'I don't suppose you have anything to drink, do you? I'm parched.'

She stilled. 'You don't have any water? How long have you been here?'

He shrugged. 'Hours, I suppose.'

'You suppose? Don't you know? Do you have *any* supplies with you?'

Her voice married concern with a scolding edge and Strato found himself imagining her dressed as a buttoned-up school mistress. It wasn't a fantasy that had ever appealed before. It didn't last long now. He preferred the prospect of seeing her in her swimsuit again, or naked, than with her figure obscured.

'I don't have anything at all.'

Now he thought about it he *was* thirsty. He should have returned to the yacht, because his staff wouldn't seek him out, knowing he wanted solitude.

Not as clever as you thought, Doukas.

He was rewarded with another frown, more like a scowl this time, and a mutter he didn't catch.

'What are you doing without supplies? It's madness.'

He nodded, fascinated. It had been a lifetime ago that anyone had taken him to task. The last had been his aunt, who'd fretted over him, worrying about him till the end. As if her worry could change the inevitable and turn him into someone different, someone not—

'It may not be high summer yet but you can't afford to get dehydrated. Especially if you're alone here.' His Nereid paused, looking beyond him as if expecting to see someone else emerge over the crest of the small hill. '*Are* you alone?'

'I am. But I'll be picked up at sunset.' That was the standing arrangement with his crew.

Her mouth firmed into a disapproving line as she slid a stained canvas bag from her shoulder. 'That's sheer stupidity. *Anything* could happen in that time.'

His gaze tracked from her wide, kissable mouth, now primed with disapproval, down the slick dark hair dripping around her shoulders and lower, reaching towards her waist. Past bountiful breasts to those horribly baggy shorts that made her hips look over-sized, to toned, glorious legs.

Oh, yes, anything could happen in that time.

'I don't suppose you've got any food in there too? I haven't eaten today.'

CHAPTER TWO

CORA PAUSED IN the act of rifling through her bag, her head lifting at the sound of that oh-so-nonchalant voice.

She didn't trust it. She didn't trust *him* further than she could shove that outrageously spectacular body. She was tall and fit but he looked taller and fitter.

Her gaze slid down across that broad chest with its light smattering of hair. Just dark enough to emphasise his defined pectoral muscles and—

Damn! She dragged her attention back to his face.

It gave nothing away. In fact it was suspiciously blank of expression, which would have made her hackles rise even if she hadn't seen the knowing gleam in those sea-green eyes.

He was laughing at her.

The sensible thing would be to leave him to his amusement. Cora had an inbuilt hatred of being the source of any man's amusement. Once bitten…

But she had a strong sensible streak, as well as too much experience of people coming to grief, especially in and near the sea. People who thought it would be okay to try scuba diving without lessons, or drive jet skis while drunk. Or get so badly sunburnt they needed medical care.

At least Poseidon had enough sense to lie in the shade, and from the bronzed colour of his skin he wasn't going to burn any time soon.

She sucked in a breath, realising her attention had dipped to those wide straight shoulders. And he'd noticed.

She wanted to wipe the smirk off his face. Okay, he might not be overtly smiling but inwardly he was laughing at her expense. Her nape tightened at a flash of memory. Adrian, golden haired and blue eyed. Laughing.

Her nostrils flared as she inhaled deeply.

If her instincts were right, this man and Adrian had a lot in common.

But you don't know for sure. And you can't leave him here without even a drink.

Cora wanted to ask how he came to be here, alone, naked and without provisions, but no doubt it would be some story of a stupid joke by friends. Besides, she suspected any show of curiosity would feed his ego.

She sighed. 'You can have some of my lunch if you like.'

Doris always packed too much food, believing that a *big girl* like Cora needed a lot of fuel. It was true that when she worked in the field, Cora burned up a lot of energy and needed extra calories. Yet she hated being categorised as a *big girl*. Even at twenty-six those words hurt. Just as well motherly Doris had no idea. She'd be upset if she knew.

'That would be excellent. Thank you.' He propped himself up on one elbow and gave her a flashing smile that would have weakened her knees if she wasn't immune to gorgeous, self-centred men.

She shifted her weight in the sand. Okay, maybe there was a little melting of the tendons, but she had this man's measure. Forewarned was forearmed.

As for being the butt of his amusement…

'On one condition.'

Cora almost laughed at the way his dark eyebrows shot up in a look of astonishment that was clearly genuine. It appeared nobody was in the habit of denying Poseidon what he wanted, or setting limits on his games.

Interesting to know. That could explain his aura of casual confidence. But then, people gifted with amazing looks were usually confident.

'What is it?' His eyebrows lowered and eyes slitted so his stare looked full of suspicion.

Cora couldn't prevent her huff of laughter. 'Don't fret. I'm not asking for a share of all your worldly goods.' She gestured at the empty sand around him.

When she met his eyes again he wore a curious expression she couldn't identify.

It struck her she was spending far too much energy puzzling over a stranger she'd never see again.

'I prefer not to eat lunch with a naked stranger. I'd rather you covered up.'

'To preserve your modesty?' His long mouth twitched in a way Cora found too attractive. Until his gaze moved to her damp shirt, where her wet hair and swimsuit made the fabric cling to her breasts. 'I'm afraid I've got nothing to cover myself with.' He paused and she felt the silence with each ponderous beat of her pulse. 'Unless you could spare me some clothing?'

Cora swallowed a smile. Someone should warn him about overplaying his hand. It was obvious he wanted her to strip off her shirt. She hadn't missed those quick glances at her breasts where, to her chagrin, her nipples were tight, hard peaks.

'You don't have hang-ups about wearing a woman's clothes? Some men might feel their manhood compromised.'

'If it's that or starvation, I'll opt for the clothes. My ego's not that fragile.'

She'd bet it wasn't.

This time it wasn't a short huff of laughter but a chuckle that escaped. If he was trying for soulful and half-starved he shouldn't look so strong and able-bodied. She'd never met a less pitiable specimen.

'Okay.' She swung her bag down to the sand between them, noticing from the corner of her vision the way he rose higher on his elbow as if intent on the striptease he expected. Cora straightened and put her hands to the hem of her over-sized shirt. Yes, there it was, a flash of anticipation in that hooded gaze.

For a second longer she hesitated, genuinely this time. Wondering if this was a huge mistake.

She could leave a bottle of water with him or offer him

a lift back to the harbourside town on the next island where his friends presumably were.

But she was hungry. Why should she have to leave and eat in the sun because of some thoughtless tourist?

The fact that she enjoyed the verbal sparring between them was another factor. How long since her pulse had raced like that? Since she'd felt anything out of the ordinary?

Besides, she rather liked getting one up on this self-satisfied stranger. It was time someone showed him he couldn't have everything his own way.

So instead of reefing her shirt over her head, she grabbed her baggy, knee-length shorts and tugged them off with one quick movement.

'There you are.' She bent and retrieved them from the sand, giving them a little shake before tossing them into Poseidon's lap.

His surprise almost made her laugh.

Except it was quickly eclipsed by something that made her bones soften. An eager heat in those narrowed eyes as he surveyed her legs and smiled.

Cora felt that sliding gaze almost like a caress and it banished her momentary sense of victory.

Idiot! She might not have uncovered her body but it seemed this stranger was almost as appreciative of bare legs. His smile morphed from appreciative to hungry, heading towards predatory.

Cora's amusement vanished.

She jammed her fists on her hips, grateful that her shirt covered her to her thighs.

'If you want to share my food we need to get one thing straight. *I'm* not on the menu. Got it? I'm not staying alone here with a man who thinks I'm available for his sexual convenience.'

The vibe she'd got from him wasn't the sort she'd had from men who'd take without asking. She was sure, pretty sure, that for all his smug amusement she wasn't in physical peril. Nevertheless, he needed to understand the ground rules or she'd be back at the boat before he could stop her.

Strato stared up into fiery eyes the colour of his favourite brandy. Heat drilled down his gullet, as if he'd slugged back a double measure. But it wasn't from sexual anticipation. For he read defiance in her expression and something that might have been worry. Or fear.

For the first time he viewed the situation from her perspective. Alone on a deserted island with a man she knew nothing about. A man who was far bigger and stronger than her. Who made no secret of his sexual interest. And no one within shouting distance to help her if she needed it.

It wasn't the fire of carnal attraction surging through him. It felt like shame.

He blinked, digesting the unfamiliar sensation.

Unfamiliar, because his casual flirting was always done with women who were patently eager for his attention. Who knew he wanted sex with no strings. Who knew his reputation for ensuring his partners' pleasure. In that world innuendo was pleasurable foreplay.

Now he was out of his usual environment. His Nereid didn't know she had nothing to fear. She hadn't a clue who he was, or that he'd never hurt any woman.

His mouth tightened as he slammed down impenetrable shutters that locked away ancient memories. He never opened them. Except in his nightmares.

Strato raised his hand in a placating gesture and sat up. 'I'm very sorry. I didn't mean to make you uncomfortable.' He swallowed, surprised to find his throat tight so the words emerged like a growl. 'I didn't think. I was just…'

'Flirting.' She sighed and her shoulders eased down a little.

He'd done that. Made her uncomfortable, not in a sexually aroused way, but because she was nervous.

'You have my word of honour that you are totally safe.'

A muscle in his jaw flexed as he gritted his teeth. How could he have made such a mistake? He'd become so used to the sexual promiscuity of a self-indulgent lifestyle that he took it for the norm.

Clearly his Nereid didn't come from that world.

Was that why he found her fascinating?

No, it was more than that. More even than her sexual allure. He liked that she didn't take any nonsense but said what she thought. Liked her quick thinking and humour, turning the tables on him when she guessed he wanted her to take off her shirt.

She was attracted, he knew that. He guessed she could be enticed into wanting him. But this wasn't the place or time for seduction.

He couldn't recall ever making such a mistake in seducing a woman.

Which shows how easy you've had it, Doukas. You never have to exert yourself.

'If you'd prefer to leave, I won't die of thirst, I promise.' He reached for the shorts she'd thrown at him, ready to pass them back. Stoically he ignored that they were warm from her body.

'No. Keep them. You might be glad of the cover if you're really staying here till sunset.'

Something within him sank. Disappointment? Because a chance-met woman was turning her back on him?

Strato told himself it was a novel experience and, since his life seemed so flat and mundane lately, he should welcome that.

Instead he felt absurdly bereft.

'Thank you. And thank you for coming to check on me. It was decent of you.'

He felt like a kid, reminded of his manners. Yet he doubted this chastened feeling would last.

She shook her head, long tresses sliding around her

breasts in a way that made Strato lock his jaw and concentrate on her face.

She wasn't beautiful but there was something about her wide mouth and warm, intelligent eyes that *felt* like beauty. Especially when amusement had danced across her face.

He was used to women with bleached, perfect smiles, pumped-up lips and lots of make-up. When this woman smiled he noticed a couple of her teeth overlapped and as for Botox—she had full lips but he'd swear they were natural.

'Are you really hungry, or did you just say that?'

'Starving. It's my own fault. I only had coffee this morning.'

Strato had only downed a tiny cup of coffee before heading into his office, knowing it was the one place his guests wouldn't follow.

'In that case…' She shrugged. 'We might as well eat. This is the only shade around and I usually have lunch here.'

Pleasure was a punch to his solar plexus. It was on the tip of his tongue to ask if she came here often but it was such a cliché and he'd promised not to play flirtatious games. Instead he simply grinned his approval.

Her response was instantaneous. Her eyes flared with a heat that reminded him of warmed cognac. Her breasts rose on a sharp breath that would have stoked his ego if he weren't used to female admiration.

Strato pretended not to notice. He'd concentrate instead on the simple pleasure of lunch by the sea with a fascinating companion.

Even so, he knew that in the right circumstances, he could find another sort of pleasure with this woman. But it wouldn't be simple. And he only did simple, didn't he?

Or were his tastes changing?

Was that why he'd been so restless lately? And why she appealed so much?

'Thank you for trusting me,' he murmured. 'It's generous of you. Now, do you want to turn around while I dress?'

Remarkably for a woman who'd stood up to him as no one else did and who berated him for his sexually charged interactions, rosy colour swept into her cheeks.

That blush intrigued. She was no wilting violet, scared to face a man. Yet she was a strange mix of confidence and reserve. He couldn't recall the last time he'd seen a woman blush.

Strato hadn't met anyone like her.

'Good idea. I'll see what Doris packed for lunch.' She turned, ostentatiously busying herself with her canvas bag.

Damp cotton bunched in Strato's hands. He'd originally hoped she'd strip off her shirt but he couldn't complain about the view.

Her tanned legs would feature in his dreams. They were shapely and long. Long enough that he wouldn't have to bend double to kiss her. Strong too, given all the swimming she'd done. Strong enough to wrap around him and grip hard as he drove deep into her luscious warmth.

Nostrils flaring, he shook the sand from the shorts with a snap and put them on.

If only the press could see you now, Doukas.

Billionaire sets new fashion trend! It puts a whole new spin on wanting to get into her pants.

He huffed out a silent laugh.

The shorts were ancient, faded and a terrible fit. But they were warm from her body and he had to take a few moments to battle his stirring erection as he imagined her naked and willing against him. It was an image his fertile imagination didn't want to relinquish.

Fortunately she didn't notice as she unpacked lunch.

Strato breathed deep and reminded himself he didn't want to scare her off.

He'd promised to behave.

For now.

Later, when she understood he was no threat, it might be intriguing to pursue this sudden attraction.

* * *

'Who's Doris?'

Cora looked over her shoulder and her stupid heart gave a shuddery heave then catapulted into a rackety beat.

She'd seen him sprawled naked. How could he look even more mouth-wateringly male wearing daggy old shorts?

Yet somehow the contrast between dark golden skin stretched over honed muscle and shabby, faded cotton made him look even sexier.

Maybe it was the nonchalant way he wore the threadbare shorts. His total lack of concern over his appearance, his casual confidence in his own skin were devastatingly attractive to a woman who'd spent too many years overly conscious of her body shape.

On him, tall and well-built would never be called oversized. He looked gorgeous.

'Sorry?'

'You mentioned Doris. I wondered who she was.'

'Oh.' Cora dragged her gaze back to the food. 'She's the cook at my father's hotel.'

In fact she was far more.

Cora's mother died when she was eight, and for the next six years it had just been her and her father, till Doris arrived. The newcomer had been good for them both, breathing new life into the place. She'd also taken Cora under her wing, providing a sounding board through the trials of her teen years, even trying to tame her so she didn't become a total tomboy.

Cora's lips twitched. Poor Doris. She was a dear, so loyal and caring. She'd tried her best to turn Cora into a model of housewifely virtues but with limited success.

'You live with your father?'

She caught a flash of curiosity. It wasn't surprising for multiple generations to live together, especially in traditional villages such as her own. Clearly this stranger wasn't from such a background.

Cora glanced out to sea where, in the distance, that massive cruiser was moored. It had come from Athens, Doris reported, after some crew came into harbour for provisions.

'For the moment. He hasn't been well.'

She swallowed, recalling that horrible long-distance call. The news her father had suffered a heart attack. The terrible helplessness of being more than a continent away and unable to be with him straight away.

'I'm sorry to hear that.'

She shrugged and spread the packets of food between them. 'He's improved a lot. He's doing better.'

Or he would be if he weren't so stressed about the hotel. The economic downturn had hit hard, just after he'd taken out a huge loan, investing in major improvements that he'd thought would set the business up for long-term profit. Now they faced a particularly poor tourist season, with bookings down and no idea how they'd meet the repayments.

Naturally Cora had stayed to help.

'I'm glad he's okay.' The stranger paused and Cora sensed his scrutiny. To her relief he turned his attention to the food. 'Your Doris has provided a feast.'

'She doesn't do things by halves.' Cora smiled and broke a large piece of cheese and spinach pie apart, passing him half. 'She even makes her own filo pastry.'

He took a bite and Cora watched him pause, eyes widening then narrowing to unreadable slits as he slowly savoured it. He took another, bigger bite.

Doris would approve of him. She liked anyone who appreciated her cooking. Cora turned her attention back to the food though, strangely uncomfortable watching his obvious enjoyment. His gusto made her wonder if he attacked other physical pleasures with the same enthusiasm.

Absurdly she felt that phantom brush of heat in her cheeks again. Because once more her thoughts turned carnal.

'That's real home cooking,' he said, what sounded like

genuine emotion drawing Cora's curiosity. It was more than simple appreciation. 'I haven't tasted food like this for years.'

Yet he wasn't starved. That imposing body was impressive.

'No one cooks like that for you?' She refused to ask if he had a wife. If he did she pitied the woman, for this man had the unmistakable air of someone committed to pleasure without concern for others.

'Not since I was young.' He took another bite with strong, white teeth and Cora watched, mesmerised, the rhythmic action of his jaw and the way his throat muscles worked as he swallowed.

She unscrewed a bottle of water and took a swig.

'May I?' He nodded to the bottle and she passed it, watching him put it to his lips.

Glittering eyes surveyed her over the raised bottle and she turned away, dismayed at her body's reaction. Because he'd put his mouth where hers had been. Which made her think of his mouth on hers. Which made her breasts tighten and heat stir low in her pelvis.

This was *so* not her. Maybe she was the one who'd had a touch too much sun. She certainly wasn't responding to Poseidon as she normally did to men.

With a huff of annoyance she shoved salad and olives towards him, then the bread. Normally Cora would have eaten ravenously after all her exertions. Now her appetite waned.

Sharing lunch with this man had been a mistake. He mightn't be physically dangerous but he disturbed her in ways no man had since Adrian. And even with Adrian—

'You're not eating.'

She looked up to find him watching her. For an instant everything inside sparked to alert, then his gaze slid away towards the beach as if appreciating the view and she relaxed.

Cora frowned. A single look did that? Did he realise? Was that why he turned away?

Slowly she reached for an orange. 'I suspect your need is greater than mine.'

Which was nonsense. She'd been hungry before. Frowning, she concentrated on peeling the fruit, inhaling the citrus tang and popping a juicy segment into her mouth.

Silence lengthened as they ate. Gradually Cora felt her shoulders lower, her tight muscles easing.

Someone seeing them would think the atmosphere companionable as they concentrated on the view.

Yet Cora was totally aware of the man beside her. The reach of his long arm as he explored the goodies Doris had provided. The easy shift and stretch of his long body as he got more comfortable on the sand.

Her own body kept leaning closer, till she realised what she was doing and pulled back.

Determined, Cora concentrated on her orange and thinking of something else.

It had been a tough morning with that reminder from the bank sending her father into something like panic.

Usually her trips to this tiny island helped her deal with the stress over her father and the hotel, which she feared they'd lose. Today even the sea, which always brought solace, failed her.

Because more than half her mind was on Poseidon, happily devouring her food, rather than on devising some new strategy to save her dad from bankruptcy.

Abruptly she came to a decision. Her earlier instincts had been right. This was a mistake.

Licking the sticky juice from her fingers, she reached for the water bottle and poured some over her palms. Then she rose. 'I have to go.'

'You're leaving?'

She saw surprise on Poseidon's honed features. Genuine surprise, not feigned.

Cora felt satisfaction unfurl. Given his penchant for flirting and the way he guarded his thoughts, it felt like a victory to see his astonished look.

He probably wasn't used to women leaving till he was finished with them.

She drew a shaky breath and told herself that didn't apply to her because she'd never let him start with her. There'd be no casual passion with a stranger. Not for her.

'It's time.' She hesitated then made the offer that any decent person would. 'Can I give you a lift?'

His narrowed eyes caught hers and she felt a frisson of awareness skid down her spine and curl into her belly. She swallowed. Given her history she'd prided herself on her defences against predatory men. This man made a mockery of those. With just a look!

'Thank you, no. I'm fine.' His hand dropped to those ancient shorts. 'You'll want these back.'

'No!' Did her voice sound strangled? 'Thanks, but I don't want them.'

Even if she could wear them with half the panache he did, she'd rather not see them again. They'd remind her of today's madness. That sudden surging hunger. For a complete stranger!

For a second longer Cora looked at him. Trying to imprint his image in her memory? Abruptly she turned away.

Strato watched her cross the beach, the loose sand turning each step into an undulating sway of curvaceous hips that dried his mouth. He groped for the water bottle and gulped.

Now she was on firm sand and her walk became an athletic stride, the movement of her long, gilded legs mesmerising.

Oh, yes, he'd dream about those legs.

He took another gulp. But his dry throat had nothing to do with the need for water.

It was all down to *her*.

When was the last time a woman walked out on him?

He understood that she was wary of a complete stranger. So he'd masked his thoughts and projected an aura of calm.

It had worked. They'd sat companionably. Long enough for him to become addicted to the sight of her eating that damned orange. He'd swear she didn't realise how the sight of her pink tongue, swiping up drips of juice, teased him. Or how he'd watched her licking her fingers and wished she'd lick him instead.

His frown became a scowl.

Strato had a reputation as a playboy but the gaps between lovers grew longer and even he had never dumped a woman or, in today's case, two, and instantly pursued another! He didn't understand it.

There was something about this woman that called to him.

Sexual allure, obviously.

But more too. Character. That was it. Feistiness melded with…decency. Her concern for him had been real, even through her annoyance. That concern had made him feel things he hadn't experienced in a long time.

That didn't say much for the people he mixed with, did it?

Even the lunch she'd shared had stirred unfamiliar yearnings. That cheese pie reminded him of his mother's. A tantalising flavour he hadn't tasted since he was eight. It had been like biting into sunshine and rare memories of happiness. No wonder he felt unsettled.

His eyes narrowed as his Nereid disappeared around the point without a backward glance. She had no interest in prolonging their acquaintance.

Or did she know that by leaving she'd pique his interest?

Whatever the reasons, this woman fascinated him, far more than anyone he could recall.

Strato reached for the segment of orange she'd left. He

bit into it, tasting the bright sunburst of sweet, tart citrus. His tongue tingled as he sucked up the juice.

Strato closed his eyes and imagined it wasn't an orange he was feasting on but her.

The question was, would he give in to temptation?

CHAPTER THREE

CORA WAS WIPING down outdoor tables on the vine-shaded terrace when she heard a boat.

It wasn't unusual to hear motors early in the morning as the fishing boats returned. Yet this motor approached the hotel, not the harbour further around the bay.

She shaded her eyes. On the water's dancing gold and silver dazzle she saw it approach. Not a traditional fishing boat but something sleek and modern.

They weren't expecting guests today, sadly. Besides, this boat was too small to have come from the mainland. Cora scanned the bay and noticed the luxury motor yacht she'd seen yesterday, now anchored off the point. If someone was coming ashore for supplies, surely they'd head to the harbourside shops?

The engine stopped and the boat kissed the end of the hotel's jetty. Someone slung out a rope, mooring it with the ease of long practice.

She moved to the next table. Yet instead of cleaning it, she watched the man walk down the jetty.

The low sun was directly behind him and she had an impression of height and athleticism, and wide, straight shoulders. He didn't hurry but his long stride covered the distance in no time.

Cora's nape tightened and the cloth crumpled in her hand as she watched that easy, confident walk. More saunter than stride.

She didn't recognise his gait, yet premonition stirred like a strong current in still waters. Some primal sense told her—

He stepped into the shade of the tamarisk trees edging the terrace and Cora's chest grabbed.

Poseidon.

The amused, intriguing, dangerous man from yesterday.

Her eyes ate him up. From the dark hair swept back off his high forehead to the chiselled male beauty and carved arrogance of his face. He wore reflective sunglasses and she wondered if behind them he was smiling again.

One sweeping glance told her he looked almost as good dressed as he did naked. He wore designer loafers, a white short-sleeved shirt, and pale trousers that must have been tailored to fit those powerful thighs and long legs.

Instantly Cora regretted her choice of clothes. Old tennis shoes, cut-off denim shorts with uneven, ragged edges and a black T-shirt proclaiming *Biologists Do It in Their Genes*.

He stopped on the terrace, surveying her. Then slowly, so slowly she felt each tiny, incremental change like the stroke of velvet on bare skin, his mouth curved up into a smile that made her pulse throb and her toes curl.

A flourish of something she couldn't name stirred and Cora snatched a desperate breath, schooling her features.

She tilted her chin higher. She'd been right. He was tall, far taller than her. It was unusual for her to have to look up at a man. Unusual and…not unpleasant.

'Good morning. Can I help you?'

Sleek eyebrows lifted and he took his glasses off to reveal eyes the colour of the sea, shimmering with warmth.

'You don't recognise me?' His smile curved even higher on one side, creating an apostrophe of amusement, a tiny groove in the tanned flesh beside his mouth.

It was like an invitation, that tiny curl. Beckoning Cora to reach out and trace it. To respond to the invitation in his eyes.

Remarkably, her fingertips tingled as if she'd done just that. As if she'd brushed them across his face.

Horrified at her vivid imaginings, she reached for the cloth that had dropped to the table.

'Of course. We met yesterday.' Her voice was appallingly

husky but she ploughed on. 'So you got picked up from the beach all right.'

He inclined his head, his eyes not leaving hers. 'You were worried about me?'

'I…' Why did her mouth dry under that wickedly arousing gaze and her words stick in her throat? She was twenty-six, not sixteen. 'It was an unusual situation, being left without supplies.'

She'd almost returned yesterday evening to check on him, but her father had felt fretful, worrying about money, and Doris had been out so Cora had been forced to stay here. That was why she'd started her morning chores early, so she had time to take the boat this morning and check the stranger was safe.

'Why are you here?'

'To see you.'

Fervently Cora hoped he couldn't read her delight at his words. She had no interest any more in uber-sexy men. Her dear dad was the only man in her life these days.

Yet excitement throbbed in her accelerating pulse.

'Really?' Willpower kept her voice flat. 'How did you find me?'

He shrugged. 'I knew you must be local.' Then she noticed he held something in his hand. He offered it to her.

'Thank you for the loan.'

Cora's lips twitched as she took the familiar, worn-thin fabric. 'You *ironed* my shorts?'

His smile widened, a long groove appearing in his cheek, and Cora had to focus on taking the clothing rather than melting at the knees.

She'd known attractive men, sexy men, but never one to affect her like this, so devastatingly. Not even Adrian had had this instantaneous impact.

'They've been washed too, but I admit I didn't do it. One of my staff was responsible.'

He had staff? Once more her gaze flickered to that massive yacht. Surely not. He couldn't be the owner. He must have come from elsewhere.

'Well, thank you.' She didn't mention she'd been on the verge of throwing out the tatty shorts.

'Join me in a coffee?'

Cora blinked.

'You do serve coffee here?' He nodded to the small tables and blue-painted, rush-bottomed chairs.

'Of course.' It was before normal opening hours but...

'Then two coffees please. If you'll join me?'

Looking into that confident face, Cora wanted to say she had too much work to spare the time. Any man who made her feel hot and bothered with just a smile should be avoided. It had been a hard-won lesson that she wouldn't forget.

Yet the adventurous Cora she'd stifled so long urged her to agree. The Cora who'd revelled in new experiences, new places and the opportunity to work in the field she loved. The work she'd had to give up while she helped out here.

Lately she'd imagined that Cora had disappeared completely, broken by disappointment, duty and worry. Now, feeling her blood effervesce, she knew better.

Caution vied with pleasure. How long since she'd had a conversation that didn't centre on the hotel, her father's health or their financial woes? At least this man distracted her from reality, even if only fleetingly.

What harm could a coffee do? It was only polite to thank him after he'd made the effort to wash and return her clothes.

Nodding, trying to look brisk and businesslike, she turned away. 'I won't be long.'

Strato subsided onto a chair where he could watch the shadowed doorway through which she'd exited.

Contentment filled him, and a little jiggle of anticipation he hadn't experienced in a long time.

If he'd known coming to these smaller islands would prove so diverting he'd have come sooner. Athens was predictable and New York palled. Monte Carlo was passé and he wasn't in the mood for Rio's flamboyant parties.

What did appeal was his Nereid.

He liked that she didn't gush when he appeared. That she treated him as an equal.

Even her addiction to appalling clothes intrigued him. He laughed, thinking of the difference between designer string bikinis and tatty shorts. Today's shorts were infinitely better for they clung close. The jagged hem rose high on one side, to just below her buttock, catching and holding his gaze as she walked away. Amazingly he found the sight of that extra sliver of thigh more arousing than either of the women who'd paraded naked on his yacht.

As for her T-shirt... It clung lovingly to her magnificent breasts and made him more than ever determined to pursue their acquaintance.

Besides, he'd never had a biologist.

Class act, Doukas. Ticking them off by profession now?

Strato breathed deep, ignoring the tang of self-disgust on his tongue. Far from ticking off professions he was intrigued by her chosen field.

Anyway, he set limits around his relationships for an excellent reason. If that meant those relationships seemed increasingly shallow and unsatisfactory, that was the price he'd pay. The alternative was impossible.

Yet he wondered what would happen if he chose not to swim in the shallows but to venture into deeper water. If he pursued a woman who seemed complex and challenging and far removed from what he was used to.

He was sprawled, legs stretched out beyond the small table, his attention not on the sea but on the door to the hotel.

A little thrill wound its way down Cora's spine then around to her breasts and lower as their eyes locked.

He sat up as she approached. Did he notice she'd taken time to brush her hair? She'd wanted to change her clothes too but pride forbade it. His ego was big enough without her primping.

Cora recalled those times Doris had set her up to meet some prospective boyfriend. Inevitably when Cora appeared, Amazonian in height and stature, usually taller than the stranger Doris had invited, the guy would stare in dismay.

Then there were the ones drawn to Cora's generous figure. Whose eyes devoured her so eagerly her skin crawled.

Her skin didn't crawl now.

Poseidon's gaze might be meshed with hers but she hadn't missed that all-encompassing survey. He'd seen *and* approved. Instead of being discomfited, she revelled in his interest.

Why? That was the million-dollar question.

Cora moved between the tables, head up. Her shoulders were back, not curving forward as if trying to minimise her chest.

Bizarre that she should react like this to a stranger's gaze when blatant sexual interest usually annoyed her. This time she felt something like pride. Delight. Anticipation at spending time with him.

'Here you are.' She placed their tiny coffee cups, glasses of water and a plate of biscuits on the table and took a seat opposite him.

'You've been baking?'

Cora laughed, the sound a little too loud. 'Hardly. I'm no domestic goddess. These are Doris's. Try one. The combination of honey and walnuts is delicious.'

He took one and bit into it, still holding her gaze. And, like yesterday when she'd watched him eat, Cora felt something flutter to life inside her. Something powerful and utterly feminine that she hadn't experienced in ages.

She'd told herself Poseidon couldn't be as attractive as

she remembered and even if he were, it had to be surface gloss, the sort of shallow gloss she'd been inoculated against with Adrian and his friend.

Yet she looked at this man and felt something visceral. A yearning she couldn't identify.

She blinked and looked away, reaching for her coffee cup. Suddenly even sitting across the tiny table from him felt like an act of recklessness.

'So, you're not a cook. I assume you're a biologist?'

Cora looked up into that steady gaze and was momentarily lost. She had the weirdest floating sensation, as if she'd dived into warm, tropical waters and forgotten her bearings.

'Your T-shirt.' His words fractured the fantasy as he nodded towards her top. 'Or isn't it yours?'

She shook her head. 'It's mine and I am…was a biologist. A marine biologist.' She stifled momentary sadness. She didn't regret coming here. Her father needed her and that trumped everything. Theirs had always been a close-knit family.

Poseidon nodded. 'This must be a fascinating location to work. Isn't there a turtle nesting site around here somewhere?'

There was and its precise location was a carefully kept secret. Even though she thought she saw real interest spark in his eyes.

'Yes, it is fascinating. Though I'm not working as a biologist at the moment.' She reached forward and took one of the biscuits, biting into it, appreciating the sweetness.

When she met his gaze again he was watching her mouth. Not leering, yet with an intensity that made her supremely self-aware.

'That's right, your father's been unwell. So you're helping here?'

'Yes. What about you? What do you do?' She knew all the locals, or thought she did. He had to be a visitor.

He shrugged in a lazy movement that drew her attention to the strength in his broad shoulders and powerful chest. 'Right now? As little as possible.'

So he was on vacation.

'What's your name?' His deep voice took on a different quality. Like whisky—warm with a rough edge that nevertheless slid easily through her. She had a premonition she could grow addicted to the sound of it.

'Cora. Cora Georgiou.'

'Cora.' His mouth lifted the tiniest fraction at one corner and in response she felt a blast of heat right through her middle. 'I like it. It's a good name for a Nereid.'

'A sea nymph?' She snorted and shook her head. 'Hardly. They're usually depicted on more delicate lines.'

He tilted his head to one side and Cora had the impression that he wasn't sizing up her body so much as exploring her mind.

It was an unsettling sensation. So few of the men she'd known bothered with the cerebral. They took one look at her body and categorised her as either over-sized and therefore dismissible or an easy lay.

Yesterday she'd have put this man in the second category. Now she wondered if there was more to him than she'd thought.

'It's my fantasy, and as far as I'm concerned you're perfect for the role.'

Cora raised her eyebrows and sharpened her stare but he sounded genuine.

Her mouth curled wryly as she realised that, if he *had* been Poseidon, he'd have chosen sea nymphs to suit his personal preference.

'What is it?'

Cora shrugged. 'The coincidence that you thought of a Nereid and I thought of Poseidon.'

Too late she realised that would only feed his already

healthy ego. Because Poseidon was always portrayed as the epitome of fit, powerful masculinity.

Yet instead of that puffing him up, she read genuine amusement in his glittering eyes. For a moment she felt a bond of shared humour, warm and...nice.

'I'm flattered. But I'm more interested in the fact our minds thought along similar lines.'

So was Cora. She couldn't recall the last time that had happened.

She sipped her coffee to hide her widening smile. The sharp taste of caffeine hit, revving her brain into gear and reminding her not to make assumptions.

'So what's *your* name?'

'Strato.' He paused. 'Strato Doukas.'

Cora felt her eyes widen.

Poseidon, indeed! For the god of the sea was also known as Earth Shaker, responsible for earthquakes. And it felt right now as if the world tilted and shook around her.

Strato Doukas! Surely it wasn't possible.

Yet she'd heard via Doris that staff from his giant luxury cruiser had visited the harbour yesterday, buying fresh seafood and local produce. She'd even suspected this man was off that same yacht.

But Strato Doukas himself?

'*The* Strato Doukas?'

He shrugged. 'It's possible you've heard of me.'

Possible! The man was famed, or perhaps infamous, not just in Greece but far beyond. Mega-wealthy and renowned for his sybaritic lifestyle. He was rarely seen at the headquarters of his international logistics empire. Despite old stories of him taking his family's enterprise from moderately profitable to phenomenally successful, it was said he didn't bother with business any more.

These days he was too busy having a good time. The stories about him grew more and more salacious. Not that

Cora read them, but Adrian and his friends had talked of the man, half envious and half admiring.

She took another sip of coffee, grimacing as the rich flavour turned bitter in her mouth.

'This doesn't seem your sort of place, Mr Doukas.'

Surely a multibillionaire playboy didn't frequent struggling little family hotels or pass the time with ordinary people like her.

Unless he was slumming it?

She remembered the gleam of amusement dancing in his eyes yesterday. She'd found it attractive. Too attractive. Now she realised he probably relished the novelty of her reaction to his nudity and his undeniably glorious body. Had he been laughing at her all the time? This man mixed with glamorous models and socialites. Women who'd look slim and elegant against her ample curves. No wonder he'd smirked over her ancient, baggy shorts.

The skin between her shoulders crawled and a shudder rippled down her spine.

She knew all about privileged men who found amusement with naïve women.

'Strato, please.' He paused, eyes narrowing when she didn't respond.

But suddenly the hints of shared intimacy, the repartee and amusement seemed one-sided rather than mutual.

Cora knew men like him didn't really view women like her as equals. Clearly he was bored. Then she remembered another snippet of gossip Doris had picked up in town. That Strato Doukas had not one but two Scandinavian lovers keeping him company on his luxury yacht.

She shoved her chair back so hard it screeched across the flagstones.

'I'm afraid I don't have time to sit and chat. There's a lot to do.'

He frowned.

To her horror, the expression didn't detract one iota from his attractiveness.

'It doesn't seem busy. You don't have many guests, do you?'

It was a reminder she didn't need. Business was poor with the economic downturn and the ferry from the mainland laid up for repairs. If things didn't improve it was only a matter of months before they'd have to close their doors permanently and sell. If they could find a buyer.

Then what would happen to her father?

Fear scraped her gullet.

And anger. Anger at this man who'd come here for light relief when his sophisticated playmates palled. As if Cora was some diversion.

What hurt most was realising how willingly she'd played along. How fascinated she'd been by this man. How eager.

'Nevertheless, I'm busy. You mightn't realise it but a lot of hard work goes on behind the scenes to provide the comforts others take for granted.'

His frown became a scowl and any trace of indolence disappeared from his big frame.

'You think I don't appreciate hard work?'

'I'm sure you appreciate a lot of things, Mr Doukas.' Like orgies with Scandinavian models and amusing himself with the yokels for a bit of variety. 'Now, if you'll excuse me I need to go. But please, take your time. The coffee is on the house.'

She'd taken a single step when he rose.

'Wait.' Instead of lazy indolence there was a note of command in that deep voice and, despite her intentions, Cora responded to it, halting.

When he spoke again the authoritative note was gone, or at least masked by a coaxing tone. 'I'd much rather you stayed.'

Cora shook her head. Her heart hammered high in her chest. 'I'm afraid that's impossible.'

He moved to stand before her.

She could walk around him yet his absolute stillness and that stare held her where she was. Once more she had the sensation he saw more than she wanted. Strange that a man renowned for his devotion to personal pleasure should have such a searching gaze.

'Why, Cora? Because you really have work, or because you're afraid of me?'

'Afraid?' Her chin jerked high and her hands planted on her hips. 'I'm not afraid of any man.'

No man had the power to hurt her any more. Because forewarned was forearmed. She'd never again be so gullible.

'No? Then maybe you're afraid of this, between us?' He raised his hand in a gesture that encompassed the pair of them.

For a second Cora felt relief that she hadn't imagined that connection between them. The invisible thread of shared amusement and camaraderie that had attracted her even more than his gorgeous body and bone-melting smile.

But it was no such thing. He was a handsome, too handsome, man with an aura of potent masculinity that would attract any woman. He'd set out to snare her and she'd fallen for it. Because he wanted a little rustic entertainment.

'There's nothing between us, Mr Doukas.'

He moved so fast she didn't have time to back away. Suddenly they were standing toe to toe and she had to arch her neck to maintain eye contact.

Cora couldn't remember ever being close to such a man. So much bigger than her, all powerful muscle and brooding intensity. The heat of his tall frame enveloped her.

Yet it wasn't fear she felt as he scowled down at her.

It was jubilation. And against her better judgement, anticipation.

A voice in her head told her she was mad. Reckless. Asking for trouble.

But she was no longer a victim. She'd rather infuriate

Strato Doukas than run from him. She'd rather feel the way she did now, challenging him, than turn her back on this glorious feeling.

'Isn't there? Are you absolutely sure, Cora? Because it feels to me as if we share…something.'

He lifted his hand, hard fingers spreading over her jaw, his thumb a mere heartbeat from her mouth.

Heat drenched her. Heat and want. So intense she didn't know what to do with herself.

She struggled to keep her voice even. Admitting he was right would be a fatal error. 'Sorry, Mr Doukas. You must be imagining it.'

His nostrils flared on an indrawn breath and something flashed across his features. It didn't look like anger.

'Maybe you're right. After all, what could we have in common?'

Cora didn't move. She couldn't, because while her brain told her to leave, every cell in her body screamed that this was exactly where she wanted to be. A quiver ran through her as she waited, watching. Then she felt a band of warmth around her waist. He'd looped his arm around her. 'Unless, of course, it's this.'

His head swooped down to hers and her lips parted on a silent sigh of relief.

CHAPTER FOUR

STRATO PAUSED, HIS mouth a bare breath from hers, reading her emotions. Disdain morphing into expectation. Eagerness so bright it was like petrol thrown on the fire of his own desire.

Her eyelids flickered and that lush mouth opened a fraction. Not, he was sure, to spew contempt, but because, like him, she craved the kiss he delayed giving her.

He sensed part of her wanted to push him away. She was spiky and disapproving, and for the first time in for ever he found himself annoyed at being judged on his reputation. Usually Strato didn't give a damn what people thought of him. He lived life on his own terms because that was the only way to survive.

He could walk away, except those golden-brown eyes blazed up at him with such expectation.

His Nereid was complicated and he made it a policy never to bother with complicated.

And yet...

And yet he couldn't move back.

Couldn't release her. Because something dark and primal inside refused to let go.

The urge to taste her mouth became a need. What had begun as teasing amusement became something elemental.

Why else would he put up with thinly veiled insults? As if this woman had the right to criticise him?

Was that why he held back? Forcing her to acknowledge that, far from trying to escape his hold, she was breathless with desire. Her breasts rose and fell with short, choppy breaths and her woman's scent, warm and rich, took on a deeper tang. Arousal. His nostrils twitched appreciatively.

Taking his time, Strato bent and set his open mouth on

the pleasure point where her shoulder met her neck, nuzzling. Then, as the texture and taste of her filled his senses, sucking greedily at her satiny flesh.

She gasped, stiffening then instantly sinking against him, bending her neck to one side to allow him free access. She tasted like the distillation of summer—heat, sunshine and golden honey with a touch of sea salt.

Her hands fastened on his upper arms, fingers digging into biceps so needily that his arousal notched higher.

Elation filled him, and the expectation of profound delight to come. Despite her dismissive attitude, Cora had surrendered. She would give him exactly what he wanted.

Nuzzling his way up her neck, Strato registered her little hums of encouragement. Would she be vocal when they were naked together? This was a passionate woman. Not one worried about getting messy hair or trying to second-guess his every move. From her responsiveness he guessed she'd meet him halfway in any erotic venture.

His erection stirred in anticipation and was rewarded with the press of her soft body. Cora moved her hips restlessly and he dropped his palm to her buttocks, pulling her hard against him.

There.

Better.

But he wanted far more.

Strato trailed kisses to corner of her mouth and she turned her head, lips seeking his.

So much for rejection. He stifled a huff of triumph, settling his mouth over hers.

And discovered something new.

Shock stormed his senses. His hold tightened and he braced his feet wider as an invisible blow rocked him from his scalp all the way down to the soles of his feet.

The taste of her, the melting sweetness of their mouths fusing, was a revelation.

He scrambled to gather his wits and catalogue the difference between this and past experience but his thoughts wouldn't fix on anything except a silent mantra of *Cora, Cora, Cora.*

And *more, more, more.*

Strato took her mouth and she reciprocated, welcoming, inviting and demanding.

She gave as much as he took and more, leaving him wanting so much more than a kiss. He wanted all of her, all to himself. He wanted to give her everything he had, not because he always felt duty-bound to please a lover, but because nothing less than everything would do.

Not with her.

He wrapped both arms around her, gathering her close so their bodies melded. She was a perfect fit. Strato could kiss her for hours and not get a crick in his neck and the feel of her voluptuous curves up close made him desperate to explore in minute detail.

The thought of their bodies joining…

He bowed her back over his arm and she clung, her mouth mating with his as if they'd been lovers for ever.

That was what felt so different. The ease and rightness of them together. As if they'd done this before and their bodies already knew each other intimately.

Strato's belly tightened and his groin grew heavy as he devoured her with languorous intent. He wanted Cora as he couldn't remember wanting any woman. But he had enough functioning brain cells left to realise that couldn't be here and now.

Regretfully he lifted his head, rejoicing in the way she rose against him, following his mouth, trying to prolong their kiss.

Oh, yes, my beauty. Soon. Very soon.

His breath came in great gusts and his muscles burned from the tension of standing still instead of hoisting her over his shoulder and carting her to the pier. They could be back on the yacht in fifteen minutes and naked in his bedroom fifteen seconds later.

Her eyes opened and it was like sinking into a pool of molten gold. Strato had never seen anything as powerfully enticing as that heavy-lidded stare and her lips, swollen and deep pink from passion.

Something twisted his gut. Something unfamiliar. Strato ignored it and concentrated on his next move.

'I want—'

Her finger on his lips stifled his words. Even that, a gesture not in itself erotic, sent a tremor of longing through him.

For a second longer they stood body to aching body. Then, on a sigh that sounded more like a groan, Cora stepped back and Strato let her slide out of his arms.

Instantly he felt bereft. He wanted to haul her back where she belonged, against him.

But this wasn't the place. Not with her father likely to appear at any moment. Seducing his daughter in full public view wouldn't be a good move. Besides, Cora deserved better. Strato knew that ravishing this delectable woman thoroughly would require time and privacy.

She stood, staring up at him, slumbrous eyes, heaving breasts, hands hanging loose against the cut-off edges of her shorts. She wore no make-up and wasn't dressed to entice yet Strato couldn't conceive of any woman more attractive than she was right now.

Even with that prickly attitude, Cora was something special. In fact, he liked that she didn't make everything easy for him.

But the time for games was over. They both knew what they wanted.

'I'd like you to go now.'

Her words froze the smile forming at the corners of his mouth.

'Sorry?' He felt as if he were underwater, sound muted by the blood rushing in his ears.

She backed up a step and folded her arms. He wished she wouldn't. It tugged the cotton tight over those abundant breasts and made it hard to think about anything else.

'I'm not interested in what you're offering, Mr Doukas.'

Strato stiffened. Each carefully enunciated word hit like a slap. The only fire in her expression looked like anger.

Why was she angry? He'd given her a chance to walk away before kissing her. She'd been a more than willing participant. It was too late to pretend otherwise. Her mews of pleasure had been impossible to miss, as had her enthusiastic body-to-body response.

He drew himself up and watched her eyes widen, fixing on his swelling chest. 'I don't recall making any offer, Ms Georgiou.'

At least not verbally.

She'd made one. The way she'd ground her pelvis against him spoke more clearly than any words.

Her eyes narrowed, her stare sharpening. 'My mistake.' She hefted a breath that looked painful, her mouth twisting. Strato wanted to reach out and…

What? Pacify her? Reassure her?

'Let's get one thing clear.' She paused. 'I'm not here to amuse you. If you're after a diversion don't expect me to provide it.' Her gaze skated down his body then back up, her expression dismissive. 'I hear you have quite a smorgasbord on your yacht, Mr Doukas. Don't come here looking for extras. I'm not interested in playboys.'

Strato felt every nerve and muscle stiffen. He relished a challenge but there were limits.

He crossed his arms, fighting the urge to reach for her and remind her how *interested* she was.

'That would be more convincing if you hadn't rubbed yourself against me like a cat on heat.' Deliberately he let his gaze drop to her proud breasts. 'Your nipples still give you away. I know for a fact you're not cold. The attraction is mutual.'

Her indrawn breath was a hiss. 'It didn't mean anything.' Her voice was hard and regret pierced Strato's annoyance. He wanted her soft and eager, not spitting ire. 'I admit I was…curious but I have more self-respect than that.'

His eyebrows arched and his mouth tightened. He didn't care what people thought of the way he lived his life but he wouldn't stand for direct insults.

What was her problem? All he'd done was kiss her. By her response she'd been hanging out for just that. Either they were phenomenally well-attuned physically or she was suffering from a desperate level of sexual frustration. Maybe both.

'Have you finished?'

She nodded, the movement jerky, her mouth a flat line.

'Good. Then let me clarify. If ever I make an offer to a woman, it's for shared pleasure, no strings attached. I have no interest in women who consider sex an insult or some sort of test. I find martyrs unattractive. If my lifestyle bothers you, look away. I don't have time for women who play hot and cold because they're too scared to confront what they feel.'

That hit home. He saw her register it like a blow. But instead of cringing back she jerked her chin up as if daring him to continue.

Strato was torn between admiration and annoyance.

She really was unique.

He moved into her personal space. She swallowed hard and he repressed a smile. Despite her veneer of outrage everything about her broadcast repressed hunger.

'I don't want someone who's afraid of herself or her physical needs. But if ever the other Cora returns, the sexy, confident woman who kisses like a goddess, let me know. *That* woman I'd like to know better.'

He let that sink in, watching with gratification as Cora's

pupils dilated. 'I'd gladly offer *that* woman the most memorable interlude of her life. I'll be on my yacht. The smorgasbord is gone so there'd be just her and me. And more rapture than she's ever known.'

Strato didn't wait for a response but strode away.

Two weeks later he stood on the terrace of his Moroccan hotel suite, watching the sun sink over the sea in apricot and amber splendour. When he turned he had a perfect view of the Atlas Mountains. The best money could buy.

The fountain beside him and the exclusivity of his accommodation in the gracious palace-turned-hotel meant he couldn't hear the noise of the opening night party.

Which suited him. Because, now he was here, he found he wasn't in the mood to party.

You've got it all and still you're not satisfied?

He stared at the glass in his hand.

What was wrong with him? The ennui that had dogged him was worsening.

For a week he'd stayed on his yacht, expecting Cora to contact him, his frustration increasing daily. Finally he'd headed to Canada on the spur of the moment for white water rafting, then Africa for off-road racing.

Neither had dimmed his discontent.

Strato had accepted this invitation anticipating the usual distractions. A sophisticated atmosphere. Like-minded acquaintances and enough gorgeous, willing women to entice any man.

Amber Harris, the sexy actress he'd met in the Bahamas, had greeted him in the lobby when he arrived. Her welcome had been warm and the invitation in her eyes and voice abundantly clear.

Then there was the French socialite he'd met on the ski slopes last year. Nadine had wit, charm and a lithe athleticism that appealed to his earthier side. She'd rung to check he was coming to this party, but he couldn't see himself beginning a liaison with her or Amber.

As for the sultry Brazilian singer taking the world by storm, maybe six months ago he'd have been diverted by her obvious interest.

Now though...

He swallowed his drink and put the empty glass down with more force than necessary.

Strato was unsettled. For years he'd had everything he wanted. Success. Wealth. Luxury. Beautiful companions. Yet increasingly he felt dissatisfied.

Globetrotting, extreme sports and self-indulgence palled, leaving what?

His dead uncle would have called him an empty shell of a man, refusing to create a family to which he could pass his wealth. His dead aunt would have looked at him with sad eyes and prayed he'd find peace and a good woman.

As if Strato would ever find that sort of peace.

His aunt and uncle, of all people, should have understood the baggage he carried made that impossible. How could they not have understood?

Thinking about a family of his own, of settling down with a woman, good or otherwise, curdled his belly and created a seam of sweat across his hairline and down his spine.

Bile rose in his gullet and Strato stalked to the edge of the terrace, needing to move. To escape the graveyard of memories beginning to stir.

He shoved his hands in his trouser pockets and told himself he'd feel better when he joined the others and lost himself in the usual distractions.

Except he knew, as he'd known for a fortnight, that it wouldn't work.

Whenever he thought of losing himself in a woman it was his Nereid who came to mind.

His pulse quickened as he remembered the flash of humour and even the glint of disdain on her features. Remembered the sway of her hips as she walked along the sand and the feel of her hourglass figure against him. Her taste, like nectar from the gods…

His listlessness wasn't boredom. It was because he wanted *her*. Cora. And no one else.

He wanted her to eat her disapproving words and beg for the pleasure only he could give her. Pride still smarted at her dismissal.

He wanted more of her banter, her quick intelligence, even her feisty attitude.

Almost as much as he craved her body.

With a sigh of resignation he hauled out his phone and dialled his head of security.

'Petro? I want everything you can get on Cora Georgiou.' He detailed everything he knew about her.

'This woman's bothering you?'

'No.' Strato almost laughed. She was, but not in the way Petro meant. 'She's not a security threat. But I want a full dossier. History, employment, financial situation. Anything and everything, and I want it straight away.'

'I'll get onto it.'

Strato ended the call and tossed the phone onto a seat. He rolled his shoulders, feeling the stiffness that had settled in his bones after two weeks of being denied what he wanted.

Jaded, spoiled and tainted too. Is it any wonder she doesn't want you, Doukas?

He had the unnerving suspicion that when Cora Georgiou looked at him she saw more than anyone else. Not the hedonist or the head of one of the world's most successful logistics companies, but right down to the nothingness deep inside. To the dark maw of dread and hollow emptiness that most of the time he managed to ignore.

At thirty-three he'd had twenty-five years to camouflage it. To appear like everyone else. Sometimes he went whole days without thinking about it, deliberately diverting himself with work and play and one enticing distraction after another.

But though he still worked, he'd achieved a level of success where he could delegate most day-to-day decisions and he always employed the best. As for distractions, they didn't gratify as they once had.

Maybe you only want her because you can't have her. Because if you have her you'll feel like you've conquered the emptiness for a little longer. So it won't consume you.

Strato's expression set in a scowl.

He prided himself on his honesty but sometimes self-reflection was overrated.

He toed off his loafers and hauled his shirt over his head. A few quick movements and his clothes dropped to the flagstones. He strode across the sun-warmed terrace and dived into the pool.

What he needed wasn't a party. He needed to numb his mind with exertion until Petro came through with his report and Strato could make his next move.

CHAPTER FIVE

'CORA, YOU NEED to come outside.'

Quickly she minimised the financial spreadsheet on the computer before it caught her father's eye. He was stressed enough without seeing her pore over their stubbornly bad projections for the summer.

She turned on the swivel chair and smiled. 'I thought you were heading to the harbour to meet your friends?'

Usually they came here, the older men spending hours on the shady terrace, setting the world to rights over coffee and backgammon. But today they were going to inspect the new motor on Niko's son's fishing boat.

'I am. I got delayed.'

From his grin, it wasn't some chore that had held him up. Cora saw his shining eyes and the way he stood with his shoulders back and felt her heart twist in her chest.

The last few months, recovering from two heart attacks and burdened by financial worry, her darling father seemed to have aged a decade. Now though, he looked almost as strong and healthy as he'd once been.

'What is it?' She rose and went to him. He gathered her hands in his gnarled ones and kissed her cheek. The reassuring scents of coffee and mints enveloped her. The same scents that coloured her earliest memories.

She squeezed his hands. It was so good to see him looking happy.

'Someone to see you, out on the terrace.'

'Who is it?' She wasn't expecting visitors.

Her dad winked and his smile grew. 'Someone you'll want to see. We've been having a good chat. But I need to get on now.' He tugged her hand. 'Come. Don't dawdle. We don't keep guests waiting.'

Whoever it was they'd impressed her father.

But to her surprise, when they reached the end of the corridor, her dad kissed her on the cheek and headed for the hotel's front entrance, motioning her towards the doors that led onto the terrace.

He wasn't even going to introduce her? Which meant it was a friend waiting. Eagerly she pushed open the door, wondering who'd come for a surprise visit.

She rounded a corner and slammed to a halt, heart pounding.

Surely not.

Cora told herself she was imagining things, that the bright sunlight dazzled her vision. Because she couldn't be seeing Strato Doukas sitting with his legs stretched out, sipping coffee and taking in the view of the bay.

Strato Doukas would never return here, not after what she'd said to him. Besides, the chef from his yacht who'd come into harbour yesterday for supplies had mentioned his boss had flown out and wasn't expected back soon.

Did she gasp or did he sense her presence?

Mirrored sunglasses turned in her direction and heat scorched her skin. Not just her cheeks and throat but across her breasts and stomach and deeper, right down in her feminine core.

'Cora.' Just that in a voice that sounded like a caress, its deep notes sliding through her and creating disturbing eddies of awareness.

She took a slow breath. None of this made sense. Especially the fact her father thought she *wanted* to see this man.

She turned her head but a swift scan showed the terrace was otherwise empty. In fact the whole hotel was empty, she realised, her dad on his way to the harbour and Doris spending the morning helping a friend who was recovering from illness. Their current guests, a couple of couples, had headed to the other side of the island.

Cora's pulse seemed to slow and the air in her lungs thicken.

'What are you doing here?'

One dark eyebrow rose but he looked more speculative than annoyed. 'Drinking coffee. Your father makes a particularly fine one.'

Protective instincts stirred. She wanted to tell him not to talk about her father. Or talk *to* him.

Slowly she paced across the flagstones. 'What did you say to my father?'

Strato pulled out a chair. 'Sit down and I'll tell you.'

He was maddeningly at ease and Cora was too aware of her emotions, anger, suspicion and...surely not eagerness?

Because she'd thought she'd never see him again.

And because, despite everything she knew about indulged, selfish rich men, she'd missed the sizzle in her blood when he was around. She'd even missed that intense awareness of her own femininity.

Whatever his game she wasn't interested. But she had to find out why he was here. What lies he'd told her father. She yanked the chair further out from the table and sat down, crossing her arms.

'There. That wasn't so hard, was it?'

'I have work to do, Mr Doukas. I can't spare long.'

'Really?' He took off his glasses and fixed her with a piercing stare that pushed her back in her seat. She'd told herself his eyes couldn't be nearly as mesmerising as she remembered, but they were. 'Surprising when you have so few guests and no prospect of many in the near future.'

Digesting his words took longer than it should have.

'How do you know about our bookings?'

He lifted his shoulders. 'I made it my business to find out.'

Cora opened her mouth then shut it again, too stunned to think of a riposte. He shouldn't even *be* here. Why bother to investigate their small family-run hotel? It didn't make sense. It wasn't the sort of place a billionaire took an interest in.

As she met that unblinking stare unease feathered her backbone. She didn't like the feeling that things careered out of her control.

Her hackles rose as she sensed a threat. 'What have you done?'

She leaned forward, unable to suppress foreboding, even when he spread his hands, palm up, and shrugged.

'Nothing.'

Cora didn't believe him. His expression might be innocently amiable but there was nothing innocent about this man.

'Then why are you here? Other than to drink coffee?'

'To see you, of course.'

Cora reminded herself she wasn't interested. Yet there was no denying her quiver of excitement. Part of her had regretted his departure. The part that had actually considered heading out to his status-symbol yacht and taking him up on his offer.

To have the most memorable interlude of her life. And more rapture than she'd ever known.

What woman wouldn't be tempted?

Especially as she was pretty sure Strato Doukas could deliver exactly that. If only a little of the gossip about him were true he was well versed in the art of lovemaking.

Such thoughts circled through her mind each night as she lay restless and frustrated in her lonely bed, even though her saner self knew she'd regret giving in to such an impulse.

He'd haunted her. The rumble of his deep voice. The light in his eyes when he'd shared a joke with her. The times when it had felt as if they were on the same wavelength, totally attuned.

The feel of his magnificent body hard and shockingly aroused against her. The bliss of his kiss.

She swallowed hard, remembering it all. And to be told

she kissed like a goddess! Even though she knew it was a line he must have used with others, Cora's defences had trembled.

She smoothed damp palms across the cotton covering her thighs.

At least, for a change, she looked presentable in a bright summer dress.

Except she wasn't trying to attract him! She stiffened and sat straighter. 'What are you up to?'

'Are you always so suspicious?' His expression remained unreadable but his eyes danced.

'Are you always so devious?'

His mouth crooked up, revealing that beckoning groove in his cheek, and Cora's heart beat faster. Because his amusement felt approving, like shared merriment. Not a laugh at her expense.

'That's harsh, Cora. I might strategise but I'm honest.' He paused, his eyes on hers. 'Can you say the same? Or are you still trying to deny the sexual charge between us?'

Cora's chin jerked up. 'There are more important things than sexual attraction.' Belatedly she realised what she'd admitted and silently cursed her choice of words.

'Now we're making progress. What's important to you, Cora?'

'Family. Loyalty. Honesty.'

Probably all things he wasn't interested in.

He nodded. 'I can promise you loyalty and honesty, for the time we're together. As for family, I don't have any and I don't intend to settle down with a wife and children. *Ever.* It's important to remember that.' Something flashed in his eyes but before she could identify it he continued. 'However, I appreciate your desire to support your father.'

What did her father have to do with this?

'You speak as if we're going to be together.' Cora's voice rose.

Did he really think she'd change her mind? What was

wrong with the man? It must be a case of wanting something because he'd been told he couldn't have it. It meshed with what she knew of his type.

Cora's lip curled. 'I thought I'd made it clear that won't happen. I don't even like you.'

It wasn't true. She liked him too much. But she knew men like him, spoiled, vain men who thought they could take whatever they wanted but didn't appreciate what they took so greedily. Cora valued herself too highly to be taken in by such a man again.

Strato shrugged, not looking in the least perturbed. 'I can live with that. I'd rather have your passion.'

Her mouth dried as wonder filled her. That she was having this conversation with Strato Doukas of all people!

She stiffened in her seat. 'It's not on offer. *I'm* not on offer, Mr Doukas.'

This time his smile held a secretive quality that stirred another premonition of danger.

'Ah, but you haven't heard my proposal, Cora.' He said her name in a deliberately slow, caressing tone that, despite her wariness, did disturbing things. She was sure something vital melted inside.

Her heart pattered faster. 'Go on, then. Tell me. Then you can go.'

But he seemed in no hurry, savouring the last of his coffee before setting down the tiny cup.

'Are you always this forthright?' he asked finally.

'Always.'

'Excellent.' He sat forward, making her even more aware of the shimmering magnetism of that big, powerful body. 'I like a woman who isn't afraid to ask for exactly what she wants. It can be very arousing in the right circumstances.'

In bed, he meant.

Cora swallowed as she read the carnal heat in his eyes and felt that same heat lick through her. But instead of rising to the bait she shook her head. 'You have one minute to tell me why you're here. Otherwise I'm leaving.'

'I thought that would be obvious. I want you, Cora. You know that. But since you refused to come to me I thought it time to provide a little…persuasion.'

The skin between her shoulder blades prickled. 'What sort of persuasion?'

Strato and her father had been talking. Her dad wouldn't have mentioned his precarious financial situation. Yet her hackles rose.

'What have you done to my father?' If he'd inveigled him in some way…

Strato lifted his hands palms out as if in surrender. 'No need to be so fierce. I've done nothing.'

Yet. The unspoken word hovered between them.

'Go on.' Her voice was thick with foreboding.

'I know you want me, Cora.' His words stole her voice. It was true, but the thought of him knowing it… 'Yet for some reason you deny yourself.' He paused. 'So I have a bargain for you. Something you want for something I want.'

Cora waited, her shoulders hitched high.

'Spend the next month with me on my yacht and I'll see to it that your father's hotel is filled to capacity till the end of the season. I plan to cruise the Ionian Sea then back to the Aegean and I can't think of a companion I'd rather have with me.'

She felt her mouth drop open in shock. She'd expected some sort of outlandish invitation but nothing like this.

'You're trying to bribe me into your bed.'

He shook his head emphatically. 'I'm creating an opportunity for us to get better acquainted. The rest is in your hands. You'd have your own stateroom and my word that I won't enter it except at your invitation. It will be your choice when we finally have sex.'

When, not *if*.

His arrogance outraged her.

A pity it also thrilled her.

Not because she liked arrogant men, far from it. But because the idea that sex between them was inevitable appealed on some primitive level she didn't even know she possessed.

He continued. 'The decision to have intimacy will be yours. I'm not interested in a woman who feels she has no choice.' His mouth curled in distaste. 'I'd never force a woman.'

His words rang with a steely quality that cut through her whirling thoughts. She *did* believe him. His body language as well as his tone proclaimed his sincerity.

Once more she was astounded by this flash of certainty about him. It had happened when they first met and it was happening again.

'You really believe no woman can resist your charm?'

'You find me charming?' He smiled and this time Cora knew he was laughing at her. 'That's a start.'

Cora shot to her feet and strode to the edge of the terrace, trying to calm herself, but the idyllic view failed to soothe her. Her mind was too full of his outrageous narcissism.

When she swung round he was where she'd left him but he sat straighter, not as relaxed as his earlier pose suggested.

'And if after four weeks I still won't share your bed?'

He shrugged. 'I'm flexible, it needn't be in bed—'

'You know what I mean!'

The man was impossible.

Or maybe that was her unruly imagination, picturing them stretched naked together out on the white sand beach where they'd met. Or right here in the dappled shade. She pictured sitting astride him, sharing another of those mindblowing kisses, riding him till they both found ecstasy.

'I said it would be your choice and I mean it, Cora.'

Yet he expected to seduce her. It was there in his eyes. Unfortunately for his schemes that look reminded her of another man who'd viewed her as his for the taking.

'You're assuming I'd be persuaded. What happens if you're wrong. If I went aboard…?' Because who wouldn't be tempted by this man and the prospect of a month of luxury exploring the seas around Greece? 'And then you discovered sex really is off limits?'

Strato spread his hands wide. 'That's a risk I'm willing to take. I actually *do* want your company, not just your body.' Heat flared at his words but she concentrated on reading his serious expression. 'Look at it this way. In a contest of wills, if you decide not to sleep with me, you win and I learn a lesson in humility. Now *that* would appeal to you.' He grinned. 'And if I win, then believe me, Cora, we'd *both* be winners.'

Scary how tempting it sounded. Outrageous but tempting. A reckless part of her revelled in the idea of besting him in such a battle of wills. She'd like to puncture that ego, just a little.

'It's ridiculous. Even someone as rich as you wouldn't waste your money helping a small-time hotel owner out of debt.'

Strato's head cocked to one side in that assessing way she'd come to know. For a long time he said nothing, leaving her too aware of the hurried in-and-out rush of her breathing, her hands fisted at her sides, and the curling heat low in her pelvis that she assured herself he couldn't know about.

'Why not? As you say, I've got plenty of money to spend as I wish.' Another lift of his shoulders and outspread hands.

'You actually mean it?'

'Say the word, *Coritsa*, and the bookings will start.'

The diminutive pet version of her name sounded like a caress in his dark velvet and whisky voice. Nothing at all like when her father or Doris called her that. It took her a moment to gather her wits.

'Even you can't conjure guests out of thin air.'

His complacent smile should have annoyed her but this time Cora found it almost reassuring. 'I head a very large company. I've decided to offer vacations as performance bonuses, and for employees recuperating from serious illness.'

'That's very generous.' In other words, she found it hard to believe.

'I expect loyalty and dedication from my staff but in return I offer excellent conditions. It's how we attract and retain the best.' He paused. 'As for the bonus holidays, the suggestion came from a recent staff survey and my advisers believe in it.'

No humour in his voice now. Cora heard pride and the voice of a man who knew what he was talking about. Strato Doukas didn't sound like a lazy playboy now, but a corporate manager. Like a man who'd taken his family transport company and turned it into a multinational corporation.

Cora hadn't been able to resist looking him up online. She'd tried to ignore the breathless gossip about his debauched lifestyle, curious instead about the man himself. Surprisingly for someone at the centre of so much publicity, there wasn't much of substance. He'd grown up in Athens but there was little information on his early life. By his late teens he'd been learning the family business, eventually inheriting it and expanding it enormously. These days, though, others ran the company while Strato Doukas swanned from one pleasure spot to another, living off the profits.

Except what he'd said indicated he still took an active interest in the business. Even more curious.

'You'd really do all that to get me on your boat?' She didn't know whether to feel complimented or insulted.

'I don't waste time doing anything against my will, Cora. Life is too short.'

Once more she had a fleeting glimpse of something more than uber-confidence in his expression. For a second Cora saw something stark in his gaze. Then he smiled and she was too dazzled to think straight.

'An offer too good to refuse, eh?'

Cora jammed her hands onto her hips. 'What lie did

you tell my father? He seemed…happy after meeting you.' Which he wouldn't be if he understood Strato's intentions.

'I told him how much I wanted you to accompany me. I explained I planned an extended cruise and that I'd value your marine biology expertise, particularly when we visit marine reserves.'

Cora forced down a fillip of pleasure at the thought of returning to the work she loved. 'So you lied.'

Strato shook his head. 'I told him the truth. I'll look forward to seeing the places we visit through your eyes. I suspect you'd give me a new perspective. As for our sexual magnetism, that's a private matter between us.'

'He thinks you're *hiring* me for my expertise?'

'I could pay you a cash salary, but I thought you'd prefer to see the hotel full.'

He was right. Cora shook her head, trying and failing to take it all in.

'It's a crazy idea. No one would go to so much effort to get…' Her words died under the weight of that steady stare.

She told herself it had to be a joke. But he looked serious. Goosebumps rippled over her arms and she rubbed her tight flesh. He wanted to buy her.

It was outlandish. Unbelievable.

Intoxicatingly exciting.

She blinked and looked away, past the tamarisks to the harbour town on the other side of the bay, so quiet now with the economic downturn and the lack of regular ferry services.

If they could hang on till next year bookings would pick up and they'd manage to repay the debt. But next year was a long time away. By then her dad would be bankrupt and heartbroken, losing the hotel he and Cora's mother had run together.

'How do I know you'll follow through with your promise? That the guests will come?' She turned around.

Strato sat forward, elbows on the table, as if sensing victory. The sight made Cora feel trapped and angry. And more determined to withstand this man's terrible magnetism.

'Check your reservation requests in an hour and you'll see that I mean it. While we're away you can call your father every day. If I renege on my promise, I'll have you brought straight back here.'

Could she trust him?

The sparse information available about his work style indicated a man who followed through on promises. Whose word was his bond. But that had been in corporate deals. This was something else.

She caught the direction of her thoughts and her breathing fractured. Was she really thinking about agreeing?

As if sensing her confusion, Strato rose from his seat. 'You need time to consider. I'll be back this afternoon for your answer.'

He moved to stand before her. Close enough that she could read the speculation in his eyes and almost feel the warmth of his tall frame.

'Have a bag packed, *Coritsa*. We leave today.'

Before she could conjure a suitable response, Strato turned and walked away, that lazy, loose-limbed stride deceptively fast.

Not once did he look back. Every movement reinforced his supreme assurance. That almost unbelievable confidence that he'd get his own way. She wanted to despise him for that yet instead was transfixed by the sight.

And by the yearning to throw aside life's hard-learned lessons and say *yes*. Yes, to sheer self-indulgent pleasure.

Because this man wasn't like Adrian. He might be a selfish, spoiled rich man. But, in offering her choice and negotiating, offering something of immense value for her time, he made her like an equal, not a plaything.

He turned an indecent, outrageous proposal into something almost acceptable.

She shook her head. Acceptable? She must be insane!

Cora's breath sawed in her lungs and she pressed her palm to her abdomen, trying to quell the hot, coiling tension of sexual desire.

In moments he was out on the pier, casting off. The motor started and the tender headed out across the bay.

Still Cora stood, feet planted where he'd left her.

It was only as the tender reached the yacht that she went inside, her thoughts awhirl.

Forty minutes later she opened the online reservations portal and found a request for accommodation from a familiar-sounding company. *His* company. The booking was for two double rooms, two singles and two of the new family rooms her father had added and fitted out at such cost. All the bookings were for three weeks, beginning next Monday.

With a couple of quick keystrokes she accepted the booking, her heart hammering. Half an hour later a sizeable deposit appeared in their account.

Cora sat back in her seat, wide eyes fixed on the positive balance.

He was serious.

Strato Doukas had the power to save her family home, her father's business and his pride. If she agreed to spend the next month with him.

What's the worst that can happen? You want him as much as he wants you. He's not pretending love or raising hopes of anything long term. He's been upfront with you from the beginning.

Not like Adrian.

Still Cora stared, refusing to make a decision.

Because this man made her feel too much. That was dangerous. She could get hurt if she gave in to his charm and phenomenal sex appeal. She'd be better off keeping her distance. Not seeing him again.

But the thought of him sailing away and never returning made her stomach cramp. And the idea of the hotel being sold by the bank to cover her father's debts made her hunch over welling nausea.

Finally, what seemed a lifetime later, Cora sat straight, her mind made up.

If the hotel was going to be full, and she wasn't going to be around to run it, they'd need to rehire trusted staff from the village. She reached for the phone.

CHAPTER SIX

STRATO CUT THE engine as the tender neared the yacht. Before either he or the waiting crew member could do it, Cora rose, balancing easily in the small boat, and secured it to the larger vessel.

Her movements were economical, betraying the ease of long practice. According to the report he'd received, she worked off boats all the time, and had even spent a season between research jobs crewing a luxury yacht.

But it wasn't her nautical skills that held his attention. It was the way her khaki capri pants clung to her hips and buttocks as she moved, the supple twist of her body and the swell of her full breasts against her top.

She left him breathless.

It was so long since any woman had stolen the air from his lungs that he couldn't remember it happening.

Careful, Doukas. These are uncharted waters.

As if he cared. He'd been in a lather of anticipation for days, since he'd decided to make her confront the magnetism between them.

He'd crossed to the shore in a state of mixed eagerness and anxiety.

Anxiety! Him! Because it was just possible this woman might reject his offer.

It was unheard of.

But his response to Cora Georgiou was unlike anything he'd known.

He'd tried to tell himself it didn't matter if he didn't bed her. If he couldn't capture that energy, that spirit and that sexy body in his arms. Or trade banter with her again in a way that made him feel energised, not enervated. Yet as he'd strode up to the hotel his heart had been in his mouth and his belly clenched as if anticipating a blow.

Till he'd seen her kiss her father in the doorway and stoop to pick up a single suitcase. Then Strato had felt a rush of relief.

The thought of not seeing her again, not discovering why she challenged and delighted him so, had disturbed him.

Cora reached for her case but he forestalled her, grabbing it before she could. Her fingers brushed his and a jolt of energy shot through him. And through her too. Her eyes widened and she curled her hand protectively close to her body as if that spark between them burned.

'Allow me.' Strato smiled as he gestured for her to go first. She felt this connection as much as he.

Cora's seduction would be swift and satisfying.

As well as carnal satisfaction, it would be a relief to conquer the unsettled mood he'd been in since they met. His reaction to her was surely heightened by uncertainty. Surely it would lessen with familiarity...

His thoughts frayed as she climbed up onto the yacht, all toned muscle and delicious femininity.

Did she really think covering herself from neck to calves would stop him appreciating her stunning body?

She couldn't be so innocent.

Yet Strato carefully suppressed his smile as he followed her. She was skittish enough without him making it obvious he wanted to take her straight to bed.

Skittish but delightfully aware of him.

Strato passed the surprisingly light case to his crew member with a word of thanks and turned to Cora. She might be at home aboard vessels but there was a quaint awkwardness about the way she stood, hands clasped, that pierced his smugness.

It reminded him that despite the sexual charge thickening the air, Cora had doubts about being here.

He stepped close and her head swung up, eyes wide.

Strato stopped and surprised himself. 'Why don't you have a rest before dinner? Vassili can take you to your stateroom.'

He'd intended to offer her champagne on deck as they watched the island slide by. But her wary expression and stiff pose made him feel strangely protective.

Of the woman he intended to seduce.

Another first.

'Thank you. I'd like that. It's been a busy day.'

Strato pasted on a smile, as if he didn't mind she'd agreed so readily. 'Vassili can give you a tour of the yacht so you can find your way around. I'll see you on the upper deck in an hour and a half.'

He stood, watching her go, revising his plan, telling himself it made sense to give her space. Instead of pushing her, which would make her dig her heels in, he'd keep his distance. Let her stew. Let her feel the torment of unfulfilled desire till she was desperate for him. Then she'd come to him.

Then and only then would he give her what her body craved.

Cora stared in the full-length mirror of her marble and glass bathroom and grimaced.

Seeing herself in such surroundings sent tremors of unease down her spine. She looked so ordinary, wearing a plain white top and khaki pants, her face devoid of make-up. So not at home in this extravagant setting.

She knew the women who stayed on yachts like this. Women who didn't work for a living, unless you called snaring and keeping a rich husband or boyfriend work. Women who'd shriek at wearing chain-store clothes or chipping their nails by doing actual physical labour.

It reinforced her suspicion that Strato was interested because she was a curiosity. She didn't fit the mould.

Her resolve strengthened. She wasn't about to become one of his women. If he thought she'd be so awed by luxury that she'd fall into his bed, he was about to learn a lesson.

Cora didn't fit here, unless it was as a deckhand, working to keep this superyacht in sparkling condition. It made Adrian's yacht, or more precisely his father's, look like a minnow beside a shark.

Her hand strayed to the smooth, sweeping lines of the custom-built vanity unit. She'd bet all the money she didn't have that the stone was Pentelic marble. Sunlight pouring through the large window highlighted a warm golden tinge to the stone she'd initially thought pure white.

Only the best for a man like Strato Doukas. Why wouldn't a billionaire demand the same stone as that used to create the Parthenon?

She shook her head, remembering her tour of this floating mansion. There'd been a pool and spa, several lounge rooms, small dining room, large dining room and a bar big enough to host all her village. A cinema, library, billiards room, sauna and an enormous gym and massage suite that, despite its pristine condition, had the air of being well used. She'd lost count of the staterooms and that was without descending below decks to the staff quarters.

Cora brushed her hair then yanked it back in a tight ponytail. Then she wrapped it deftly around her fingers and secured it in a no-nonsense bun.

She wouldn't dress up for dinner. Soon Strato would tire of playing a game he couldn't win.

Because Cora wasn't the naïve woman she'd been before. Adrian had seen to that. Opulent yachts didn't impress her. For she knew about the men who owned them, their strain of seedy indulgence and sense of entitlement.

Yet her nerves strung tight as she moved into her enormous stateroom and shuffled into her deck shoes. She felt too wired.

Rest had been impossible. She'd tried. Except lying on

the king-sized bed she'd kept imagining Strato sprawled beside her, naked, with that devilish glint in his eyes and the smile that made her feel as if the two of them shared a secret.

Finally she'd got up and had a shower, hoping to cool her overheated body. But she kept visualising him there with her. Those long-fingered hands playing across her, that muscular body sliding against her as he—

With a huff of annoyance Cora opened her door and headed out to meet her host. Some bracing sea air would clear her head.

She found him on his private deck, along with a table set for two, complete with a centrepiece of fragrant roses.

Cora wanted to curl her lip at the predictability of the romantic setting. Except it *was* beautiful. Not fussy but the best quality. The tablecloth wasn't snowy linen but a rustic cloth with a Greek key design that looked handwoven. The silverware shone and the glassware, while elegantly made, didn't teeter on overlong stems that would be dangerous on an unstable sea.

She noticed all that because she didn't want to notice *him*, over against the railing, looking out to sea as they cruised past a small island.

The view was spectacular, the sun low over the water, turning the air golden.

Finally, unable to resist, she slanted a look at Strato, her gaze snagging on his straight shoulders before roving further.

He hadn't changed for dinner either. In long shorts that hugged his buttocks and thighs, and a short-sleeved shirt that left his sinewy arms bare, he looked fit, strong and mouth-wateringly masculine. Even the way the breeze ruffled his dark hair enhanced his attractiveness.

He was talking on the phone and she caught drifts of conversation. To her surprise it seemed to be about labour negotiations in the Far East.

Not what she expected from a hedonist who spent his life chasing pleasure.

He turned, gaze colliding with Cora's, and something shifted inside her, as if he'd untied something vital.

'I have to go. We'll talk later.' Putting the phone away, he smiled, and that curling dimple appeared beside his mouth. 'Welcome, Cora. You feel rested?'

'A little.' It was a lie, but better than admitting her inner turmoil.

'Would you like a drink?' He lifted his glass of sparkling liquid and her nerves settled a little. Because now he was following a predictable pattern, trying to use champagne to turn this into a celebration and weaken her resolve.

'I'd rather have water, thanks.'

His eyebrows arched and his smile grew as he crossed to a bar. 'Good. That's what I'm having. Still or sparkling?'

Cora blinked. He was drinking water? And talking business? Was this the man who kept a harem on his yacht and spent the day lolling naked on the beach?

'Sparkling,' she croaked. It was easier when he acted to type. Then she could dismiss him, or try to.

When he turned and held out a glass, Cora's chest squeezed. Not in fear or dislike. But because, looking into those dancing eyes, she acknowledged what she'd tried to ignore.

She wanted to be here.

Wanted to bask in his smile and stand close to that imposing body that drew her like a swimmer to a warm current.

'Here's to a memorable cruise.' He clinked his glass against hers and Cora nodded and sipped.

That was the beginning of an utterly unexpected evening. At every turn Strato defied expectations.

They moved to the railing and he asked her about the island they were passing, what she knew of its history and the marine life in the area. From there the conversation headed to marine conservation areas in the region, the best places for diving, and her recommendations. Strato mentioned some places he'd thought of visiting and asked her opinion.

Instead of flirting he conversed sensibly and listened to her responses. Gone was the teasing light in his eyes and his gaze didn't once drop below her neck. Cora found herself relaxing, slowly dropping her guard as they talked.

By the time they were at the table, feasting on fresh seafood and a bottle of crisp white wine from a small Greek vineyard she'd never heard of, she was no longer watching every word. For there was no sexual innuendo. No sly smiles. Just pleasant company in gorgeous surroundings. Even if she was constantly aware of the man opposite, her eyes drawn to his compelling features.

She sighed. 'The sunset is gorgeous from here. There's something about being on the water that makes it special.'

'I agree. It's the best place for sunrises and sunsets.'

Hours ago Cora would have scoffed at the idea of Strato being up to see the sun rise, but now nothing would surprise her.

She leaned back in her seat, enjoying the view, even if she had to work not to keep glancing back at the man opposite her. The sea looked like liquid silk, peach and an intense fluorescent pink that should have looked unreal against the gathering indigo.

Cora realised that for the first time in ages, she felt completely relaxed. Not stressing about the hotel or finances or how looming bankruptcy might affect her father's health.

If Strato hadn't sauntered into her life with his outrageous proposition, can-do attitude and phenomenal wealth, able to fill their hotel with a few phone calls, she'd be steeling herself to talk to her father about selling the family business.

She hated Strato's sense of entitlement, believing she'd fall into his hands, but the hard truth was he'd saved her father's business and, Cora believed, his life. For she feared her dad would fade away without the hotel that generations of his family had built.

Cora blinked, frowning as she realised how much she owed Strato. He'd given them the breathing space they needed to make good by the time next year's hopefully normal tourist season came around.

'What's wrong, Cora?' That deep voice caressed her, comforting yet exciting at the same time.

She took a moment to gather herself, conquering the weakness that made her want to lean into him, seeking comfort. Tonight it was too easy to forget he wasn't a friend.

'Thank you, Strato.' She met his gaze squarely. 'I didn't thank you for what you've done for my father, making it possible to keep the hotel running. That means a lot. I've been so worried about him.'

His eyebrows angled down as he frowned. 'I'm glad it's helped. I like him. But my motives are selfish. You know why I did it.'

His expression dared her to think well of him.

Cora nodded. 'I'm not likely to forget.' How often was a woman, particularly an ordinary working woman, proposi-tioned in such spectacular fashion? She was no *femme fatale*.

Yet she didn't see that familiar speculative gleam in his eyes. The glint of sexual interest and invitation she'd asso-ciated with him from the first. He looked genuinely con-cerned she'd mistake him for someone benevolent.

Her mouth twitched.

'What's so funny?' He looked wary and that made her smile broaden.

'You. Worried I might mistake you for a good guy.'

He wasn't. He really, really wasn't.

His actions were prompted wholly by self-interest.

Yet he was upfront about it. He wasn't deceitful. Cora could cope with Strato's sort of selfishness. As long as she didn't fall into the trap of believing there was more to his actions than an attempt to get his own way.

'That's not the way I'm usually described.' His mouth rucked up at the corner in that almost-smile that had fascinated her from the first. She felt her breath slow and made herself look away.

'I can imagine.' She'd read the headlines.

'Would you be sorry to lose the hotel? If it weren't for your father?'

Cora shrugged. 'I can't imagine it not being part of my life. My earliest memories are there.' It had seemed a golden place when her mother was alive. Then, when it was just her and her father, they'd been a tight-knit unit, drawing on each other for strength as they fought grief and found a way to go on. 'It's been in the family for generations and it's a special place. We have guests who come back year after year.' Though fewer this year, due to circumstances beyond their control.

'Do you *want* to run a hotel?'

She shook her head. 'I'm used to it but, no, it's not my dream. Unless I could install a manager and spend most of my time working on a marine project.' She shifted in her seat. 'Sadly funding for marine research isn't easy to come by.' Which was why she'd done a stint working on a yacht. 'Especially not near our island.'

'So it's your father keeping you there.'

Cora slanted a look at Strato, surprised at his curiosity. Was he, like Adrian, feigning interest to make it easier to get her into bed? Yet that wasn't the vibe she got from the big man sitting there so relaxed, twisting his glass on the table.

'He isn't forcing me to stay. I want to. He's my father and I love him.'

The light changed. At least she assumed it was that, because for a second Strato's face darkened, turned stark and brooding. But a moment later the impression was gone and he looked just the same.

'How about you, Strato?' She felt hyper-conscious of

his name on her tongue. 'Are you sentimental about your family home?'

'No.' The answer came swiftly. 'I don't have a family home.'

'Really? There's nowhere special you feel attached—'

'Nowhere. No family home, no family. And I'm not sentimental.'

Cora heard the warning note and stiffened. Gone was the companionable man she'd begun to relax with. Gone the easy conversationalist. His tone was as welcoming as a *Trespassers will be shot* sign and his features set hard.

Strato saw her double take, that instant of shock when she read the grimness he couldn't hide, and silently cursed.

He was used to deflecting interest in his personal life, and particularly the past, with ease. A casually dismissive comment, a change of subject and it was done. Tonight for the first time he could remember, that skill eluded him.

Because Cora touched a part of him that no one else did? Because he'd felt a flicker of jealousy over her relationship with her father and her obviously happy family life?

Strato dismissed the notion. His past was dead and buried. He didn't yearn for family. Instead the thought sent a glacial chill through him.

But he saw Cora's recoil and regretted his curt tone. A moment before she'd been relaxed and happy to share.

Pushing aside instinctive distaste, for he *never* spoke of this, he said, 'I was orphaned.' The words stuck like shards of glass in his throat.

Cora's tight features softened. 'I'm sorry. That must have been dreadfully hard.'

He made himself shrug, as if his neck and shoulders hadn't seized up. 'I was lucky enough to be adopted.' He paused and repeated, 'I was very lucky.'

It was what he'd told himself over and over. What others had said in those early days. Somehow, though, he'd never believed it.

'So you were happy with your adoptive parents?'

Another question he never answered in public. Not because his aunt and uncle had been anything other than kind, decent people, but because talk of family screwed him up.

'They cared.' He swallowed a mouthful of wine. 'They gave me stability and safety.' But no matter how hard his aunt in particular tried, they couldn't replace what he'd lost. 'My adoptive father took me into his business straight from school and taught me everything he knew. When he died I inherited the company and built it into what I have now.'

Cora watched a smile that wasn't really a smile stretch his features and felt the hairs rise on her nape.

Something was wrong. Something that turned this sexy, self-assured man into a shadow of himself.

It lasted bare seconds. He caught her gaze on him and sat straighter, his expression shifting into something approximating amusement.

At her or himself?

'Sorry. I don't talk about the past much. I prefer to focus on the present. And prospects for the future.' His intimate smile told her he was thinking of his goal of persuading her into sex.

Yet the blankness in his eyes belied that inviting smile.

She nodded, knowing it was time to change the subject. 'I understand that. So, are you going to tell me how you turned your adoptive father's medium-sized transport company into a global corporation?'

If she'd expected eagerness, she didn't get it. It seemed Strato wasn't the sort of man who needed to broadcast his success. Why would he? His wealth spoke for itself. Nevertheless, his body language changed as he refilled her glass and started talking, briefly outlining his strategies and successes and sharing some amusing anecdotes.

Even as she smiled and responded, fascinated by the different world he described, Cora's thoughts returned to the brief but real emotion she'd seen. The grim darkness that had engulfed him.

It had made her want to reach out to him. Not because Strato was the most attractive, charismatic man she'd ever met, but because for an instant she'd seen something that made her want to comfort him.

She couldn't shift the idea she'd had a glimpse of the man behind the headlines. A man who kept himself hidden.

Who was Strato Doukas? She could no longer put him in a box and label him as simply a shallow party animal. That was one side of his character. Maybe one he played up?

Or was she projecting because she wanted him to be more? Because the man she'd seen this evening was one she liked too much. One who intrigued her.

Strato confused her. She wanted to understand him—the man who thought he could bribe her into bed!

The trouble was, the longer they were together, the more she realised the idea wasn't as outrageous as she'd told herself. It was actually…tempting.

CHAPTER SEVEN

CORA LOWERED THE anchor of the small tender and turned on her bench seat to find Strato pulling out the snorkels. He hauled off his T-shirt, leaving her with a view of his tanned chest and sculpted torso. Of the slight fuzz of dark hair that accentuated the shape of his powerful pectorals. Of the way his lean, muscled form tapered to a flat belly and narrow hips.

She was so *aware* of him. Felt it like an electric charge humming from her fingertips to her toes.

That hadn't changed, despite discovering last night that he was more complex and intriguing than she'd first imagined.

Despite the fact that, all morning, as they cruised past a scatter of islands, Strato had kept his distance, allowing her space. When they were together he'd chatted without any hint of sexual interest.

It was a relief not to be pestered.

Yes, a relief!

She was *not* disappointed to be virtually ignored after she'd spent the whole night thinking of him.

Of him and her together.

Besides, Strato didn't ignore her. He'd been a perfect host. Offering every amenity, yet not fussing around her.

Not by so much as a sidelong glance or teasing comment had he made her feel uncomfortable.

She'd done that all by herself.

After a restless night in her vast bed, imagining how it would be to share it with him, Cora was strung too tight.

'You've changed your mind about swimming?' His voice cut through her thoughts and Cora yanked her gaze up from where it had stuck on his dark swim shorts and powerful thighs.

Heat warmed her cheeks. She'd been caught staring.

Yet when her eyes met Strato's his expression didn't register anything but mild curiosity.

No doubt lots of women checked out his body.

All the time.

Cora gritted her molars and told herself she'd have to do better if she were to maintain a pretence of not wanting him.

'No. I haven't changed my mind.'

She undid her shorts and rose a fraction off the seat to pull them down. Then she shucked off her deck shoes, placing them with her neatly folded shorts.

The sooner they were in the water, and she had something to concentrate on other than this man who could have modelled for a Greek god, the better.

Gripping the bottom of her T-shirt, she yanked it up and over her head and folded it, leaning down to place it with the rest of her clothes.

'You play dirty, Cora.' Strato's voice was low and a little rough, making her think of gravel and suede. At the sound of it her body softened as if caressed.

'Sorry?' She looked up to find him watching her.

This time, his gaze raked from the top of her scalp down to her soles and back up again, lingering along the way before rising to focus on her face.

'I promised our affair would go at your pace, but then you wear a swimsuit with a front-opening zip. A *long* front-opening zip.' Strato shook his head, his expression mournful but his eyes hot. 'Underhand tactics, Cora, very underhand.'

She told herself she did *not* feel adrenaline pump through her blood at that look. As for the thrill tickling its way along her spine and down between her legs, making her shift on the seat...

'I'm sure you're used to seeing women wearing much less than this. It's a perfectly respectable one-piece.'

Because when she'd flung in clothes for this trip she'd avoided packing a bikini. She'd grabbed two one-piece swimsuits instead, telling herself she'd give Strato no encouragement.

He leaned back on his hands in a move that spread his shoulders and bare chest and made Cora swallow convulsively. He really was superbly made.

Just as well he didn't know she'd spent the night fantasising about him.

'True. But didn't you know there's a delightful piquancy about what's hidden from view? Topless string bikinis leave nothing to the imagination and I've lost my taste for the obvious.'

His voice dropped to a bass rumble that made Cora shiver. Not with fear but something like anticipation.

That tickle between her thighs strengthened, teasing, and it took real effort not to twitch where she sat. Because after a morning of treating her like a sister or elderly aunt, Strato was suddenly looking at her with blatant sexual appreciation. His nostrils flared as if scenting her arousal. The skin across his cheekbones tightened and those remarkable eyes looked slumbrous and secretive. Inviting.

Cora shook her head, making her tone as disapproving as she could. 'It's got a high neckline. It needs the zip for access.'

A slow smile began at the corner of his mouth then travelled across his face. 'Precisely. It's designed to tempt a man into reaching out and tugging that silver loop down...' His gaze dropped from the base of her throat to her breasts and slowly, infinitely slowly, to the spot low on her abdomen where the zip ended.

Cora searched for a dismissive response but her throat had dried. She felt her nipples bead and thrust towards him and hoped the black fabric would hide the sight.

'It makes me think...' his eyes locked on hers and lightning sheeted through her out of the clear sky '...you wore this to tempt me.'

She swallowed. There was an element of truth in that.

She'd pulled out both swimsuits this morning, taken one look at the brown with its traditional style and dull colour and couldn't bring herself to put it on. Because the black with the high-cut legs, the sharp angle in towards her neck that left her shoulders completely bare, and its long zip, made her feel feminine and powerful. Sexy.

She'd told herself she didn't want to attract his attention but at the first chance she'd dressed to catch his eye.

What did that say about her determination to keep her distance?

She *liked* it when Strato looked at her with that smouldering stare.

She *liked* feeling desirable.

Cora had warned herself not to weaken when he tried to seduce her. She hated the idea of being manipulated. Yet this wasn't him seducing or manipulating but her demanding his attention.

Pride and common sense told her not to fall for his practised charms because all he offered was shallow physical passion. But the rest of her clamoured that physical passion with Strato would do her fine, thank you very much!

She'd been sensible so long, guarding her heart. At least with him there was no pretence of hearts being involved. It was about lust and for the first time in her life Cora discovered how phenomenally powerful that could be.

Powerful and attractive.

Her whole body seemed to throb in time with her quickening pulse. Stoically she ignored it.

'I dress to please myself, Strato.' That was true. Seeing the rampant appreciation in his eyes made her feel wonderful. Even if it was wonderful tinged with danger. 'But if you'd rather not swim with me—'

His raised palm stopped her. 'On the contrary. I'm looking forward to it very much.'

He passed her a mask and snorkel and she took them, carefully not touching his fingers.

Did he notice? She feared Strato noticed most things. Cora was only too ready to get into the water and away from this conversation. She primmed her mouth and went through the usual safety checklist with him.

For, despite his seduction scheme, ostensibly she was here because of her marine expertise, helping him explore an area he didn't know. It salved her pride to think she was different from the other women he took on his yacht. More than simply someone to flirt with.

'Remember, stay close,' she concluded. 'Don't go into one of the sea caves alone.'

The sea was calm today but accidents happened and she was the expert. If she didn't know where he was…

'Don't worry, *Coritsa*. I intend to stick to you like glue.' His face was grave but the gleam in his eyes made her breath catch and her knees wobble.

Cora grinned as she hauled herself up onto the sun-warmed rock above the tiny, secluded inlet. What a brilliant afternoon. She rolled her shoulders, filled with that good feeling of muscles well used, and bent to scoop up a towel.

'That was fantastic!' Strato's voice made her turn in time to see him hoist himself up out of the water and onto the broad rock platform in a demonstration of upper-body strength that she envied.

The sight of him, all streamlined strength and toned masculinity, was enough to dry a woman's throat. Even one who hadn't been immersed in salt water for hours.

His eyes snared hers, black eyelashes spiked around bright green eyes, and the blaze of exhilaration she saw there stole her breath. Water dripped from his hair, running down his features and his broad chest and for an insane moment she wanted to plaster herself against him and kiss him, trying to absorb some of that vitality, that charge of energy that radiated from him.

Instead she tossed the towel to him and bent to get another for herself before he guessed her thoughts.

Because in that second of connection she'd read no sexual intent in Strato's expression. Only the pleasure of someone delighted with what they'd experienced.

As she'd been moments ago. Despite their conversation in the boat, she and Strato had spent a companionable couple of hours exploring sea caves, secret bays and even a sunken wreck. They'd seen more varied sea life than she'd expected and, instead of her amateur companion flagging from exertion and wanting to return to his luxury cruiser, Strato had been as eager as she to investigate further.

It had been fun, far more than she'd anticipated. There'd been no awkwardness or accidentally-on-purpose attempts to crowd her. Nothing sexual.

Not until she turned to see him beside her on the flat rock where they'd left their supplies. Sexual awareness had hit with all the finesse of a tsunami.

She rubbed her fluffy towel briskly over her face, then concentrated on her hair, the bane of her life.

'It must take ages.'

'Sorry?' She looked up from where she was bent over, rubbing her long tresses.

Strato nodded at her hair. 'It must take a long time to dry.'

Cora nodded and straightened, pushing her wet hair behind her shoulders and drying her arms. 'It does. It's a nuisance.'

'But beautiful.' He turned away, leaving her to deal with the silly jolt to her pulse at the compliment. As if she'd never received one before. 'If it's a nuisance, why not cut it?'

He finished using his towel and spread it in the shadow of the white cliff that loomed behind their seaside platform.

Cora looked around for somewhere to lay her own towel while they sat and shared the food they'd brought, but space was small and there was nowhere left but beside Strato's.

Telling herself it didn't matter because he'd dropped that sexually charged attitude, she spread her towel next to his.

It made her wonder if perhaps he wasn't as attracted as he made out, that he could turn it off so easily whereas she…

'I promised I wouldn't cut it.' Cora settled on the towel and nodded her thanks as he passed her a water bottle. 'When I was younger Doris was afraid I'd turn into a complete tomboy and made me promise not to cut it. I wasn't good at cooking or sewing, or behaving like a good Greek housewife, all the things she tried to teach me, so it seemed a fair compromise. My father backed her up. Said it reminded him of my mother's long hair.'

That had been enough to convince Cora. Even now, the regret in her dad's eyes whenever she mentioned cutting it short stopped her.

'You're a sentimentalist.'

She looked up but he wasn't watching her. Instead he was hauling the cold bag closer.

Well, she'd wanted him to drop the flirting, hadn't she?

Except she couldn't ignore what he'd said in the boat or the way he made her feel about her body and its increasingly clamorous needs.

'I'm not sure I'd say that.' She paused and took a long draught of blessedly cool water. 'But my father and Doris are special. I care about them.'

Plus there were times, like when Strato complimented her on her hair, that she privately revelled in the flagrantly feminine look. Mostly she was too busy working to think of herself as a sexy woman. Unless she was dealing with sleazy men who thought the generous size of her bust was inversely proportionate to her IQ and that she wanted nothing more from life than to fall into bed with them.

She'd thought she was good at giving them the brush-off. Till Adrian, who'd tricked her.

Cora took another swallow of water, rinsing away the

sudden sour taste on her tongue, then handed the bottle to Strato.

His eyes held hers as he lifted it and drank. That now-familiar corkscrewing sensation tightened inside her, drilling down to the aching emptiness within her pelvis. She shifted and looked away, reaching for a tiny tomato and popping it into her mouth.

It burst in a pop of tangy deliciousness and she tried to concentrate on that, not the fact she'd prefer to taste Strato.

He'd taste of salt water and—what was the flavour of that dark golden skin? She imagined licking the line of his sternum, straight up the centre of his chest to his throat. Sucking on that full lower lip.

She gave a shuddery sigh and tried to ignore her tightening nipples.

'More water?' Strato held out the bottle again.

'Not at the moment.' Because putting her lips where his had been seemed too intimate.

'There's wine and beer.'

'I'll stick with water, thanks.' It became clearer by the moment that she needed to keep her wits about her. Lest she give away how aware she was of Strato beside her. It was as if a switch had flicked in her brain, as if the companionable hours they'd spent together meant nothing. Because now her mind filled with him and sex.

Cora passed him a container. 'Chicken wing?' Her thoughts strayed to the day they'd met, with him stretched out, naked and mind-bogglingly attractive, and her offering refreshment. It felt a lifetime ago.

'Thanks.' He took some chicken, biting into it with strong, white teeth.

Cora took some herself and tried to concentrate on the spicy, marinated meat. But the silence crowded around her.

'You've done much snorkelling?' Maybe she could distract herself with conversation.

'Some.' He dropped chicken bones into an empty container, his hairy arm not quite brushing hers, making her quiver.

Cora shot him a sideways glance but he was focused on the aqua and green depths of the sea.

'How about scuba diving?' she asked eventually. 'I know an ideal place. Another wreck, but in deeper water.'

Strato nodded but didn't turn. 'Sounds good to me.'

Yet from this angle he looked to be frowning.

Cora subsided into silence, her usually reliable appetite fading. Her gaze strayed across his broad back to the scar he'd dismissed as the result of an old accident. Curiosity welled but it was fleeting. She wasn't concerned with old scars but with what had gone wrong in the last few minutes.

He was distracted. That wasn't her problem. It wasn't her job to entertain him. Yet the change from enthusiastic companion and would-be seducer, to a man barely aware of her presence, jabbed her ego.

She leaned back on her elbows, looking on the view of their tiny cove. Apart from their small boat there was no sign of people. They were utterly alone.

Strato continued to ignore her. Last night and this morning they'd spoken easily and he'd been a pleasant companion. This afternoon their communication had mainly been via sign language and occasional nods and grins as they swam. Now they didn't communicate at all.

Odd how bereft that made her feel.

Lying back like this, Cora couldn't see his face, except for his cheek and the line of his jaw, which she realised was clenched. It matched the hunched line of his shoulders. She shifted, trying to get comfortable, and noticed the tic of Strato's pulse at his temple. Whatever was on his mind it didn't look like anything relaxing.

Maybe she should head back into the water while he worked off what looked like abstraction or a bad mood. But she'd swum enough. It felt good to relax. Or it would if she didn't increasingly feel tension in the air.

She shifted again. Her flat rock wasn't as flat as she'd thought.

Cora opened her mouth to speak then realised she'd been going to fill the void with chat because Strato's silence felt brooding. But if he had a problem, it wasn't up to her to fix it. He was an adult. Let him deal with whatever bothered him.

Stifling a sigh, she folded her hands behind her head and searched for a comfortable position. That was better—

'If you've finished eating we should go back to the yacht.' His tone was terse.

'The yacht?' She frowned. 'You've barely rested or eaten anything.'

'I'm not hungry and, believe me, I'm not in the mood to rest.' His voice held a rough edge, emerging almost as a growl.

It shouldn't bother her, but his mood tarnished what had been, for her, a lovely couple of hours. Stupid to feel hurt. The illusion of companionship between them, even liking, flickered and faded. Just as well. She wasn't looking for a friendship, or anything else from this man.

Cora rose a little, bracing herself on her elbows. 'What's the problem, Strato? You sound like a bear with a sore head. I thought you liked our swim.'

He nodded but she saw his fist clench at his side, and the tendons stand proud beneath his skin. 'I did.'

Just that. No explanation of why they needed to get back to the yacht. Cora sighed and was about to move to pack up their mini picnic when her obstinate side reasserted itself. She refused to tiptoe around this man, second-guessing what she'd done to trigger his temper.

'Then what's up? Or am I expected to put up with your sudden mood swings? At least you owe me the courtesy of telling me why you've suddenly turned sour.'

'You don't want to know.'

Cora's breath hissed between her teeth. She did want to

know or she wouldn't have asked. But she refused to labour the point. She'd met enough selfish men to waste time with this one. She sat up with a jerk and began jamming their provisions into the bag they'd brought ashore.

In her haste her hand brushed Strato's arm.

He stiffened. His head swung round and her breath jammed back in her throat.

For the man whose gaze pinioned her to the spot wasn't the debonair pleasure seeker she knew, or the charming companion of earlier. There was a fierce light in his eyes while his arched nostrils and tightly drawn mouth hinted at strong emotions.

He looked…elemental. As if spawned from the depths of the ocean or carved from the rock on which they sat. Except he was flesh and blood. She saw the heavy rise of his chest and felt heat radiate from him.

Cora's breath seized and his hot gaze slid down to the rise of her breasts, swelling against the black fabric.

'Cora.' There it was again, that rasping note. A growled warning.

Suddenly she realised she wasn't the only one beleaguered by sexual arousal. It was there in the etched lines of Strato's face and the shimmer of tension between them.

'What don't I want to know, Strato?'

She knew, but she wanted to hear him say it. Because suddenly caution and common sense didn't matter a jot in the face of her compulsion to get close to him.

His mouth twisted in what she might have thought a sneer if she hadn't seen the sweat beading his brow. Strato wasn't bored or moody. He was racked by tension.

'That you're driving me crazy lying there beside me. That we need to return because I promised I wouldn't touch you and I don't break my promises. But I can't take much more.

'Every time you shift I imagine the feel of your bare skin against mine. The slide of our bodies together. The taste of your orgasm in my mouth. The sound of you screaming when I make you come.'

He paused, his breath audible in the thick silence. Cora's own breathing had disintegrated as the visions he conjured stopped her lungs working. Her fingers curled into damp towelling as she clung on tight.

'From the first I've wanted you, Cora. From the very first moment.' His deep voice and frowning face imbued the words with a gravity she felt deep inside. Felt and welcomed because wasn't that how she'd felt too?

'I want to feel your tight heat welcoming me inside. I want to suck your breasts and ravish every inch of your body until you can't remember being with any man but me.'

His massive shoulders rose and fell as he dragged in a slow breath.

'That's why we need to leave.'

Yet he made no move. Maybe he too felt glued to the spot.

Finally she spoke. 'You haven't asked me what I want, Strato.'

His eyes narrowed. 'What do you want, Cora?'

For a second she paused, waiting for her protective instincts to kick in. Obviously they were on holiday, or overwhelmed by the inevitable.

'All of the above.'

She reached for the zip at her throat.

CHAPTER EIGHT

HE'D DIED AND gone to Heaven.

Except Strato didn't believe in Heaven. As he didn't believe in love or fate or anything except the present and what he could see, hear, taste and touch.

His lips curled in a smile so tight it hurt his face. He intended to do a lot of looking, listening, tasting and touching.

He wanted Cora. All of her. In so many ways he'd never be able to satisfy himself today. It would take days, weeks, to work through his fantasies.

His smile widened as he brushed her hand away and took control of that silver loop on her zip.

Good thing he had her for the next month. That would give him time to indulge this gnawing hunger.

He'd planned slow and gentle the first time they were together. Instead he watched his hand tug hard, dragging the zip open with a sibilant hiss, right to the bottom, just above her pubic bone.

Was she bare down there or was there a triangle of dark silky hair over her mound? He wanted to find out. Except gravity distracted him, in the form of her swimsuit parting over her bounteous breasts, a little further with each short, sharp breath.

Strato's gaze fixed there, drawn to those perfect breasts and the way the slick fabric clung to her nipples despite the growing swathe of skin he'd revealed.

He heard a gasp and dragged his attention to her face. Her lips were parted and eyes narrowed in an unmistakably carnal look.

He licked his lips, imagining the taste of her mouth, her breasts, her sex. Her eyes widened and so did the gap between the edges of her zip as her beautiful breasts rose and fell sharply.

Strato knelt astride her, not daring yet to lower himself and lie over her. He might be desperate with want but not so desperate he'd allow this to be over in seconds.

His penis throbbed at the thought of covering her body with his. Instead he lifted his palm to her throat then stroked down and out, pushing the wet fabric aside to uncover one breast, its pert nipple begging for attention.

Strato was a generous man. He liked to please his lovers. Obligingly he lowered his head and fastened his mouth there, shaping her breast with his hand as he drew, gently at first, then harder.

So generous, Doukas! When you've been aching to get your hands and mouth on her breasts from that first day!

She writhed between his knees, hands fastening on his bare shoulders then slipping up to cradle his head. But there was nothing gentle in Cora's touch. She clamped his skull to her as if fearing he might be lunatic enough to pull away.

He smiled against her skin, scented with honey, warm woman and the sea, smoothing the fabric off her other breast. It was perfect in his hand. Gently he squeezed as he nipped her flesh and she made a tiny growling noise in the back of her throat that almost undid him.

Her patience was as fragile as his.

So he slid his hand down her restless body, past ribs, navel and soft belly, underneath clingy fabric to downy hair and a slick cleft that drew his fingers to her core.

Another breathy growl and her pelvis tilted, inviting him in. Strato didn't hesitate. He slid a finger deep, then two, and felt her grip him. He paused, breathing hard, reminding himself to wait.

But she couldn't. Her hips rose, her breath coming in frantic puffs, and he pressed down on her bud, circling till she jerked beneath him and cried out.

Her rapture went on and on, tempting him to join her. But he wanted this to last. For his own pleasure, and, he realised, to imprint on her the fact that he, Strato, was the lover who could give her such delight. He wanted her craving his touch. Not once or twice because maybe it had been a while for her, but because no other man could give her what he could.

He stilled, stunned by that alien idea. It was almost… possessive. Nothing he'd experienced before. But he was too aroused to spare time thinking.

Instead, after one last, luscious lick of her breast, he drew his hand up her shuddering body, lifted his head and surveyed his Nereid. Her eyes were closed and her mouth slack with pleasure.

Good but not good enough. He wanted her eyes fixed on him, alight with the knowledge it was he, Strato, taking her to the stars.

Gently he moved her arms, helping her out of the swimsuit, dragging it down her yielding body to bare her ribcage, waist and hips, then all the way down and off.

He'd known she was magnificent. That hourglass figure had snared his attention even covered by baggy shorts and a T-shirt. But knowing and seeing were two different things.

Lightly, not trusting himself to linger lest he get distracted, Strato skimmed his hands over her, following curves and indents. Her waist was narrow and her hips and breasts beautifully symmetrical. And those legs, long and shapely with toned muscle.

He was going to enjoy every moment with his new lover.

He should be crowing at his success, seducing the woman who'd scorned him. But he didn't feel he'd scored a point. Triumphant yes, but with anticipation. He was too aware of his own hungry yearning.

His gaze flicked to the supplies he'd brought and the condoms secreted there. Not yet.

He pushed open her thighs and settled between her legs,

inhaling the perfume of sated woman. But not as sated as she was going to be. One hand beneath her rump angled her pelvis and the other reached to tease her breast as he nuzzled her cleft.

Instantly her legs tensed around him. Her eyes shot open, dazzled and unfocused. They glowed a rich golden brown that made him think of treasure. Slowly he licked, long and deep, and found his own treasure.

Cora scrambled up on her elbows, frowning. He licked again, holding her gaze, and he felt her quiver.

'Don't you want—?'

'Oh, I want, *Coritsa*. I want all of you. Starting here.' Holding her gaze, he lowered his mouth.

There it was again, the glimmer of gold between lustrous dark lashes. Her lips were parted, her face flushed with passion and her eyes intent as he stroked her. She looked beautiful and something in his chest swelled.

Her eyelids flickered as he nuzzled, devouring the taste of salt and aroused woman. Her breasts rose, peaked nipples jerking high as he caressed her.

'Strato, I...' Her voice disintegrated on a gasp but the sound of her hoarse voice saying his name was a gift. It echoed in his ears as he took her to the edge. Her toned thighs clamped around his shoulders, her pelvis rising to meet his caresses in a needy rhythm, her heat warming him.

Through it all, his eyes held hers, watching as, by degrees, she slipped closer to—

'Strato!' The waves of her climax broke upon her. He felt it so intimately it was like riding the wave himself. Except his groin, rock hard and aching with need, told him otherwise.

Yet he wouldn't have missed this. Not when her shout became a moan of delight, formed around his name. Not when her dazed eyes held his as if there were nothing else in the world but him.

What was this imperative to mark her as his? To fill her consciousness with him so she didn't think of anyone else?

Later he'd wonder about that. For now, he rose to his knees and reached for protection.

He was so aroused and sensitive that sheathing himself became a test of willpower.

She watched him from slumbrous eyes. That golden-brown stare was a potent aphrodisiac. Her limbs were limp as he settled again between her thighs, gritting his teeth as their bodies touched.

He leaned forward, propping himself on one arm, his erection sliding against slick folds that felt so good he had to focus on his breathing. Guiding himself, he entered, slow, deep and so easy it felt as if they'd done this before.

A flutter of sensation surrounded him, turning into a tight clench that threatened to dissolve his control.

That was when he saw Cora's mouth tilt into a smug smile. As if she liked seeing him on the verge of losing himself.

Most often these days he found his lovers more appealing in anticipation than actuality. Not Cora. Especially when she encircled him with her legs, squeezing him closer to her soft body. Her hands were on his shoulders, fingers digging tight as she urged him to move.

It was exactly what he wanted, to find oblivion in her sweet body. But he wanted more, wanted her enslaved again to an ecstasy she associated only with him.

Slowly Strato moved, withdrawing then thrusting, luxuriating in the feel of them together and the shock in her eyes as he moved to a slow tempo that took every bit of control. If the damned could find Heaven, he almost believed he reached it as he took them both higher.

He'd known they'd be good together but this was...

Thought short-circuited as her hands slid down and gripped his buttocks, urging him higher.

Strato obliged with hard, sharp thrusts that made Cora

gasp. Tension rolled through him, tightening his skin, his groin, his whole being, till he knew he had seconds left. Sliding his hand between them, he found her clitoris and circled it hard as he let go and pumped right to her core, again and again and again.

Liquid gold burst around him, melting his brain while his body pounded deep into that luscious body as it convulsed around him. Fire consumed him. Sensations so exquisite they bordered on pain. As he sank into ecstasy it was with the sound of Cora screaming his name.

The sun was noticeably lower in the sky as he spooned behind Cora.

They'd drowsed, limbs tangled, for a long time. Till inevitably he'd needed more and he'd lifted her, tired but delightfully willing, onto his lap and urged her to ride him. Again that powerful rush of ecstasy hit simultaneously. Again it had been phenomenal, like a charge detonating deep in places he was barely aware of any more.

What was it about Cora that made him so needy? Recently his interest in women had waned. Yet with Cora he'd struggled to focus on anything but possessing her from the moment he'd seen her.

The sense of post-coital well-being far surpassed what he'd experienced before.

The novelty of a new lover? That didn't ring true.

She stretched and he watched the sinuous shift of her body, skin gleaming like silk. Cora might have the shape of an earth mother, with lush breasts and hips, but she was slender elsewhere and toned from physical activity.

He slid his palm down her shoulder blade, telling himself not to think about physical activity. Cora was tired. She'd fallen asleep in his arms and he'd been content to hold her, ignoring the hard rock jutting into his hip through his beach towel.

'You're awake.' Her voice was husky with sleep. Had she dreamt about him? About them together?

'I am.' He hadn't slept. He'd lain here, basking in the afterglow, caught up in the profound sense of peace and well-being that was so rare.

He let his hand drift across her back then frowned. 'What's this mark?'

She shrugged. 'Am I bruised? There was a knob of rock under my towel that dug into me.'

Strato feathered his hand across the spot, frowning. 'You should have said. I don't want to hurt you.'

'It's okay. I *wanted* you. It didn't matter.'

He recalled the force of his body slamming into hers, his weight pushing her down, and tasted something metallic on his tongue.

'Even so, I don't want to cause you pain.' He was so much bigger and more powerful. It was why he never set aside all caution, even with the most responsive lovers. The thought of hurting a woman made his blood congeal. 'Next time tell me.'

She shrugged. 'Okay.'

Strato was about to demand she promise but caught himself. Cora would wonder at his insistence. He'd have to be more careful.

Which meant ignoring his libidinous thoughts till they returned to the yacht.

'Are you ready to go back?'

She shot him a look that made his heart thud. The woman was a siren, when even a glance roused him.

As if you weren't already aroused, lying naked against her. Just thinking of her gives you a hard on.

'You don't want to stay here longer?' Her expression and the slide of her body against his sent desire spiralling through him.

But Strato wouldn't be persuaded.

He sat up, ignoring the discomfort in his groin and her challenging pout.

'No. Let's get back. Aren't you looking forward to a hot shower?'

Cora stifled disappointment at his impatience. He'd rather be on his luxury yacht. Despite his getting a buzz out of their snorkelling expedition, she suspected he'd only suggested it to put her at ease, given how reluctantly she'd agreed to this trip.

Strato Doukas was used to a sybaritic lifestyle of indulgence. Not open-air sex on a rock above the sea.

Her throat constricted.

She'd thought it exciting and elemental, that they hadn't been able to resist the magnetism dragging them together.

But maybe for Strato there'd been a feeling of novelty? Something different from sex in luxurious surroundings.

For her the experience had felt life-changing. As if she'd never known rapture till today. He'd definitely enjoyed it too. There'd been no faking that.

Yet for the first time, Cora felt gauche. It was all very well getting swept up by desire, but now, naked with a stranger, especially a stranger used to glamorous, sophisticated women and every sort of luxury...

'Of course. I'll find my swimsuit.'

His arm stretched out over her shoulder, black fabric dangling from his fingertips. A substantial amount of fabric.

For a second she wished she were the sort to wear a topless string bikini. That she were a petite woman who wore mere wisps of material. Then she set her jaw. She'd learned there was no point wishing to be someone she wasn't. Her body was fit and strong. It served her well. She wasn't ashamed of it.

'Thank you.' She plucked the fabric from his fingers and sat up.

'Would you like help?' His voice held a rough edge that sent heat pooling low in her body. Again!

She twisted to look over her shoulder and what she saw made her heart thud against her ribs. Not a bored man thinking of cocktails on the deck. Strato watched her so intently it felt as if he noticed nothing but her. Not the bright sea or vast sky or the little boat that would take them back to his superyacht.

'Scratch that.' His gaze dropped to her bare breasts and he shut his eyes. 'If I touch you we won't get back for hours.'

His words thrilled her. 'Would that matter?'

Strato's eyes snapped open and fixed on hers. Something shifted inside. She told herself it was the aftermath of phenomenal sex. Strato made her previous sensual experience fade into nothing.

'I don't want you getting more bruises because I can't control myself.'

'*That's* why you want to go back?'

He worried about her discomfort? She'd never thought him an ogre but what was one tiny bruise compared with the sexual conflagration they'd shared?

Or maybe what had been so stunning for her was the norm for Strato?

His mouth curved ruefully. 'Well, it's not because I've lost interest. You have a potent effect on me, *Coritsa*.'

Cora struggled and failed to suppress a smile.

This wasn't the sort of relationship she wanted. It was short term and purely physical, yet she enjoyed hearing he found her desirable.

Maybe she'd let Adrian's attitude affect her self-esteem after all. Maybe that was why she responded so avidly to Strato, because he made her feel strong.

'Okay. Give me a minute to get dressed.' Suddenly she noticed how far the sun had moved. She'd had no idea it was so late. 'I promised to call my father this afternoon.'

To check on him and that those further hotel bookings had come through.

Cora wriggled into her one-piece, wishing she could do it more gracefully, trying to ignore Strato's gaze on her. When they'd shared their bodies she hadn't minded his flagrantly appraising stare. Yet she wasn't used to being naked with a man, subjected to that intense scrutiny.

'You and your father are close,' Strato murmured. His tone made her wonder about his relationship with his adoptive father.

'He's my dad. There's only been us since I was young.'

Once more that green gaze shimmered with something she couldn't identify. 'Then let's not keep him waiting.'

Strato held out his hand and pulled her up against him. Cora felt that jangle of awareness as their bodies brushed, even though the bones in her legs had jellied from so much pleasure.

His slow smile told her he recognised how she felt. Understanding mixed with smugness and a hint of promise. 'Maybe you should rest when we return. Because I'd like to spend the whole night with you.'

CHAPTER NINE

HE DID. THAT NIGHT and every night after that. And Cora didn't for a moment think of objecting.

What they shared left no room for false pride. Strato might have used outlandish tactics to get her aboard his yacht, but she *wanted* to be here. She wanted him and relished the woman she became with him.

It wasn't that he'd changed her. It was more that with him she was free to be herself as never before. There was no judgement, no expectation.

All Strato demanded was honesty. After her past experiences it had taken her a while to believe that, but it was true. Her honest responses, physically and in conversation, were never dismissed and always welcomed. It made conversations stimulating and lovemaking unique and special.

In return, Strato was straightforward to the point of bluntness. He had a way of telling her exactly what he'd like to do with her sexually that made her pulse skyrocket and her body throb in anticipation.

The only exception to his forthrightness was that he rarely spoke of his past and then in only the most general terms, so Cora learned not to raise the subject, respecting his desire for privacy.

She'd moved from her guest stateroom to Strato's vast suite with its enormous bed. It was the most comfortable bed she'd ever slept in. Or maybe it was because she was always exhausted from exertion and pleasure when sleep claimed her.

For a lazy hedonist Strato had so much energy! And not just for sex. Every day they explored, either an island or underwater.

Yesterday it had been a sunken ancient temple, an amazing place she'd never visited. Exploring it with him had felt special. As if they shared something remarkable. Afterwards, as they dined on the deck, and later as Strato gathered her close, Cora had felt herself soften. Not just physically as her body shaped itself to his, but mentally.

Strange as it might once have seemed, she *liked* Strato. And he…

No, she wouldn't go there, second-guessing his feelings. They were more than halfway through their month together. When the time was up they'd go their separate ways. Strato was an amazing lover but he'd made it clear their relationship was time-limited.

No long-term ties. No happy-ever-after. Those had been his conditions from the first.

Now though, four weeks seemed an incredibly short time. She couldn't imagine going back to her island, or to another research project, and never seeing Strato again.

Cora rolled over and stared at the space beside her, ignoring the dull feeling of disappointment like a lead weight in her middle.

She'd known Strato wasn't still in bed. If he had been they'd have been touching. Either spooned together or with her sprawled across his chest in what had become one of her favourite positions. Head on his shoulder, arm and knee across him as if to stop him moving away.

They were always touching. Even when they weren't making love. Strato was the most tactile person she'd met. She loved the connection. The brush of his fingers across her arm as they shared some new discovery. The weight of his hand at her breast or waist as he slept.

You'll miss him when you leave.

You miss him now, waking up to find him gone.

What will you be like in eight days' time, knowing you won't see him again?

Cora frowned as she focused on the dented pillow. What would life be like without Strato?

Less exciting. Less pleasurable. Less…warm.

There was something about sharing with him, not just sex, but small things like her joy in a glorious sunset and her weakness for sweet pastries, or big things like her hopes of working permanently in research at a marine reserve. He listened and understood. She had that with her father but there were things she couldn't share with her dad that, to her surprise, were easy to discuss with Strato.

And though he wasn't one to talk about himself, he sometimes told her snippets about his business interests that fascinated her. The complexity of the corporation astounded her, as did the suspicion that he ran it all from aboard his yacht. Clearly he delegated, but there'd been enough video conferences and hours when Strato was shut in his study to convince her that the stories about him as a louche playboy didn't paint the whole picture.

She knew him so well yet there was so much she didn't know. So much she wanted to understand.

Cora pushed back the sheet and swung her legs out of bed. It was early but she wouldn't get back to sleep.

It had been a mistake getting into the habit of falling asleep with Strato. Now it felt wrong, trying to sleep without his solidly muscled body beside her.

She smiled. Maybe she could convince him to come back to bed.

Strato pulled on the handles of the rowing machine, feeling the stretch of muscles in a pleasing rhythm that would, eventually, exhaust him.

Eventually but not soon. He'd woken with Cora spooned against him, her buttocks cushioning his morning erection and his hand at her plump, perfect breast.

He grimaced and pulled harder on the machine, feeling tension rack his shoulders, torso and legs.

He'd been about to wake her for dawn sex as he usually did, when he realised what had begun as a delicious treat had become habit. Each day he woke and reached for her. Not simply because of his almost permanent state of readiness these days, but because he was becoming addicted to giving her pleasure.

Sweat beaded his brow as he worked harder, forcing his body to the limits. As if a gruelling workout could obliterate his craving for Cora.

The desire for sex he could understand. But this was more. He liked being with her. Even arguing some point of disagreement, he felt energised as he hadn't for years. As for pleasing her, physically, or with some treat like the dive yesterday to the temple, he spent more and more time thinking of ways to make her smile.

Strato frowned as he hauled on the handles.

His month with her wasn't turning out as expected. It was becoming complicated.

You don't do complicated, remember? Not in your personal life.

Personal complications equated to emotional engagement.

Strato had devoted the last couple of decades to ensuring he never made the mistake of getting emotionally involved. Because he knew the risks that came with that. The *danger*. He'd vowed that no one else would suffer that danger, that devastation, with him.

'I thought you might be here.'

He halted, heart hammering, as Cora walked barefoot across the gym.

Her hair was pinned up in a haphazard arrangement that made him want to see it spill around her shoulders and back. But it wasn't her hair that snagged his attention. She wore an ultra-short tank top, or perhaps it was a sports bra, and a pair of shorts. Brief shorts that clung. Different from the ones she usually wore. Between the two garments was a swathe of smooth skin and a narrow waist.

His breath slid out in a sigh of approval that snatched

in sharply as she bent to drape a towel over a bench near the window. The view from behind dried his mouth. Long, toned legs and tight, perfectly rounded buttocks.

Strato released the handles and the rowing machine stilled.

'What are you doing?'

Good one, Doukas! Asking the obvious is a sure sign you've lost the plot.

'Same as you. Exercise seems a good way to start the day.' She smiled as she bent into a long, slow stretch, though her eyes didn't meet his. Instantly he wondered why.

Maybe she'd missed him, waking to find him gone. Maybe she wanted him as much as he wanted her.

Yeah, and maybe you've got a one-track mind.

Strato grabbed his towel and rubbed his face, neck and arms.

Cora followed the movement and he felt a spark of excitement.

He pushed aside the notion that had disturbed him only seconds ago—that his involvement with this woman was getting too complex and he needed to pull back. Now he was faced with the reality of her, all his years of pursuing pleasure told him there'd be no pleasure more complete than what he'd experience with her.

He planted his feet on the floor and rose, watching her eyes widen before she turned her head and apparently concentrated on the stretch to her toes.

Strato suppressed a smile. She was supple as well as strong and he appreciated both.

He was always cautious with lovers, given his superior size and power. Yet Cora met him as an equal, revelling in the male strength he always sought to harness. Her size, taller and more robust than most women, though far smaller than him, made it feel as if she were designed specifically to please him, or he her.

That was why sex felt so good. They...matched.

Strato made an executive decision not to pursue that thought further.

Because the implications might make him uncomfortable and he had more pressing concerns.

He slipped his hand into his pocket and found the condom he'd put there. These days he had them on him at all times. Cora tempted him even in the most prosaic of places, including yesterday on the floor of his walk-in wardrobe.

He'd followed her in there to grab a fresh T-shirt and had accidentally brushed against her, inhaling that intriguing scent of hot, honeyed woman. Abruptly hunger had consumed him. Consumed them. They hadn't made it as far as his bed, mere metres away. Their coupling had been hard and furious, then slow and sweet. Thinking of it made his groin ache and tighten.

'Where are you going to start?' He slung his towel over his shoulder as he approached.

Cora shot him a sideways glance then slowly straightened. When she stood she barely had to tilt her chin to meet his eyes and Strato liked that. He was sick of bending double to kiss a woman.

'Maybe some Pilates work.' She looked around the room. 'I'm not really into weights.'

'No, not weights. Something more holistic, I think.' His thoughts raced ahead and so did his pulse.

'You have a suggestion?' Cora turned, expectation in her expression. Could she read his mind?

'I have. If you'll put yourself in my hands.'

Her gaze dipped to his mouth and, remarkably, Strato felt his chest tighten, his throat constricting. Her eyes met his, shimmering golden brown.

'Why not?' She paused. 'I'm always happy to take advice from an expert.'

She moistened her bottom lip with the tip of her tongue and Strato felt as if she'd swiped that moist tongue across him. She'd done that last night, so effectively he'd shattered far too quickly. He shuddered at the erotic memory.

Sometimes it felt as if *she* was the experienced one, not he, evoking responses so profound they stunned him.

Not because Cora used sexual tricks. It was that, with her, none of this felt stale or second-hand. Everything was fresh and...

Strato sucked in a sharp breath.

Meaningful was the word that came to mind. But that wasn't possible.

There was no hidden meaning here. It was pure sexual chemistry at its best. As he was about to prove.

'Excellent.' He took Cora's hand, his fingers brushing her wrist where her pulse thudded fast. 'Over here.' He drew her to the window beyond which the blue-green sea extended towards the distant mainland.

Strato planted her right hand on the large pane of reinforced glass. Her breath hitched as her eyes caught his in a smoky sideways stare that shot heat to his groin.

'Now what?'

He moved behind her, taking her left hand and planting it on the glass in front of her, then he put his hands on her hips, fingers gripping hard, and tugged her back towards him.

He heard a sigh. Hers or his?

'Comfortable?'

She nodded, then shuffled, hips wriggling, till she came up against him. 'Very.'

Witch! He heard her breathless laugh and grinned. He slid one hand round her hip and down to cup her mound and instantly she pushed into his touch.

'You like that?'

She nodded and when she spoke she sounded breathless. 'You really think this will give me the workout I need?'

Strato bent forward and nipped the side of her neck. 'Count on it.' His other hand moulded her breast, discovering her nipple already peaked hard. It was one of the things he liked about Cora. She was always as eager for him as he was for her.

She gave another little wriggle of her hips against him and Strato's patience for this game waned. He tucked both thumbs in the waistband of her shorts and dragged them over lush hips and down till they fell at her feet.

His gaze fixed on her bare buttocks, perfect as a peach. 'Now that *is* naughty,' he murmured. 'Not so much as a G-string to preserve your modesty.' He was already shucking his shorts and tearing the condom wrapper.

A gurgle of laughter reached him. 'I didn't think it was my modesty you were interested in.'

She'd be surprised. He loved her naked. But he was almost as aroused seeing her buttoned up, or zipped up, in the case of that wickedly tempting swimsuit.

He slid a palm over the pale globe of her buttock then down between her legs, finally encountering slick folds.

'Aren't you going to take off my top?' Her voice sounded stretched and he could relate. He felt as if his groin were caught in a vice, gripping harder and harder.

'Next time,' he growled as he slid his other hand up her ribcage and under the tight fit of her top. Something like relief engulfed him as her breast filled his hand. That was better. That was what he needed.

'More,' she demanded, pushing into his hands. 'Give me more.'

'I've created a monster,' he teased. 'First you pretend you don't like me and now you're insatiable.'

'You like it. You know you do.'

She was right. Strato couldn't remember delighting in anything more than being with her.

Cora didn't pry or connive for a permanent position in his world. She accepted him as he was. There was no evidence now of hesitation, or of the calculation he'd read in other lovers.

It was as if she didn't give a damn for his money.

Or sense the darkness at the heart of him.

As if that darkness didn't exist.

Strato shivered at the heady illusion.

It had been a long, long time since he'd experienced anything like it.

The powerful realisation tempered his hunger with rare tenderness. He bent his head, feathering kisses across her bare shoulder, trying to slow the surge of need building in his loins.

Her hair tickled him but he couldn't bring himself to let her go long enough to release it. He loved Cora's long tresses, soft and enticing, but not as enticing as her almost naked frame, backing up into his groin, hips circling.

'Stop teasing, Strato!'

He smiled against her skin. This feisty woman really could be imperious. That called to something inside him. As did her sense of humour and her generosity.

'Well, if you're sure you're ready...' He bent his knees and guided himself to her, pausing to give them both a moment to anticipate what was to come. Then with one long, sure thrust he went deep, embedding himself. Her heart pounded beneath his hand and he felt the hot, slick grab of her muscles around him.

For a second they were still, as if the glory of their union took them both by surprise. As if this wasn't simply about two aroused bodies seeking ecstasy but two souls finding each other.

Strato grimaced and let his forehead rest against Cora. He breathed deep and strived for sanity. From the age of eight his life had been firmly rooted in reality. No flights of fancy. No cosy fantasies. No sentiment.

So when Cora angled her body, pushing back against him, hips circling needily, Strato shoved aside the outlandish thoughts and set about giving her what she wanted.

First with his hand between her thighs, till she trembled and cried out, her inner muscles convulsively clutching him.

Then, when her sighs had died, unleashing his own need, powering fast and hard till the view of sea and sky blurred and exquisite sensation filled him.

On the cusp of losing himself, he knew a moment's hesitation, an atavistic warning that this was something other than simple sex.

Then it was too late and Strato lost himself in bliss and Cora's welcoming body.

Later, when finally they could make their bodies move, he carried her to the spa on his private deck. She slumped in his arms, her head tucked beneath his chin as he stared out at another magnificent new day.

Occasionally she snuggled closer, nuzzling his throat or shifting her weight on his thighs, and heat drenched him. Not heat from the spa or even residual heat from sex, but something deep in his gut.

Strato frowned. They had just over a week left together yet he was no nearer being ready to let her go. With any other partner he'd be impatient to end their liaison.

Why not now?

'That's what I meant to ask you. You keep distracting me and I keep forgetting.' Cora moved as if to draw back from him, probably so she could meet his eyes, but he tightened his embrace. He was comfortable like this, enfolding her against him.

'What did you forget?'

'Something my father said.'

'Is there a problem with the hotel bookings?' According to his information, that had gone smoothly. The boat chartered to take guests from the mainland and back had even become the unofficial public ferry for the island while the government-funded one was repaired.

'No. That's fine. Everyone's busier than ever with all these guests. The businesses along the harbour are reporting increased income too.'

'So?' He slid a finger up her throat and around the back

of her ear where she was particularly sensitive and was rewarded with a quiver of response.

'Do you know an organisation called Asteri?'

Strato stilled. 'Why do you ask?'

'The bulk of the bookings are from your company, but my father mentioned someone from a place called Asteri also reserved quite a few rooms.'

'So?'

Once again Cora shifted as if to look up at him, but he held her where she was.

'I wondered if that's you too, under a different name.'

And there he'd been, congratulating himself on the fact that Cora didn't pry.

Strato chose his words carefully. 'I don't own a company called Asteri.' He paused, seeking a change of subject to distract her. 'Surely you and your father are happy to have bookings from a range of places.'

'Oh, we are. And now there's transport to the island again, we've had more private bookings. The season is looking to be our best ever. Thank you, Strato.' She turned to plant a kiss at his collarbone.

'You're welcome.'

He didn't refer to the fact that was the only reason Cora was here, because he'd presented her with a deal too good to refuse.

As for the question about Asteri, it wouldn't be disastrous if she learned about his involvement. Except it was something Strato kept strictly private. Only a very trusted few knew of his links to the organisation.

Because it was the one thing in his life that he felt strongly about. Even building his uncle's company into a mega-successful corporation wasn't as important as Asteri.

If the press became aware of his involvement, there'd be endless curiosity and possibly someone, finally, would dig up the past he preferred to forget.

'Strato? Are you okay?' Brandy-coloured eyes held his

and it felt, remarkably, as if it wasn't a throwaway question. It felt as if Cora really was concerned. As if she tried to see deep inside him.

'Never better, *Coritsa*.' Deliberately he brushed his hand over her bare breasts and watched her shiver. Yet still her gaze held his.

The potency of that look, and of his yearning response, hit him like a blow. Almost as if he wanted to share things with Cora that he'd never shared with a soul, not even his well-meaning aunt or the experts who'd probed him.

His breath jammed and backed up in his cramping lungs.

He refused to go there. Not ever again. It was unthinkable.

Which meant something had to change. He'd created a hothouse atmosphere, alone on the yacht with Cora. That was why he was plagued by unfamiliar thoughts about sex becoming something more. And about unburdening himself.

They needed a distraction. Then Cora wouldn't have time for curiosity.

Strato slid his hand past her soft belly to the curls between her legs. She gasped, thighs opening instantly for him, and he smiled his approval.

He *did* like this woman. So much.

But he couldn't afford to let her upset his well-ordered life or unleash old hurts.

'Remind me to tell you later about the surprise I have for you.' Then, before she could question him, he took her mouth and seduced her all over again.

CHAPTER TEN

CORA INHALED THE scent of sea and flowering geraniums. The latter were a burst of bright red in painted olive-oil tins clustered against the last whitewashed house in the village.

'I like your surprise.' The tiny harbour and bright fishing vessels, the sunlight dancing off clear water and the joy of walking hand in hand with Strato made a perfect end to the day. 'I've never been here.'

Strato's gaze caught hers and heat danced inside. 'I'm glad to bring you somewhere new. But this is just a stop-off. The surprise is tomorrow—'

A cry wafted on the late afternoon breeze. A seabird? Cora turned but saw nothing. It was Strato who spotted it, a bundle of colour at the bottom of the steps to the harbour.

Before Cora had even taken it in, Strato loped across and vaulted off the stone wall.

When Cora caught up she discovered the bundle was a child. A little boy with huge, overbright eyes and two badly skinned knees, red with blood. Beside him a girl, a little older, scolded him for jumping off the steps. 'I told you not to. You're not big enough yet.' Despite her words, she was clearly upset and Cora guessed both children had had a nasty fright.

Strato squatted before them, introducing himself and discovering the siblings were Costa and Christina. He was friendly, but matter-of-fact, and Cora sensed his attitude stopped a flood of tears. He asked Costa if he could stand.

The boy did, but winced with pain.

'I'm all right,' he said, blinking hard.

'I can see that,' Strato responded, checking he had no other injuries. 'But it might be hard climbing the steps.'

The girl twisted her hands. 'I'll have to call Mamma. I said we'd play outside while she fed the baby but—'

'We don't need to bother your mother yet,' Strato said as Cora opened her mouth to say the same. They shared a look and again she experienced that sense of connection as if they read each other's thoughts. It happened more and more frequently.

'We could help you up the stairs,' she said. 'I'm Cora and my friend Strato is very strong. He could carry Costa.'

'I'm not a baby!' That dried the boy's tears.

'Of course not,' Strato said, 'but it's sensible to accept help when you need it. Cora and I are going to buy ice cream, if there's somewhere that sells it.'

'There is.' Costa looked suddenly eager. 'I could show you.'

'Costa! We can't. Mamma—'

'Maybe,' Strato said, 'you could ask your mother if it's all right. If you show us the way, I'd be grateful. Perhaps you'd both like ice cream as a thank you?'

Minutes later, after Christina had dashed into the house with the geraniums and checked with her mother, the four proceeded to the village store. Christina walked beside Cora, asking where they came from and whether they liked the island. Costa, on Strato's shoulders, grinned and shouted all the things he could see from so high.

By the time they settled down with their ice creams, Costa allowed Strato, rather than Cora, to tend to his scrapes and both children chattered about their island, the fine church, the huge underground cavern and the bay where legend said a local boy once rode dolphins.

The interlude revealed a new side to Strato. His patience and good humour with the children intrigued Cora. But she'd already known he wasn't just the careless playboy he made out. He'd shown genuine concern and an appreciation not only of Costa's pride, but of Christina's need to check in with her mother for permission. His patience, thoughtfulness and unflappable attitude were typical of the man she'd begun to know.

'What are you thinking about?' Strato asked as they walked alone to the tender that would take them to his vessel.

'You with those children. I never imagined you with kids.'

His smile stiffened. 'You imagined right. I don't intend to have any.'

There it was again, that blare of warning. The same as when he'd said he'd never settle down with a family.

'But you understand them. You're used to being around kids.'

'Not at all.' When he read her curious look, he sighed and finally added, 'I had siblings, one older and one younger. I remember what it was like, being with them.'

His voice dipped and Cora felt the gravity of his words. That was when they sank in.

He'd *had* siblings. Past tense.

Her pulse throbbed. The articles she'd read implied he was an only child. Had they died before or after he was adopted?

She couldn't ask. Not when it was clear he didn't want to discuss it.

Silently Cora tucked her hand in his. She felt privileged he'd shared so much when she knew he disliked talking about his past. Maybe one day he'd share more. The fact he'd told her this was surely proof of their growing trust.

But though she didn't ask, her thoughts raced. Was that why he didn't want a family? Because he'd experienced loss early in life? Was he scared to love and lose again?

Where Strato was concerned, her curiosity was boundless.

Cora had approached Athens by sea multiple times. Usually by ferry or occasionally a research vessel. This time, instead of landing at the public dock, she was at a private marina of luxury boats.

For the first time in weeks she felt out of her comfort zone. What was she doing in a place like this?

Amazing how swiftly she'd acclimatised to Strato's superyacht. Not just the yacht, but him. It felt natural to wake in his arms then spend all day and night with him.

A shiver skated down her spine despite the sunshine. She resented coming into Greece's capital, because it meant less time solely with Strato.

When had he become so important that the prospect of being surrounded by others, not having him to herself, bothered her?

She told herself it was the stupendous sex, a revelation to a woman who hadn't realised how deep her own carnal appetites ran. Strato awakened a sexually confident woman she'd initially found hard to recognise.

Yet Cora felt more than physical desire. She liked the man, and had developed an intimacy with him plus a level of trust she'd never known before.

Maybe it was as well they were in Athens. Time alone with Strato messed with her mind.

'There you are, *Coritsa*.' Warm arms wrapped around her and she felt his hard frame at her back. She inhaled Strato's spicy scent and something in her eased. She let her head drop back against his shoulder. 'Ready to go ashore?'

She nodded, telling herself Athens would be a nice change. A shame she didn't believe that.

'Excellent. I've got business to attend to but you'll find lots to keep you amused. Then tonight we're invited to a private dinner.'

Cora froze. They weren't spending the day together? She'd imagined...

That Strato would spend the day visiting crowded tourist sites with her? Or sit in a simple *taverna* with her when his onboard chef produced the most amazing meals every day?

Of course he had people to see, a reason for coming here. If she'd been thinking she'd have organised to catch up with old colleagues. It might still be possible, even at short notice.

Yet bitter disappointment lingered on her tongue. She turned. 'A private dinner? Where?'

'A business contact. Damen Nicolaides. He and his wife, Stephanie, are having a dinner at their Athens home.'

'Damen Nicolaides, the shipping magnate?'

'You've heard of him?'

Heard of him? He was more famous than the prime minister. Like Strato, his name was synonymous with wealth.

'I know of him.'

Cora breathed deep. Dinner with a couple of world-famous billionaires instead of just one. Strange how daunting that seemed.

Suddenly she realised how little she'd really seen of Strato's life. There was another side to his world about which she knew nothing. What a novelty she must be to him. A change from the usual sophisticated socialites.

'Are you okay?' His rough voice scraped her skin.

Cora swallowed, shoving aside the idea that that was really why Strato wanted her. Because she was a change from the usual. But it was true. She'd let herself forget she and Strato came from separate worlds.

'Of course. What are our plans?'

For a moment longer he stared deep into her eyes but Cora was prepared now, drawing on the protective reserve she hadn't needed in weeks.

'We'll go to the Nicolaides home first as that's where my meeting is. That way you can meet them before dinner tonight. I know dinner with complete strangers can be daunting.' He stroked his hand down her cheek in a gesture that made her heart squeeze. That, and his intent gaze, made it feel as if he was genuinely concerned about her. 'We'll meet on board around five. There'll be time to…relax before we leave for dinner.' His mouth curled in a familiar smile that spoke of sex and Cora's blood heated to flashpoint.

Just like that!

Even knowing she was only with Strato as a temporary diversion.

You can't complain. You're revelling in it. You're using Strato for your own pleasure as much as he's using you.

Yet the thought of their month ending and them going their separate ways loomed like a dark cloud on the horizon. A disaster she didn't want to think about.

'Sounds good. I have plenty to keep me busy.'

Like buying something to wear tonight. In a fit of pique at being manoeuvred aboard Strato's yacht, she'd packed only casual clothes, mainly shorts and T-shirts. Nothing for dinner with a bunch of billionaires. Pride dictated she find something better than the olive-green capri pants and cream top she wore now, even though she knew she couldn't compete with the other guests' designer clothes.

'That reminds me. I have something for you.'

Strato fished out a credit card.

Cora stiffened. She flashed a killing look into those enigmatic green eyes. 'I don't need your money.' Her tastes were simple and she had no intention of spending a fortune.

His dark brows rose. 'I know women, Cora. You'll feel out of place tonight unless you wear something sophisticated like the others. I don't want you feeling uncomfortable. You're only attending to keep me company, so I'll buy the new outfit.'

She was torn between indignation at his *I know women*, as if she were the same as all his other lovers, and something far softer at his consideration. He knew he put her in a difficult position and tried to make things easier.

Then don't force me to go somewhere I'm not comfortable!

But she couldn't say that. He had a right to meet friends and associates. She was a competent woman, able to hold her own amongst strangers, even ones born with silver spoons in their mouths.

'Thanks for the thought, but I'll manage. I don't want your money.' It felt like being bought.

Which might have made sense if she hadn't accepted his deal to fill her father's hotel with paying guests. Was that why she felt so outraged? Was she trying, belatedly, to salvage self-respect?

Strato stared down at her. 'Don't let pride stop common sense. Buy something for tonight.'

'Absolutely not.'

'Damn it, Cora. I'm not trying to buy your soul, just make tonight easier!'

Before she could stop him he shoved the card in the tiny pocket of her top and took her arm, turning her towards the gangplank.

One glance showed his jaw set like granite. But his tension didn't ameliorate hers. She wanted to rip out his credit card and toss it in the harbour. Except that would be childish. She'd simply use her own money and return the card, untouched, at the end of the day.

Yet her temper simmered all the way to the Nicolaides' estate. Possibly because Strato remained tight-lipped too. Gone were the charming smiles and the camaraderie, much less intimacy.

Was he so used to getting his own way that he got in a temper when crossed?

She wrapped her arms around herself. Clearly she didn't know him as well as she'd thought. All she knew was the side he let her see. The carefree, sexy man who was surprisingly thoughtful and great company. But he maintained definite barriers. He erected one whenever his family was mentioned. He'd shoved up another now, when she refused to do as he ordered.

Her mood worsened as she watched the city go by while Strato devoted himself to his phone as if she didn't exist.

It was a long time since she'd thought of Strato as like Adrian. Now she wondered if she was mistaken and Strato was just as egocentric. He hadn't seemed so before, but she'd been in such a haze of well-being...

When they arrived at a gated property with lush gardens and a winding drive that led, finally, to a breath-stealing mansion, Cora's heart dived. She could just about face this with Strato's support. Right now, though, his expression was cool.

Great! She breathed deep and moved towards the huge bronze front door that swung open at their approach.

Now she felt Strato's hand at her elbow and some of her nerves eased.

He was still miffed. She felt the tension in his tall body. But he was perfectly polite to the housekeeper who showed them into a stunning sitting room of ivory and gold with black accent pieces.

'Mr Nicolaides will be with you shortly. Please make yourself comfortable here or on the terrace.' Then, with a promise of refreshments, the woman bustled out.

Strato's hand dropped and with it Cora's heart.

Was she so dependent on his approval? The idea shocked her. She'd never been dependent on a man. It worried her.

Instinctively Cora moved towards the wide terrace with its spectacular view over the city to the sea.

'Wait, Cora! We need to talk.' She turned and Strato's expression made her pulse leap. He didn't look angry now. She thought she saw her own longing reflected there.

Then his phone rang. He pulled it out and glared at the screen, swearing under his breath.

'It's okay. Take the call.' She'd gathered from his calls in the car that today's business was important.

'But *then* we talk. It's important.'

Cora wasn't sure if it was an order or a promise but she nodded. She was unsettled by the way their harmony had fractured, but it seemed Strato wanted to put that behind them too.

She strolled along the paved area, towards a magnificent azure pool fringed with brightly blooming shrubs. A taller shade tree beckoned and she approached it, admiring the setting.

'Damen, you should have asked me first.' From above came a woman's voice. 'I'm happy to invite Strato to dinner. But to have to entertain one of his bimbos today! How could you? I had other plans for this afternoon.'

Cora froze as she realised the woman was talking about *her*. One of Strato's bimbos.

Ice crackled along her veins and into her bones. Her stomach hollowed.

She saw someone move on a balcony above and swiftly turned away, plunging deeper into the garden.

Stupid to feel hurt. Yet the words caught her on the raw, like pressure on a bruise, after what had happened this morning. She was Strato's woman, but only temporarily. That didn't make her a bimbo, but she didn't like to think what it *did* make her.

She wasn't wanted here. She felt her skin crawl, knowing she was an unwanted guest. She'd leave as soon as she could. But first she had to face her reluctant hosts.

Eventually she forced herself to return to the house.

Cora found a couple talking to Strato, a handsome man who smiled and introduced himself as Damen and his petite wife, Stephanie, who looked at her gravely and offered a fleeting smile, her hand on her baby bump.

For ten minutes they chatted. Then Damen invited Strato to his study to discuss business.

Yet Strato lingered, surveying Cora as if he sensed her distress. Instead of following Damen he moved towards her and she had the horrible feeling he'd ask if she was okay. Which she wasn't. Her emotions were too close to the surface. From his frown she guessed he thought it was because of their spat earlier.

Cora pinned on a smile that felt too tight. 'Enjoy your discussions. I'll think of you stuck inside while I'm out in the sunshine.'

Strato stopped before her, his gaze searching. Then he pulled her up into his arms and kissed her soundly on the mouth. Her knees softened as she clutched him needily.

'I'm sorry about earlier,' he murmured against her ear. 'I acted like a fool. Forgive me?'

Stunned, she pulled back and nodded. The apology was unexpected. She'd assumed he was too used to getting his way to see her side.

'We *will* talk later.' He paused. '*Are* you okay?'

'I am.' Now her smile was real. 'Go and do your business.'

Strato kissed her again. Then with a lingering, molten look that singed several vital organs, he followed their host.

Wiping her hands down her capri pants, Cora swallowed. She turned to her hostess. Damen had invited her to spend the afternoon with Stephanie, saying his wife was looking forward to the company, but Cora wouldn't stay where she wasn't wanted. 'Thanks for the invitation to stay, but I—'

'No! Please!' The other woman looked horrified. 'Not before—'

'It's okay, really. I need to—'

'Please!' Stephanie shot to her feet and actually wrung her hands. 'Not before I apologise.' She breathed deep and colour washed her cheeks. 'I was dreadfully rude. What I said on the balcony... I felt about an inch tall when I realised you'd heard me.'

Cora bit her lip, feeling incredibly uncomfortable. 'You weren't to know I was there.'

'It was ungenerous of me. For what it's worth, I see that I was wrong. You're not what I expected.' She shook her head. 'I was upset and the thought of being stuck all afternoon trying to make conversation with a...'

'Bimbo?'

Her face turned grave again and Cora realised it wasn't disapproval making her look that way but embarrassment.

'I'm so sorry. That will teach me to control my temper.' Her mouth wobbled and suddenly Cora felt sorry for her.

'Maybe you should sit down, Stephanie.'

'Steph, please.' She sighed and subsided onto a lounge. 'Please, take a seat.' She waited till Cora did before speaking again, smiling ruefully. 'You sound like Damen. He's always telling me to put my feet up.'

'It's nice that he's concerned for your health.'

'It is, but he's smothering me! He keeps finding reasons to stay at home with me.' Her eyes glowed and her smile grew. 'There are *definite* benefits to having Damen being attentive. But he tries to stop me going out alone. Says I do too much and I should be resting when I'm perfectly healthy and full of energy.'

Cora tried to imagine what it would be like having a loving partner hovering, looking after you that way.

It wouldn't be a man like Strato, since he didn't believe in long-term relationships. She repressed a sigh.

'So I'm afraid when he asked me to stay and keep you company I lashed out. I thought he suggested it to keep me in when I'd planned to go out.'

'You can still go. I have to do some shopping myself.'

'You do?' Steph sat forward. 'Maybe we could go together.' She frowned. 'Although I'll understand if you don't want to. After the dreadful thing I said...'

'Stop it! You're beating yourself up over nothing.' It was true. Hearing the other woman's explanation, Cora knew she'd be foolish to take offence at her earlier words.

Steph's eyes widened and Cora spread her hands. 'Sorry. I have a habit of saying what I think.'

There was a gurgle of laughter. 'So do I. You have no idea how often I have to bite my tongue.'

Cora felt a smile pull her mouth wide. 'I suspect I have some idea.'

'Seriously, feel free to do your shopping alone,' Steph said. 'But if you'd like company, I know my way around Athens, even if I am a foreigner. If you tell me what you're looking for I might have suggestions.'

'Something to wear tonight. I didn't bring any dresses. Just shorts and trousers.'

Steph's eyes gleamed. 'I know a couple of places. I could show you.'

Cora eyed the gorgeous aqua dress the other woman wore. It looked simple but even she knew such simplicity came at a high cost.

'I'd like that. There's just one thing.' She lifted her chin. 'I'm on a budget.' At Steph's steady look she continued. 'I pay for my own clothes and I'm a currently-out-of-work biologist.'

Steph grinned. 'You *really* aren't what I expected. No wonder Strato is smitten.' Her words rocked Cora. Strato? Smitten? 'I think I know the place to find what you're after.' She shot to her feet. 'Shall we go?'

It turned into a lovely day. Steph was funny, friendly and so down-to-earth Cora found herself relaxing. It helped to learn the vast Nicolaides wealth was new to Steph and that she was still coming to grips with it, though she was over-whelmingly happy with her adoring husband.

They went to a boutique in an upmarket area that looked alarmingly expensive, but Steph said there might be bargains to be had. Typically, there wasn't much in the store in Cora's size, but instead of waving them goodbye, the sales-woman asked them to come back in an hour.

They filled in the time lunching and talking non-stop. They were laughing as they returned to find the saleswoman beaming. Two dresses had been procured especially for

Cora and she was ushered straight into the change room where she stopped, staring.

'I'm afraid they're not quite what I had in mind.'

'You don't like them?' The saleswoman's eyebrows shot up. 'The colours are perfect for you.'

Cora shook her head. The bronze silk with its narrow shoulder straps and flirty skirt was so gorgeous she almost feared to touch it. The vibrant red with the plunging neckline and slim fit would turn her into someone sophisticated and sexually confident. Someone who could turn any man's head.

'It's not that. They're beautiful. But the price…' There was no price tag on either but they were obviously out of her range.

The saleswoman smiled. 'Mrs Nicolaides said you need something for her dinner tonight. She's a very good customer so there is a substantial discount. Plus, if anyone were to ask where you got your dress…' She shrugged. 'Word of mouth is better than paid advertising.'

In the end Cora couldn't resist. Both were amazing. She felt glamorous and confident in a way she never did in her usual little black dress. When the saleswoman produced mid-height strappy sandals to match each dress, Cora had a rush of blood to her head, buying both outfits.

Fortunately, with the hotel making a profit, her father had transferred money into her account in lieu of the wages she hadn't drawn in months.

From there she and Steph searched for curtain fabric for Steph's nursery. Then had foot massages and pedicures. After that it was nearly five and the traffic was manic. Steph suggested Cora get ready at her house, instead of trekking to the port and back. It seemed sensible and Cora had time to soak in a scented bath before facing the dinner with a bunch of privileged strangers. Though, if they were like Damen and Steph, it wouldn't be so bad.

And Strato would be there. Her pulse accelerated as she thought of him and that wonderful, mind-melting kiss.

She'd missed him when she took the logical option to return to the Nicolaides house rather than the yacht. She'd rather have bathed with him, even if it meant a rush to get ready because they'd been busy doing more interesting things than dress for dinner.

Cora smoothed her hands down her dress. She'd spent ages getting ready, not wanting to look out of place amongst his friends and acquaintances. But mainly because she wanted Strato to look at her in admiration.

You want him to look at you the way Damen looks at Steph. Not just with sex on his mind but as if you're the one and only woman in the world for him.

Horrified, Cora bit her lip.

She couldn't be so naïve.

Yet as Cora took one final survey of her reflection, she avoided her eyes in the mirror. Because she feared what she might see.

CHAPTER ELEVEN

STRATO PACED THE sitting room. He'd arrived early and Damen and Stephanie weren't down. Nor was Cora and, short of knocking on every door in this vast place, there was no way of finding her.

His discussions with Damen had gone successfully yet he'd found it difficult to concentrate.

That argument on the yacht and Cora's obstinacy over a little thing like buying a dress! He'd been trying to protect her from a potentially uncomfortable position.

The women tonight would be dressed expensively and he didn't want them looking down their noses at Cora. She was worth a dozen of them. He'd dragged her into this world. It was up to him to look after her.

Strato paused mid-stride. Was that why he was agitated? He wanted to look after Cora?

He breathed deep, controlling a ripple of unease.

It was a long, long time since he'd tried to look after anyone. Tried and failed abysmally.

His gut clenched so viciously it was like a hammer blow.

He set his jaw and yanked his thoughts to the present. This was different. He was doing the right thing by his current lover. Despite what the press said, he had at least a thread of decency in him. His mouth quirked cynically.

Cora was proud and independent yet it irked him that she didn't trust him enough to accept his help without argument. She trusted him with her body. Why fuss over a credit card?

Other women would happily spend his money.

Maybe that was why he was restive. He wasn't used to unpredictability. Cora hadn't returned to him at the yacht. When Damen said the women were late and Cora would get ready at the house, Strato had wanted to demand she meet him. Except he didn't have her phone number! He refused to use Damen as a go-between, passing a message via his wife.

Strato had felt powerless and he didn't like it.

A sound made him turn and he lost his train of thought.

'Cora.' His voice was so thick her name sounded unfamiliar.

She stood in the doorway and for the life of him Strato couldn't move. His feet were soldered to the floor, his tongue stuck to the roof of his mouth.

He knew her body intimately. He ran his fingers through her long hair daily and never tired of watching expressions chase across her lovely face. Yet she surprised him.

Her olive skin glowed and her hair was a gleaming curtain over one shoulder. She'd done something that made her eyes smoky and her lips…her parted lips made him want to devour her.

That dark red dress accentuated every dip and curve. The V neck plunged deep but not outrageously. The fabric clung to breasts and hips but flowed freely around her as she shifted her weight on pretty shoes that gave her added height.

His stasis broke and he strode closer. He hungered for her lush body, her mouth…

'Strato.' She sounded breathless.

Good. He'd hate to think he was the only one.

But when he wrapped his arms around her, she put her palm to his chest and glanced over her shoulder.

'Someone's coming.'

'And I should care because…?' He lowered his head.

Her smile sent relief shooting into his bloodstream. He'd missed her. He hadn't liked it that they'd parted without properly resolving their argument.

Though, looking at her ravishing form, he could see she'd clearly accepted his help. That outfit was worth every penny of its no doubt exorbitant cost.

Before he could kiss her she whispered in his ear. 'I'm

nervous enough. I'd rather not meet the others wearing smudged lipstick.'

Strato didn't care what others thought. He didn't care about her lipstick. She should be thankful he didn't pick her up and take her straight back to the yacht. Yet he stopped.

He closed his eyes, breathing deep. Her delicate scent wafted to him and he pressed his mouth to her neck, nibbling and kissing. Cora sighed and arched in his hold, grabbing his biceps as if afraid she'd fall.

Now Strato felt better. Now he held Cora close and felt her eager, yielding body.

Crazy that he'd wondered if she'd had enough of him. That she'd rather browse the shops than be with him.

His plan to bring her to the city where there'd be distractions had been madness. He wanted her completely to himself.

'Strato. What do you think of Cora's dress?' He lifted his head to see Stephanie enter on her husband's arm. She wore a mischievous smile.

Reluctantly he straightened and turned, holding Cora to his side. The silky material beneath his hand slipped across firm, rounded flesh and he swallowed hard.

'Beautiful. Almost as exquisite as the woman wearing it.' He felt Cora start as if he'd surprised her.

How could that be? She knew he was fascinated by her body. So much so that he contemplated negotiating an extension of their time together. Though he suspected little negotiation was necessary. The way she leaned against him suggested she'd be as eager as he.

Belatedly he focused on his hostess. 'I'm lucky to be in the company of two such gorgeous and clever women.'

Stephanie's grin widened and Damen made a smiling comment about not trying to sweet-talk his wife.

If Strato weren't so eager to have Cora to himself he'd have enjoyed an evening in their company. He respected

Damen's business acumen and liked him and his wife. But soon they were joined by more guests.

The evening didn't go as Strato had envisaged.

He'd imagined being in company would lessen his pre-occupation with Cora. The opposite was true. The guests were pleasant, witty and well informed but he wasn't inter-ested. Not when, for the first time, he felt jealous.

It took a while to realise what it was. That sour tang of annoyance, that tightening of his shoulders whenever the art collector across the table looked at Cora as if he'd like to add her to his private gallery. Or the young archaeolo-gist, who shared her passion for scuba diving, kept trying to monopolise her.

Strato told himself it didn't matter. She'd go home with him. Yet he prickled with discomfort when she smiled at another man, or got absorbed in what they had to say.

Possessiveness was unprecedented. Never had he cared enough about any woman to feel jealous.

It was illogical. Yet he couldn't conquer it. Could only weather it and warn off her admirers with glares and bla-tant signals that Cora was *his*.

Strato's consolation was the way she leaned close to him. And the tremor he felt run through her when he stroked her leg beneath the table. And her smiles, that promised so much.

So he endured it. He talked with the other guests, ate his meal, and complimented their hosts on a pleasant evening. But at the first chance after dinner he pushed back his chair.

'I'm afraid you'll have to excuse us. It's time we left.'

'Left?' The art collector frowned. 'But it's early.'

Cora turned, a question in her eyes. He held her gaze, his mind full of the things they'd do when they got back to the yacht. Colour flushed her cheeks.

'We're sailing tonight.'

'Tonight?' That was Damen. 'But you just arrived today.'

'It was a flying visit.'

'But surely—'

Cora moved her chair back. 'You're right. We don't want to miss the tide.' As if that mattered. She turned to their hosts. 'Thank you so much, I've had a lovely evening.'

Strato took her hand and felt the pulse at her wrist jump. Was she wound as tight with need as he?

The goodbyes took too long, but he contained his impatience, again thanking Damen and Stephanie, and watching as the two women said fond farewells. He wasn't sure what he'd expected, bringing Cora here, but she'd been unhappy earlier and it was good to see she'd bonded with the other woman.

Finally, as his patience reached its limit, they were on their way. Strato folded his arms across his chest, took a deep, shuddering breath and released it.

'What's wrong?' Cora looked from the soundproof glass separating them from the driver to Strato, who avoided her gaze. What had happened to the man whose molten stare had promised passion ten minutes ago?

'Nothing.'

'Strato, I can *feel* the tension radiating from you.'

Finally he turned his head, and she saw in the passing streetlights that his face was set.

He breathed deep, his chest and crossed arms rising. 'What's wrong? Apart from the fact I had to sit for hours while every man there ate you up with his eyes?'

Cora's heart leapt in disbelief. Strato was jealous?

She'd wondered if their relationship was morphing into something new, but told herself that was because her feelings for him were changing. She'd never expected his to alter. Strato had made it clear, and reiterated often, that he didn't want anything long term.

'I wasn't attracted to any of them.' There was no need to tell him that. Yet it felt important to make that clear. 'I enjoyed the conversation and the interesting company but the only man I want to spend the night with is you.'

'I'm glad to hear it.'

He took another breath, yet kept his arms folded.

Cora frowned. '*You* were the one I let touch me under the table.' She'd done some touching too, her hand straying to the rock-hard muscle of his thigh. She'd revelled in his twitch of response. 'It's ridiculous to get grumpy about men looking at me.'

She refused to apologise for having a good time. Even if the best part had been seeing Strato's stunned reaction to her appearance. That had given her confidence, and a thrill, feeling her feminine power so blatantly.

'There's no need to sit with your arms crossed and your jaw clenched as if I've done something wrong.'

'You think that's what I'm doing?'

'What else? You're keeping your distance.'

She'd grown accustomed to his touch and missed it now, especially after the way he'd looked at her earlier.

Abruptly he laughed, the husky sound curling around her in the darkness. 'I'm sitting like this, *Coritsa*, because I'm trying, very hard, to resist ravishing you in the back seat of this limo.'

Cora's eyes widened and heat speared deep into her pelvis. 'Oh!'

'Yes, oh. I might have a reputation as a profligate but I refuse to strip that delectable dress off you in full view of our driver or anyone on the street.'

Cora opened her mouth to say he could ravish her without stripping her naked, then thought better of it.

'I like that you're tempted, but I think I'd rather wait till we have privacy.'

'My thoughts exactly.' His voice dropped to a growling rumble that did devastating things to her.

No man had affected her as profoundly or as easily as

Strato. Not even the man she'd once believed herself falling in love with.

The difference between him and Strato, whose muscles bunched as he fought not to touch her, couldn't be greater. How had she thought them similar?

On impulse, she wanted to tell Strato how much that meant. He'd done so much for her. Not just saving her father's hotel. Or giving her the holiday of a lifetime, or even the most wonderful sexual pleasure. He'd helped heal wounds that had festered too long. He'd given her back her confidence as a woman, her sense of her own power, and, most surprisingly, her ability to trust.

She'd been so busy cutting herself off from her past, she hadn't given herself permission to process what had happened or move on from it. Instead she'd pushed it into a locked box labelled 'Adrian' and tried not to think of it.

Cora swivelled on the seat to look directly at Strato. 'There's something I like even more than your passion.' She paused, feeling as if she crossed a bridge with this confession, but feeling she owed it. 'That's your honesty.'

'Because I admit I want to have wild, unrestrained sex with you in the back of a moving vehicle?' His voice was harsh as if he really suffered from the effort of holding back. In the gloom she caught the glint of his eyes on her.

'That's part of it.' She gathered her thoughts. 'From the start I knew where I stood with you. You never try to hide things I might dislike, or dress things up in fancy words.' She paused, realising she still hadn't got to the nub of it. 'You respect me. That first day on the beach you realised I might feel threatened and you deliberately set out to ease my fears and put limits on your behaviour. Some men wouldn't have done that.'

Some men would have tried to force her into acquiescence.

'It's a small enough thing. I don't like people who say

one thing in public and do another in private.' His voice sounded grim, as if she'd touched a nerve.

'Exactly. There are too many who lie to get what they want. I admire that you don't, Strato.'

Even if increasingly she wanted more than he offered.

She yearned to understand him. Would he one day trust her enough to share his feelings and his past?

'Thank you, *Coritsa*.' He unfolded his arms. In the darkness his gaze held hers. 'Are you going to tell me about the person you're comparing me to?'

'How do you know there was someone—?'

'You speak so passionately. From experience. Someone hurt you.'

She'd never spoken about it, never wanted to. But suddenly she wanted to share. To feel less alone. Maybe that would complete the healing Strato had unwittingly begun. Perhaps it might encourage him to share too.

'His name was Adrian and I worked on his father's yacht in the Caribbean between research positions.'

'Let me guess.' Strato's voice hardened. 'He seduced you.'

Cora nodded. 'He was handsome, rich and privileged, used to getting whatever he wanted. You reminded me of him that first day.'

'I suspect that's not a compliment.'

She shrugged. 'He was also attentive, polite and friendly. I was wary, though. We came from separate worlds and I refused to fall for his charm.'

'Which increased his determination to have you.'

'I didn't realise it at first. I thought his persistence and patience meant he cared. I was naïve.'

'What happened?' Cora couldn't pinpoint the change in Strato's tone except she wondered if he spoke through gritted teeth.

'We had an affair. I thought it was more. I was falling for him and thought he felt the same.' She felt anger and something like shame at being so gullible. 'It wasn't till his friend came on board that I realised that for him I was just a convenient body. A notch on his bedpost.'

A shudder scraped her spine as she remembered over-hearing Adrian talking to Brad about her. Not as his girl-friend but in the crudest terms about her body. Comparing her to other women he'd had. She'd felt like an animal at market, appraised by potential buyers.

'He offered me to his friend as if I were...'

A large hand covered hers, squeezing hard. 'I get the picture.'

Cora's heart hammered but she was determined to finish. She should have told someone long ago. She didn't want sympathy, but finally sharing this would ease the hurt she'd felt so long.

'When I refused, Adrian was annoyed, as if I'd insulted him or let him down. Later, after he'd given the rest of the crew the night off to go ashore, he came to me full of apolo-gies, saying he hadn't meant to insult me. He said he knew I'd like Brad once I knew him better and suggested a three-some *to break the ice*!' She almost gagged on the words. 'He wasn't happy when I refused.'

'Did he hurt you?' No mistaking Strato's tone now. He was furious, yet his hands grasping both of hers were gen-tle. 'Tell me his name and I'll deal with him.'

'No need.' Though remembering Adrian's ugly look and his friend Brad's excited leer, she knew she'd been lucky to get away. Adrian wasn't used to being denied and the pair had cornered her. 'One of the crew was still aboard, heard the argument and came to help me. I left straight away.'

'You were all right?'

'I was fine.' She'd been shaken and sick with disgust but okay. Strange that *she'd* been the one to feel shamed by what had happened.

'It's a wonder you even spoke to me that first day. If you thought me like him.' Strato's voice was tight.

Cora shook her head. 'My brain was trying to warn me but the truth was...'

'Yes?' He leaned nearer.

'I was fascinated.' She'd never known such a profound or instantaneous reaction to any man. 'Logic told me to be careful but there was something about you I couldn't resist.'

Strato threaded his fingers through hers. 'That's how I felt. Fascinated. Even after you sent me packing I spent weeks thinking about you.' His voice dropped to a low note that scoured her soul. 'I couldn't get you out of my head. It was a new experience.'

Her breathing shallowed. She wanted to ask if it still felt unique to him. Because her feelings for Strato were unprecedented. She knew with a certainty she couldn't explain that for her this was serious.

'Ah, here we are.'

Disappointment mingled with relief filtered through her. No time now to ask about his feelings, but that meant he wouldn't disappoint her by saying his emotions weren't involved and for him this was still purely sexual.

It didn't feel as if it was simply lust between them as he ushered her aboard, his arm protectively around her. Nor when he led her by the hand to his bed and stood, staring down at her with gleaming eyes, as if seeing right into her heart.

Lust was there in the faint tremor of his hands as he unzipped her and in the harsh angle of his jaw. But so was tenderness and respect as he brushed his lips slowly across her bare shoulders, taking his time to caress her till she shivered with eagerness. In the way he slowly skimmed the crimson satin off her body then stood with something like wonder in his eyes as he took her in. As if she weren't an ordinary woman but some goddess who'd struck him dumb.

There was delicacy in the way he knelt to undo her sandals, and in the skimming, tantalising, delicious kisses he imprinted on her calves, knees and thighs.

There was even something like reverence in Strato's sigh as he hooked his thumbs into her thong and slid it down her trembling body.

And when he scooped her up in his arms, his eyes holding hers, Cora felt her heart swell against her ribs as if her bones had shrunk, or the feelings she harboured grew too big to hold in.

Soon she was naked on the bed and Strato made short work of his dinner suit. Even shorter work of protection. Still he didn't rush, but prowled up her body, nuzzling, kissing, stroking, till she was gasping for breath and pleading.

Strato wouldn't be hurried. But this wasn't like other times when she'd seen a teasing gleam in his eyes. Now his expression was intent, each caress considered and careful.

Was it crazy to think he was *showing* her his feelings though no words passed his lips? That those feelings were deeper than light-hearted flirtation?

When, finally, he settled between her thighs, propped on his elbows so she didn't take his full weight, his expression was grave. Cora saw furrows on his forehead and deep grooves bracket his gorgeous mouth and felt a moment of unspoken communion when she could swear their pulses beat as one.

Then his mouth broke into a slow smile that undid the last, fragile thread of her defences.

Cora smiled back.

Nothing in her life had been as good as this, here, now, with Strato. He undid her. Yet, as their bodies merged in one slow, sure stroke, she didn't feel undone but complete and stronger than she'd ever been in her life.

Together they made a whole that surpassed everything.

Cora planted a hand on his thrumming heart and lifted her other hand to his cheek, losing her breath as he turned his face into her touch and kissed her palm.

Tenderness welled along with anticipation.

She'd fallen for Strato. So deeply, so completely it put

what she'd felt for Adrian in stark perspective. He'd flattered and tempted her, playing on her natural curiosity and burgeoning sexuality. But he'd only hurt her pride, not anything more significant.

Strato's fluid, powerful movements had her clinging, lifting her body into his rhythm and holding tight, eager not just for bliss but also for these moments of profound connection that felt as if they changed her for ever.

Did they change him too?

No time to think about it as he gathered her closer, his body leading hers deeper into pleasure, his eyes holding a promise she couldn't look away from.

'Coritsa.' His voice, velvet-wrapped gravel, was a caress in itself. The heated glow of his gaze as it held hers felt portentous.

'Strato, I…'

Suddenly it was upon them. The lightning bolt that turned the world iridescent. The shimmering wave upon wave upon wave of completion so exquisite it stole her voice. And still Strato held her eyes. Till finally, on one last explosive shudder, Cora tumbled into darkness.

As she sank into oblivion the words she hadn't said aloud echoed in her head.

Strato, I love you.

Her world had changed for ever.

CHAPTER TWELVE

DAYS LATER THEY were on the island of Aegina and Cora couldn't stop smiling.

Since leaving Athens things between her and Strato felt different. He was as attentive and passionate, as charming and as much fun. But there was an unspoken undercurrent that fed her excitement.

She didn't try to label it, for it had been scary enough, naming her feelings for him. She didn't want to con herself into believing he felt more than he did, or build too much upon his various kindnesses. Or the fact he'd asked her to stay past the agreed month.

It had been that night when they'd left Athens. Cora was sprawled, boneless, across Strato's big frame, his heart beating beneath her ear, when he'd asked her to stay. Not for a set time, but simply to stay.

Eagerness had vied with practicalities, like worries over her stalled career and the need to see her father, but her biggest concern was of digging herself deeper into an emotional hole.

What if Strato never returned her feelings?

Yet Cora hadn't been able to say no. She knew this man, enigmatic as he could be, was the man for her.

Add to that her father was well and had help at the hotel. Strato had also promised to sail back so she could check on her father in person instead of via her regular calls.

As for her career as a marine biologist, that was harder. She'd left work to help her father and there weren't many other positions around. She should be looking but for now she couldn't think past the present and Strato.

It was a shock to realise they'd been together just over a month.

A month during which she'd had no period.

They stood before the beautiful Temple of Aphaia, high on a hill overlooking the Aegean Sea, the scent of pines and sea salt wafting on the breeze. Strato was beside her, strong and solid. Just as well, for she rocked back on her heels as realisation hit.

Frantically she recalculated the weeks, flicking through dates in her head, and with each recalculation shock edged further along her bones, like the shadow of a cloud creeping across the sun.

Her periods were clockwork-regular.

Which meant…

'Cora, are you okay?'

Sea-green eyes met hers and a warm hand gripped her arm. The concern she saw in Strato's expression calmed her.

'Yes, absolutely fine.'

There was no need to panic.

This had been the most amazing, unusual month of her life. Would it be so surprising if her body didn't follow its usual rhythms? She didn't feel different physically.

And even if there *was* a reason for her delayed period, she and Strato weren't passing strangers. They'd moved on from their original insta-lust. Pregnancy might even be the impetus for acknowledging a deeper relationship.

Yet, thinking the word *pregnancy* sent a quiver of shock through her.

She'd assumed that when she had a child she'd be in a secure relationship like her parents had shared.

But she was getting ahead of herself. First she had to find out if there was a child.

Would the small town where they'd come ashore sell pregnancy test kits? Cora took a slow breath, trying to calm her racing thoughts. She'd have to get to a bigger town and find out if she was pregnant.

Then, well, she'd think about what came next if it happened.

* * *

Strato stood on his private deck, a cold beer in one hand. Where was Cora? Usually she'd joined him on deck by now. The sun was low in the sky.

He felt restless because, after their early morning sight-seeing trip to the temple, he'd devoted himself to work while Cora took a hired car to the other side of the island. Usually they explored together. This was the first time they'd been separated for any length of time, apart from that afternoon in Athens.

Strange to think he'd become so accustomed to her company that he noticed an absence of a few hours. He sometimes worked alone in his study and that didn't bother him.

Because always she'd been nearby. Accessible.

His glass stopped halfway to his mouth then lowered. Suddenly the taste in his mouth wasn't the tang of beer but something bitter and dank.

He wasn't becoming obsessive about her, was he? Needing to know where she was every moment? Needing to control her movements?

His belly clenched as if in response to an invisible blow. His stomach curdled.

Strato waited for logic to reassure him. Obsession was impossible. It had to be. Because he, of all people, knew how dangerous it was. His skin prickled and searing pain shot through his shoulder, even though the scar tissue there was old.

Again he swallowed.

Could such a fatal flaw run in families? He'd told himself it couldn't, not if you did everything you could to guard against it. And Strato had done everything to prevent that happening.

Still he frowned. It was true his relationship with Cora had altered. She was no longer a casual sexual partner.

As if! From the first he'd felt anything but casual about her.

But he'd been sure that though she'd become a friend as

much as a lover, she only occupied a specific part in his life. Strato had honed the ability to compartmentalise his world.

Yet today he'd found himself wondering what she was doing. Whether he wouldn't rather be with her. Regretting their time apart.

Movement caught his eye. It was Cora, emerging on deck. He turned fully and was instantly swamped by his response to her.

Good old sexual desire. Admiration. Joy.

Surely they were all positives? Surely that negated the secret fear that his feelings verged on something dark?

'You look fabulous.' His voice was gruff with appreciation. Instead of her usual casual clothes she wore a bronze-coloured dress, gleaming like silk. Its narrow straps left her shoulders bare and its cut followed her body, cinching in around her narrow waist before spilling gracefully over her hips and thighs.

Beyond her stretched the green-blue sea and above it, at the top of the hill overlooking the coast, the white marble columns of the ruined temple.

The setting suited her. He'd first imagined her as a sea nymph, so much more than an ordinary mortal woman. Seeing her against that backdrop reinforced that feeling.

Cora was special.

Want rose in him, the familiar tide of desire, but something extra too. Something warm and tender.

Strato refused to analyse it. Instead he put his glass down and approached her, taking her hands in his. 'I approve. You bought it today?'

She shook her head and for the first time in weeks he couldn't read her expression. 'I got it in Athens.'

She'd spent his money well.

'And you waited till now to wear it?' He bent his head and kissed her, slowly and thoroughly, only drawing back when he realised he was on the verge of sweeping her into his arms and straight to bed.

He was determined to prove he could control his feelings around Cora.

She shrugged and he realised that, despite the way she'd melted into his kiss, the movement looked stiff.

'Have you spoken to your father today? Is all okay at the hotel?'

'Yes and yes. Both are thriving. Thank you, Strato.' Her expression eased. Maybe he'd imagined tension because he'd been distracted by his own troubling thoughts.

'Good. Now, what would you like to drink?'

'Sparkling water, thanks.'

He nodded and made himself release her, knowing that he'd much prefer to keep touching her. Again that tiny quiver of concern flickered through him.

Strange that the silence as he went to the bar and got her drink felt heavy. Usually he and Cora chatted easily but didn't feel the need to fill every moment with talk. He turned, her glass in his hand, and saw he hadn't imagined it. Something was wrong. Cora bit the corner of her mouth and her shoulders were hunched.

'What is it, *Coritsa*? Is something wrong?' He couldn't imagine what. Things were good between them.

Yet to his dismay she nodded. 'Not wrong exactly but…' She drew a deep breath that made her breasts rise high. 'We need to talk. Maybe we should sit down.'

Perhaps it was his unresolved tension from earlier, or a sixth sense for trouble, but Strato felt his own shoulders tighten. 'Don't prevaricate. Just tell me.'

She swallowed and finally nodded, her eyes not leaving his. 'I'm pregnant.'

There was a crashing sound but Strato didn't really register it. He was too busy watching the woman before him looking so earnest as her words, her unbelievable words, echoed in his brain.

Something inside him plummeted.

Had he really thought she was different?

Had he really believed in the happiness he'd found with her?

She'd prepared carefully for this moment, he realised, looking again at that slinky, seductive dress that was so different from her usual outfits. It turned her into a different woman. More like the others who'd tried over the years to catch him.

Had the woman who'd snared his interest on that tiny island, the fascinating, forthright woman who cared more about protecting sea turtle nesting sites than about jewels and his vast fortune, been an illusion? Had their chance meeting and her initial rejection been part of a deliberate ploy, to attract then hook him?

Pain stabbed his chest as his lungs failed.

How many times had a woman stood before him, claiming to carry his child?

Strato shut his eyes because even now the sight of Cora, gorgeous and tempting, messed with his head. As if what she said could be possible.

That only made things worse because the idea of him fathering a child was the stuff of nightmares. Clammy heat crept across his skin and nausea welled.

He snapped his eyes open.

At least he was spared that horror. He'd made sure there'd be no children. He was the last of his family.

But that meant Cora was lying. Like those others who'd tried to snare him in marriage.

He hauled in a rough breath.

He didn't want to believe it. *Not Cora.*

But Strato knew about betrayal. He knew it so well it was inked onto his very bones, etched on his skin.

He understood you could rely on no one but yourself.

How had he forgotten the lesson that shaped his life?

Yet watching Cora, as all the good things he'd experienced with her crumbled into dust, felt like a blow from which he'd never recover.

Because he'd let her get under his skin. Let himself be tempted into feeling too much.

It was his fault as much as hers.

Cora watched the glass drop to the deck and shatter but Strato didn't seem to notice.

The concern in his eyes died, replaced by the shock she'd expected and something else. It looked like pain.

She frowned, heart hammering, trying to gauge his response. It couldn't be pain. That made no sense.

Then he shut his eyes, breathing deep, nostrils flaring and hands curling at his sides. He looked like a man struggling with strong emotion.

Cora wanted to go to him, touch him, *connect* with him. But she stood rooted to the spot. Something about the starkness of his features and the lines ploughing his forehead held her back.

Then he was staring at her again, eyes narrowed and hard as chips of stone.

Not a delighted father-to-be, then.

'You're the third.' His voice was barely recognisable. Raw and rough and once more she sensed pain. Yet his eyes were frigid with accusation.

'Third what?'

His mouth stretched wide in a humourless smile that made her heart twist.

'Third woman to tell me she's having my child.'

'You've already got children?' Her hand went to her throat in shock. It was only when his gaze lowered that she realised her other hand had gone instinctively to her stomach, as if comforting the new life deep inside.

Even now, hours after confirming her pregnancy, Cora reeled from the revelation. It didn't seem real. Her body felt the same as ever.

Yet, in the short space of time since she'd learned about the baby, it seemed she'd acquired protective, maternal instincts. Instincts that urged her to retreat from this big man.

Except she knew Strato. Knew he'd never hurt her or their baby.

Nevertheless, his tight smile perturbed her. She'd never seen him like this.

'No, I don't have kids. I told you, I'll never have a family.'

Cora waited for an explanation but none came. Had the babies died? Horror filled her. 'What happened?'

'Nothing. The women left when I wouldn't marry them.'

She shook her head. 'The babies! What happened to the babies?' She felt as if she were underwater, sounds blurred and distant, struggling to make herself understood.

'There were no babies.' He flicked a glance at her abdomen once more then back to her face. 'One woman wasn't even pregnant. The other was, but to someone else.' His lips drew back in something like a snarl. 'They made a mistake thinking they could lie their way into a share of my fortune.'

Shock slammed into her. 'You think I'm lying? You think I invented this?'

After what they'd shared, not only their bodies but the growing emotional intimacy, Cora felt sick at his implication.

'I *know* you're lying.' Before she could protest he went on, his expression grim. 'I should have known. Believe it or not, I thought you different.' He shook his head and she almost believed she saw sorrow on his face.

'Listen, Strato, I know this is a shock. I was stunned too when I found out today.' Cora told herself it wasn't surprising a man who'd faced false paternity claims should react badly, though something within her shrank at his forbidding expression.

'You only found out today?' He shoved his hands into his trouser pockets. 'How convenient that you happened to have a sexy new dress to wear while you announced the news.'

His tone dripped sarcasm. 'What did you expect? That I'd be so overcome by lust that I wouldn't care you're lying? That I didn't mean it when I said I'd never have a family?'

The shivers rippling across her flesh became shudders and she folded her arms, partly for warmth and partly in anger at his hurtful accusations.

'I don't know what I expected. But it wasn't this... viciousness.'

Strato folded his arms too. On him the gesture didn't look defensive but aggressive, showcasing the formidable strength in his arms and upper body. 'Lady, you have no idea if you think *this* is vicious. Be thankful you don't.'

Her chin hiked higher. 'I have no wish to see it. This is bad enough.' She swallowed hard. 'I understand you've had bad experiences but I'm not lying, Strato. When have I ever lied to you?'

For a moment she wondered if she might have got through to him. Until he spoke.

'That's one of the things I admired about you, Cora. That you were honest. Or appeared to be. But I *know* this is a lie because I can't have children.'

'Sorry?'

'I had a vasectomy. I'll never have children.'

Cora stared, trying to take this in. Her sense of unreality, which had begun with the news of the pregnancy, then crested when Strato turned into a man she didn't know, battered at her.

'But I'm pregnant. The baby is yours.' He said nothing, merely lifted one eyebrow haughtily. 'You used condoms against pregnancy.'

'No, I used them because I've had multiple partners. It's a common-sense health precaution.'

Cora reeled. That put her in her place. One of his multiple partners. Her skin crawled. She'd actually begun to believe they shared something special!

Then the implications sank in. He'd had a vasectomy

and used condoms and *still* she'd got pregnant? What were the chances?

For a second she was tempted to think maybe he was right and there was a mistake. Except she'd bought two test kits, two different brands, and each time got the same result. Plus there was that time weeks ago when the condom broke.

'That's silenced you, hasn't it?' Strato's voice was flinty, yet she imagined she heard something more than anger there. She peered up into his eyes, but could see no softening.

It was like looking into the face of a stranger, a stern, disapproving stranger.

Incredible how much that hurt. So much that she felt it as a searing physical pain right through her middle. The change in him, from caring, fun, attentive lover to brooding enemy was too much to take in.

'No, Strato, it hasn't silenced me, because I'm telling the truth.' She gulped a deep breath and focused on keeping her voice even. 'I bought a couple of pregnancy kits today and took multiple tests to be sure. Because, believe it or not, pregnancy wasn't in my plans. At least not yet. I can show you the results.'

Still he said nothing, just looked down that straight nose at her as if he were a judge and she a criminal.

She'd been right to be nervous about breaking the news. So nervous she'd taken refuge in fancy clothes, hoping to boost her confidence. From his expression it wouldn't matter what she said, Strato wouldn't believe her.

She was torn between outrage and sorrow. It was obvious she'd deluded herself, thinking he might return her feelings.

'I haven't been with a man in years.' Not since Adrian, who'd hurt her so badly. 'Until you.'

Her eyes flickered shut for a second. The pain Adrian had inflicted was nothing to the damage Strato was doing now.

Oh, she could sure pick men! Her lips pulled back in a

grimace. First Adrian and now another arrogant rich man, who, it seemed, didn't care for her either.

Why, oh, why hadn't she followed her instinct and refused Strato?

Because from the start he fascinated you. Because with him you felt like a stronger, better, happier version of yourself. Not the cautious, hemmed-in person you became after Adrian.

Much good that had done her!

'It's no good, Cora. Whatever so-called proof you have, I know it will be manufactured. It won't stand up to scrutiny.'

'But you can't brush it off like that! Not after what we've shared. This is a *baby*, not a con! You're going to be a father.'

She'd hoped to crack that icy control and she succeeded. But not in the way she hoped. Strato didn't soften. He didn't offer to submit to a paternity test. Instead that cold stare turned to flashing fire and a look that scorched her to the soles of her feet.

'If you think to appeal to my emotions, you've misstepped, Cora. I can't think of anything that horrifies me more than the idea of fathering a child.'

Her throat constricted, making it difficult to swallow. There was no trace now of the charismatic man she'd fallen in love with. No tenderness. Only harsh, horrible words and a terrible blankness in his eyes.

'Now get out of my sight. I'll arrange for you to leave in the morning.'

CHAPTER THIRTEEN

CORA DIDN'T WAIT till the morning. Strato emerged next day, red-eyed from too much brandy and lack of sleep, to be told she'd gone ashore the previous night.

Something grabbed at his vitals, twisting till pain screamed through him.

He told himself he was angry she'd run off in the night. Yet beneath the multiple layers of fury at her for lying, at himself for falling for those lies, and anguish at the terrible memories she'd stirred, was fear.

Fear that something bad might happen to her.

Logic said that she'd easily find accommodation in the little coastal town. Of course she was safe. This wasn't a dangerous area and she was a capable woman. She was probably already crossing the island to catch the Athens ferry.

Yet anxiety lingered. She was alone and upset.

As if her story were true! Strato reminded himself Cora had spun a deceitful tale. Yet she'd been almost convincing with that stark look of dismay and dawning hurt.

He'd almost fallen for her game. Though clearly her story was impossible.

Strato hated being played for a sucker, especially as, for the first time he could recall, he'd come to like having a woman around. Cora wasn't precisely restful, but with her he felt…

He ground his teeth at the way his thoughts kept straying to the good times they'd had. How could that be when those were obviously manufactured like her tale about a child?

That was what really undid him. He'd been lied to so often by scheming women, but for a second when she broke her news he'd actually imagined it might be real. Imagined he might be on the brink of fatherhood.

Him, a father. Carrying the legacy of his father before him.

Horror hurled him back in time to the atrocity he'd made it his life's work to forget.

You'll never forget, Doukas. The best you can do is pretend it never happened.

It had worked for twenty-five years.

Yet the one time he'd shut his eyes last night, nightmares of the past had taken him straight back to hell.

He spun around. He needed another drink. Something to deaden the hurt Cora had caused and stop the traumatic memories she'd unleashed.

Except how could he hide with the memory of Cora standing before him with those earnest, soulful eyes, telling him they were going to have a child?

Even so, he called Manoli to him and told him to go ashore and check that Cora had spent the night at one of the local hotels.

'And if she didn't?' His assistant's expression was stiff, a reminder that he, too, had liked Cora. From his withering stare Strato knew he blamed his boss for her sudden disappearance.

The downside of having an employee who was so close, as close as Strato got to a friend, was that he wasn't afraid to share his opinions.

Now he thought about it, all the staff had liked her.

'Then use your initiative, damn it! I need to know she's safely on her way home.' Even if he had no intention of seeing her again.

Slowly Manoli nodded. 'And shall I give her a message if I find her…sir?'

The fake obsequiousness of that *sir* was a deliberate provocation from a man who'd used his first name for years.

'Don't push it, Manoli.' Strato growled and headed for the bar. 'I had my reasons for sending her away.'

Excellent reasons.

Yet that didn't make him feel better. Even when Manoli reported that Cora had spent the night in a budget hotel then caught the first bus to the other side of the island to catch the Athens ferry, Strato couldn't settle.

So, on the spur of the moment they sailed to Alexandria. Though once there Strato found he didn't feel in the mood for Egypt's attractions. Instead they went to Monte Carlo. It was only when they arrived that he recalled he was bored with the place. Spain was next but Strato couldn't find the distraction he sought.

Work didn't fulfil him. He found himself constantly distracted, even in high-level negotiations, till he forced himself to step back and delegate more, rather than undo the good work of others with rash decisions.

He was on the point of flying to Rarotonga, simply for a change of scenery, when he realised what he was doing.

Running away.

Looking for something to fill the void in his life left by Cora. Not that he was searching for another woman. Hell, no! But the ennui that had dogged him before he met her was back full force. The listless sense of pointlessness. Nothing, not even business, interested him. He couldn't settle to anything.

Because even now you can't quite believe she's like the rest, can you, Doukas?

He gritted his teeth and took a long swallow of iced water, having decided to stop drinking alcohol when that did nothing to ease his mind or his mood.

Music reached him across the marina. Someone was having a party on one of the nearby superyachts. But the sound of laughter didn't entice him.

He frowned into the twilight, trying to remember which port this was. There'd been so many in the last few weeks.

It didn't matter. What mattered was that niggling sense of something left undone.

Strato prided himself on following his instincts. When he got the feeling something wasn't right about a deal he delved deeper and always discovered a sound reason for that warning burr across his nape.

He felt it now but it had nothing to do with the company. It had to do with Cora.

He didn't understand it. It was impossible that he'd got her pregnant. There was no way, no way at all. Not after a vasectomy and then condoms…the idea was laughable.

Yet that sixth sense bristled the hairs across his nape and all the way down his arms.

Finally Strato grabbed his phone. It took a while to get the person he wanted. It was out of business hours but his name made most things possible. Finally he put his question.

It was as he'd thought. Impossible that he'd impregnated Cora.

Well, the doctor amended, *almost* impossible. There were occasional, rare cases…

Strato's mind blanked, the voice at the other end of the line blurring.

The music from across the marina became a buzz of white noise. The lights dimmed. There was a sound in Strato's ears, a hammering that grew faster and louder, till he realised he'd forgotten to breathe and dragged a desperate breath into aching lungs. Immediately the thump of his pulse eased enough for him to hear the medico's words.

'So you're saying…' Strato found his voice '…that it's extremely unlikely but you can't rule out the possibility.'

'Exactly.'

Strato braced himself against the deck's railing with a trembling hand as regret washed through him. Regret at how he'd treated Cora.

And fear. Fear that the one thing he'd been determined to avoid might actually come to pass.

* * *

Cora was helping Doris tidy the kitchen after evening service when one of the part-time waitresses came in from the now-empty restaurant.

'There's someone to see you, Cora.' Her breathless voice made Cora look up from the plates she was stacking.

'Who is it?' Clearly someone interesting, given the gleam in her dark eyes.

'A man. And what a man.' She shook her hand as if it burned. 'A tall, handsome stranger. And that sexy voice!' She gave a little shiver.

Cora barely noticed because she was too busy staring at the empty doorway behind the woman, heart in mouth as she imagined who could have caused such a reaction.

The answer was obvious. Strato.

But that was impossible. He'd washed his hands of her. He'd all but tossed her off his yacht, ordering her out of his sight.

The memory stirred indignation as well as hurt. Cora's shoulders tightened and her hands clenched. He might be rich but he had no right to treat her that way.

For the first time in her pregnancy she felt nauseous.

Could it be Strato? Who else could cause such a stir?

'Well…' Doris watched her from shrewd eyes '…aren't you going to go and see who it is?'

Cora was tempted to say no, she wasn't.

She didn't want to talk to Strato ever again.

Who are you kidding? You might be fuming with anger, but you've got unfinished business with him. Despite everything, you want to see him, don't you?

Actually, she wanted to punch him and rant at him for what he'd done but part of her actually missed him. It had been almost impossible to settle in the weeks since she'd left him. She'd been so distracted she knew that only the fact the hotel was frantically busy had saved her from her father noticing. But Doris clearly sensed something was wrong.

'Of course. Are you okay to finish up?' She untied her apron and tossed it into the laundry basket.

'Sure. We're almost done. Don't you want to tidy your hair?'

She did. She'd like to face this man looking poised and elegant, but she refused to let him think she'd put in a special effort for his sake. So she shook her head, wished the others goodnight and marched out of the kitchen and into the restaurant. It was empty so she went out onto the terrace.

Most of the lights were off, leaving the illumination from a single rope of fairy lights strung along the edge of the vine-laden trellis. In the distance the lights of the village spilled across the bay's still waters and out at the point she picked out a large vessel.

'Hello, Cora.'

It was him!

She swallowed, hating the way her throat constricted with emotion.

Cora turned and there he was, tall and still, hands thrust in his trouser pockets. Her gaze tracked his wide shoulders and firm chin. His mouth set hard and tight, the frown furrowing his brow.

If she'd had any thought that he was happy to be here she could forget it. He looked anything but.

Cora folded her arms. 'Why are you here?' Her tone was sharp. Good, she didn't want him realising how conflicted she felt.

'To talk. To apologise.'

Her heart skipped a beat, yet nothing in his voice indicated he wanted to be here. So much for her fantasy of him begging her forgiveness because he realised how much she meant to him.

She drew herself up sharply. 'Not here.' With the hotel full, they could be overheard by anyone in the floors above. Not looking at him, she strode across the terrace, out past the tamarisks towards the water.

Strato fell into step beside her as she followed the path away from the harbour, towards the deserted promontory, bright moonlight illuminating the way. Cora tried not to notice how familiar it felt, walking beside him, his tantalising scent teasing her.

'You left your visit very late. I'm about to go to bed.' Instantly she regretted the words, thinking of all those evenings that had ended with them together in bed, lost to everything but the delight they'd shared. How she'd felt cherished.

Until he'd brutally rejected her, calling her a liar and worse.

'I just arrived and came straight to see you.'

'If you expect me to be impressed, I'm not.' She drew a breath, trying to slow her racing heartbeat. 'Just say what you came to say.'

Silence followed her words.

Had he expected a warmer welcome?

Her mouth twisted as she thought of her anguish because the man she'd fallen in love with despised her. He hadn't even considered the possibility she told the truth.

'I'm sorry, Cora. I shouldn't have ordered you off the yacht like that.'

To her amazement, Strato sounded as if he really meant it. As if, like she, he was stressed and worried.

Her step faltered and she forced herself to look at the sea rather than at him. They'd stopped near a stand of dark trees that hid them from the hotel. All was silent except for the soft shush of the water and, floating across the bay, the faint sound of music.

'Really? You left it a long time to apologise.'

The first week she'd been on tenterhooks, hoping he'd contact her. But he'd meant every cutting word about her lying and trying to snare him.

As if anyone could snare this man who didn't trust!

'I was utterly convinced I couldn't father a child.'

'What changed?'

In her peripheral vision she saw him raise his arm to rub the back of his neck. 'I got medical advice. It's rare but occasionally a vasectomy isn't successful.'

He paused and she said nothing. After all, she already knew he'd fathered her child. She'd had weeks to convince herself it was as well he wanted nothing to do with her baby. She'd bring it up herself, here on her island, where it would be loved and cared for.

'And?'

'And I had a check-up. It turns out that mine is one of those rare cases.' His tone was so sombre it raised the hair on her arms and across her neck. 'There's an outside chance I could father a child.'

Cora felt like shouting it wasn't a chance. It was a reality. One she lived with every day, as she fought to acclimatise to the fact she was pregnant. Early next year she'd be a mother.

She'd alternated between fear and excitement. She knew nothing about babies and this was going to affect her plans to return to marine biology. But her father and Doris would stand by her when she told them. Her child would have a stable, loving home, even without its father on the scene.

'You don't say anything.'

She swung around. 'What do you want me to say, Strato? You're not telling me anything I don't know. *I'm* the one whose whole life has changed because I'm carrying *your* child.' Her index finger drilled hard against his breastbone.

Before she could pull back he covered her hand with his. Cora was shocked at how warm and familiar it felt. Shocked at how something in her eased at his touch. How much she wanted from him, even now.

The realisation made her yank her hand free and step back. This man destroyed her in so many ways.

Pain engulfed her. She'd fallen for Strato, believing him to be something he wasn't. Which confirmed her appalling taste in men. Twice she'd made a terrible mistake, gulled into believing someone selfish and over-privileged might care about her.

She tilted her chin to meet his stare. 'You've said you're sorry. Now what?' His apology didn't change anything fundamental. 'I notice you admit you *could* be the father, not that you are.'

Strato lifted his shoulders. 'There's a big difference between the two.'

Cora's hands jammed on her hips. 'You really are some piece of work, Strato. You come all this way and admit you overreacted but still you don't believe me.' She dragged in a rough breath, made difficult by the way her lungs cramped, pain shooting behind her ribs. 'It's as if you *want* to believe I'm lying.'

To her surprise, he shifted, his gaze leaving hers.

She was right! He'd prefer to believe she was a gold-digger. The realisation loosened her knees and she had to concentrate on staying upright.

'The one thing in this world that I want to avoid is becoming a father.' His deep voice was rough with what sounded like genuine emotion.

Why was that so important to him? She'd pondered that from every angle and had no answer.

'What are you after? A paternity test? You're trying to prove, even now, that the baby isn't yours?'

As soon as she said it she realised she'd hit the nail on the head. It was there in his stillness, that searching scrutiny so intense that she felt it even in the silver wash of moonlight.

'Is it so unreasonable?' He spread his hands palm up. 'The odds are against it, since I used a condom every time. And I've already had two women claim to be pregnant with my child.'

But I'm not like them!

Cora wanted to shriek the words, barely managing to hold them back.

'I see.' It took everything she had to keep her hands on her hips rather than wrapping her arms defensively around herself.

He cared so little for her that he *wanted* her to be a liar, so he could walk back to his hedonistic life without a backward glance. Her baby deserved better than this man as its father.

'And if I refuse?'

'Why would you refuse the chance to prove I'm the father? There's no risk to the child. All it takes is a blood test from you. And if I am the father...' he paused and she watched him breathe deep as if collecting himself '...then I'll provide support.'

'Money, you mean.' Because clearly he wouldn't be a real father, bonding with their baby and being there through thick and thin.

The fight went out of her. Cora's shoulders slumped as exhaustion hit. She'd known they had no future, yet she'd hoped. Now she saw how futile those hopes were.

She shook her head, about to turn away, then stopped.

Was that the responsible thing to do? She remembered how close they'd come to losing the family business, how tenuous her scientific career would be once she took more time off to have a child. What if there was another downturn and they lost the hotel? Sometime in the future her child might need financial help from its father.

So she made herself ask about the paternity test.

Unsurprisingly Strato had someone on his yacht who could visit the next day to take a blood sample then return to Athens to have the results processed.

For what felt like a full minute she hesitated, fighting outrage. Finally she nodded. 'I'll do it. But just send the doctor. I don't want to see you.'

She'd prove this baby was Strato's in case their child ever needed his support, but then she'd cut him from her life. He didn't want her and didn't want to be a father. Well, that was fine with her.

It *had* to be fine. For she had no choice in the matter.

Cora spun on her heel and marched, alone, along the well-trodden path home. She ignored the wetness trailing down her cheeks and the terrible pain inside as if her heart had cracked in two.

CHAPTER FOURTEEN

DAYS LATER CORA took a couple of hours off for an early morning trip to her favourite islet. It was probably too early to see turtle hatchlings, but she needed time alone.

Since seeing Strato she found it impossible to settle. Even when she was busy working at the hotel her thoughts strayed to him. To his apology that was only half an apology, for he still didn't trust her. To the feeling she'd had that something was badly wrong, the tension in his tall frame evident even in the moonlight.

Wrong? Of course there was something wrong! He was convinced she was a gold-digger. It was crazy that she felt even a spark of concern for him. *She* was the injured party, and the one who'd bear the consequences.

Setting her jaw, she lifted her water bottle and drank, grateful for the shade of the trees at the edge of the tiny beach.

Surely in this peaceful spot she could think clearly about her future as a single mother. As yet she hadn't noticed any physical changes but soon they'd come. She needed to think about preparing for the baby. Until now her thoughts had been a jumble, as concerned with her failed relationship with Strato as with the baby.

'Hello, Cora.' The deep voice came from behind her. She spun around, spilling water, and gaped.

For this was Strato as she'd never seen him. Still tall and handsome in his casual clothes, but his features were etched with lines that carved deep around his mouth and furrowed his brow. He looked sombre. More than that. He looked like a man on the brink of disaster.

'Strato!' Her voice cracked. 'What is it?' She made to get up but he gestured for her to stay where she was, seating himself nearby.

'I've had the test results.' His voice was different, no longer smooth but scratchy and tense. 'I'm sorry. You didn't deserve my anger that night when all you did was tell the truth. I treated you very badly.'

'You did.'

'I apologise unreservedly.' His mouth hitched up at the corner in a smile that held no amusement. 'You needed support, not anger.'

Slowly she nodded. Yet it wasn't the way he'd treated her then that concerned her as much as his intentions now.

Cora knew they could never be a couple, no matter the hopes she'd held, or the fact that even now she saw him and wanted to smooth away that scowl and have him hold her as if he'd never let her go. But surely, sharing a child, they could build some trust, some level of friendship?

Stoically she ignored a piercing ache at the thought that was all they'd ever be. Strato had made his feelings, or lack of them, clear.

'I don't lie, Strato. I was always straight with you.'

'I know.' He shook his head. 'I tried so hard to believe you were like all the others, lying for personal gain. I even told myself the fact you accepted my money to buy those dresses was another proof against you.'

'But I—'

'It's okay, I know, Cora. I know now you didn't access my money, because you're too independent.' He shook his head and for a second she thought she read warmth in his expression. 'The fact was I simply didn't want to believe you.'

Cora put down the water bottle and clasped her hands. 'Because you don't want a child.'

He nodded but didn't offer anything more.

She waited, telling herself he'd eventually explain. There had to be a reason he'd turned from caring, considerate lover to fierce enemy in the blink of an eye.

'I'll support you,' he said finally, his shadowed gaze

catching hers for a moment before moving on, looking down the beach in a way that made her think he didn't see it.

'What do you mean by support? Money?' *She* didn't want his money but wouldn't refuse the possibility of him helping their child when it was older. 'Moral support? Shared parenting?'

Cora couldn't miss his recoil at her last words. The way his jaw clenched so hard she saw the quick flick of his too-fast pulse.

'I'm not cut out to be a father. I told you that.' His eyes sought hers for a moment but instead of filling her with the usual warmth, that look left her chilled. 'But anything else I can provide. Money, security, a home—'

'I have a home. We'll live with my father and Doris, where I grew up.'

The idea should make her happy. Except for a brief period she'd imagined a future with this man, this lover turned stranger.

'But what about your career? You can't get a marine biologist's job here.'

Cora frowned at his concern. How could the man who'd treated her so outrageously worry about such a thing? He confused her more than ever.

'I can't work elsewhere and keep the baby with me, so I've no choice.' Her smile was tight. 'It looks like my future will be in the hotel business.' It had been a dream to pursue her scientific work but some dreams just didn't come true.

'But I'll help financially. You can hire a full-time nanny. Live wherever you like—'

'No.' She breathed deep before continuing. 'I don't want your money, Strato. We'll do well enough.' She lifted her hand when he made to protest. 'I won't object to you providing support later, maybe for university. But I'll live on the island where I grew up. It's more important that our child has people who love it than a fancy house and a paid nanny.'

Strato's frown deepened at her words but he didn't object. Why should he? She was letting him off lightly.

'But there's one thing I do want.' Cora lifted her chin and fixed her gaze on his. 'I know you don't want to be a hands-on father.' Even though she sensed the man she'd fallen for, the caring, fun-loving man who'd ensured she had regular contact with her father and who'd worked so hard to seek out experiences she'd appreciate, would make a terrific dad. 'But I want our child to know you. To have a bond with you. I don't want our baby growing up only knowing you as a distant stranger in the news.'

Family was important. Cora cherished those years when she'd had her mother. Though her relationship with her dad was special, she was grateful she'd had the chance to know and love both her parents. Strato might not be the man she'd hoped but she knew he had a caring side.

'All I ask is that you spend some time getting to know our child. Even just a couple of days now and then but on a regular basis.'

She resisted the urge to wrap her arms around herself, because what she was asking wasn't much for Strato but for her it would be torture, seeing him again and again, thinking of what might have been if he'd really been the man she hoped.

'I'm sorry, Cora. But I can't.'

'Can't?' Her temper flared. 'Surely you mean *won't*! Do you really care so little about the life we've created together, our *child*, that you can turn your back on it?'

'It's better that way.' His voice was harsh. 'Some people shouldn't be parents. Our baby will be better off without me.'

Cora heard it then. Pain. Strato's voice sounded scraped raw, as if it hurt to talk. If that weren't enough, the tension in his big frame spoke for itself.

'I don't believe that. Not of you, at any rate.' Strato was no Prince Charming, but he had lots of good qualities. So many she still, angry as she was, couldn't wash her hands of him.

He turned sharply, green eyes clashing with hers. For a second she thought she saw surprise there. Then his expression turned guarded and she couldn't read anything.

'It's true.' He paused. 'But I'll arrange for funds—'

'No!' Cora scrambled to her feet. 'I don't want your money. I want the truth. You owe me that. Why don't you care enough to be a father to our child? I'm only asking for a couple of visits a year.'

She didn't know if she sounded furious or pleading. Maybe both.

Strato rose in a single lithe movement. 'You're going to keep prodding, aren't you?' His chest expanded mightily as if he struggled to contain his feelings.

'I'm simply asking you to explain. One day our child…' her throat tightened '…will want to know why you didn't care. I don't want them believing there's something wrong with them that made their father refuse to see them.'

His eyes widened as if he hadn't thought about that. But instead of answering, he took out his phone and typed something. Then, in silence, he scrolled, frowning, and scrolled some more.

'Here.' He handed it over.

Cora blinked at the screen then back at him, but he'd already turned away as if he didn't want to watch her read.

Man slays family!

The headline stopped her breath.

It was an old newspaper report from Brisbane about a murder-suicide. A man had been fighting his estranged wife for custody of their three children. There were accusations of violence and stalking against him. One night he got into the house where she was living, killed her, drugged their children and set fire to the house before killing himself. He'd intended them all to die together.

Cora shuddered at the appalling story, her flesh crawling. She'd heard of such violent acts but couldn't stifle a gasp of sheer horror. The only positive piece in the whole, dreadful tale was that one child had survived.

'I don't understand.' She lifted her eyes.

Strato stared straight back, his taut, beautiful face so grim her stomach curdled.

'I remember my grandfather, just. He made his wife's life hell. He died when I was young but he taught my father well.' Strato paused, and Cora realised he looked physically sick. 'That's my father in the article. The man who killed his family.'

'Your *father*?' She goggled up at him, as if she couldn't process his words. Strato couldn't blame her. It was such an obscene crime.

'Can you see the resemblance? I've got his looks, his height and strength.' Strato gritted his teeth, every word paining him. It was torture even to think of his father and grandfather, much less talk about them. 'There's a twisted streak in my family. I refuse to pass it on or hurt another generation.' He paused, letting that sink in. 'I don't dare risk being a father. It's too dangerous.'

Cora gaped. She looked down at the article then back at him. 'But this was in Australia and the family name isn't Doukas.'

Strato shrugged. 'My mother was Greek but we were born in Australia.' He paused, his mouth twisting. 'After *that*, I was adopted by my Greek aunt and uncle. I took their surname. I refused to use my father's name again.'

Changing his identity, putting the past behind him, had been the only way to survive. Even then, for years it had felt like a half-life. He'd wanted to connect with his aunt, who'd tried so hard with him, but something held him back.

The fear of getting close. The fear of caring too much. Of losing everything again.

Was it any wonder he was a loner? He socialised, he

partied. There were even a few, a very few people he liked and trusted, like his faithful secretary Manoli and Damen Nicolaides, who could have been a competitor but instead was something like a friend. Or would be, if Strato trusted himself enough to have friendships.

Yet here was Cora, wanting him to be a *father*! As if that were possible.

The thought of it unwound something inside him that he couldn't allow. To the outside world Strato Doukas was the epitome of louche debauchery and self-indulgence. No one guessed at the soldered-shut lid he kept on his emotions. The fact that his inability to maintain permanent relationships was by choice, because he feared what they might reveal about him.

For his father's and grandfather's blood flowed in his veins.

That alone wouldn't make him dangerous. Upbringing accounted for a lot. But he'd been eight by the time of his father's crime. Eight years to embed his father's twisted thinking. Who knew what that had done to his own psyche? What sort of father *he'd* be?

'I…' Cora shook her head. 'I don't know what to say.'

To his amazement, instead of keeping her distance, she stepped closer, taking his hand in hers, threading their fingers together.

Strato's breath snagged in astonishment. He still recalled the weeks after the fire, the number of people who'd watched him with repugnance or fascination, as if he wore the visible taint of his father's crime. The only exceptions had been the professionals who were paid to be kind, and his aunt.

Cora squeezed his hand and warmth flooded from his hand up his arm. His skin tingled. He couldn't tell if it was pain as if frozen muscles thawed or something else.

He should step away but couldn't. He looked into her grave eyes and couldn't tear his attention away.

'I'm so glad you survived. Though I can't imagine how tough it's been.' Her voice resonated with feeling and Strato found himself wanting to reassure her that it was okay. But things weren't okay and he couldn't raise her hopes that his story had a happy ending.

'How *did* you get away? Or don't you want to talk about it?'

What did it matter? He'd been haunted by memories since the paternity test results. Besides, she was the first person he'd spoken to about this in over two decades and he wanted her to understand.

'I was sick that day with a stomach upset. I hadn't been able to keep down food and I was resting in bed. I woke to noise, but I couldn't make out what it was. Then it all went quiet and my father came to the room, bringing hot milk to help me sleep.'

Strato had been stunned. His father wasn't supposed to be there and he'd never before brought a bedtime drink. But Strato knew better than to ask questions of his father so he'd obediently sipped the sweetened milk.

'He'd drugged the milk.' Strato swallowed hard. 'But it made me feel sick, so after he went out I tipped it out the window.' He'd been terrified his father would find out. 'I waited for my mother to come and say goodnight but she didn't.' He felt his jaw clench.

'Strato. You don't have to tell me. I'm sorry I asked.' Cora held his hand with both hers now, stroking and comforting.

He curled his fingers around hers. Her touch, and her understanding, felt so good.

'There's not much more. Eventually I heard noises and noticed a funny, sharp smell. When I saw smoke coming under the door I tried to get out but it was locked, so I pushed out the screen on my window and got out that way.' It sounded simple, but every moment had been fraught with fear and confusion. At eight he hadn't known what was happening or what he should do.

'When I got outside I saw the fire. I tried to get in another window to help Melissa and Alex, and my mother, but couldn't get it open. So I turned to go next door for help but there was an explosion. The next thing I remember was being in a hospital bed.' He'd been frantic about his family and for a long time no one would tell him what had happened. That dreadful limbo had felt like an extension of the nightmare.

'That's where you got the scar.'

Strato blinked and focused on Cora. 'Sorry?'

'The scar on your shoulder. It looks like a burn.'

'Yes, it's a memento of that night.'

'Oh, Strato!' Cora released his hand and stepped in, wrapping her arms around him. Her hair tickled his chin as she pressed close and more of that delicious warmth seeped into his rigid body. Oh, he could get used to this.

That was half the problem. He already was.

Even knowing he did the right thing, deciding to break with Cora, it was a struggle. Part of him wanted to forget about being responsible and grab her close. Grab everything she offered and more. As if this one remarkable woman could turn his life around.

He closed his eyes and let his arms fold around her, lightly at first, then strongly, hauling her hard against him in a convulsive movement.

He wanted her. So badly. Wanted the joy and light she'd brought him. The sincerity and honesty.

Had his father ever felt like this? Had he craved happiness and been unable to resist the allure of that one, special woman? Had he known the damage he'd do, yet been unable to resist?

Firm hands cupped the back of his head, pushing through his hair and pulling him down. Her lips, soft and intoxicating, whispered against his and the ache in his chest burst into a fiery blast of longing. Of need so deep it channelled through his bones.

Strato teetered on the brink of giving in. He *needed* to give in, for the force of his yearning was stronger than any temptation he'd felt in his life.

His lips opened, brushing hers and he drew in the taste of her, sweet and alluring. Peace beckoned. He bent closer.

Abruptly realisation slammed into him.

He was taking. No matter that Cora offered. That was what the men in his family did. They took and took. They demanded. And when they couldn't have everything exactly the way they wanted...

His fingers clamped on Cora's arms. For a second longer he lost himself in the glory of her kiss. Then he stepped back, holding her at arm's length and looking down into drowned golden-brown eyes full of compassion.

Strato locked his jaw.

He didn't want her compassion.

He wanted *everything*.

Which was why he couldn't allow himself to have anything.

'Cora. No. I can't.'

Her eyes narrowed as if she looked deep into his soul. 'But you want to.' She said it as if it were a revelation.

'Of course I want to. I haven't stopped wanting you for a second! Even when I thought, hoped, you lied about being pregnant, I still craved you.'

He'd said too much. Strato saw that in the flare of emotion in her expression.

He released her and stepped back even further, making it clear there'd be no more physical contact. Though he yearned for it with a ferocity that astounded him.

Proof that he could easily become obsessive about her? He hated to think it. He'd told himself for years that he wasn't like his old man. Yet he couldn't take the risk.

Especially now she carried his child.

Strato had spent most of his life denying he wanted a family. It was a shock to learn how wrong he'd been. How the new life Cora carried made him think, not only of his monstrous father, but of his beloved mother and his siblings. Of the times the four of them had been happy. Of the bond they'd shared and how he still missed them.

Why had he escaped when they hadn't?

'Strato?' He realised his gaze had dropped to Cora's abdomen where she cradled his child.

'Sorry?'

'I still want you too.' Her smile was an endearingly crooked line.

It was more than he'd let himself hope, after the way he'd treated her. 'I don't deserve you, *Coritsa*.'

The terrible thing was that, even now, he was tempted to do something irresponsible and dangerous, like pretend he was an ordinary guy, and persuade her to stay with him.

'You see now why I can't be a father. Our child deserves better.'

So did she.

'You can't—'

'I can and I will.' He forced his shoulders back, standing straight and shoving his hands into his pockets. 'Don't you see, I can't afford to take the risk? Not with you or our baby.'

They meant so much to him. More than he'd dreamed possible. Imagine how possessive of them he'd grow as time progressed. He had to cut these ties before they twisted into something ugly.

Slowly Cora shook her head. 'You're not that sort of man.'

'Aren't I? How do you know?'

'I know something about you, Strato. It wasn't just sex we shared, remember?' A flash of temper warmed her gaze and he felt it as a delicious shiver down his spine. He'd give everything to bask in that freely. 'I know a lot about you. Enough to know you're not cruel or—'

'Manipulative? Have you forgotten how I coerced you

into being my lover? How I used your concern for your father for my own ends?'

'I haven't forgotten, Strato. But I had a choice. I could have said no. You didn't force me.'

His mouth tightened. How had he forgotten her obstinacy?

'It doesn't concern you that I'm possessive?'

'You are?' Instead of looking worried Cora's face brightened.

Strato frowned. 'I spent all that evening in Athens fuming whenever another man tried to flirt with you. I hated the way they salivated over you in that red dress. I wanted to shove them all away, or, better yet, take you somewhere private where only I could admire you.'

'I like that you didn't want to share me with other men.'

'Don't you see? That's not a good thing. Jealousy is a curse. It's a step on the way to obsession.'

The trait of his father's he most feared. The man had been a control freak, seeing his wife and children as extensions of himself. They were supposed to do what he said at all times.

Cora shook her head. 'Not necessarily. I felt jealous of those women eating you up with their eyes. And *I'm* not obsessive.'

'What women?'

She made an impatient sound. 'The women at the dinner in Athens. I'm sure some of them would have gone with you if you'd invited them.' She looked away then darted a sideways glance at him. 'Then there are all those other women you've been with. I don't like them. Any of them.'

Astonished, Strato rocked back on his heels.

Cora sounded jealous.

Where had that come from?

'*I think* the fact you didn't like other men looking at me is positive. It means you feel the connection between us too.' Now she looked him straight in the eye, chin up and hands on her hips. The sight made something in his chest roll over. He liked her feistiness, her determination.

Liked? There was an understatement. He felt too much for this woman. The temptation to ignore the risk and pursue what sounded like an invitation was too alluring. He had to end this, now.

'I'm sorry, Cora, but it can't be. Ever. I know where feelings like that could lead me.' Because his father's taint loomed like a shadow. Strato's next breath felt like a blade slicing his lungs. 'I experienced it. You didn't. I refuse to take a chance of something like that happening to you or our child.'

The fire in her eyes dimmed. Her pugnacious attitude softened. 'Oh, Strato, you—'

'My lawyers will be in touch about a settlement.' He turned away, knowing he had to go before he reached for her again.

'Wait!'

He paused, but didn't turn back.

'Please, give me one more day before you leave. There may be things we need to discuss. Things I'd prefer to talk with you about, not a lawyer.'

Strato narrowed his eyes against the glitter of sunlight on the sea. But it wasn't the view he saw, it was Cora. She filled his mind, his soul, even the heart he'd tried to tell himself he no longer possessed.

'Very well. I'll stay another twenty-four hours.' But he prayed, with a fervour he hadn't felt for decades, that Cora would see sense and not drag this out. Better that he leave and never look back.

CHAPTER FIFTEEN

CORA'S LITTLE BOAT puttered out in the early morning light. As it drew in close it was completely dwarfed by the magnificent lines of Strato's luxurious yacht. Cora didn't care. She was well past being intimidated by his wealth.

Strato was just a man, as flawed as any other, even if he was also magnificent.

Her heart squeezed as she thought of him yesterday, doing what he believed to be the right thing by their unborn child, looking all the while like a man on the edge. His fortune was no protection against unhappiness or the terrible burden he carried.

The story of his past had undone her. What must he have suffered? It put his determination to remain unattached in a different light. His voice when he'd mentioned the family he'd lost…

It was obvious his guilt over surviving when they didn't was real and raw.

So here she was, gambling her future on the slim chance Strato felt more than protectiveness for her and the baby. Hoping he felt even a little of what she did.

For what she'd learned yesterday had made her bruised heart open even further. She'd loved Strato when he was strong and sexy, when she felt cherished and sheltered in his arms. But her feelings were even stronger now, knowing how much he'd suffered, how much he'd missed out on and still did. How he thought not of himself but of her and their baby.

How could any woman who cared turn her back on him, having heard the truth?

The odds were against her. He was so fiercely determined to protect her and their child from himself. All she had on her side was his admission that he still wanted her. And the strength of her feelings.

So she'd taken her time to work out her strategy. It didn't amount to much, a few arguments she hoped might convince him, and her sexy red dress that had distracted him in Athens.

Strato was no fool, he'd realise she'd dressed up for a reason, but she'd use whatever tools she had.

As she neared the yacht Manoli, Strato's assistant, waved and took the line Cora tossed him, securing it.

'It's good to see you, Cora.' He lowered his voice as he held out his hand to help her aboard. 'I'm worried about him.'

She nodded. 'So am I.' Distress over Strato's story, and the slim chances of making him see sense, had kept her awake most of the night. He couldn't go on like that, cutting himself off from everyone, believing he was evil incarnate when he, more than anyone, was a victim. 'Where is he?'

'In his study, though he seems to be brooding more than working.'

'I'll see myself in if that's okay.'

'Great idea. If you don't improve his mood, nothing will.' Manoli's sweeping glance and appreciative smile boosted her confidence.

Her dress was the sexiest thing she'd ever worn and she'd spent ages washing then brushing her hair till it shone. She'd even put on enough make-up to give her eyes a smoky look and emphasise the shape of her lips. She wore a delicate chain necklace in the shape of a bow with long tails that fell low and drew the eye to her cleavage.

Yet her stomach was full of butterflies as she pushed open the door to Strato's study. His back was to her as he stared out to sea. For a second she had leisure to take him in, broad straight shoulders beneath a white shirt and pale trousers pulled tight over his perfect rear by the hands shoved in his front pockets.

'Strato.'

He spun towards her and for a fleeting moment she read welcome in his expression, before a scowl descended. 'I'd hoped you'd make this easy for both of us, Cora.'

She stepped into the room, shutting the door behind her. 'You promised you'd hear me out if there were things we need to discuss.'

'Well?' His look, his stance were pure arrogant billion-aire. As if she took up too much of his precious time. But Cora wasn't fooled. This man felt deeply, too deeply, and he cared, even if he tried to give the impression he didn't.

'I have a proposition, Strato. I want you to live with me, not as a temporary lover, but as my partner.'

His eyebrows shot up and his eyes widened. 'Didn't you hear *anything* I said yesterday? I can't live with you, what if I...?'

'And what if you don't, Strato? You're denying us all, you, me and our baby, the chance of happiness, because you're afraid of something that's not going to happen.'

He stepped closer then stopped abruptly as if fearing to get too close. 'You ask me to forget the danger to you both? I can't do that.'

Cora folded her arms and saw with a flicker of hope the way his gaze followed the movement, lingering a fraction on her breasts.

'You're making assumptions, Strato, and any scientist will tell you that's unwise. You're acting without proof.'

He shook his head. 'The proof being an act of violence? I refuse to risk it.'

'Don't you see, your thinking is flawed? I understand your fear about learning behaviour patterns from your fa-ther and grandfather. But have you stopped to consider that the very fact you refuse to take this chance points to you being different?'

'You haven't known me long enough to form an opinion,

Cora.' His dismissive tone might have stopped her once. Now she saw it as camouflage for his pain and doubt.

She paced closer, glad she'd taken time to pull together her information and marshal her arguments.

'I did some research yesterday, Strato. There are plenty of press reports about you but not one mentioning violence or abuse of women.' He opened his mouth but she kept speaking. 'I also rang Steph Nicolaides, who spoke to her husband.'

'You did what?' He looked stunned.

'Don't worry, I didn't share your past. I told her how I felt about you and asked if she was aware of anything I should know about you.'

Not because Cora doubted him for a second. But so Strato could hear what others thought of him. He respected Damen and trusted his acumen. She hoped Damen's feedback would make Strato stop and think instead of instinctively rejecting what others saw and he couldn't.

'How do you feel about me?'

His eyes bored into hers. Cora swallowed and reminded herself this was no time for pride.

'I love you.'

Strato moved towards her then stopped abruptly.

'You can't!'

He was breathless, his voice cracking, and all the feelings she battled to contain surfaced. She wanted to hold him and comfort him. Rock him in her arms, take him into her body and whisper soothing words to erase his pain. She wanted to take those lovely, wide shoulders and shake him!

'I can and I do.' When he would have spoken, she raised her palm. 'You can't control my feelings, Strato. I've loved you since well before I learned about our baby. My feelings are true and real and I wouldn't change them if I could.'

She watched him reach for his desk as if he needed support. Good. Maybe a few shocks would knock some sense into him.

'Steph said you were kind and generous and that you'd make a terrific father if you could be persuaded to settle down.' Seeing Strato's shock, Cora hurried on. 'Not that she knows about the baby. She said Damen thinks highly of you and trusts you. He said you're a truly decent man, masquerading as someone who doesn't care.'

Cora agreed.

Strato's mouth twisted in a jeering smile. 'Much as I appreciate the praise, none of that counters my concerns.'

'What about Asteri?'

He stiffened. 'Asteri?'

'Don't look so surprised. I know you're associated with it, even if you don't run it. I told you I'd been digging.'

Strato's lowered brows told her he wasn't happy.

'Where did the name come from? Since it means *star*, it made me think of a bright light to guide you in tough times. Is that it? It's appropriate for an organisation that gives on-the-ground support to victims of family violence.'

'You *have* done your homework.' He didn't sound pleased.

'I kept seeing hotel bookings from Asteri, for single women or sometimes for women with children. I got curious.' She'd found a charity that provided safe housing and services to families affected by violence. 'Those holidays you've paid for aren't just for employees. Some are for survivors of trauma.'

'I don't see the relevance.'

He was *so* stubborn. 'Do you really think a man who sees women as possessions to be controlled would champion that cause? Not with a tax-deductible payment, but with a meaningful contribution like holidays they wouldn't usually be able to afford? A break when they most need it?'

Cora closed the gap between them and put her palm to his chest, pushing. A tremor ran up her arm and encircled her chest at the thrill of touching him again.

'Don't, Cora.'

'Or what? What will you do?'

His hand closed on hers and he gently pulled it away. Yet he kept hold of it. Was it imagination that turned his touch into a caress? His grim stare into one of longing?

'Would you beat me or—?'

'Don't, Cora! This isn't a game.'

His pain created an ache that ripped through her own chest. Cora lifted her other palm to his face, cupping his jaw, feeling the roughened texture of his unshaved skin.

'I know. But you're not like your father. I look at this scientifically, look at the facts, and draw sensible conclusions.'

She didn't mention the very unscientific fact that she also followed her heart. Her instinct that Strato was the man she believed him.

'You're not violent, Strato. On the contrary, you help victims of violence.' And went to considerable trouble to do it quietly so that the public wasn't aware of his interest. 'You're incredibly protective, of me and our baby. I admire you. I care for you. I *love* you, and I want you to take a chance on turning your life around and being with me.'

She had no idea what she did.

Asking the impossible. While at the same time holding out shining hope.

Strato had never let himself think of being loved again. He knew how precious it was. Still remembered the warmth of his mother's love and his siblings'. He'd spent his life locking away what was left of his broken heart. Now Cora strode into his life, smashing barriers he'd thought impenetrable, and said she loved him. She trusted him. She wanted a future with him.

A great shudder racked him from head to toe. He tried to move back, find space to think, but couldn't bring himself to release her.

The tender touch of her palm on his face was every hope, every dream he'd tried not to harbour.

But it seemed dreams weren't so easily killed. Beneath his adamantine control something welled, hot and strong. A yearning. A need. A sense of inevitability.

Because he loved her.

Cora had worked a miracle, awakening feelings he'd never thought to experience. That was what he'd fought against recognising all these weeks.

He loved Cora with every part of his shadowed soul. With every breath he took and would ever take.

Not just because she offered the elusive promise of a future to a man who'd never allowed himself to think long term.

But because of Cora. She was everything he needed. Sensible. Sexy. Giving. Funny. Determined. Frustratingly determined.

'Strato?'

Eyes the colour of cognac held his and he felt himself on the brink of falling. He wanted to fall. To trust she was right and all would be well.

But it wouldn't be him paying the price if this ended in disaster.

'I…care for you, Cora. That's why I can't do what you want.'

He stepped away, far enough that she couldn't touch him. She didn't follow. She looked winded, as if his rejection had undone her.

Strato wanted to tug her into his arms and tell her it would be all right. But she was too precious.

'What would your mother say, Strato?'

His head jerked back as if she'd slapped him.

'Don't bring my mother into this!'

He still grieved for her. For the fact he hadn't been able to save her.

'Would she want to see her boy turning his back on happiness? Wouldn't she want to see you with your own family, feeling joy and tenderness? Do you think she'd be happy seeing you pursuing meaningless hook-ups that diminish you instead of sustaining you?'

How had Cora known? That was exactly how it felt. He'd realised in the time they'd been apart that he could never go back to those brief sexual encounters.

Because what he wanted was Cora. For ever.

His nemesis continued. 'I suspect she'd hope that, despite what happened to your family, you'd find true peace and happiness. That you'd love.'

Strato drew a slow breath and released it.

Cora was right. His mother had been positive, despite her abusive marriage. She'd told him to reach for the sky and dream big. That was why the charity he'd established was called Asteri. That and the fact she'd always called him *asteri mou*, my star.

'You're right.' The words ground from his constricted throat. 'But I can't seek happiness at your expense.'

The dawning light in Cora's eyes dimmed as her mouth thinned. She planted her hands on her generous hips, drawing his unwilling attention to the marvellous curve at her trim waist and up to those magnificent breasts.

'You don't think I have the strength to stand up for myself, Strato?' Her chest heaved and he looked up, discovering her eyes narrowed in anger. 'Well, I can.' She paused and he wondered what argument she'd try next.

She dropped her arms and breathed slowly, as if through pain.

Had he convinced her? Why didn't he feel pleased? He knew an unreasoning urge to bar the door to stop her going.

'If that's your final word, there's nothing left to say.' Her gaze held his and he read distress there that matched his own, making him even more miserable. 'But know this, Strato Doukas. I want my baby to have two loving parents like I did. It may take a while, years even, but I'll find a man who's not afraid of commitment. A man who'll truly care for me and help me raise my child.'

Unbelievable pain filled Strato's chest, clogging the space behind his ribs till he couldn't breathe.

'You wouldn't.' The thought of Cora with another man, a stranger raising his child...

'Why not? I'm not going to live like a hermit because you don't want me.' She looked away. 'You might have broken my heart.' She paused, swallowing, and his own heart shattered. 'But thanks to you, I've discovered I like sex. There are decent men out there who could be a father to this baby. It mightn't be a love match but, as you've also taught me, love doesn't guarantee a happy ending.'

'You're bluffing!' She had to be.

Cora turned towards the door, the hem of her skirt flaring, teasing him with a glimpse of toned thighs.

'Someone like Manoli maybe. I like his sense of humour. And he's got infinite patience. He has to have, working for you—'

Strato's hand on her arm stopped her mid-step.

Go to Manoli indeed! When she professed to love *him*.

Cora swung around and he couldn't help himself. Fear and desperation melded into an unstoppable force. He hauled her close and put his mouth on hers, the threads of his control finally tearing.

Firm hands captured his head, holding tight as if she feared he'd pull back. All that wonderful womanly softness pressed against him, splintering any thought of self-control. And her kiss...

Strato sighed. She kissed like a woman in love. As desperate as he.

He wrapped his arms securely around her and gave himself up to the inevitable. Amazingly, it didn't feel like defeat, but victory, optimism.

It was a long time before he could summon enough control to lift his head and find his voice.

'Witch.' Even to his own ears the growl sounded like an

endearment. 'You had no intention of pursuing Manoli or anyone else, had you?'

'You expected me to fight fair when our happiness is at stake? Our whole future and our child's?' Her eyes shone overbright. 'Kiss me again, Strato. Please?'

Her wobbly voice undid him. It matched his own shuddering wonder.

How could he refuse her? Even knowing she'd played him, had him dancing to her tune. She'd broken him down to his most elemental being and reassembled him so he felt trembling belief in the possibility of a future.

He just couldn't relinquish it, or her. Not now.

Finally, it seemed hours later, he sat with her bundled on his lap, warm and luscious in his arms. Strato inhaled the scent of wild honey as he nuzzled her neck and knew that whatever the future held, *this* was right. She was right for him.

'I love you, Cora.' It felt amazing to say it aloud.

She turned, eyes shining with wonder.

Strato swallowed, pushing down fear and clutching at hope. The precious gift Cora brought him.

'Oh, Strato!' Her eyes brimmed with tears, but she smiled through them and the sight of her joy gave him hope for the future.

'I want to make you happy, always. But I don't know how.'

She shook her head. 'For a clever man you have a lot to learn. Just keep on being you and I'll be happy.'

'That I can do. I just wish—'

Her finger on his lips stopped him. 'How about we promise to take it a day at a time? You're not the only one who has to learn about building a future together. And being a parent.'

Strato lifted her hand to his lips. 'But we're in this together.' The power of that thought sustained him against the shadows of fear. He'd do everything he could to build a wonderful future for them all. There was no other possible alternative. 'You and me together, *Coritsa*. We'll make mistakes but we'll learn. If I have your love that's all I need.'

Cora's tender smile eased a little of his ancient hurts. Who knew what a lifetime of them together could achieve?

'You have it, *agapi mou*. Always.'

EPILOGUE

'Look, Daddy, look!' Melissa turned her gap-toothed grin and bright eyes on Strato and he felt that familiar hit of joy. 'There's another. Isn't it cute?'

She pointed to the tiny, just-hatched turtle, crawling across the sand towards the sea.

'Absolutely,' he murmured. 'Almost as cute as you.'

She giggled and threw herself at his legs, hugging hard. 'I love you, Daddy.'

As ever, those words made his heart turn over. Even though he was now part of a family that spoke openly about such emotion.

'And I love you, my little princess.' He scooped her up in his arms, whirling her high till she giggled.

'Shh! You'll scare them,' Alex cautioned. Strato turned to see his son at the water's edge with his grandfather and Doris. Serious, warm-hearted Alex and carefree Melissa. The twins lit up Strato's world, as their namesakes, his siblings, had years before.

'We promise to be quiet. Don't we?' Melissa nodded and he put her down, watching her skip off to the others.

This was a regular outing. All the family came to Cora's island when it was time for the hatchlings to appear. Strato had built a house on the main island across the headland from his father-in-law's hotel and this was just a short boat ride away.

'Thank you, *agapi mou*.' An arm slipped around his waist and there was Cora, his wife, his love, his life. He pulled her satisfyingly close, his smile widening.

'What for? The island?' He'd bought it in her name, as part of a successful proposal to turn the area into a marine park. Now it was protected from development and a new

research facility did important work, also providing oppor-
tunities for researchers like his wife.

Glowing golden-brown eyes met his and desire stirred.
'That too. And for inviting Steph, Damen and the kids to
visit next week for our anniversary party.' She paused, her
mouth curling in a tender smile. 'But mainly thank you for
believing in us. For trusting yourself, and me. I love you,
Strato. I can't tell you how much.'

Her misty eyes and sweet smile told him. As did the ache
of pure joy that filled him.

'As much as I love you, *Coritsa*.' His love for her filled
him to the brim and always would. 'I give thanks every day
that we found each other.'

She'd saved him from himself and taught him how to
live in the sunlight instead of the shadows. He leant in and,
here at the place where they'd met, Strato kissed his own,
special Nereid with all the love in his heart.

* * * * *

COMING SOON!

MILLS & BOON

THE HEART OF ROMANCE

A ROMANCE FOR EVERY READER

MODERN

Prepare to be swept off your feet by sophisticated, sexy and seductive heroes, in some of the world's most glamourous and romantic locations, where power and passion collide.

HISTORICAL

Escape with historical heroes from time gone by. Whether your passion is for wicked Regency Rakes, muscled Vikings or rugged Highlanders, awake the romance of the past.

MEDICAL

Set your pulse racing with dedicated, delectable doctors in the high-pressure world of medicine, where emotions run high and passion, comfort and love are the best medicine.

True Love

Celebrate true love with tender stories of heartfelt romance, from the rush of falling in love to the joy a new baby can bring, and a focus on the emotional heart of a relationship.

Desire

Indulge in secrets and scandal, intense drama and plenty of sizzling hot action with powerful and passionate heroes who have it all: wealth, status, good looks…everything but the right woman.

HEROES

Experience all the excitement of a gripping thriller, with an intense romance at its heart. Resourceful, true-to-life women and strong, fearless men face danger and desire - a killer combination!

To see which titles are coming soon, please visit

millsandboon.co.uk/nextmonth

MILLS & BOON

Coming next month

REDEEMED BY HIS NEW YORK CINDERELLA
Jadesola James

"I'll speak plainly." The way he should have in the beginning, before she had him ruminating.

"All right."

"I'm close to signing the man you met. Giles Mueller. He's the owner of the Mueller Racetrack."

She nodded.

"You know it?"

"It's out on Long Island. I attended an event close to it once."

He grunted. "The woman you filled in for on Friday is— *was*—my set date for several events over the next month. Since Giles already thinks you're her, I'd like you to step in. In exchange, I'll make a handsome donation to your charity—"

"Foundation."

"Whatever you like."

There was silence between them for a moment, and Katherine looked at him again. It made him uncomfortable at once. He knew she couldn't see into his mind, but there was something very perceptive about that look. She said nothing, and he continued talking to cover the silence.

"You see, Katherine, I owe you a debt." Laurence's voice was dry. "You saved my life, and in turn I'll save your business."

She snorted. "What makes you think my business needs saving?"

Laurence laughed incredulously. "You're a one-person operation. You don't even have an *office*. Your website is one of those ghastly pay-by-month templates, you live in a boarding house—"

"I don't need an office," Katherine said proudly. "I meet

clients in restaurants and coffee shops. An office is an old-fashioned and frankly completely unneeded expense. I'm not looking to make money off this, Laurence. I want to help people. Not everyone is like you."

Laurence chose not to pursue the insult; what mattered was getting Katherine to sign. "As you like," he said dismissively, then reached for his phone. "My driver has the paperwork waiting in the car. I'll have him bring it round now—"

"No."

It took a moment for the word to register. "Excuse me?"

Katherine did not repeat herself, but she did shake her head. "It's a kind offer, Laurence," she said firmly, "but the thought of playing your girlfriend is at least as absurd as your lie was."

Laurence realized after several seconds had passed that he was gaping, and he closed his mouth rapidly. He'd anticipated many different counteroffers—all that had been provided for in the partnership proposal that was ready for her to sign—but a refusal was something he was wholly unprepared for.

"You're saying no?" he said, to clarify.

She nodded.

"Why the hell would you say no?" The question came out far more harshly than he would have liked, but he was genuinely shocked. "You have everything to gain."

She tucked a lock of dark hair behind her ear, and he was momentarily distracted by the smooth slide of it over her skin. The change in her was truly remarkable. In her element, she was an entirely different person than the frightened teenager he remembered, and she carried herself with a quiet dignity that was very attractive.

Continue reading
REDEEMED BY HIS NEW YORK CINDERELLA
Jadesola James

Available next month
www.millsandboon.co.uk

LET'S TALK
Romance

For exclusive extracts, competitions
and special offers, find us online:

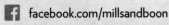 facebook.com/millsandboon

@MillsandBoon

@MillsandBoonUK

Get in touch on 01413 063232

For all the latest titles coming soon, visit
millsandboon.co.uk/nextmonth